A
Wedding
in Italy

ALSO BY TILLY TENNANT

A Wedding in Italy

TILLY TENNANT

bookouture

Published by Bookouture
An imprint of StoryFire Ltd.
23 Sussex Road, Ickenham, UB10 8PN
United Kingdom
www.bookouture.com

ISBN: 978-1-78681-167-7
E-book ISBN: 978-1-78681-166-0

This book is dedicated to some very special people, nominated by my readers. Here are their messages:

To Jodie and Mark Rothman, thank you for all your support through everything. I love you both so much, I hope you will treasure this dedication to show that you mean the world to me, forever and always, love Mum xx

To Emma Crowley, thanks for always being there even though you've already got a lot going on in your own life, from Sharon

To Craig Weafer-Hand 11/01/2001 to 17/11/2006
We miss you always, we will love you forever, the brightest smile in our lives, now the brightest star in the sky.
Love always Mammy and Daddy

My dedication is for my wonderful husband Richard Clark, who as well as being my soulmate is my absolute rock. His love and support gives me the strength to stay positive when dealing with difficulties

To Hazel Budd, such a strong woman and a wonderful mum to all of us xx

One

Kate threw open the curtains and the morning sun washed the room in gold. It was winter in Rome, but that hadn't diminished the brightness of the days. Nor had the constant drip of her kitchen tap, the fact that the lock of her front door got stuck from time to time, or that the electricity went down at the most inconvenient moments. Nothing could dampen her enthusiasm for her new home. Her neighbours complained of the cold, of how they wished that summer would hurry and return, but Kate, once she'd got the gist of the conversation (and it sometimes took a lot of effort with her still very rudimentary grasp of Italian), would smile and think to herself that if they'd ever suffered a winter in Manchester they'd count themselves very lucky to be basking in their current temperatures. Christmas was six weeks away and would mark a little less than six months since she'd first met the man of her dreams on a balmy evening at the Spanish Steps. Her journey to becoming a fully-fledged Italian citizen had been even more fraught than her journey to Alessandro's heart, and it had taken her until late autumn to finally make the move, but now that she was here those troubles all seemed like a distant memory. The only thing that sometimes tugged her towards home was the fact that she hadn't seen her sisters, Anna and Lily, since the move, and she missed them more than she'd thought she would.

Alessandro smiled up at her from the pillows where he was currently propped. It was rare for him to spend the night at her flat – partly due to his largely antisocial duty shifts as a police officer and partly due to him wrestling with his good Catholic conscience. His sexual appetite was as healthy as the next man's but he would often talk about his mother's views on couples living together unmarried and how concerned she was that Kate and Alessandro would end up doing just that. She was equally concerned by Kate's status as a Protestant and foreigner, though she was coming round to accepting that now, won over by Kate's best efforts to charm her with a multitude of hand-sewn gifts, from cushion covers to dresses for church. Each new creation seemed to wear Signora Conti down a little more, and Kate was certain (as was Alessandro) that she would eventually forget Kate was British and a raging Church of England heathen at all.

'Come back to bed,' he said, patting the space beside him with a wicked grin. 'You have time.'

'No, I don't.' Kate tried to look stern but it was impossible. How could she look stern at such an invitation? 'And you need to ask me in Italian. I need the practice. . . remember?'

'If I ask in Italian you will pretend you do not understand and I will not get my Kate in these arms.'

'I would never do that.'

'*Va bene. Torna a letto.*'

Kate gave him a shrug, accompanied by an impish smile. 'Sorry . . . not a clue. I guess I'll just have to go and make breakfast . . .'

He leapt from the bed with astonishing speed, and Kate shrieked with laughter as she bolted from the room and he tore after her, catching her breathless in the living room and whipping her onto her back on the sofa. Closing in for a kiss, his hand found its way beneath her dressing gown and travelled up her thigh, causing her to shudder with pleasure. What this man could do to her. . . she didn't think she could ever get enough. Even now, with a million jobs to think about in the day ahead, she was lost. It didn't look as though she was getting breakfast any time soon.

'You do know that your landlord speaks English?' Alessandro raised his eyebrows over the top of his coffee cup as they sat at Kate's tiny dining table.

'He doesn't speak very much. It's hard to make him understand and he's busy looking after so many tenants.'

'He speaks it perfectly. He is trying to make you go away and it is working. If there are things wrong in your apartment, he must fix them . . .' He placed the cup very deliberately back onto the saucer and looked up at Kate. 'I will speak to him. There will be no misunderstanding then.'

'No, you won't. I don't need you fighting all my battles.'

'Then you must learn to fight them yourself.'

'I do!'

Alessandro said nothing, but he didn't need to – the look on his face said it all.

'I know I could be a bit more assertive, but I like it here and I like Salvatore, and I don't want to upset him or he might decide to give me my marching orders.'

'Your marching orders? What does that mean?'

'He might tell me to leave the apartment so he can rent it out to somebody else.'

'He would not do that; I would speak to him—'

'And here we go again,' Kate interrupted. 'You can't be seen to be using your position of authority in that way.'

'I would speak to him as a citizen of Rome, not as a policeman.'

'But it might be viewed that way if Salvatore chose to take offence. I'd never forgive myself if it got you into hot water and I'd rather not take the chance.'

'Hot water is what you are not into right now. That is why we are having this conversation.'

Kate couldn't help a grin. Alessandro's English had been pretty perfect before, but the nuances of conversation with an actual English person, complete with jokes and sarcasm and wordplay, had been lost to him. Since they'd started to spend all their free time together he was slipping into those idiosyncrasies with ease and at times sounded almost like a native Mancunian. There were phrases she often had to explain to him despite this, but his grasp of English was certainly developing a lot faster than her grasp of Italian. She had asked him and his family to speak to her in Italian often so she would be forced to learn it, but the process of any conversation had been so slow and painful that they often just reverted to English so they could say what they needed to and get on with their lives. Which wasn't particularly helpful in terms of Kate's education, but she could understand their frustrations nonetheless. Only Alessandro's mother persevered with her native tongue when addressing Kate, but that was because her English was even worse than Kate's Italian. It made for very long and laborious conversations, with quite bit of inadvertent charades thrown in.

'What time did you say you'd go to help with the wedding preparations?' Kate asked, very deliberately changing the subject to that of his sister Lucetta's impending nuptials to her long-term and hopelessly enamoured boyfriend, Gian.

He glanced up at the clock. 'I have an hour, maybe a little less. Why do you ask? Do you want me to come back to bed again?' He waggled an eyebrow at her, and she threw the teacloth she was wiping the table with at his head.

'No, I do not!' she laughed. 'But I *am* nervous as hell about all those new family members to meet.'

He shrugged. 'It's not so many.'

'You've got twenty cousins arriving to help decorate this hall and you don't think that's many? I'd call that quite a few! And that's without all the aunts, uncles and second cousins due tomorrow at the wedding! It's alright for you to be chilled about it, but you know them all and you have no need to make a good impression.'

'Neither do you. My family will love you just as you are.'

'Try telling that to your mother,' she replied darkly. 'I think she's been studying that family tree pretty hard to see which cousins might be removed enough for you to marry.'

'She would not do that. Mamma knows that we are in love.'

'That wouldn't stop her from trying to tempt you away if she thought she could. We both know that she tolerates me but she still doesn't think I'm suitable marriage material . . .' She held up a hand to silence any argument that might arise. 'And before you make some flippant remark about how we're not getting married yet, you know full well that ultimately we'll have to make a decision on that, and it won't ever be soon enough for your mother, who seems to think that if you're not married by the time you're thirty-one you'll turn into a vampire or something.'

'She wants to see me make a good marriage before she dies.'

'Your mother will live forever; she'll certainly outlive both of us!'

Alessandro raised an amused eyebrow. 'You are full of fire this morning.'

'I'm full of nerves. It always brings out my neurotic side.'

He pushed himself up from the table and two strides saw him at her side, where he took her into his arms. '*Ti amo troppo . . .*' he said, and kissed her tenderly. 'It does not matter what anyone else wants, only what you and I want.'

'I know what I want,' Kate said, melting into his embrace. 'You.'

'And I want you, so we have nothing to fear from a thousand cousins at the wedding, not even if they came with the biggest dowries in Italy.'

Kate gave a playful frown. 'I have to pay a dowry to marry you? Suddenly I'm not quite so keen.'

He laughed and tapped the tabletop with a knuckle. 'This will do just fine.'

'Ah, well, in that case. . .' Kate reached to kiss him again, 'I'm all yours. . .'

Alessandro had gone off to the wedding venue, taking along a few police colleagues to meet with the cousins who were waiting there for them, having also agreed to lay out chairs, decorate the marquee and help with all the other preparations for the reception. That left Kate with plans to go to his mother's house and assist three of Alessandro's sisters – Lucetta, Abelie and Maria – with the packing of sugared almonds into delicate muslin bags as favours, binding floral arrangements and writing out place cards. Not that she was brilliant at any of those things, but Lucetta seemed to be labouring under the illusion that being able to sew meant Kate was good at everything remotely creative, and Kate hadn't been able to say no when asked. She was also shrewd enough to realise that saying no would have won her no favour with the family anyway, and she needed all the help she could get. Despite this, Kate wasn't exactly enamoured by the prospect of a day with Alessandro's oldest sister, Maria, who still hadn't quite forgiven her for scuppering the union she'd clearly hoped for between her only brother and her friend, Orazia. Of all the resistance their relationship had encountered from the Conti family, Maria's was perhaps the greatest. If Kate had announced today that she was packing up and moving back to England, she was quite sure Maria would have been throwing the party to end all parties. It wasn't all-out hatred, but it was sniping comments and filthy looks when she thought nobody else was looking, and any excuse to show Kate in a bad light she grabbed gleefully with both hands.

There was cinnamon on the air as Abelie opened the door of the Conti home to admit Kate, warm and welcoming. If only it reflected the welcome Kate would get once she was inside. Abelie kissed her on the cheek.

'*Ciao*, Kate. *Come va?*'

'*Sì. . .*' Kate replied with a stiff nod. '*Grazie.*'

Abelie frowned and stepped back to appraise Kate more fully. 'I do not think you are telling the truth. You seem troubled.'

'I'm fine,' Kate said hurriedly. 'A little tired.'

Abelie raised her eyebrows. 'Alessandro was at your house all night? Do not tell Mamma you are tired. . .'

'I won't,' Kate said, laughing despite her anxieties. Alessandro's sisters were surprisingly open about their love lives, and they had no qualms at all in sharing conjecture about Alessandro's either, even if that was with Kate herself. Signora Conti, however, was a different matter entirely.

'So there is nothing else to worry you?' Abelie asked. She lowered her voice as she glanced down the hallway and then back to Kate. 'Mamma has said that Maria must not be rude to you today, because you are a guest and you are kind enough to help us with the wedding.'

Kate wondered if Signora Conti had had the same conversation with herself. Although it wasn't exactly rudeness that bothered Kate in that quarter – more her ongoing covert operation to find Alessandro alternative marriage material, while simultaneously engaging in pleasantries to Kate's face. To her, Kate was like a bout of chicken pox that her son had been unfortunate enough to catch, meaning she was faced with no alternative but to patiently suffer the spots until it passed. That said, she was a sweet lady who didn't have it in her to be overtly mean to anyone, but it was no secret that she didn't think Kate was the woman for her only son and was keeping a keen eye out for a replacement model – preferably Italian. If she could have Catholic, well-off, respected old family, good childbearing hips and still a virgin into the bargain, then all the better. There were regular conversations over meals about this person's daughter, or that person's sister, or somebody else's granddaughter – on the surface innocent enough but obviously meant to pique Alessandro's interest. They were often in Italian, and perhaps Signora Conti thought Kate wouldn't cotton on, but she had picked up enough now to get the gist, even though Alessandro would deny it afterwards in a gallant bid to protect Kate's feelings.

She gave Abelie a grateful smile. 'There was really no need on my account. I know it will take time to get to know you all properly, and some people take longer than others to feel comfortable with a newcomer.'

That reply was as diplomatic as she could manage. The truth was that on occasion she had been sorely tempted to shove Maria's head into one of Signora Conti's tureens of tortellini broth. But the broth was so very good, and it seemed a shame to ruin it with something that would leave such a bitter taste.

'But you are Alessandro's choice,' Abelie said stubbornly. 'We all respect that, apart from—'

Her sentence was cut short by Signora Conti hailing them from the end of the hall.

'*Ciao*, Kate,' she said and smiled as she stepped forward to kiss her on the cheek. To a casual observer they could have been best friends. The fact was, it was difficult to be annoyed at Alessandro's mother, despite her meddling, because she was so bloody nice.

Abelie gave a tiny shrug and an apologetic smile as Signora Conti beckoned Kate to follow her down the hall. Kate returned it with a small smile of her own. At least she had some allies in the camp, and she was grateful for them.

'Any luck on the job front?' Abelie asked as they reached the living room and Signora Conti, signalling that they should wait, went into the kitchen. It looked as though Kate had arrived earlier than Maria, and as Lucetta was also missing she wondered whether they'd gone out together to fetch some last-minute supplies.

'Not yet,' she replied. Before her move to Italy, many people had offered to speak to this contact or that friend to try and get her some work before she arrived. But despite their best intentions and promises, they had all come to nothing and Kate was having to do the legwork herself. 'It's very hard to convince people that it's a good idea to hire me. I mean, I can wait tables and serve English-speaking customers, but I'm not going to do so well communicating with people from other countries who don't speak English. But I have sold two dresses, so that's a start on the business front.'

'You have?' Abelie clapped her hands together. 'But that is wonderful!'

'I had to do a discount, of course, because they were for my landlord's wife. . .'

Abelie's expression darkened. 'Why a discount? He has plenty of money.'

'I don't think he has quite as much as you imagine. He said—'

'Does he give you cut price on your rent?' Abelie demanded.

'Well, no, but—'

'If he wants you to pay all the rent, he must pay you full price for dresses!' She stamped her foot in a manner that was so petulant it was almost comical. 'I will speak to him!'

'No, please don't do that!' Kate groaned. This was Alessandro all over again. She didn't need anyone talking to her landlord on her behalf and she didn't want to rock the boat and risk losing an apartment that she liked. Well, perhaps *like* was stretching it, but it would do her well enough, and she would much rather avoid the stress and upheaval of trying to find another place when she was barely settled in this one. 'I wish I hadn't told you now. . .'

Abelie rubbed her arm. 'Come now, I do not want you to feel sad. I want to hear about your dresses; it is exciting and soon the whole of Rome will be talking about them.'

'I doubt that, but I appreciate the sentiment. It's a start at least, and it's more than I've managed to do in the last month of trying to get my business off the ground.'

'You will be a success; I know it. But you must be patient.'

'I know. Patience is hard when the money is bleeding from my bank account faster and faster every week.'

Abelie frowned. 'It is not like you to be sad about things. You are always hopeful, always happy. What happened?'

Kate shook her head. 'Ignore me. Of course I'm not sad – I'm living a dream that few other people get to live. I'm in Rome, with the most fantastic boyfriend and his wonderful family. You're right – if I keep working on it and I'm patient, I'm sure it will all come good. I just thought that people might be a bit more enthusiastic about what I do, that's all. I didn't imagine that it would be such hard work to convince people to buy from me.'

'You need a shop. People cannot buy what they cannot see.'

'Right again, but that won't happen any time soon.'

'*Va bene*, but for now I have made these cards to get you some alteration business. See. . .' Abelie reached for a stack of cream business cards sitting on a nearby table and handed them to Kate. They were inked in an elegant slate-grey font, the details written in Italian apart from Kate's name. Underneath the main body of text was a short paragraph in English:

English-speaking seamstress – repairs and alterations undertaken, reasonable rates and excellent work.

'That is for the expatriates and the tourists,' Abelie explained, indicating the final sentence with a perfectly manicured nail. 'There are many in Rome and they would be glad of an English woman to help them, I'm sure.'

Kate looked up at her and beamed. 'They're fantastic! Where on earth did you get them? You didn't make them, surely?'

'Bruno. He works for the print shop and he made them for me.' She gave a coy smile. 'He can be very useful.'

'Is this Bruno who got dumped but is still madly in love with you?' Kate said, trying but failing to give her a look of disapproval. 'Shame on you.'

Abelie's smile turned into a broad grin. 'I may decide to let him ask me to dinner again. He is not horrible.'

'You are, though,' Kate said, but then she broke into a grin too. 'I suppose if I was as pretty as you I'd be stringing a whole heap of men along.'

'*Stringing a whole heap of men along?*' Abelie frowned. 'I do not understand. . .'

'Never mind,' Kate said, putting the business cards back on the table and giving Abelie a warm hug. '*Grazie*. It's a wonderful thing for you and poor Bruno to do for me.'

'*Prego.*' Abelie beamed, clearly happy to have done Kate a service. If only all Alessandro's sisters could be so easy to win over.

'Where are Maria and Lucetta?'

'Getting their hair cut.' Abelie patted herself on the head, as if just to be clear on it.

'Oh.'

'Yes, they are supposed to be here,' Abelie confirmed. 'Mamma is unhappy. She says Lucetta maybe she can spare because she is getting married and everybody will look, but Maria is not the bride and no-body will be looking at her hair.'

'I suppose we should make a start without them, then,' Kate said, choosing not to comment on Maria and Lucetta's absence. In the circumstances, she wasn't exactly broken-hearted about it – at least, not about Maria anyway.

Signora Conti returned, staggering under the weight of a huge box. Kate and Abelie ran to take a corner each and helped her place it on the table.

'Wow, they're heavy,' Kate said. She looked at Abelie. 'How do you say heavy in Italian?'

'*Pesante.*'

'*Sì.*' Signora Conti nodded. '*Molto pesante!*'

'These are the almonds?' Kate peered into the box. 'They look lovely.'

'Mamma has candied them all herself,' Abelie said, the pride obvious in her voice.

'She has?' Kate smiled at Signora Conti. '*Molto bella!* They look amazing!'

Signora Conti waved away the compliment, but it was clear from the way she was beaming that she was enjoying the praise just the same. Disappearing into the kitchen, she returned a few moments later with a pile of tiny muslin bags and a crate of delicate pink flowers that looked a little like forget-me-nots, though Kate wasn't sure what they actually were.

'We will put five almonds in each bag and tie them up with a ribbon and a flower,' Abelie said.

Five almonds each didn't sound like much of a gift, but when the guest list was close to four hundred people, Kate supposed that was actually quite a lot of almonds. They were probably lucky they were getting almonds at all.

Signora Conti said a few words to Abelie that Kate didn't catch, and then went back into the kitchen. Abelie dragged the box of almonds towards her and produced a scoop from within.

'I will count the nuts into the bags and I will pass them for you to tie and make pretty with the flowers. You will do that better than me.'

'Where's your mother gone?' Kate asked as she took a pile of bags.

'She has to prepare lunch.'

'This early?' Kate glanced up at the clock.

'Yes.' Abelie nodded cheerily. 'A special lunch for Lucetta. It is her last as an unmarried woman.'

'I suppose so,' Kate replied, though it didn't make much sense to her that Alessandro's mother should be faffing around in the kitchen all morning when they had so much to do and were down two pairs of hands already. It wasn't like Lucetta would never have lunch there again once she was married. But what didn't make sense to her obviously did to Signora Conti, and there was no point in dwelling on it – a lot of things Signora Conti did or said didn't make much sense to Kate. . .

The next half hour passed pleasantly, Abelie describing some of the more eccentric family members Kate could expect to meet at the wedding – like Uncle Carlucci, who just loved telling new listeners about his extra nipple, and after a few drinks would be even happier to display it, and Cousin Sophia, who led everyone to believe that she travelled the length and breadth of Italy singing opera, though Cousin Flavia knew someone who knew someone who had seen her performing at a rather less cultured lap-dancing club. There was Aunt Speranza, who sat in her garden day after day listening to her vegetables growing, and ninety-year-old Uncle Michele who lived up north. While other pensioners of his advanced years were expending all their energies simply on staying alive, he still belonged to a boxing club that he attended five times a week and bombed around the shores of Lake Garda on a motorbike salvaged from an army base during the Second World War. Kate thought they sounded like a wonderful, if slightly daunting, bunch, and she was looking forward to getting to know Alessandro's extended family better. The only thing that caused her a great deal of anxiety about it all was how they would receive her, particularly if Maria or Alessandro's mother had primed them beforehand. It was a worry that she expressed to Abelie (whilst leaving out the parts about Maria and Signora Conti's potential influence) but Abelie merely smiled warmly and exclaimed that she couldn't see how Kate could possibly fail to charm them as she had everyone else. Except for Maria, she added, but everyone knew that Maria could take issue with the Virgin Mary herself, and nobody would know the reason why, not even Maria. The idea of Maria picking a fight with Jesus's mum made Kate giggle, and then Abelie giggled too, until they were helpless at the idea. Then Signora Conti came through from the kitchen with coffee and biscotti for them, so they downed tools for a short while and engaged in small talk while they enjoyed their refreshments.

And just when Kate had completely relaxed, happy to be in the company of Abelie and her mother, Lucetta arrived. She smiled broadly as she greeted Kate, and then Maria appeared, her greeting far more stiff and formal and clearly made as a grudging courtesy. Kate could cope with that, but her breath caught in her throat when another figure entered, and she looked past Maria to see that Orazia had followed them in.

'You remember my friend Orazia?' Maria asked Kate, with a smile that spoke of her delight at seeing Kate squirm.

'Yes. . . *buongiorno*.' Kate gave Orazia a brisk nod, unsure of the etiquette here. While she and Orazia had met before, it was in a professional capacity when Kate had gone to the police station to report a robbery during her first visit to Rome, and Orazia had been the officer in charge of the front desk who had first dealt with the complaint.

It wasn't until later – after a great deal of scowling and black looks in Kate's direction, along with a rather rubbish anonymous and threatening phone call – that Kate discovered Alessandro's sister and Orazia were best friends, and that both of them had very definite plans for Alessandro's future, which involved Orazia getting her happy ending with him – at least until Kate had turned up to throw her English spanner into the works. She hadn't seen Orazia since the phone call, and she was fairly certain that she wasn't forgiven one bit, but this was a family situation, and didn't they at least have to pretend for the sake of courtesy that they liked each other?

She was spared any further torture on this point by Signora Conti rushing towards Orazia and embracing her, while Abelie simply raised her eyebrows slightly at Kate and Lucetta looked very awkward about the whole situation.

'It was a great surprise – Orazia was at the hair salon when we arrived,' Lucetta explained hurriedly to Kate. 'Maria asked if she would like to see Mamma.'

Kate did her best not to show her despair in the smile she gave to Lucetta. Poor Lucetta was doing her best to keep the peace, and she didn't need this sort of stress on the eve of her wedding when she would have enough for twenty people already. As for Maria, Kate was pretty sure that Orazia's presence at the hairdresser's was no surprise to her at all. And she was quite certain that the only reason Maria had brought Orazia home was to taunt Kate.

At Signora Conti's beckoning, Orazia, Lucetta and Maria all took a seat at the table, and Signora Conti rushed to the kitchen – presumably to get more coffee and biscotti. Orazia and Maria both directed penetrating stares at Kate, with fake smiles plastered to their faces, while Lucetta glanced from one to the other, and Abelie, with an impatient sigh, turned her attention back to counting out almonds. Kate wished she could do the same, but she understood that she was compelled to make some kind of conversation in this situation – she just didn't know what it should be, and she didn't particularly want to in any case.

'You are living in Rome now?' Orazia said, the smile that was all show still stretching her face wide.

Kate nodded. 'Yes.'

'You like it? You are brave to come back after you were robbed on the street.'

'It wasn't so scary. . .'

'Hmmm. I thought you looked very scared the day you came to the *Questura*.'

'Did I? Well, I didn't mean to give that impression. And the police made me feel a lot safer.'

There was a stifled guffaw from the direction of Abelie, who simply buried her head deeper into the box on the pretence of scooping out some more almonds. Kate supposed, on reflection, that her comment had been inadvertently funny. One policeman in particular had made her feel a lot safer and she had ended up dating him, and it must have sounded as if Kate had just scored a point against Orazia for apparently reminding her of that little outcome, even though that wasn't what she'd intended at all. 'I'm very happy living in Rome,' she added.

Orazia nodded stiffly. 'You have work?'

She knew Kate didn't have work yet – Maria would have told her that. But Kate didn't take the bait. 'Not yet. But I'm hopeful to get something soon.'

'You will have to go back to England if you do not get work?'

You wish, Kate thought as she aimed her most saccharine smile at her nemesis. *I'm not going to make it that simple for you. . .*

Maria jumped into the conversation before Kate could come up with a suitable reply. 'No money, no rent,' she said, looking at Kate. 'It is sad but that is how the world works.'

'Oh, I've got some money I borrowed from my sister if things get bad,' Kate said.

'But that will not last forever,' Maria insisted, and Orazia clucked in agreement.

'No,' Lucetta broke in, 'but we would help Kate to stay in Rome. After all, she is almost family now.'

'Not yet,' Maria said firmly.

'But when Alessandro marries her she will be. . .' Lucetta replied, and aimed a surreptitious wink at Kate, who had to fight hard to suppress a smirk. There was no love lost between Orazia and Lucetta, and thank goodness Kate had at least one ally in her bid to stave off the competition. Alessandro himself was quite adamant that he would rather chew off his own ear than go on another night out with Orazia, and he had seen quite enough of her tempers and mood swings during their brief relationship for him to know she wasn't someone he could make a future with. But it was the fact that they *had* been involved in a relationship, and that Orazia was a policewoman who could understand the demands of Alessandro's job in a way Kate never could that sometimes troubled Kate in the wee hours of the morning. And not necessarily just Orazia, but any woman who had a lot more in common with him than she herself did – which was pretty much any woman Signora Conti tried to foist upon him. She and Alessandro had been brought up worlds apart and their life experiences had been so different – would those differences one day become problems for their relationship? Her head told her no, but sometimes her uncertain heart made her judgement very poor indeed. Once, she had imagined that her marriage to her ex-husband Matt was rock solid, and all it had taken was one particularly cruel Friday the thirteenth to show her that all she'd believed of that life had been a lie. Now he was living with a girl who'd become pregnant almost as soon as she'd met Matt – ironic when you considered that Kate had been desperate for children but Matt had been dead against the idea. As far as she knew, he still was, but it was a bit too late for that particular lament now.

The warmth from Lucetta's show of solidarity faded quickly as Kate reminded herself of all this. She looked across at Maria and Orazia and forced a careless smile. But inside there was sudden turmoil. When she really looked at Orazia, the woman was gorgeous. Not a vague, fragile prettiness, in the way that Kate regarded herself on a good day, but Orazia was handsome – fire in her eyes, full-on sex appeal and the kind of figure Hollywood stars paid thousands for surgeons to give them. She was the sort of woman who made strangers in the street stop and stare. Try as she might, Kate found it difficult to be relaxed about the fact that she and Alessandro saw each other every day at work. How hard was she trying with Alessandro when Kate wasn't there? She was finding it hard to shake the little barbs that sank into her heart as she looked at the woman who would be her rival. Why had Orazia chosen to come here today of all days, just when Kate had been settling and having fun with Abelie? Who knew, if she hadn't turned up to ruin everything, perhaps Kate could have made progress with Maria too as they worked together?

'Kate has only just arrived in Rome,' Maria said, indignation in her tone. 'Alessandro cannot marry her so soon.'

'I think Alessandro will never marry,' Orazia said nonchalantly, but she looked slyly at Kate as she did so, and it was clear she was hoping for a reaction. Well, Kate wouldn't give her one.

'Marriage is overrated,' she said airily. 'And if Alessandro never asks me I won't care.'

Lucetta stared at her, her mouth now open. Even Abelie looked up from her task and blinked in disbelief. Immediately, Kate realised she'd said the wrong thing. The fabric of their entire family was built on marriage, and she knew very well how important and sacred the institution was to them all, especially Signora Conti. She might as well have said that she was going to tie Alessandro up and keep him in the cupboard as a sex slave. But she couldn't take it back now without looking weak in front of Orazia, and so she pretended that she meant perfectly well what she had said and dared anyone to challenge it. 'It is the twenty-first century, after all,' she added for good measure.

'I wonder if Alessandro knows your feelings. . .' Maria said. 'I am sure Mamma will be interested to hear them.'

Lucetta turned on her, an argument erupting in rapid Italian. Kate made out something about Maria being a troublemaker, their mother being sent to an early grave and Alessandro being in love, but then Abelie and Orazia joined in, and with so many other voices all speaking at the same time, she lost the thread and fell too far behind to translate any more. In all honesty, if the same argument had been raging in English, she would have been hard-pressed to keep up with that too. Her own sister, Anna, could be opinionated, and she, Kate and their youngest sister, Lily, had their disagreements, but the Conti sisters were something else.

It was as Signora Conti rushed in to see what all the clamour was about that Orazia pushed her chair from the table and stood primly.

She said something to the room that Kate couldn't catch and then swept from it. Maria glowered in Kate's direction before chasing her friend, while Signora Conti stood, open-mouthed, staring at the direction they had both just disappeared in. Maria and Orazia could be heard quite clearly from the hallway, and even though their conversation was still in their native tongue, Kate could tell that she featured rather heavily in it. The problem was, so could everyone else, and when it got to the bit where Orazia made no secret of the fact that she thought Kate wasn't good enough for Alessandro, that she was already causing the sort of trouble in the family that threatened to cause a real rift, and that she had insulted Orazia, who was their guest (although Kate couldn't see how she'd managed to do that in the short time Orazia had been there, and was quite regretful that she hadn't been told beforehand she was going to get accused of insults, because she would have thought of some really juicy ones to justify the accusation), Signora Conti's expression had darkened. For a split second, as she watched, Kate could see exactly where Maria had inherited her scowl from. And Lucetta, though Kate suspected they had different reasons for looking angry.

The sound of the front door slamming echoed down the hallway and into the room, and Kate almost leapt from her seat. Seconds later a furious-looking Maria marched back in. Without a word to anyone, she yanked the box of almonds away from Abelie and dug her hands in, tight-lipped as she counted out groups of five and shoved them at Kate. Abelie gave a hopeless shrug, glancing between Lucetta and Kate, and then looked at her mother. But Signora Conti didn't say a word either and took herself back to the kitchen. Perhaps she was in mind of the old adage that if you didn't have anything good to say, don't say anything at all, or perhaps she just didn't know how to react to the fracas. But Kate wished she'd say something because right now she didn't have a clue where she stood with the Conti matriarch, and she really needed to if she was going to have any chance at all of winning her favour. As for Maria, it looked as if the best she could hope for was a ceasefire, at least for the next couple of days while they celebrated Lucetta's wedding, because it was clear from her face that Maria was not in the mood to make friends any time soon.

Kate had been so preoccupied by the altercation with Orazia that, for once, she'd barely noticed how the glorious winter sun bounced from gleaming terracotta rooftops, or the way it gently warmed the pavements dotted with planters of olives and herbs as it clung to the horizon, or the way the branches of gnarled vines on the trelliswork of pavement cafés cast scrolling shadows along the walls. Fairy lights like first stars in a rose sky popped into life over restaurant doorways as dusk drew in, pearly lanterns at the corners of streets flickering to join them. She'd spent many evenings exploring her neighbourhood with Alessandro, and every time it revealed some new wonder to her. She'd been driven home in this way many times by one of his sisters too since she'd arrived in Rome, but this was the first time the glory of her new home had failed to rouse her. She was tired, and for the first time wondered if perhaps Signora Conti had a point about Kate's suitability for Alessandro. She was an alien to his world, and tonight she felt it might be a very long time before she began to understand how it worked.

She'd bid Abelie a distracted goodnight at the door to her apartment, keys at the ready before she'd even left the car in her haste to get home and put the day behind her. But the day wasn't finished with her yet.

'Oh, hello, Salvatore. . .' Kate squeaked as she rounded the corner from the stairs and emerged into the main corridor of her apartment building, almost slamming into her landlord, who was coming the opposite way. 'I mean, *buongiorno.*'

'*Buonasera*, Kate,' he said amiably.

Kate couldn't help a fond smile. He was an odd little man, sprightly, very thin, in his early sixties, with thinning hair and a wispy moustache that clung to his top lip, as if someone had applied glue and then blown a handful of eyelashes at him in the hope some would stick.

'There's no problem, is there?' she asked. 'I mean, you weren't looking for me for any reason?'

'*Scusi?*'

'Did you need me?' Kate asked. The problem with her Italian was that, at the moment, she was getting listening and interpreting a lot faster than she was getting the actual speaking bit. So while she could often get the gist of what people were saying, she found it difficult to remember the words for a reply. Often, conversations with her landlord descended into this strange farce where he spoke in Italian, and she replied in English, and then he would reply in English that was as terrible as her Italian, so that she would be forced to try and switch to her own bad Italian, which would get them both precisely nowhere. In the end, a lot of nodding and smiling happened, but not a lot of actual communication. Which was why Kate chose to avoid the little matters of faulty boilers and leaking taps, deciding that it was easier just to live with them than trying to explain.

'Ah!' he exclaimed, the war medals that he wore pinned to his grey woollen jacket clanking together as he wagged a triumphant finger. Alessandro had told her that Salvatore had never actually won the medals and had never seen action in any war anywhere in the world, but since inheriting the medals from some distant uncle over twenty years ago, he had taken to wearing them himself at almost all times. At least, that was the version of events the local gossips held to be the truth – gossip that Alessandro had grown up hearing. The reasons for this were a complete mystery to those same local gossips, but something they had simply decided to stop worrying about. Nobody gave Salvatore's war chest so much as a passing glance these days. 'My wife. . . her dress. . . *molto bella!* She likes very much!'

'Oh. . .' Kate said, relaxing a little. 'I'm glad.'

'You make more?' he asked, holding two fingers up in a V sign, presumably to indicate the amount of dresses his wife wanted, although in Manchester it would have had an altogether ruder meaning.

Kate nodded, and briefly the conversation she'd had with Abelie about the pricing of her work popped into her mind. As she internally framed the words to bring the matter up, he interrupted her thoughts. '*Molto bene!* Same price, eh? *Sì? Molto bene!*'

She shrugged slightly, and then nodded. What was the point in trying to argue when she wasn't even equipped with the words to begin it? Alessandro and Lucetta could tell her off, but they weren't the ones looking into Salvatore's funny little face as he grinned hopefully up at her. She couldn't help but like the man, whether he was ripping her off or not, and he and his wife had been very sweet to her since she first moved into the building.

'*Grazie!*' He beamed. 'When?'

'You mean when can I do them?'

He nodded eagerly. 'Nunzia, she has party. Big party!'

'When is the party?'

He scrunched up his face for a moment. '*Dicembre. . .*'

'December? Beginning or end?'

'Soon. . .'

It was early November now, so that gave her four or five weeks at best. Quite why Nunzia needed two dresses for one party was a bit of a mystery too. Kate supposed she might get better information from Nunzia herself, who would no doubt come over shortly to peruse Kate's pattern books, or else bring some ideas of what she wanted from her own magazines. Nunzia's English wasn't perfect either, but it was still a lot better than Kate's Italian.

'OK,' Kate said. 'I'm not home tomorrow. . . Lucetta Conti's wedding. . .'

He grinned and nodded. '*Sì, sì. . .*'

'But I'll be here next week all the time so Nunzia can come any time to see me.'

'*Va bene. . . Grazie.*'

Kate nodded. '*Prego.*'

After bidding him goodbye, Kate was grateful to finally unlock the door to her flat and close the world out behind it. As tough days went, it had been one hell of a prime specimen. The place felt empty without Alessandro's presence filling it, but she was glad of the quiet and the opportunity to take stock.

With Signora Conti preparing such a huge lunch for Lucetta, there was little need for Kate to cook much for her evening meal. As she grazed on some bread and cheese, she couldn't help but dwell on the events of the day. The atmosphere at what should have been Lucetta's celebration of her last day as a single woman was subdued, and try as she might to feel otherwise, Kate couldn't help but feel that it was all her fault and she had ruined a day Lucetta could never get back. It had only been Jolanda and Isabella, two of Alessandro's older sisters, arriving with their youngest children, who had lifted the mood, being completely oblivious to what had gone before, and Kate was thankful for them. At least after lunch they had all pitched in to get the preparations for the wedding finished, and with the extra bodies the atmosphere had become a little more jovial again, though it was far from perfect. Goodbyes with Kate had been strained all round, and she had been glad to shut the door behind her and leave the household to discuss her freely, which they undoubtedly would. At that point, she was simply too tired and fed up to care.

Kate's mobile phone sat on the kitchen worktop next to where she was perched on a stool eating as the late evening sun warmed her back. The sound of an incoming call shook her from her musings and Alessandro's warm tones greeted her as she answered.

'Kate. . . Lucetta has called me. What has happened today with Orazia?'

That hadn't taken long. Kate had been hoping she wouldn't have to go over it again tonight. But it was obvious that Lucetta or Abelie would call Alessandro about it. It wouldn't be a huge surprise to learn that Maria or Orazia had too, but their version of events would have been very different.

'I don't really want to talk about it. Will I see you tonight?'

'But Orazia insulted you?'

'Not exactly. She wasn't what you'd call friendly—'

'Maria was rude too. . . I will speak to them!'

'Always with the speaking to people!' Kate snapped. She rubbed at her temples. 'I'm sorry. . .' she said, evening out her tone. He was looking out for her and she was just lashing out at him because there was nobody else there. Why did things have to be so complicated? What happened to boy meets girl and everyone is happy for them?

Why did Signora Conti want her son married off to just about any woman under the age of forty apart from Kate, who wouldn't actually mind the job so much?

'I just don't want you to speak to anyone about it,' she continued. 'I don't want people thinking I have to hide behind you all the time. I need to deal with it and I will.'

'Mamma likes you,' he said, though Kate could hear the frustration in his voice. They both knew that Signora Conti did like Kate. She would love Kate as her personal seamstress, as a neighbour, as the quirky English woman who came to dinner every so often to entertain her with stories of a rainy Manchester, but as a daughter-in-law. . . that, not so much. And it was frustrating, for her and for Alessandro.

'I know that. Maria, on the other hand, is not so keen, but I suppose no family is perfect.'

'Maria is trying, but she is disappointed.'

'That Orazia won't be her sister-in-law after all? The funny thing is I can see why it bothers her, which doesn't help. I suppose the idea of your best friend being part of your family is a nice one.'

'Orazia is trying too.'

'She's that alright. . .'

'What do you mean?' he asked simply. Kate found herself giving the phone a tight smile, even though he couldn't see it. The language barrier again, though sometimes it was lucky he didn't quite get her immediate response to a comment, particularly when it made her look sulky and unreasonable.

'I'm sure she thinks she's being perfectly lovely to me – at least, as nice and courteous as she can be. But it's obvious to anyone with eyes that she hates me.'

'She does not hate you.'

Kate was silent for a moment, certain that he was wrong but not wanting to provoke a disagreement. She'd had quite enough of those for one day. 'I just want a chance to be accepted by your family, that's all. And by family I mean all of them, even Maria and your mother. Right now it feels as if nothing I do endears me in the slightest to them.'

'Perhaps Lucetta's wedding will be that chance. When the whole family meet you they must love you, and their good reports will persuade Mamma and Maria too.'

'I'm not convinced, but maybe you're right. I hope so.' She let out a sigh. She suddenly realised how badly she wanted him with her, to hold her and kiss her and tell her everything would work out. Because when she was with him, she felt she could face anything. 'So, will you be able to come over tonight?'

'I am sorry, so much to do for the wedding. I am still at the wedding villa and it will not be ready for some time. I must speak with my cousins too. . . you will be OK?'

'Yes. . . yes, of course I will be. I should have realised – this is a big family occasion and you need to be involved. I'm sorry I asked, it's just. . .'

'I would want to be with you, more than anything. But tonight is impossible. Tomorrow, early, I will come for you, and we will go to the wedding together.'

Kate nodded. 'It'll be a nice day – I'm looking forward to it.'

If he could hear the lie in her voice, he didn't say so. '*Va bene.* Sleep well tonight and do not worry. *Ti amo.*'

'*Ti amo*, Alessandro. See you tomorrow.'

Ending the call, Kate pushed her plate of food away and leaned on the counter, gazing around the tiny kitchen. The flat was not luxurious, but it was good enough and she made the best of it, considering the trade-off a small price to pay for living her dream in Rome. At times like these, however, when the dream didn't seem quite as sparkly as she'd once hoped, the faded décor that she told everyone was characterful, and the dated, worn furniture that she insisted cheerfully was vintage and quirky, didn't seem quite so appealing. At times like these she missed the beautiful house she'd had in Manchester and the friends and family she'd left behind. As for a walk to remind her of why she was trying so hard to make a new life here, her apartment was so far from the city centre it would take her hours to walk it, and the magnificent architecture and breathtaking splendour of the city itself was a world away from the post-war blocks of the suburb she lived in.

She shook herself. Tomorrow was another day, and Alessandro was right – she needed to use the occasion to get to know everyone and win them over while they were all in a party mood. There was a lot of family to meet, and it was going to be busy, but it might just be the answer to her prayers. It was a wedding, in a beautiful church, followed by a spectacular reception venue, in one of the most romantic cities in the world, and she had the man of her dreams by her side. Why wouldn't it be amazing? It was a wonderful excuse to cut loose, let her hair down, remind herself why she loved Italy so much and why she had chosen to live there.

Reaching for her phone, she dialled her sister Anna's number. She had spoken to her younger sister, Lily, earlier that day, but her older one, Anna, had been busy and she had promised to call back. It was probably wise to do it now, get showered and get an early night ready for the long day tomorrow.

Anna picked up on the first ring.

'Bloody hell, did you have it glued to your hand?' Kate asked.

Anna's laughter was the most wonderful sound, and it lifted Kate's spirits immediately. It also made her yearn for her sister's company.

'Not quite, I just happened to be unplugging it from the charger. How are you?'

'I'm good,' she replied. There was a pause.

'Is your nose OK?' Anna asked.

'What?'

'Not poking vases from sideboards or anything? Because it must be growing at a rate of knots. . .'

'Ha ha, funny.'

'I can always tell when you're lying. What's wrong?'

'Nothing's wrong,' Kate said. She let out a sigh. 'Nothing is wrong with day-to-day living. It's just. . .' How did she explain the arbitrary and irrational jealousy she was fast developing about Orazia? There was no reason in the world to fear her, even less to question Alessandro's heart, so why did she feel so threatened? It was bad enough convincing Signora Conti that she was the right woman for Alessandro, but that just needed a little gentle coaxing, maybe a few more gifts and kindnesses. Orazia was something else, however – something Kate didn't know how to deal with. She had never once felt threatened by the women that her ex-husband, Matt, came into contact with, and she had never been filled with such a forceful sense of distrust. The fact was she thought Orazia capable of anything, and for some reason, even though Kate had been in Rome for a month now, her old nemesis had suddenly decided to show her face, despite not having done so up until this point. It could have been a coincidence, Maria and Lucetta casually running into her at the hairdresser's, but somehow Kate doubted it. It smacked of a set-up. Perhaps Maria had sat by, thinking that Kate and Alessandro would blow their relationship out themselves – a holiday romance that wouldn't stand the test of becoming something more real – but then she had seen Kate making headway, and their relationship getting stronger, and had decided to do something about it.

'Alessandro's family are still proving a bit tough?' Anna asked gently. 'You'll get there. He won me over, and I'm sure you can do the same with his mum. After all, if he's in love and happy that's surely all any mother wants for her son?'

'Yes. . . of course, you're right. Like always.' Kate rallied for Anna's sake. There was no point in causing her anxiety when distance prevented her from doing the one thing she would be desperate to do if she thought Kate was in trouble, which was come to her aid. 'At least the preparations for the wedding are going well.'

'Lucetta's? It's tomorrow, isn't it? God, what I wouldn't give for an invite – I bet it'll be fantastic.'

'I think it will be. It certainly promises to be memorable. And big. And very rowdy.'

'I'll bet!' Anna laughed. 'I want photos, and lots of them. What are you wearing?'

'I've got two dresses – a little tea dress in Wedgwood blue for the day and a dove-grey strapless one for the evening.'

'They sound lovely. It's such a shame I can't nip round to yours and borrow them any more.'

'Come over any time.'

'Actually. . .' Kate could hear the smile in Anna's voice, 'I was thinking I might.'

'Come over? To see me here?'

'It's not such a weird concept!' Anna replied, laughing lightly. 'When's good for you?'

'Well. . . My diary isn't exactly full but even if it was I'd move *everything* to fit you in. There's not much room at the flat but—'

'Don't be daft. We wouldn't hear of putting you out. Christian and I will be just fine in a hotel somewhere nearby.'

'Are you sure?'

'Of course. Besides, you might find it a bit tricky to fit Lily and Joel in too. . .'

'They're coming too!' Kate squeaked. 'When was this decided?'

'We talked about it last night – thought it was about time we came to your new home and saw what all the fuss is about.'

'Oh, I can't wait! How long will you come for?'

'I'm not sure yet. We're going to put our heads together, check out the flights and hotels and base it on the costs. The cheaper we can do it for, the longer we can stay. Mum says she's going to try too, but I don't know whether she'll make it as our hypochondriac stepdaddy Hamish has been suffering with his gout again. You know how it is, so we won't make any promises there. I'm really looking forward to meeting Alessandro's family too. . .'

Kate's smile slipped. She'd forgotten about that little scenario. Under normal circumstances she'd have been excited about that too, but after today? With Lucetta's wedding around the corner and the chance that represented to smooth things with Signora Conti and Maria, it was too early to tell yet how a meeting with her own sisters might go. Perhaps it wasn't worth worrying about yet. But she was looking forward to showing Anna and Lily the sights. They wouldn't take much convincing about the beauty of Rome, and they'd understand once they saw it for themselves just why Kate had fallen in love with the city.

'There's so much I want to show you, it would be great if you could do the whole week. But whatever you manage we'll cram in as much as we can.'

'I'm looking forward to a bit of sister time.'

'I'm not sure Christian will be with you on that.'

'Oh, he can do whatever he wants. I expect he'll find a bar to prop up somewhere. Maybe Alessandro can take him out to do blokey stuff.'

'I'm not sure they'll be into the same blokey stuff, but that's not a bad idea.'

'Italians love their football. So does Christian. They'll be absolutely fine.'

An unexpected yawn suddenly erupted from Kate.

'I heard that,' Anna said drily. 'Am I keeping you up? Or has Alessandro been doing that?'

'No, cheeky. It's just been a long day.'

'Early start tomorrow too?'

'Yes.'

'I'll ring off, let you get ready for bed.'

'I'm not going to bed this early, no matter how tired I am. Please. . . don't go yet. Talk to me for a while – tell me what's going on there.'

'Are you sure you want me to? It hasn't got any more exciting than it was before you left.'

But it's safe, Kate thought. Boring, but safe: no boyfriend-stalking, bunny-boiling Amazonian policewomen hiding around every corner and waiting for the first opportunity to trip you up and steal your man. No watching the money in the bank drain away while you struggled to get work in a city that had enough workers of its own. No constant fear that you'd made a huge mistake. Nice and safe.

'I can take a bit of boring,' Kate said. 'Hit me with your worst.'

Two

Kate reached across the bed. Empty. She'd been dreaming that Alessandro was there and had woken, convinced she could hear his voice. But the sun slanted through a gap in the curtains and lit up crisp white sheets, untroubled by the presence of anyone but herself. Flipping herself over, she squinted at the clock on her bedside cabinet. It was almost six, and her alarm was set to go off in a few minutes anyway. Switching it off, she rolled onto her back with a deep sigh and stared up at the ceiling.

Lucetta's wedding day had arrived, and although part of her was excited for the spectacle and glamour of an Italian wedding, the rest of her was rather more apprehensive. She had no need to be – Alessandro, Lucetta, Abelie, Anna and Lily had all told her she had nothing to fear and no reason not to gain the approval of Alessandro's wider family. But it wasn't easy to feel as confident as they all did.

Her dresses hung on the rickety old wardrobe doors. She turned onto her side and gazed at them. At least she was happy with those, and perhaps, when she told people she had made them herself, they'd be impressed enough to want her to make things for them too. . . and actually get paid the going rate for her work. Reaching for her phone from next to the clock, she checked for messages.

Are you awake?

Kate smiled.

Yes. Are you excited for today?
Lucetta is. She woke everyone at four thirty. Mamma is tired and unhappy.
Oh dear. Are you tired?
I am never tired. I am like a horse, remember?
My Italian stallion – yes!

Kate giggled. It was a private joke, something she'd said the very first time she and Alessandro slept together.

I will come for you soon.

Kate tapped out a reply: *I can't wait. Give me a clue, though. How soon is soon?*

Alessandro and his entire family had this annoying habit of making social arrangements without any sense of a schedule whatsoever, and they seemed to assume that everyone else could just fit in with it. At least it would have been annoying if there hadn't been something quite carefree and endearing about it. How on earth Lucetta was going to be standing at the altar within any kind of chronologically accurate timeframe was a mystery for the greatest minds of the age, but Kate was curious to see if she would manage it or not. And if the extended family were as bad, it would make for a very interesting day indeed.

One hour.

Great. She might have known that six wouldn't be early enough. Why didn't she learn to iron these things out beforehand? But it was pointless and a complete waste of precious time sitting arguing about it.

OK. See you in an hour. x

Locking the phone, Kate scrambled out of bed, now wide awake and full of nervous energy. She had an hour to make herself presentable – it looked as though breakfast was going to have to wait.

As she opened the door to her apartment, smoothing down her dress, the smile on Kate's face turned into a frown. The man made a little gesture, as if tipping an imaginary cap.

'*Buongiorno*. I have come to take you to the wedding.'

She had never seen this man before in her life. Instinctively, she backed away slightly, retreating into the safety of the doorway with a hand firmly gripped on the door, ready to slam it shut. 'Where's Alessandro?'

'He sends apologies – he could not come. Signora Conti needs help.'

'What sort of help?'

He shrugged. 'She wobbles.'

'Wobbles?'

'*Sì*. . .' He did a little mime, as if he was feeling faint. Kate could only assume that the stress of the day had already got to her, but in all honesty, it could have meant anything. If Signora Conti was wobbling, didn't she have plenty of other children in the vicinity to help her out? Why did it have to be Alessandro?

'Is she alright?'

'She needs to rest. But the church is not ready.'

'But I thought they did all that yesterday,' Kate replied obstinately. 'Why couldn't somebody else do it? He said he would come for me this morning.'

'*Sì*. . . he sends apologies,' the man repeated. 'But I can take you now.'

'I'd rather call him first,' Kate replied. 'Wait there.'

Shutting the man out, she dug in her clutch bag for her phone and dialled Alessandro's number. It rang out. Typical. Why did he have to be so frustrating? What was Kate supposed to do? What was so important that he couldn't come? And who the hell was this man standing in his place? Was she just supposed to get into a car with him? How did she know he was who he said he was? Come to think of it, he hadn't said anything about who he was at all. Her mind was in a whirl, and she was beginning to feel as if she'd somehow stumbled into the plot of a thriller novel. Who else could she call to verify the new arrangements? Lucetta and her sisters would all be busy getting dressed and pampered and she doubted they would answer their phones. With a mental shrug, she tried Abelie anyway, and then Jolanda and Isabella, but, as she suspected, they didn't answer. As for trying Maria, Kate decided that she would rather fight off a potential abductor than phone her.

'This is ridiculous,' she muttered to herself and opened the door again to the man, who simply stood smiling at her. He looked harmless enough – in his late forties to early fifties, slightly built, a good head of curly hair and eyes that reminded her an awful lot of Alessandro. Come to think of it, now that she looked closer, he did bear a resemblance. A relative?

'Are you a wedding guest?' Kate asked, the question rather stupid considering the suit he was wearing. But it seemed politer than asking *Who the hell are you?*

'I am Marco. . . Alessandro is my nephew.'

Kate smiled. It would have saved a lot of time if he'd simply told her that at the beginning instead of being so vague. And as for trusting him, she didn't see that she had a lot of choice. Refusing his lift would probably be an insult if he was Alessandro's uncle, and she didn't want to start her introduction to the extended family that way. Although none of this changed her vexation at Alessandro for dropping her at the last minute without any warning or letting her know what plan B was.

'I'm Kate.'

He nodded amiably. 'I know this.'

'Of course you do,' Kate said. 'Silly, aren't I?'

Sweeping a hand towards the corridor, he beckoned her out. 'Please, we go. The wedding is early; there is much to do.'

There was nothing else for it. Kate locked the door of her apartment and followed him to a white car waiting outside. It looked as if it was at least thirty years old, but it seemed in a good condition nonetheless. It seemed loved too, waxed to a finish so mirror-like that the early morning sun bounced from its bonnet, gleaming chrome wheels and immaculate tyres. Marco opened the passenger door for her.

'*Grazie*,' Kate said as she got in. She watched as he got into the driver's seat and started the engine

'Are we going to the church straightaway?' Kate asked.

'Yes. Alessandro is there now.' Marco shot her an appraising glance, and then quickly shifted his attention back to the road as they pulled away from the kerb. 'You are the English woman who has stolen Alessandro's heart?' he asked, staring straight ahead.

Kate paused. Was he going to add more to that statement? Say he was glad, express disgust, ask her more about her intentions for the future? But he offered nothing else.

'I suppose so,' she said lamely.

'Maria does not trust you, and Giuditta wonders if you will run away to England.'

'Giuditta?'

'Alessandro's mother.'

'Oh!' Kate couldn't help a smile. It was like being back at school and finding out the teachers had real names other than Sir or Miss. She had always known Alessandro's mother as Signora Conti and couldn't imagine calling her anything else. For a start, it would seem discourteous, but other than her children, it was all anyone she had encountered so far called her. It was weird to imagine her as a girl, running the backstreets of Rome with her friends calling her proper name. But the smile faded. What exactly had Maria said? She made no secret of her dislike to Kate, but prejudicing her family before they'd had a chance to meet Kate for themselves wasn't helpful, even though she probably should have expected it. And for someone who had only just met Kate, Marco was being very open about their discussions. *No messing, straight in, this is what we think of you.*

'I think you will be good for him,' he said into the gap. 'You want to stay in Rome?'

'That's the plan.' Kate looked at him, but he was still staring at the road ahead, and his expression gave nothing away. 'I love it here.'

'You may want to go home when it no longer feels like a vacation.'

'I'm not here because it felt like a vacation in the first place. I'm here because I want a new life, not an extended holiday.'

He nodded. '*Va bene*. Then you will be good for Alessandro. Giuditta is afraid for him.'

'She is?'

'She does not want to die and leave him alone.'

'But that's silly! She's not going to die any time soon and he has lots of family and friends.'

'Not the same. She wants him to have a good wife.'

Kate frowned. 'Abelie isn't married yet.'

'Abelie did not lose the love of her life; she has never had her heart broken. She will make a good match because her heart is not injured.'

'And you think Alessandro's is?'

'Giuditta does.'

'He's always seemed happy to me. I know about Heidi, of course, but I thought he was over that.'

'Yes. He acts well, no?'

'You mean he's still mourning?'

He shrugged. 'Perhaps.'

'He's never said anything to me.'

'He is a man.'

Oh, well, that explains it, Kate thought wryly. But was Alessandro still scarred by the death of his first love, Heidi? The woman he'd planned to marry had drowned in a Swiss lake. That had been eight years ago, but perhaps you never really got over something like that. Kate and Alessandro, though – they were happy, weren't they? He wasn't looking at Kate and wishing she was Heidi, was he? It didn't feel like it, but over the last few days, it seemed as if she couldn't be certain of anything between them.

'You will marry him?' Marco asked.

What was it with this family and marriage? They were obsessed by the idea and seemed to be arranging the church the minute someone of age looked at a member of the opposite sex. 'I don't know. Maybe in time.'

'Maria says you do not want to marry anyone. She says you told her this.'

Kate grimaced. It was only a matter of time before her flippant comment came back to bite her on the bottom, and Maria had made sure to spread it as quickly as possible. It was a fair bet she'd embellished it a great deal along the way too. But did the fact that she had told her uncle mean that she had also told Signora Conti?

'That wasn't exactly what I meant. I just meant it's too early to think about marriage.'

'So you will? In a year perhaps?'

'I don't know.'

They lapsed into silence again. As introductions to the family went, this was a strange one. Kate had imagined them standing around outside the church, kisses and smiles, not an interrogation during an unexpected car journey.

For the remainder of the journey, Kate desperately tried to instigate more fluffy small talk, but though they both engaged, covering the weather, new taxes and good places to eat, it felt like hard work. The creams and greys of Rome flashed by, the streets strangely subdued so early on a Sunday morning. She could almost imagine the city in reflection – thinking back on the week just gone and looking ahead at the week to come.

Marco found a space a few streets from the church and parked up.

'We must walk a little,' he said, hopping out and racing around the car to open the passenger door for her.

Three

It was the first time Kate had seen the church of Santa Maria in Trastevere. More like one of Rome's many tourist attractions than a church at first glance, the approach was through a piazza, a beautiful raised fountain at its centre adorned with decadent detail and the lifelike figures that were so commonplace around the city they became almost unremarkable. The stonework of the church itself was in faded pastels, glittering mosaics depicting holy figures drawing the eye upwards to their eaves, symmetrical arches marking the entrance and a great bell tower standing sentry over it all. The sun skimmed the rooftops, sending blades of light to the ground, the shadows dense where they fell. Something about it felt so holy, so special, that the sight made Kate's neck hair stand on end.

Without even realising she had, she stopped and stared.

'Beautiful, no?' Marco said with a faint smile.

'Gorgeous.' It was a far cry from the poky registry office where she had married Matt. She shook herself, her gaze drawn to a group of figures at the entrance. There were seven or eight men in suits, Alessandro standing a head taller than them all. Throwing a glance across to where she stood with Marco, he handed a huge swathe of what looked like white ribbon to one of his companions and jogged over.

She had been prepared, determined even, to show him how annoyed she was about the unexplained change of plans, but seeing him looking so handsome in his black suit, his expression bright with anticipation and pleasure, the irritation melted from her and she couldn't have held onto it if she'd tried. He pulled her into a kiss, no care for the fact that Marco was standing watching.

'I am sorry I could not come this morning,' Alessandro said. 'The church. . .' He tilted his head to the group behind him, now swelled by the arrival of three women from inside the building. 'So much to do before Lucetta and Gian arrive.'

'Hmmm,' Kate replied, forcing a frown, but it clearly wasn't very convincing because Alessandro simply smiled. 'Lucky for you your uncle looked after me because I could have been quite upset about being abandoned, you know.' It had crossed her mind that Marco could have undertaken the duties that Alessandro had been tending to all morning, but she supposed there might be reasons she didn't know about for this not happening.

Alessandro turned to Marco and clapped him on the back. '*Grazie mille.*'

'*Di niente,*' Marco replied, with a knowing nod to Kate. 'I enjoyed meeting your beautiful Kate.'

It was perhaps best not to mention the bits where she'd almost mistaken him for a kidnapper and he'd proceeded to interrogate her throughout the journey, so Kate offered him a smile in return. 'It was lovely getting to know you too.'

'You would like to come and meet my cousins?' Alessandro asked, offering Kate his arm. 'They are not all here yet, but some. Come. . .'

Kate followed him across the square, taking care not to turn an ankle with her heels on the uneven cobbles. 'What happened to your mother this morning? Marco said she was ill.'

He waved his hand around the piazza. 'This. . . she is exhausted.'

'But she's OK?'

'Abelie made chamomile tea for her. She is at home with Lucetta, preparing for the wedding.'

'Oh. So she's not ill.'

He sighed. 'She never rests and she worries too much about everything. This morning, her head. . .' He paused, waved his hands around his own head as if trying to explain.

'Light-headed?' Kate suggested. 'As if she might faint?'

'Yes. And her heart. . .' He thumped a staccato rhythm out on his chest with the palm of his hand.

'Does that happen a lot?'

'Not so much before. Many times this year.'

'You never said.'

'She does not want me to tell anyone.'

'What does the doctor say?'

'She will not see the doctor.'

'Why not?'

'He will tell her to rest, and she does not know how. She does not want to hear it.'

'But she'll make herself worse if she ignores it.'

'Perhaps when Lucetta has gone to live with Gian life will be easier and she will feel well again.'

Kate doubted that. Signora Conti would still have Alessandro and Abelie to worry about, and from what Marco had said that morning, she could worry herself into an early grave about her family whether they lived with her or not. And even with Maria, Isabella and Jolanda all married and left home, Signora Conti still ran herself ragged preparing lavish meals for one or more of them almost every day. It wasn't exactly winding down as far as Kate could see and she didn't think for a second that Lucetta moving out would make a scrap of difference. It was a worrying development, not only for Alessandro's mother, but for Alessandro too. They were close, and if his mother became ill, it would doubtless have a huge impact on him.

'So she needs to avoid stress,' Kate said. 'At all costs.'

'It would be a good idea, but not so easy, I think.'

Kate didn't think it would be easy either, and it wasn't a comforting thought.

Overwhelming was just one word for it. In a whirlwind of names and random facts, Kate had been introduced to the members of Alessandro's family who were already at the church. As she then helped them by running little errands or indulging in last-minute tinkering with the decorations (mostly because she felt so useless standing around while everyone else did it, not necessarily because any of it was needed), more arrived. Uncles, aunts, cousins, second cousins, cousins-twice-removed, in-laws, family friends and what seemed like pretty much anyone else Lucetta had once passed on the street. At the weddings Kate had attended before, the day ceremony was busy if fifty close family and friends graced it, leaving all the other guests – perhaps one to two hundred at most – to let their hair down at the reception later on. If the same ratio applied here, then half of Rome would be at the reception.

The courtyard of the church rang with laughter and the greetings of family who had not seen each other for years. Kate had expected it to be a very chic affair, but outfits ranged from stunning haute couture to some of the more senior guests, who looked as if they had spent the morning cleaning their oven and forgot to change before they came out. But Alessandro extended the same courtesy to them all, and they all showed nothing but civility to Kate as he introduced her.

At nine thirty, Gian climbed from his scooter, looking dapper in a perfectly fitted slate-grey suit subtly edged in black, but more nervous than Kate had ever seen him.

'He looks as if he wants to throw up,' she whispered to Alessandro as members of Gian's family came forward to greet him.

'Throw up?' Alessandro frowned. 'Throw what?'

'He looks as if he might be sick,' Kate explained.

Alessandro's frown became a grin. 'He is marrying Lucetta. He is perhaps sick about all the money he will have to earn to make her happy.'

'Harsh,' Kate said, but she smiled anyway. 'She's not that bad.'

'She likes beautiful things.'

'Beautiful things don't always have to cost a lot of money. Look at this sunshine today; it's cost us nothing and it's the most gorgeous morning Lucetta could hope for.'

Alessandro looked down at her. For a moment, Kate thought he would reply, but then he simply leaned to plant a warm kiss on her lips.

'I must get ready for Lucetta,' he said. 'She will be here soon.'

Kate nodded, watching with regret as he strode through the crowds, still being greeted sporadically by new arrivals, towards the arches of the church entrance, where Gian now stood with his own entourage. She understood that Alessandro was the natural choice to give Lucetta away in the absence of the father who had been dead for so many years, and in that capacity he had duties to perform. She also understood perfectly that he felt honoured to have been asked, and that the request reflected his close bond with his sister, but it didn't mean that Kate wouldn't feel a little lost and lonely without him at her side for the service. Which, being the unabridged Roman Catholic version, promised to be much longer than any she had sat through before.

Her thoughts were interrupted by a huge cheer from the crowd, who burst into spontaneous applause as a blood-red Maserati arrived in the piazza. Kate smiled. Trust Lucetta to go for the sporty option, and as she emerged, swathes of white fabric unfurling from the car with her, Kate wondered just how stressed Signora Conti was feeling at her daughter's impractical choice of transport. Even though she had seen Lucetta wearing her dress before – and she had even worked on it, making alterations to the sleeves – Kate's breath still caught in her throat at how beautiful Alessandro's sister looked. It was one thing to see the dress when Lucetta had tried it on after a day at work, but another to see her hair pinned up, matching jewellery, veil flowing behind her and a glow of happiness that could rival the sun shining down on them. It seemed others thought so too, and there were gasps and exclamations in the crowd. Kate glanced to where Gian had not even bothered to make himself scarce by going inside the church to wait for her, but simply stared, agog, as if he was seeing her for the first time. The best man gently nudged him, and together they went in as Alessandro approached Lucetta and kissed her on the cheek. As there was pretty much only room for Lucetta and her driver in the Maserati, another car arrived a moment later, a rather more dignified-looking vintage Rolls-Royce, from which Signora Conti herself climbed, along with Abelie, wearing a stunning bridesmaid dress in Marsala chiffon, and three of her nieces in complementary dresses that were pure white tulle with matching coloured detailing.

'This will be a beautiful day, no?'

Kate spun round to see Marco standing beside her.

'I'm sure it will be,' she said, glad of a friendly face, even if it was relatively new to her. 'Lucetta looks incredible.'

'Gian is lucky.'

'I think he knows it too,' Kate said, laughing. But out of the corner of her eye, she spotted a figure – Orazia, talking to Maria and her husband – and she suddenly felt the blood drain from her face.

Of course Orazia was going to be here, but she wished somebody had thought to warn her. Suddenly the day didn't seem quite so bright, or the occasion quite so exciting. It would be all sly looks and whispers behind hands, and conversations that Kate couldn't quite grasp, and far from relaxing and starting to enjoy getting to know Alessandro's family, as she had hoped to, she would feel on edge: watched, judged and unable to defend herself.

The faint strains of violin music reached them from inside, and across the piazza Alessandro and Lucetta made their way to the entrance where they stood and waited. Marco turned to Kate.

'Come, we begin. . .'

Kate smiled as he offered his arm. She hesitated for a moment before she accepted, looking around for someone else to be making their way over to take him from her. But everyone started to make their own way in. Didn't Marco have anyone with him? He was with their huge family, obviously, surrounded by hundreds of them, but what about a wife or children? Her thoughts had been elsewhere that day and now she regretted that she hadn't asked.

'Come,' he insisted.

With an uncertain nod, she let him lead the way. They passed Alessandro and Lucetta, waiting for the last of the guests to seat themselves before they made their entrance, and he gave Kate a warm smile, while Lucetta did an excited little wave that made Kate want to burst out laughing. She may have looked like a demure and regal bride, but it was still the same feisty, outspoken Lucetta beneath all the finery. How strange that they should have become so close after their inauspicious start, when Kate had been quite convinced that Lucetta hated her. Looking at her now, Kate was glad that she didn't, because Lucetta's friendship and support had been more valuable over the past few months than Kate could possibly express.

Kate considered herself to be an emotional sort of person, but she had never cried at a wedding before, not even her own sister Anna's. But the magnificence of her surroundings – opulent golds, mosaic and marble, the altar standing beneath a cavernous and elegant dome, classical religious music echoing through the space from sublime strings – and the beauty and sentiment of the ceremony, along with Lucetta and Gian's obvious love for each other and the pride she felt in watching Alessandro bravely and reverently perform the duty that their father would have done had he still been alive, finally overwhelmed her. When the tears came, they were unexpected and unprepared for. Marco had sat next to her, and she gratefully accepted the handkerchief he offered and was glad of his company to save her from sitting alone while the main bridal party of Lucetta and Gian's closest family occupied the front rows. Lucetta and Gian had opted for a mix of newness and tradition at their wedding that spoke volumes about their personalities and their heritage, so while the unconventional transport to the church showed they were firmly rooted in the millennium, old traditions such as the smashing of a glass and releasing doves after the service were observed and cherished. And as the couple emerged from the church and into the sun-drenched square, rice raining down on them as the guests cheered and clapped, Alessandro joined Kate and folded her into his arms.

'You are happy?' he asked as he smiled down on her.

'Your uncle looked after me so I didn't have to sit alone,' she said. 'I got a bit emotional for a second in there – I suppose my make-up is ruined now?'

'No. You are beautiful.' He kissed her, and even as he did, Kate could feel Orazia's eyes boring into her back without having to look round to see if she was there, like a second sight. They broke apart and she turned to see she'd been right. Orazia averted her gaze and pretended to be in earnest conversation with Maria and her husband, but Kate wasn't fooled for a minute.

Pushing it from her mind, she turned back to Alessandro. Orazia could stare all she wanted, but he looked handsome in his suit, and his gaze was so warm and genuine that Kate just wanted to savour this moment, to store it forever, and no amount of petty jealousy was going to take it away from her.

There had been a wedding breakfast of sorts, what Alessandro called cocktail hour, and though it sounded a little like a drinks promotion in a tacky Ibizan bar, it was exactly that – a stop-off for only a select few guests at a local restaurant to take cocktails while everyone else entertained themselves until it was time to make their way to the villa for the evening reception. Kate was thrilled to have been included in the cocktail-party guests, and even more thrilled (despite fighting the feeling of smugness) that Orazia had not. More relaxed and intimate, and with a chance to chat at length to people she knew already, this had been her favourite part of the day so far. After congratulating Lucetta and Gian, and going to tell Abelie how gorgeous she looked, Kate made a beeline for Signora Conti.

Alessandro's mother sat at a table a little away from the main throng, and though she had a tall glass of something iced in front of her, she didn't seem to be drinking very much of it. Kate sat alongside her.

'*Come sta?*' she asked gently. It was about as far as her Italian would take her, so she touched at her own temples to mime a headache, and Signora Conti seemed to understand, because she patted Kate's hand and smiled.

'*Bene, grazie.*'

Kate gave her a quick appraisal. She didn't look fine, even if she said she was. She looked pale, and in desperate need of a rest. Now that Kate thought about it, Signora Conti had looked strained for some days now, and she was amazed that the fact hadn't registered before. 'Tonight. . .' She paused as she fumbled for the word in Italian. It was at times like these that her slow progress in the language frustrated her beyond measure. '*Stanotte. . .*' she continued, 'you will sleep well,' she said, laying her head on her hands and then indicating Signora Conti to explain her meaning.

'*Si.*' Signora Conti smiled, and Kate returned it. Signora Conti's monosyllabic replies weren't out of any annoyance with Kate, but simply because the language barrier meant it was pointless trying to elaborate. Kate understood it, and she was relieved to see no animosity in Signora Conti's face. So did that mean Maria hadn't repeated the conversation about marriage and Kate's lack of interest to her mother, despite telling so many others? If not, it inspired just a little respect for Maria after all. If Signora Conti was stressed, ill or tired, or whatever seemed to be ailing her, hearing what amounted to malicious gossip from Maria would hardly help her feel better and Maria, it seemed, had the good sense to realise that. And at least it meant that Kate herself wasn't the cause of Signora Conti's current malady, which Kate had fretted about in the back of her mind for most of the morning.

But then, as if on cue, a shadow fell across them and Kate looked up to see Maria standing at the table, her youngest child clinging to her skirts. Signora Conti broke into a delighted grin at the sight of her grandson and beckoned him over to sit with her. As she chatted and laughed with the little boy, it meant that Maria and Kate were forced into conversation as Maria sat to join them. She wore a smile, but not one that was in any way warm, and the one Kate sent in return was cautious. She needed to tread carefully, and she needed to find a way to win Maria over, but it seemed that as long as Orazia was prowling in the wings, exerting her influence, that wasn't going to happen. And until she won Maria over, it would be that much harder to win Signora Conti over too.

'The little girls looked lovely in their dresses, didn't they?' Kate said. Maria nodded slowly.

'Children always look lovely.'

'Of course they do. . . I just meant yours in particular looked lovely. Have you enjoyed the day so far?'

'Yes.'

'And you're looking forward to the reception this evening?'

'But of course.'

There was a pause. The conversation hadn't exactly been sparkling, but what small talk she had to offer Maria had dried up. Not that Maria was going out of her way to help, keeping her answers terse and giving Kate nothing to nurture into a conversation that might lead to them discovering some common ground.

Their attention was thankfully diverted by the arrival of Donato, Maria's husband. There was no doubting that he was a handsome man; though greying a little at the temples, he was muscular, and the laughter lines around his eyes only served to give the air of someone who knew how to live well. He gave Kate a good-natured nod, a swift glance up and down that seemed to appraise her and score her out of ten. For some reason – though there had never been any malice or suggestion, or concerning word or deed of any kind on his part in their few interactions – Kate always had the feeling that he was scoring her, and she didn't think his scoreboard was based on her ability to play Scrabble. Donato was perfectly polite, his expression mostly neutral and his enquiries after her well-being benign, but there was something she couldn't put her finger on, something that didn't sit right with her whenever they met. She supposed it must be something to do with the things she imagined Maria would be telling him about her in private that made her feel uncomfortable, but even Alessandro seemed to be on edge whenever Maria's husband was around. He'd never say so to Kate, though, and she couldn't even be sure it wasn't just her own paranoia colouring her view.

'You are enjoying the wedding?' he asked.

Kate offered a guarded smile. 'Very much.'

'It is very different from weddings in England?'

'Certainly different from a lot of the ones I've been to. You can rely on the weather here for a start – there's a good chance you'll get rained on in England.'

He grinned, showing impossibly white teeth, and though his smile was handsome, his canines were almost pointy enough to convince someone of a more nervous disposition that he was a closet vampire. 'It rained on the day I married Maria.'

'Oh,' Kate said.

'So we are not always lucky,' Maria chipped in, and if Kate hadn't known better she'd have said that, for once, her constant attitude of a wasp in September was aimed at someone other than Kate as she gave her husband a significant look. But Donato merely reached to pull her close and kissed the top of her head.

'We do not all believe the superstitions,' he said. 'We must make our own luck.'

Somehow, as Kate watched him, she got the impression that he went through life doing just that, and not always caring about any possible consequences. In the same way that Alessandro was a man who knew who he was and what he wanted, Donato was too, but whereas Alessandro's moral code was straight black and white, Kate couldn't help but feel that Donato's might be rather more greyed in the wash.

For an awkward five seconds or so they lapsed into silence. Just as Kate was about to make some banal comment about being peckish – not because she was but because she needed to fill the gap – Signora Conti motioned for Maria to collect her son from the old lady's lap.

Then she nodded across to where Gian's father stood making an announcement. From what Kate could tell, he was informing the guests it was time to leave for the reception venue. *Saved by the bell.*

With a stiff smile to Maria, Donato and Signora Conti, she got up to look for Alessandro.

The villa on the slopes of one of Rome's seven famous hills was the most perfect reception venue that Kate could imagine. The pristine white walls were like sugar decorations, giving the house the air of a giant wedding cake, and a sweeping staircase at the main gates led to an elaborately tiled portico with arches that ran the length of the house. Emerald grass, palm trees and lush tropical flowers skirted the building, making the garden a mass of singing colour, the air filled with an array of exotic scents to bewitch the senses. The open marquee on the back lawns overlooked the splendour of the city, and at night was illuminated by strings of lanterns, their light glinting from row upon row of sparkling glass and silverware. It was early November, and the evenings were cooler now, but lines of heaters bordered the tent so that everyone would be warm and comfortable no matter how long the party lasted or how the night frosted the gardens over. As the guests arrived another string quartet played them in, and the villa staff beckoned them to line a path formed of floral-decked plinths, down which the newly married couple would be paraded when they arrived for everyone to greet them.

One thing was for certain, Lucetta's wedding photos were going to be incredible, but Kate couldn't help dwelling on the fact that her mother must be very broke indeed if she'd had to stump up for all of this. Alessandro had once said that his mother was too proud to accept any help from her other children, and had somehow always managed to pay for the weddings of her married daughters, but Kate was sure, nonetheless, that Alessandro must have had a hand in helping with the costs of at least this one, if not of the others. Looking around, it was clear there was no way Signora Conti could have afforded such opulent surroundings unless she was a secret gangland boss, and that was without adding the dress, flowers or food into the equation. It was no wonder she was feeling the strain of it all. If Kate had known them to be a less traditional family, she might have supposed that Gian or his family had pitched in, but knowing Signora Conti that would never have been allowed. It had to be Alessandro, and it was just like him to deny any involvement and ask for no thanks.

He squeezed her hand and looked down at her with a reassuring smile as they lined up to greet the newlyweds. She was glad to have him by her side, because the sheer number of people she didn't know now standing around her was daunting, and for much of the day he'd had other duties to perform that meant she hadn't been able to cling on to him. The numbers had swelled, even from the huge audience at Santa Maria, and Kate couldn't imagine how Lucetta and Gian knew so many people. They were certainly a popular couple if this was anything to go by.

The early evening was fresh already, the gentle sun of the day giving way to a cool November night. Kate shivered briefly as a breeze rattled through the palm trees, but when she thought about the temperature back in England right now, it didn't feel so bad. At home she'd have been swaddled in her duffel coat and woolly hat instead of in an evening gown and light wrap, but then nobody would have been having a wedding reception outside at this time of year. It was close to Bonfire Night, and perhaps she would have been watching a firework display tonight, hot dog in her hand as the lights popped and exploded above her, the tang of burnt gunpowder on the air transporting her back to childhood.

'What are you thinking about?' Alessandro asked.

'Hmmm?'

'You are quiet.'

She smiled. 'I'm often quiet.'

'You are tired?'

She shook her head. 'Of course not; it's far too exciting a day to be tired yet.'

'Good. We will dance until the morning comes.'

'We will? In that case I'm really tired.'

'Dancing is easy.'

'Jumping about to music is easy, but not everybody would call it dancing. Dancing that actually looks like dancing might not be as easy as you think, and certainly doesn't come naturally to me.'

'I will lead, and you will soon learn.'

'These are traditional Italian wedding dances? So everyone will know them really well and will know straightaway if I'm doing the steps wrong?'

'They will not care; they know you are not Italian.'

'Well that makes me feel better,' she replied wryly.

'Nobody here would know any of your traditional English wedding dances, so you are the same.'

'Yeah, but the hokey-cokey isn't complicated as traditional wedding dances go; I mean, the instructions are practically in the song as you go along, so. . .'

He gave a tiny frown, that look he gave her when he was trying to follow something that he felt he ought to be able to follow, while in reality he had no hope of knowing what she was talking about.

'Don't worry about it,' she laughed. 'When Lily gets married to Joel you'll find out. Not that they've even got close to setting a date yet and goodness knows how long that will take them.' She paused, the smile slipping from her face. 'That's assuming you'll come with me to England for that,' she added. 'I mean, I don't want to take for granted that you'll want to. . . you might not, and that would be completely OK, of course. Not that we need to worry about it just yet. . .' She was aware that she was babbling. It had been a frequent characteristic of their earliest conversations, but as she'd got used to being around Alessandro it had lessened. Sometimes, at moments like these when she felt uncertain of herself again, and of their relationship, the babbling returned.

'Of course.' He smiled. 'It would be my honour.'

Kate relaxed. Another characteristic of their early relationship was that as often as she babbled, he would instantly put her at ease with a warm smile and a look that reassured her of his love. Somehow, he always sensed what she was feeling, and his response was always just right.

They were interrupted by a call for the attention of the guests. At least, that's what Kate thought it was as everyone stopped talking and an expectant hush fell over the crowd. Lucetta and Gian were introduced for the first time as husband and wife, and enthusiastic applause followed as they appeared from the main house and made their way, arm in arm, to the path lined with guests that led to the tent where dinner would be served. They were both beaming, thanking people as they passed through, receiving pats on the back, kisses and hugs along the way from those too enthusiastic to wait for a chance later. Kate contented herself with a smile, suddenly too shy to make any show of affection in front of the whole of the wedding party, and Lucetta gave her an understanding smile in return. It was strange, Kate reflected vaguely, how they were becoming almost as close as real sisters, and it had happened in such a short time. It was hard to know just how much testing their friendship would stand, but Kate liked to think it might be quite a lot.

Once Lucetta and Gian had been welcomed, the part of the evening that Kate had been dreading arrived. Perhaps dreading was too strong a word, but she was certainly aware of the opportunity to look very stupid indeed. The newlyweds took to the gleaming parquet dance floor first. Their dance was a traditional one, Gian sweeping Lucetta across the floor with ease, the pair of them as graceful as swans on a lake. As the next song played, it was the turn of the wedding party to join them, and Alessandro led Kate to the floor.

'Do not worry,' he said. 'I will lead and nobody will notice.'

As Kate stumbled and second-guessed, Alessandro laughed warmly – not at her but with her.

'Everyone thinks you look lovely,' he said.

'You're such a bad liar,' Kate replied, trying, but failing, to frown with disapproval.

The steps were simple, and towards the mid-section of the song Kate was beginning to master them. But even as she started to enjoy herself, she could see Maria dancing with her husband a few feet away, paying him and the steps no heed but firmly fixed on glaring at Kate. If Kate had hoped to use tonight's occasion to soften her, the outlook didn't appear to be promising. It didn't help her feel any better when they spun around and swapped positions so that Donato was now eyeing her up in the most disconcerting way, and she was certain once again that his mental scoreboard was totting up her particulars. He threw her a glib smile and Kate hurriedly looked away. Her loss of concentration made her tread on Alessandro's foot, and as she apologised, blushing, her eye caught Orazia, now sitting with the guests yet to dance, her scarlet-painted lips drawn so tight they were in danger of disappearing into her face as she watched Kate and Alessandro. He dipped into a light kiss and laughingly told her not to worry, and Kate's gaze was involuntarily drawn back across the room, where Orazia's expression darkened even further. Kate suspected that if there hadn't been a tent full of witnesses, Orazia might have taken up a fish knife and launched herself at her.

There was a sense of relief when the song ended, and the rest of the guests were invited to dance, until Kate realised that Orazia would not have a partner, and it didn't take a genius to work out where she'd be heading. But even as Kate watched her march across, almost barging the other guests aside in a bid to reach Alessandro before anyone else, another figure cut across their path, and Kate found herself staring into the remarkably pretty face of a woman she hadn't met before.

'May I?' she asked Kate sweetly. If your idea of sweet was the witch in the gingerbread house just before she shoved Hansel and Gretel in the oven, Kate thought.

Caught off guard and totally flustered, Kate gave a meek nod, then watched helplessly as Alessandro was whirled off. He didn't even look upset that he'd been separated from Kate, and in fact he smiled warmly at the woman. The sight of it made Kate's heart heavy, despite chastising herself severely for being so ridiculously paranoid. Irritated at her own stupidity, she was making her way back to her seat when there was a tap on her shoulder. She spun round to find Marco looking almost grave.

'You have no partner.' It was a statement rather than a question, because she supposed that much was obvious.

'It seems like it.'

'He will not dance with the others for long. Dance with me until he is finished?'

Kate wondered whether she might prefer to sit down, given her lack of dancing finesse, but she felt it rude to refuse Marco and she didn't want to offend him. 'Thank you,' she said and took his arm as he led her back on.

His dancing was stiffer, less natural than Alessandro's, but he knew his steps well. 'This foot here. . .' he instructed. 'Left foot back. . . right foot side. . . left foot forward. . .' he continued, until Kate's confidence increased and she could look him in the face as they danced rather than at her feet.

'Who is that dancing with Alessandro?' Kate asked.

'You think she is beautiful, no?' Marco asked, giving a vague nod behind him to where Alessandro danced with the unknown woman.

'Yes,' Kate said. 'I would imagine everyone here thinks so.'

He lowered his voice. 'Plastic surgery,' he whispered with a wicked grin.

'Really?'

'Yes.'

Kate was thoughtful for a moment. The woman's hair was a rich auburn, swept up into a loose bun, but it didn't match her almost black eyebrows and dark eyes, though it still suited her. 'Plastic surgery or not, she's still lovely.'

'She is not married.'

'Isn't she?' Kate asked, wondering why he was telling her this.

'Why do you think this is?'

'I don't know. Who is she?'

'Federigo Valvona's daughter, Cara.'

Suddenly, it all made sense. Kate had to assume this was the same woman Signora Conti had been trying to match Alessandro with before Kate had come back to Rome for good (the one matchmaking choice Lucetta had decided she didn't like because of a passing comment Cara had once made about the size of her nose). Alessandro hadn't been interested. At least that was what he'd said to Kate. As she watched them dance now, they looked at ease with each other. He was chatting as they danced, and every so often she would throw her head back and laugh at some quip he'd made.

'The Valvonas are old family friends,' Marco continued.

'I guessed that,' Kate replied, trying to tear her gaze away from them to give Marco her full attention. For some reason she was finding it very hard. As if life wasn't difficult with Orazia on the scene, she now had two gorgeous women to worry about, both of whom were infinitely more suited to Alessandro in the eyes of Signora Conti.

'But you have not answered my question,' Marco said.

Kate turned to him. 'What question was that?'

'Cara is twenty-nine, and she is not married.'

'I don't think twenty-nine is all that old to be single. I'm thirty and I'm single.'

'Perhaps not in your family. With the Valvonas. . . maybe a little. Federigo wants Cara to find a husband as much as Giuditta wants Alessandro to find a wife. A perfect match, no?'

'Alessandro's not interested in her, though,' Kate said, unconvinced by the statement even as she made it. She glanced across to where they were laughing again, his hand resting on the small of her svelte back, his other on her shoulder, their graceful movements perfectly in sync. She moved like a professional dancer and she looked incredible. How could anyone fail to be interested in her? 'He told me so.'

'No, he is not. And she is not interested in him.' He lowered his voice again and his eyes had that mischief, that gentle mocking that Kate had seen in Alessandro's so many times. At that moment she could really see the family resemblance. 'She is interested in the women.'

Kate's gaze turned sharply back to him. 'She is?'

He nodded. 'It makes you happy, no, to hear this?'

'And this is true?'

His expression was even more wicked, more playful. Kate was beginning to think that she liked him a lot. 'You should ask Abelie.'

Kate's eyes grew. 'Abelie? She didn't. . .?'

'No.' He laughed. 'Abelie wants a husband. But poor Federigo does not know his daughter wants a wife. Only Abelie and I know this secret. But I am telling you because I see you worry. She is dancing with Alessandro but you do not need to be afraid. They are old friends, and they know each other well, and that is why she wanted to dance with him. But I think she would rather dance with his sister.'

'I won't tell anyone,' Kate said, suddenly feeling sorry for Cara, having to carry this burden and keep it secret from her family. But then she looked relaxed and confident, and perfectly happy with herself. Maybe she was OK with leading a double life, and perhaps she had a lovely little circle of friends tucked away who shared her secrets, people to love and laugh with away from her overbearing family.

'Orazia, however. . .' Marco clicked his tongue and Kate's gaze went across to where she was dancing with an elderly man and looking very unhappy about it. She was flinging him around so violently to the music that it almost looked comical. But the old man didn't seem to mind, a benign smile stretching his face as she whirled him around and glared at Alessandro and Cara, and then at Marco and Kate, in turn. But perhaps that had something to do with the fact that the old fella's face was directly in line with Orazia's magnificent bosom, and it was probably the most excited he had been for a good many years. Kate only hoped that the sight didn't finish him off, because there was nothing quite like a death to put a damper on a wedding reception.

'I know,' Kate said. 'She's made her intentions very clear. But Alessandro says he isn't interested in her either.'

'Still, you should be careful.'

Kate was silent for a moment as she mused on his words. Such a simple sentence, and yet loaded with meaning. She didn't know what

Orazia could do to change things, but she couldn't help feeling that Marco's warning was an astute one.

'Do you know much about her?' she asked.

'She is not as nice as she pretends.'

'Well, if that's her pretending to be nice,' Kate laughed, 'she must be absolutely awful!'

'She will do anything to get what she wants. The same always, since a little girl. The doll, winning the race, the job, the man . . . whatever she wants she will have.'

'Thank you,' Kate said, giving him a grateful smile. 'I'll watch out for her.'

As the song came to an end, Marco gave Kate a little bow. She scanned the room, to see Alessandro making his way over. Orazia was in his wake, but Marco darted from Kate's side and accosted her. She saw Orazia nod, a sour expression barely masked by a cold smile. Marco threw Kate a quick wink as the music started up again and Alessandro hooked his arms around Kate's waist.

'Mysterious lady,' he said, a playful smile on his lips. 'Would you dance with me?'

'I would love to, handsome stranger,' Kate replied, breaking into a broad smile, and for once, as she glanced across at Orazia dancing with Marco, she felt like the winner.

The feeling didn't last long. The very next song saw Orazia steal her prize, and Alessandro was whisked from beneath Kate's nose, leaving her to dance with Isabella's husband, who was a good dancer, but whose dexterity hardly compared to Alessandro or Marco. When she looked again, they were no longer dancing but involved in an animated discussion in a corner of the tent. Kate frowned as she craned to keep watch, but with the rest of the dancers moving so fast, in and out of her line of vision, she could barely get a handle on what was going on before they returned to the floor and continued as if nothing had happened at all. *What the hell was that about?* Then again, was it something she wanted to know? Perhaps she was better off in blissful ignorance.

But then they were called for *La Tarantella*, a crazy dance that involved everyone, and Kate could only concentrate on keeping her feet as the tempo got faster and faster until they were all racing around the dance floor and almost crying with laughter.

Then the music faded, and the announcement came requesting everyone take their seats for the speeches. Kate was relieved to be with Alessandro again, a place of honour at the family table afforded her by Lucetta, which earned her glares from Maria and Orazia. If only Maria's husband, Donato, hadn't been sitting so close and studying Kate quite so thoroughly, the moment would have been perfect.

Gian's father spoke, followed by Alessandro himself. Kate picked up the odd word but struggled to follow their rapid speech. So eventually she gave up trying to understand and indulged in a bit of people-watching. Her gaze settled on Donato and, thank goodness, he was engaged in a very low conversation with Maria and Orazia, seeming to have lost interest in Kate now, which suited her just fine, though she did have to wonder if she had featured in their discussion.

As Alessandro's speech drew to a close, someone shouted: '*Evviva gli sposi!*' at which there was a rapturous round of applause, echoes of the sentiment and much cheering. Alessandro made his way back to Kate's side as Gian stood to speak.

'I will translate for you,' Alessandro said in a low voice as he sat down.

Kate smiled. 'That would be good.'

'The first moment I saw my angel, Lucetta, I was in love. God had sent her from heaven for me. . .' Alessandro began, speaking quickly into Gian's pauses. 'Today I am the happiest man on the whole of the Earth. I pray to God I can give her everything she desires and I will be a good husband, so that when we are old she will be glad she chooses to marry me. . .'

Gian turned to Lucetta, took her by the hand and led her to stand. She smiled, looking more self-conscious than Kate had ever seen her as he began to address her personally.

'My love, Lucetta, my strength is your strength,' Alessandro began. 'My breath is your breath. My heart is your heart. My world is your world. My happiness is your happiness. Everything of me is yours. . .' Kate was breathless as Alessandro spoke, echoing Gian's speech, but looking at Kate so intently that she almost imagined they were his own words, meant for her. 'Take me and make me yours, for I will never again be happy unless I am by your side.'

Hastily wiping away a tear, Kate looked up to see Lucetta do the same, and many others around the room blow quietly into handkerchiefs. And then Gian kissed Lucetta and beckoned her to sit with him as another shout of '*Evviva gli sposi!*' went up and another round of cheering and applause rippled through the room.

'Long live the newlyweds,' Alessandro translated, catching another of Kate's tears with a thumb. 'Perhaps one day people will say it to us.'

Gian's speech was followed by a short blessing of the meal, and then liquors were served, sweet and spicy and much stronger than Kate had expected. Dinner began, course after course, starting with antipasti of stuffed mushrooms, olives, pickled peppers and artichokes, calamari, prosciutto and many other delicacies that Kate didn't even recognise. Then followed more courses including broth, pasta, salads, more meat, more pasta, more broth, fruit – champagnes and wines flowing in between them all – until Kate's groaning stomach was practically begging for mercy and she was desperate for an hour somewhere private to unzip her dress and let it all hang out. And there were still many desserts to get through, along with what Alessandro called *wanda*, twists of fried, sugared dough that were traditional and meant to be a symbol of good tidings for the couple.

The air was fragrant with herbs and spices, alive with sparkling conversation and warm with the heat of bodies and good humour. Gian was slightly more flushed every time Kate looked at him, though Lucetta looked rather less affected by her alcohol intake, and Alessandro joked that he would be asleep by eleven rather than attending to his wedding night duties. The drink affected Kate too, and she giggled uncontrollably at jokes she might not have found quite so funny in the sober light of day.

At eleven thirty, as the last of the food was being cleared from the tables, Maria approached them, her youngest child slung across a shoulder, sleeping soundly despite the music that was now playing again. She announced to Alessandro that she was taking her brood home, and that she wouldn't be coming back. Kate was relieved to see that Orazia hovered behind them. Presumably, she was leaving with Maria and her family, as she had been their guest all day and would have nobody in particular to keep her company once they left. Then Maria confirmed as much – or at least, that was as much as Kate picked up as she spoke in her native tongue – but before they went, Orazia stepped forward and pulled Alessandro to one side, speaking so rapidly that Kate couldn't hear what they were saying. Nor could she even try to lip-read the odd word. Orazia looked agitated, though Alessandro didn't rise to it, and the more she seemed to lose her temper, the calmer he appeared to become. He shook his head solemnly, and again at a new question, Orazia's tone rising with vexation. And then he took her squarely by the shoulders and kissed her on the cheek.

'No,' Kate heard him say emphatically, and then he walked away.

Orazia folded her arms tight across her chest and looked for a moment as if she would call him back, but then she simply glanced at Maria instead, who was urging her family out of the tent.

'What was that about?' Kate asked as they watched them leave. She had vowed earlier not to ask, to trust that he would tell her if she needed to know, and to respect his judgement if he decided she didn't. But the drink had loosened her tongue and her curiosity, not to mention rousing the green-eyed monster that lurked in the dark places of her heart.

'Police business,' Alessandro said lightly, and Kate raised her eyebrows.

'Police business? Here? Right now?'

'She is worried.'

'Still. . . there's a time and a place. I would have waited to speak to you about it when it wasn't your sister's wedding.'

'But you are not Orazia,' he said with a faint smile.

'Is it a case? Something she needs help with working out? Is she worried about a victim?'

'No,' Alessandro said flatly. Kate waited, but there was no elaboration. Whatever it was, he had made it clear it wasn't up for discussion.

'But you kissed her,' Kate said stubbornly. She sounded like a petulant child, and she knew it, but she couldn't help it.

'Yes,' Alessandro said. 'She is my old friend.'

Kate opened her mouth. What she wanted to say was: *After all she's done?* But, of course, Alessandro didn't know half of what Orazia had done to get between them, and it probably wasn't the time to tell him – in her tipsy state it would come out all wrong and *she'd* end up sounding like the bunny boiler. No, as muddled as her thoughts were now, even she could see that it was better to take the moral high ground as far as Orazia's misdemeanours were concerned.

Alessandro seemed to recognise some internal struggle on her face, because he cupped it in his hands and planted a gentle, lingering kiss on her lips. He tasted sweet, like the pudding wine they'd had somewhere around the tenth course, his skin warm and fragrant.

'See the difference?' he asked with a faint smile as he pulled away to gaze at her. 'I did not kiss Orazia like this.'

'You kissed her like that once. . . before me.'

'Never like that, even before you,' he replied, his patience unfaltering. 'She has always been my friend and that will not change, but you are my love.'

It was all Kate needed to hear. She smiled and melted into his embrace, lost in a place that felt like home. They stood, locked together, and she was happy. In his arms, everything, no matter how wrong it had looked before, was right.

A deafening crack made them leap apart, a sound like squealing metal on metal. Kate's head whipped round to see that while they'd been busy someone, from somewhere, had wheeled in a loud speaker. Lucetta and Gian were fiddling with a music dock like overexcited children, and what had at first appeared to be the sounds of war was actually the opening riff of a heavy-metal song. Then the newlyweds grinned at each other, and the graceful classical music of the night was replaced by a thudding drumbeat and squealing guitars. Lucetta and

Gian dived for the dance floor, hand in hand, while the older of the remaining guests looked on in horror, covering up their ears, and the younger ones rushed exuberantly to join in the new wave of dancing.

Signora Conti was sitting a few seats away. She clasped her hands to her chest, as if praying for strength, while Alessandro threw back his head and roared with laughter.

'Lucetta told Mamma she would have some heavy metal at the wedding!' he shouted to Kate above the music. 'Mamma said no, but Lucetta has never listened to Mamma and why should she listen on her wedding day when she no longer belongs to Mamma?'

Kate looked at the dance floor, where now perhaps twenty people had joined Lucetta and Gian in a crazy mosh dance that was a world away from what they'd had so far that night. Lucetta's wild streak was a mile wide, and Alessandro was right – why pretend to be someone you're not? If she wanted to head-bang in her wedding dress, why not? And at least she had waited until the night was almost over, so if people wanted to leave now, they could do so without appearing rude, while Lucetta would presumably continue to party until she dropped.

'I want to dance!' Kate shouted, suddenly feeling reckless herself. She grabbed Alessandro by the hand and pulled him onto the dance floor while he protested. But he followed her anyway, and they began to bounce up and down together, laughing like loons, lost in the pure joy of the moment. This, right now, was what life was about. There would be things to fear, things to worry about, things to mourn, things to hope for, but they could wait. Tonight was about celebration, about Lucetta and Gian, and Kate couldn't think of a better way to honour their union than acknowledging the fantastic, crazy, unique people they were.

Four

Kate slept until late the next afternoon and woke to see Alessandro's side of the bed empty. Groggily, through the thick fog of her hangover, she wondered where he'd gone. But she could smell coffee, and hear the sound of steel clanking against china in the kitchen, and shortly afterwards he entered the room with a tray containing two cups. She pushed herself up and rubbed her eyes.

'I saw you were beginning to wake,' he said, putting the tray down before sitting next to her on the bed and handing her one of the cups.

'That must have been a pretty sight,' she replied, the warmth of the cup spreading through her fingers as she wrapped them around it and inhaled the richness of the brew inside. 'But thank you.'

Alessandro hopped back into bed.

'I could get used to these lazy days,' Kate said, snuggling into Alessandro's arms, the sun outside already beginning to sink below the rooftops of the city, despite the fact they had barely ventured out of bed yet. 'Do you absolutely have to have a job? Can't we just do this every day?'

'We would be very poor.'

'Poor and happy. Sounds good to me.'

'It would be a good dream.'

'It would.' She closed her eyes. 'I'm going to run that one through my head for a moment. You entertain yourself while I do that.'

She felt his lips on hers and opened her eyes to see that he was looking down at her with a grin.

'But not that,' she said. 'I swear I'll be worn away to nothing.'

'Perhaps I shall save it for when we are married.'

'What? Make me wait? I'll die!'

'Then we will marry quickly and you will not need to wait.'

'I think I need to get a job first,' she said, serious now. 'We couldn't afford so much as an olive in a dish right now, and we have a lot to compete with if Lucetta's wedding is the norm around here.'

'It was a wonderful day,' he agreed, clearly deciding that the question of their possible marriage was one he would drop for now. She loved that he respected her reticence to commit, knowing as he did how her past with Matt had scarred her, no matter how much she tried not to let it, and how careful she would be in the future. Falling in love with Alessandro was one thing, but promising a life together, that was something else entirely, and something that could not be so easily undone if it all went wrong. One divorce in her life was enough.

'Lucetta looked so happy. Gian too. And your family are so lovely. I especially liked your uncle Marco.'

'He is a good man.'

'Yes. I didn't quite know what to make of him at first, but I like him a lot now. . . I never saw him with anyone yesterday. I mean, a wife or children or anything. Doesn't he have anyone?'

'He is divorced,' Alessandro said. He let out a low sigh. Kate sensed some kind of significant truth was coming, and she waited as he paused. 'It is a surprise to you? Mamma does not like to speak of it.'

'Does it really matter that much? People get divorced, even here; there's no stigma like there used to be. I mean, I'm divorced—'

'Mamma does not know that yet,' he reminded her, and Kate wondered silently – and not for the first time – whether they would ever find the right moment to tell her, or whether Kate would have to keep that secret forever. 'And divorce matters to Mamma a great deal. She sees shame, she does not like it.'

'Did he end the marriage or did his wife?' she asked.

'She did. . . I should tell you, his wife was named Michelle.'

Kate frowned. 'She was English?'

He nodded. 'I am sorry I did not tell you this before because you will see that it matters to us too. But I wanted to respect my mother, who does not like to speak of it and does not like us to speak of it either. Marco was married to Michelle for ten years. She became sad in Italy, and she wanted to go home. Marco did not want to leave Italy. They could not agree. Michelle went home and she never returned, so they divorced. The little children went to live with her. My grandmother was heartbroken because she could not see her grandchildren every day. Sometimes she would not see them for a whole year because Michelle did not have the money or time to bring them, and when she did she argued with everyone in the family, who wanted her to return them to Italy, because it was their home. They were sad times and the children did not enjoy their visits. Soon, they did not want to come at all, and when they were old enough to decide for themselves, they stopped. Do you see now why Mamma is so afraid for us?'

Everything slotted into place, this new revelation like a huge heavy boulder rolling over the mouth of a cave and blocking out the sun. It was no wonder Signora Conti didn't trust Kate. 'But I wouldn't ever do something like that,' she said, knowing even as she did that it was an empty promise. Who could say what would happen in five, ten, even twenty years? Who could know what might come to change everything? She would mean to stay with Alessandro forever, but nobody could ever promise forever with any certainty, no matter what they meant at the time. And as for Marco's children, they were Italian but they were English too, and she couldn't help but have some measure of sympathy for a harangued Michelle who must have felt that they needed to discover their English roots and family just as much as they needed to keep in touch with their Italian ones. There was just no right or wrong in a situation like that, and someone was always going to be unhappy with the arrangements.

'Mamma has your words, but for her they are not enough. I trust you, but Mamma. . . she likes you, but she is convinced that one day you will go home, just like Michelle, and I will be left like Marco, my children living far away and me standing alone at weddings.'

Kate was silent for a moment. It was difficult to see what would change Signora Conti's mind, apart from time. And right now Kate's position probably looked more perilous than ever – she didn't even have a job yet. With no money coming in and bills piling up, most people would run for home. The only thing for it was to get some traction in her bid to get settled and show Alessandro's mother that she was here to stay.

'We can make this work,' she said finally. 'I know it's going to be hard, but we can convince your mother that we're not Michelle and Marco. I don't know how yet, but I'll think of something.'

He leaned to kiss her. 'That is why I love you; you are not afraid of anything, even when you think you are.'

'I wish that was true,' she said with a wry smile. 'I was terrified about moving here and I very nearly didn't.'

'But you did, and that is because you were brave.'

'I must have been to take you on.'

'I must go to see Mamma,' he replied, laughing as he disentangled himself from her and sat up.

'You're worried about her?'

'A little.'

'Do you want me to come?'

He paused for a moment. 'You have many things to do, and I will be ready to go much quicker alone.'

'All those things can wait. And are you insinuating that I'm high maintenance?'

He frowned as he reached for a shirt from the back of a nearby chair. 'What does that mean?'

'You think I take a long time to get ready and I take a lot of looking after?'

'Yes,' he said, and Kate threw a pillow at him.

'Rude,' she said with a smile. He swivelled to kiss her.

'If you like, you can stay in bed and wait for me.'

'If I stay in bed I'll be snoring again. I'm going to get up and call my sisters, see how things are there.'

'That is a shame,' he said.

'But we could have dinner? I mean, if you're planning on coming back tonight. . .'

'*Va bene.* I will go now and be back at seven.'

Filled with a new sense of urgency, Kate dressed quickly and logged onto a laptop borrowed from Abelie's on-off boyfriend, Bruno. At the wedding, someone had given her a name, and she had scribbled it down on a napkin, which now lay crumpled at the bottom of her bag. She had no idea who had imparted the information, or how it had come about, but recalling that she had a name, at least, she had decided to search for it. It was a long shot, and one she had dismissed at the time, but now, in light of her new resolution to get Alessandro's mother on board once and for all with their relationship, she was willing to try pretty much anything.

The napkin sat beside her on the table now, with *Shauna Davies, Piccolo Castelli* written on it in spidery, drunken script.

Google found her the website for Piccolo Castelli easily enough, and scrolling through the pages of their site, in amongst all the reams of text that she didn't understand, she managed to work out that they had a contact page, with email addresses for their staff. There was a photo of Shauna with her details beneath. She had almost white hair, curled under her face in a chin-length bob, and was perhaps in her late fifties, but the Italian weather obviously suited her because she had the most glorious tan and she looked incredibly slim and glamorous. Kate supposed that she had to keep up a certain appearance for some of her wealthier clients, but this assumption only served to fuel Kate's doubt that she would even get looked at twice for the trainee estate agent job she'd been told might be going. And it was only might, because the person, whoever they were, was not even sure at all. They simply had a name and a hunch, given to them by a friend of a friend who had once had very satisfactory dealings with Shauna and had since remained good friends with her.

She drafted and redrafted the email. Every time she was about ready to send, she felt compelled to go back over it and change something else – a word that wasn't quite right, a comma in the wrong place, something minute and insignificant that seemed to glare at her from the page. Perhaps it was a subconscious stalling; once it had gone there was no taking it back, and she was afraid that the person at the other end would laugh and question why on earth someone like Kate would even be putting herself forward in this way. But then she remembered Alessandro's faith, and how he had told her he believed in her bravery even when she didn't herself, and she took a deep breath. This was silly. She could walk around an apartment as well as anyone else, and she could read from a crib sheet and explain to clients what was on there. She assumed they would be English clients too – expats after a bit of *la dolce vita*, and who would be more perfect to show them around than someone who'd already taken the leap?

After one last read through, where she refused to let herself change another thing unless it was a genuine mistake, she clicked send.

There, it was gone. Now she just had to wait. At least she had plenty to keep her busy, starting tomorrow with a call to Nunzia, her landlord's wife, to see about those cut-price party dresses. It wasn't exactly going to make her rich, but at least it was a start.

Alessandro had called to say he was still worried about his mother and was going to stay with her that night. He'd assured her that there was no need to come dashing over, and that he and Abelie had the situation under control. Though Kate had missed him, it was somewhat of a relief, and it meant that she could get a much-needed early night. She'd slept in until the afternoon, but it had hardly been restful, and as they hadn't returned to her flat until the early hours after the wedding anyway, it hadn't taken long for Kate to start yawning again come the evening.

Salvatore, Kate's landlord, only pretended that his English was bad, or so Alessandro said, but his wife's really was. It was hard work making conversation with Nunzia, and not something she always looked forward to, but she did like Nunzia and she couldn't very well back out of her agreement with Salvatore now. So after a quick and overcomplicated phone call the following morning, Nunzia was waiting in her tiny yellow Fiat 500 as Kate hurried down the steps of the apartment building to her.

'*Buongiorno!*' Nunzia said, kissing Kate on the cheek as she climbed into the passenger seat. As odd as Salvatore looked with his funny moustache and borrowed war medals, Nunzia looked sweet and homely and absolutely, straight-down-the-line normal. At some point in her younger days, she might even have been quite pretty, her soft brown eyes decorated with wrinkles these days but full of laughter and fun, and thick hair with barely a grey showing. She was curvy, but she had a good shape and a distinct waist that suited tailored dresses perfectly. Kate often wondered how she and Salvatore had got together, and she could imagine Nunzia picking him out at something like an animal shelter for rejected men, feeling sorry for him and deciding to devote her life to making him a functioning member of society.

First stop was coffee at a sweet little backstreet café, nestled between a quaint gift shop and fragrant bakery, tables and chairs set outside on gleaming cobbles and herbs growing in window boxes on the floors above. Kate pored over some dress patterns and magazines that Nunzia had brought along to show what she wanted, and it was a pleasant hour – despite the language difficulties, nothing pleased Kate more than talking about dressmaking. She was good at it, and other people thought she was good at it, and she loved to see the looks of admiration for her finished pieces. Nunzia's face was alight with expectation as they turned the pages for ideas, and once they had settled on a couple of styles, it was time to visit the haberdashery.

It was Kate's turn to get excited as they got back into Nunzia's car. She had heard of Bassetti Tessuti before – it was the largest and most famous haberdashery in Rome, and possibly one of the biggest in the world – but despite wanting to visit, she hadn't yet managed to find the time. Partly because she knew that an hour of browsing would be nowhere near long enough to appreciate it, and she hadn't had many full days spare between getting her flat habitable and searching for work. At least this time they knew what they needed and so aimless browsing would be narrowed down to constructive browsing, which would hopefully take a lot less than a day.

A frontage of cream stone greeted them, and the glass doors set in a metal frame bearing a plaque with the shop name in a sensible font were unassuming enough that most people would pass without realising what treasure lay within. But as they opened the doors, Kate's stomach flipped in a way that was usually reserved for anticipation of date nights with Alessandro, because here the other love of her life was about to be indulged.

Oh, how she wished she had an inexhaustible credit card as they wandered room after room, craning their necks to look up to the tops of rack upon rack of cloth bolts lining the walls and reaching up to the ceilings. There was so much of this she longed to buy for herself, but she had to keep remembering that they were here for Nunzia's fabric and, besides, she could hardly afford what was in here anyway. These were the finest fabrics in Rome, with a price tag to match. She'd never paid this much at the market in Manchester, not even in Laura Ashley, where she used to go when she was treating herself to something a bit special. More than once, Kate recalled Lucetta's incensed comments about Salvatore's stinginess in his payment for Nunzia's dresses, but she tried to push her doubts to the back of her mind.

'You like?' Nunzia asked Kate, as an assistant held two bolts he'd just been sent up a dizzying ladder to fetch down for them.

Kate examined each fabric in turn. 'I think this one would sew better – a bit stiffer for the style you want too, so it would hold the structure. But this one. . .' She stroked the other. 'This has a lovely texture. You'd be better with a softer style for this.' Nunzia looked blankly at her. Kate smiled patiently and went over it again. 'This. . .' she pointed to the first one, 'this strong. Good for this style. . .' And Kate mimed a huge billowing skirt around her legs. 'And this one,' she added slowly, 'this one good for soft shape. . .' And she ran her hands down her legs with a sultry face that had Nunzia giggling. 'Sexy,' Kate continued. '*Sì?*'

Nunzia sent the assistant up the ladder again for three more swathes from the top that she wanted to look at more closely. If she hadn't known better, Kate would have sworn she was doing it on purpose, just for the hell of it, as there were hundreds lower down that looked just as nice. But then, after another half hour or so, she settled on two that she liked and that got Kate's approval as something she could work with.

'We look little more,' Nunzia said, shooing away the assistant to go and work out the cost and wrap the goods.

'But I thought we had everything.'

'Not see everything,' Nunzia said.

Kate smiled. She was stalling, so that Kate could have a good snoop around the place. But what was the point in looking when you couldn't have anything? Nunzia looked so pleased with herself for the kind gesture to Kate, however, that she didn't have the heart to say no. 'OK.'

The shop was a maze of rooms which they explored for a second time to see what they might have missed the first, each one jampacked with fabrics, from shirt cottons, to wool for suits, to silk, to designer fabrics by the likes of Versace and Valentino. Some rooms they wandered into, saw that it didn't have the sort of fabric they needed, and headed straight back out, but other rooms found them lingering as Kate admired bolt after bolt of beauty.

'Oh!' she said, pulling a modern black and grey floral from the shelf. 'That's gorgeous!'

'You like?' Nunzia asked.

'Oh, I do!' Kate said.

'*Quanto?*' Nunzia called to the assistant, who was now hovering nearby again.

'*Cento*,' he replied.

'One hundred euros,' Nunzia translated for Kate, though her rudimentary Italian had already told her as much.

'We have what we need, eh?' she replied and made a show of looking at her watch. Really, this was all getting a bit torturous, and she'd had just about enough of looking at stuff she couldn't afford.

'Go to car,' Nunzia said. 'I pay.'

'Oh,' Kate said, getting the distinct feeling she was being dismissed and not liking it much. Had she said something wrong? Was Nunzia annoyed because she had suggested they finish shopping? Clueless, she simply nodded and made her way from the shop to the pavement outside while Nunzia went to settle up at a very odd counter that looked like a bank window from a black-and-white movie.

Kate waited patiently on the pavement by the locked car. One or two people gave her suspicious looks as they passed by, and she agreed that she did look suspicious hanging around a locked car, but where else was she supposed to go? Nunzia emerged half an hour later, just as Kate was thinking she'd fallen into a rack of woollens and had been lost forever, struggling under the weight of a huge parcel.

'Let me help!' Kate said, rushing to take the weight.

'*Grazie*,' Nunzia said. She let the whole lot fall into Kate's arms, and Kate stumbled backwards.

'It *is* heavy,' she said, slightly taken aback that it was, in actual fact, just as cumbersome as it had looked. For a moment she'd wondered if Nunzia was being feeble or just feigning helplessness.

'*Si*,' Nunzia agreed, fishing in her bag for her car keys. With a pop, the locks opened and Kate deposited the fabric in the tiny boot before joining Nunzia in the car.

As they drove home, Kate was almost glad their little trip out was over. While she had loved seeing the store, and had enjoyed talking about all things sewing, chatting to Nunzia had been hard work and the more time she spent out daydreaming, the more other concerns pressed in on her thoughts. There was so much to do, and she was pratting around in what amounted to a sweet shop for her. She had a job to find, and a family to win over, and she hadn't spoken to Lily for days. Nunzia liked her well enough now, but would she be quite so keen when Kate couldn't make her husband's rent?

Nunzia pulled the handbrake on outside the apartment building. There was one last job to do before Kate could let her go back to the home she shared with Salvatore, half a mile down the road from the block he owned, and that was to take her measurements. She'd already made her one dress, of course, but it was best to be safe and re-measure every time if you could – you never knew what slight variations could arise from a week of indulgence or a week of abstinence, and every pattern was a little different anyway. Kate carried the fabric, Nunzia following, and once they were inside, she dropped it onto the table while she went to fix drinks for them.

'Very nice.' Nunzia nodded, gesturing at the room as Kate handed her a lemonade.

Kate smiled. On her limited budget she had done her best to make her flat feel like home, but as her grandmother used to say, you couldn't make a silk purse out of a sow's ear. She would hardly feature in next month's *Homes & Gardens* magazine, but Kate kept it clean and tidy, and it was bright and homely enough, and she knew she was a lot better off than some, so she took the praise with good grace and went to fetch her tape measure.

When she returned, Nunzia had unwrapped her parcel, and as well as the two swathes of fabric she had chosen for herself, the black and grey floral that had caught Kate's eye at the store sat on the table. Kate stared at the cotton, and then at Nunzia.

'I don't understand. . .'

Nunzia grinned. 'You like?'

Kate's eyes widened. 'It's for me?'

'*Sì!* For you!'

'But why?'

Nunzia shrugged. 'You are good.'

'But I can't take this—'

'*Sì*, you take!'

She stared at the fabric again. It was such a lovely gesture, and an even lovelier fabric, and she didn't really know that she'd done anything to deserve it. But Nunzia didn't seem like she'd take no for an answer, and besides, the shop was hardly likely to take it back now when they'd cut it from the roll. Though looking at it, there was an awful lot of material – probably a lot more than Kate needed to make herself a dress, and it had probably cost a small fortune. '*Grazie mille!*' she cried, hugging her. 'It's gorgeous and I love it!'

'*Prego*,' Nunzia said. As she pulled away, she gave a cheeky smile. 'No say to Salvatore. . . secret. . .'

'Yes, our secret,' Kate said, nodding. Ordinarily, she found that secrets led to trouble, but this was one she didn't mind keeping.

Five

Alessandro's night shifts had started again, so for the next five nights Kate wouldn't see him at all. They were long shifts, and though sometimes they would grab some time together during the few hours between him sleeping and starting work again that evening, it was always rather more tense, both watching the clock and knowing they couldn't wander too far because he'd have to leave soon. But it did give Kate time to get stuck into some well overdue tasks, as well as catch up with her family and friends. After phoning both Lily and Anna, who mostly talked about things that had happened at work, the weather, what their respective other halves were up to, whether Kate had found a job yet and whether her landlord was still quite mad, she took the opportunity to make herself a coffee before calling her mum. But in the gap in her schedule, the phone sitting on the kitchen counter next to her lit up, and Jamie's face appeared.

Kate swiped to take the FaceTime.

'Hey!' He grinned. 'How's it going?'

Kate broke into a broad, delighted smile of her own. Whenever she saw Jamie, she instantly felt happy. It was a strange effect he had on people, and it wasn't just to do with his handsome features. There was something unnameable but truly wonderful that shone from him, and she'd seen it the first time they'd ever met at a taxi rank at Fiumicino Airport. Everyone he met was enchanted by his wit, his charm, his good nature – everyone wanted to be a satellite in his orbit – and Kate, despite the odd drama during the early days of their acquaintance, was no different. She'd even fancied him a bit at first – looking as Adonis-like as he did, it was difficult to imagine who wouldn't – but once he'd put her in the picture that he was gay and engaged to be married to a great guy back home in New York, she quickly decided she liked him a lot better as a friend anyway.

'It's great!' she said. 'Well, not great actually,' she added, 'but not terrible.'

'That's good!' He laughed. 'Not terrible is better than terrible. Is that mean cat of a sister still giving you trouble?'

'Maria? I haven't made my way onto her list for Christmas drinks and nibbles yet, but I'm still working on it.'

'Leave her to me. . .' He winked, reaching out of shot and then putting a glass of red wine to his lips.

Kate's smile grew. 'Leave her to you? Does that mean you're coming to Rome?'

'In a week.'

'YAY!' Kate squealed and clapped her hands together. 'That's fantastic! You could stay with me if you like.'

'What, and miss out on the opportunity of making my boss cough up some dollar for a hotel? Honey, it's a lovely sentiment but please join me in the real world!'

Kate giggled. 'Aww, and you've even camped up for me.'

'Only for you.' He smiled. 'So, what has naughty Maria been doing?'

'Oh, nothing really. Just sending bad vibes and evil wishes in my direction. I can't really say she's done anything wrong as such, but she doesn't make a secret of the fact she doesn't like me.'

'What about Mamma Conti? Have you worked your magic on her yet?'

'Well, she's not won over yet, but I think we can get there. In fact, I was thinking I might pop to see her tomorrow.'

'Give her my love. And check that the invite for dinner still stands.'

'I'm sure it would; she bloody loved you. Even Maria loved you and that's saying something!'

'I'm honoured, truly. . . So, what else is new?'

'I'm still unemployed, if that's what you mean. But I did get a name from someone for an English estate agent based here who sells Italian properties to rich Brits who might want some help. I know I don't exactly have a ton of experience in that area. . . well, none, actually, but I reckon I know a bit about houses and I speak perfect English, so that's two pluses on my side, right? So I've emailed her, just to see whether she can help or if she knows anyone else. It's a long shot, but it's better than nothing and so far all the other jobs I've applied for haven't come to anything. I suppose it'll take time, but even a pot washer would do me right now.'

'But you don't want to be a pot washer forever. . . whatever one of those is, so what's the point of taking a job like that now? The real-estate business sounds like a good plan. What about your dressmaking?'

'I'm still getting that off the ground, but I am getting orders. . .' She could have added that it totalled exactly two orders, both cut price and both from the same person, but it wasn't something she wanted to share right now. Jamie didn't need to see self-pitying Kate – he deserved positive, upbeat, doing-OK Kate. And that was what he was going to get.

'That's fantastic!' Jamie beamed. 'I still feel just awful that my contacts didn't work out for you, but hey, you won't need to worry about any of that when the business starts rolling in.'

'I can do it from my apartment for now,' Kate added. 'Salvatore, my landlord, is OK with me working from here as long as I don't have lines of clients outside the door, because he says people will start to think I'm a prostitute if that happens.' She giggled. 'I can't imagine what sort of prostitutes he's ever visited if there are queues of middle-aged women outside. But at the moment I'm not getting lines of people, and if that day ever comes I suppose I'll find the money to set up at proper premises.'

'I just know that day is going to come. So, when are you and Alessandro getting married?'

Kate rolled her eyes. 'Not you as well. That's all I've heard for the last few weeks, and Lucetta's wedding has made it worse. I think Signora Conti is on a mission to clear her two remaining children out of her house so she can have it to herself. She's already started a hope chest for Abelie and the poor girl has only been in a stop-start dating arrangement with her boyfriend up to now.'

'Well, perhaps another wedding will take your mind off your own. . .' he replied.

Kate wrinkled her nose. 'Sounds rather cryptic. . . Wait! Does that mean you and Brad have finally set a date?'

'Not quite. But, we do have a pretty good idea of where we want to get married, and we're thinking Rome. . .'

'Oh my God!' Kate squeaked. 'That would be incredible! Please make it so, then I'd be able to come!'

'There's a lot to check out first, but it's such a beautiful city that we decided why not? And we get to do it again with a mirror ceremony and party back in New York for the people who couldn't make it to Italy – two parties! As soon as I told Brad that he was sold!'

'This is so exciting! You have to make it spring time, when there'll be blossom and lovely cool days and I'll get time to make a new dress. And I'll have to get a hat too! You're doing the full works, aren't you?'

Jamie chuckled. 'I have no idea. I think Brad will want to go for all-out glamour. We're going to start doing some research – see who will marry us and who won't, and at what kind of venue. Then we'll worry about the party. I'm glad you're excited.'

'Excited? I can't wait! I'm so happy for you.'

'Thank you.'

'Hang on,' Kate said, reaching for the mug of coffee she'd just made and holding it up. 'A toast, to Jamie and Brad getting married in Rome!'

'Possibly,' he said, and laughed, but he raised his wine anyway. 'I'll drink to that!'

Hi Kate,

Thank you so much for your email. Your friend was right – I am very busy at the moment and help would be much appreciated. I'd be interested in having an informal chat with you, to get an idea of your background and tell you more about what we need. Would you like to meet for coffee? I have lunchtimes free during the next week, so let me know and we'll get together.

Yours,

Shauna Davies

Kate read the email again. It sounded promising, though she tried not to get too excited about it. After all, she was going to have to come clean about the fact that her 'very little estate agent experience' actually meant none at all. But she could negotiate that, and she was sure that if she met up with Shauna she could create a rapport good enough to convince her she was the woman for the job. After all, nobody got anywhere without taking risks and sometimes being just a smidge economical with the truth, did they?

She quickly typed a reply, expressing her delight at Shauna's interest and suggesting some days and times when she could meet. Twenty minutes later they'd fixed a meeting for the coming Friday, so Kate had four days in which to read as much as she could about property buying and selling in Italy and expat residency laws.

As she clicked send, she reached for her phone. Alessandro would be thrilled at the news. But then she hesitated. It was hardly in the bag yet, and what if she didn't get it? Better not to jinx it by assuming success. She put the phone down again. Her insides were fluttering, though, and if she was keeping this to herself for the time being, she needed to get all this nervous energy out of her system somehow. Her gaze flicked to the swathes of fabric on the table, still there from her shopping trip with Nunzia the day before. Those dresses wouldn't make themselves, and if she needed to take her mind off her coffee with Shauna, this was as good a time as any to start them.

Shauna looked exactly like her photo. Sometimes Kate struggled to recognise people from online headshots, but there was no way she was going to mistake Shauna, whose statuesque figure and striking white hair drew every eye in the café as she entered. Kate stood from the table she'd settled at to wait, having been around twenty minutes early in her bid to look efficient and enthusiastic, and beckoned her over.

'*Ciao*, Kate,' Shauna said, kissing her on the cheek like a true native. 'It's lovely to meet you.'

'You too,' Kate replied, feeling flustered and wondering whether she ought to kiss, hug, or offer a good old-fashioned handshake. In the end, she was saved the stress of making the decision by Shauna taking a seat at the table and shrugging off an expensive-looking forest-green woollen jacket. Kate, always with a keen eye for a good sew, couldn't help but admire how exquisitely tailored and finished it was as Shauna draped it over the back of her chair. 'Thanks so much for coming to meet me.'

'On the contrary, I should be thanking you. I'm glad you got in touch. If we can come to some agreement you may have saved me a lot of admin.'

Before she had a chance to elaborate, a waiter glided over and took her order for espresso, while Kate went for plain and simple white coffee.

'So,' Shauna continued as he left them again, 'tell me about yourself.'

'I can type fast, I've got lots of experience in administration and for ten years I ran a busy department in a high-end pet-care distribution business.'

Mr Woofy, Kate's previous employer, was being flattered immensely by her description, and her job as an office clerk even more so. But the fact was that, although she was embellishing the truth a tiny bit, her colleagues in the office were so lazy, and the boss so perpetually and mysteriously absent from duty, that she might as well have been running the place.

'Oh. . .' Shauna waved a nonchalant hand, 'I'm sure your credentials are all wonderful, and we can certainly talk about those later, but what I really want to know is what brings you to Italy. You're obviously planning to put down roots if you're talking to me about a job.'

'Yes. I divorced from my childhood sweetheart, back in England.' She shrugged. 'At his instigation, not mine. Moving felt like the right thing – a new start somewhere far away from the constant reminders.'

'That's an awful long way to go. He must have smashed your heart to smithereens.'

'I suppose it is a long way. . .'

'So you still love him?'

'Oh, God, no!' Kate smiled. 'No, that's all water under the bridge. In fact, he's about to have a baby with someone else – probably any time now.'

'Was it amicable? The split, I mean.'

'I tried at first. But he. . . well, he made things difficult. These things are never quite that simple, are they?'

'No, I don't suppose they are. I've never managed to stay married myself. Too much of a control freak, I expect. I can't be bothered with men now.'

'I suppose your business occupies a lot of your time.'

'It does.' The waiter returned and Shauna thanked him as he left their drinks. Then she turned to Kate again. 'So you're looking to stay permanently in Rome? No plans to go back to England?'

'No.' Kate gazed into her cup for a moment as she stirred her coffee. She shook herself and looked up with a bright smile. 'I love it here, and I'm going to make it work no matter how hard it gets.'

'I take it that means it's been hard so far?'

'A little.'

'If you don't mind me saying, you might have made it harder by waiting until you were here to look for a job. More pressure on you, and they're not exactly easy to come by.' She took a sip of her espresso. 'Why aren't you teaching?'

Kate frowned. 'You mean English?'

'It's what a lot of the other expats of your age do and there's plenty of teaching work about. Everybody in Rome wants to learn English; it's good for business.'

'I would, but my Italian is terrible, and I think I'd need to be able to communicate with my students in their own language too. Besides, I don't think it's for me. I wouldn't know where to start.'

'And you would with estate agency? You told me in your email that you didn't have much experience.'

'No, but I do know how to talk to people, especially British people. Half an hour's debate on the weather and we're best friends, aren't we?'

Shauna chuckled as she placed her cup back on the saucer. 'Well, a sense of humour certainly helps.' She folded her hands over one another on the table, a huge aquamarine ring glinting on her middle finger. 'We manage properties not just in Rome, but in the surrounding areas too: Tuscany, Umbria. . . how would you feel about driving out to those places to meet people?'

'I don't have a car, but I can drive. I've not actually driven in Italy yet but. . . Well, I can't say I'm super confident but I expect I'd get the hang of it if I had to.'

'And the hours would be long. When we're closing a sale it's intense, then there's all the after-sale legalities to keep an eye on. If the buyer runs into problems, we're the first port of call whether it's our responsibility or not, and often they don't care as long as it gets sorted. Clients can be rude, snobby, quick to blame and often resort to threats along the lines of us losing the sale to get what they want. Sellers will lie about their properties and buyers will lie about their cash flows. They play us for devil's advocate at times. And the Italian property laws can be your undoing if you're not absolutely on top of your game. Not to mention all this dreadful Brexit business hanging over us, and none of us can be certain how that will go right now. It can be a very pressured environment.' She took another sip of her coffee. 'You understand, I'm not telling you all this to put you off, but so you're aware of exactly what you'd be taking on.'

'I just want a chance to prove myself. I realise that you don't know the first thing about me, and I can write all the CVs in the world but you wouldn't be able to get the measure of me until I've worked for you. I'd be happy with a trial at this point, but I understand that I don't have any experience and neither of us knows if I'll be suited, so I completely get it if you don't want to take the risk at all.'

'The problem for me is that I can't afford to carry someone. If you're on my payroll then you must be making money for me, and an inexperienced agent won't be doing that. However, I do have a feeling that you could be a good fit for the position.' She paused, regarding Kate steadily before speaking again. 'How about you shadow me for a while as I work? I'll go out to meet clients and you come with me, learn as much as you can. I won't be able to pay you for this time, but you can look on it as an investment, and if things move in the right direction, I might be able to take you on as a fully-fledged member of the team. How does that sound?'

'That sounds OK,' Kate said.

'You don't seem certain.'

'It's just. . . how long do you think that arrangement might last for?'

'I would say as long as it takes for me to feel confident you could operate on your own. It's impossible to judge at this point. If you're not comfortable with that, I completely understand.'

Kate chewed her lip, deep in thought. It was a risk, and the time spent training without pay would mean she wouldn't have much spare to look for another job if it went pear-shaped, or to earn enough to keep her afloat while Shauna decided whether she was going to employ her at the end or not. But it could be a golden opportunity, at least until she made some real progress with her dressmaking business. And who knew, perhaps she might grow to love working at Piccolo Castelli so much she'd settle into it and not want to pursue riskier self-employment?

'Can I think about it?'

'Of course. I'm sorry if you came here under the assumption that you would leave with a job—'

'Oh, no!' Kate cut in. 'I didn't think that at all! It sounds like a fantastic opportunity, but I'd like some time to work out if I can do it. . . you know, with the no pay and all. I'm not exactly rolling in it and though I have funds, they won't last forever.'

'I understand that. Think it over, talk about it if you like with any significant other and let me know. You have my email address, and you can ring me at the office any time if you need to chat more about it.'

Shauna drained the last of her coffee and reached for her jacket. 'It was really lovely to meet you, even if we don't end up working together. And if we don't, then all the best for whatever future you build here in Rome.' She smiled as she collected her handbag from the table. 'You never know, our paths might cross again anyway. There aren't that many of us Brits living here that we can miss each other so easily.'

Kate watched as Shauna turned to go. What was wrong with her? Here she was, being handed an opportunity to do something really different, to meet people, to do a job that commanded some respect, to work with a lovely lady like Shauna, to get to travel the countryside of Italy and wander around gorgeous homes. She was crazy not to say yes straightaway, if only for the experience. And she could prove her worth, she was sure of it – then Shauna would employ her properly. What was that old saying: you have to speculate to accumulate? She could knock on the doors of Rome's backstreet restaurants until those proverbial cows came home, and maybe eventually she'd get a little job that would just cover the rent every month, but this was a real opportunity not to be missed.

'Wait!' She almost leapt from her seat in her haste to halt Shauna's exit. 'If you'll have me, I'd love to come and shadow you for a while. I'll do my best to be a good pupil.' She gave a tiny shrug. 'And it's not like I'm doing a lot else at the moment.'

Shauna smiled. 'That's fantastic news!' She took off her jacket and sat down again. 'In that case we'd better get some more coffee and make some concrete plans.'

Six

'NO!' Alessandro shouted. 'She thinks you are a fool! And she is right!'

Kate's arms tightened across her chest and she scowled at him. 'It's alright for you! You have a good job, and you would find one easily if you wanted another. I have to take what I can get!'

'This is not a job! This is slavery! People do not work for no money!'

'People have a right to choose, though! And I wouldn't really be working, I'd be training – there's a difference.'

'When I learned my police work, I was paid. They want you to learn, they pay – that is how it works.'

'Shauna can't afford to do that. You're talking about the police, who have all that public funding for trainees. But this is worth taking a chance on even without money. . . you must be able to see that?'

'You must telephone Piccolo Castelli, tell this. . . this woman that you will not be her slave! If you want to work for nothing, there is a house for the poor in the city where you can give them soup and at least they will be grateful for you!'

'I can't,' Kate replied, steel in her voice that her quivering insides would betray if she let them. 'I've already said I'll do it now and how would it look if I backed out?'

'It would look as if you had been given some brains!'

'I am not backing out! You don't get to tell me what to do – not now, not if we're married, not ever! I had enough of that with Matt – and never again. I am going to join Shauna next week and that is an end to it.'

'You will not listen to sense?'

'I have listened but I won't change my mind.'

Alessandro threw his hands into the air, swore under his breath in Italian and then stalked out onto Kate's tiny balcony, slamming the French doors shut behind him. She could see him through the voile curtains, hands gripping the rail as he stared out over the streets below. It would be easy to go to him now, apologise, take back everything she'd said and agree to break her arrangement with Shauna – but she wouldn't. She loved Alessandro, but that didn't mean he was right about everything. The Pope himself could ask her to back down now and she wouldn't.

So why did she feel so utterly wretched about the whole thing? Perhaps because she'd been so looking forward to the weekend, when his night shifts would halt for a few days and they could spend some proper time together, but their disagreement had cast a shadow over everything now, and even if they ironed it out, precious hours had been lost that they could have been enjoying.

More for something to take her mind off the atmosphere that hung heavily over the apartment than for the need, Kate went into the kitchen to make a coffee. It was as she stared at the kettle, watching as the bubbles fizzed up and down the transparent casing, that she felt the hand on her shoulder.

She turned, and in his eyes she could see that he hated this as much as she did.

'I'm not sure you understand how hard this is for me,' she said. 'I will make mistakes, but I'm bound to. I'm trying to make a new life and it's so different from my old one. . .'

He shook his head. 'I was wrong to shout. You have given up so much to live in Rome. I know this but sometimes I forget. And this is not home for you. . . not yet, but it is hard for me to remember because it is home for me. I cannot say I think you are right about this job, but I understand why you told this woman you would do it.'

'Then I have your blessing?'

'We must see how long it takes. I will not be able to keep my opinions to myself if she does not decide quickly whether she wants you or not.'

'But you'll let me try?' Kate insisted, sensing some resistance still, despite his attempts to smooth things over. All she wanted was a yes, for him to recognise that she needed to find her own way, and that sometimes it wouldn't be his way.

'It is not for me to let you try or no. I am your lover, not your king. . .' He gave a wry smile. 'Just as you said before. . .'

She smiled. 'I don't recall the lover bit. And I think I said you weren't the boss of me. . . a bit like I used to say to Anna when I was five. Probably not my most mature moment if I'm honest.'

'We were both angry.' He folded her into his arms and she leaned her head on his chest. But she could still feel the distance between them, even there as she listened to the steady thrum of his heart. He had made the first move to a reconciliation, but that didn't mean he was happy about it. 'Come,' he said, pulling away and kissing her lightly on the forehead. 'Mamma will be waiting for us.'

* * *

Kate was getting used to riding pillion on the back of Alessandro's moped, but her heart still missed a beat every time he slalomed past a truck or took a corner just a little too fast. And she could sense that his concentration wasn't entirely as it should be today; more than once they'd had horns blasted at them as he got a little too close to another vehicle.

So she was relieved when he killed the engine outside the building where his mother lived and helped her off.

Alessandro opened the front door and stepped back to allow Kate in first, and then followed. The apartment was quiet, quieter than Kate could ever remember it being, and it momentarily threw her. Was everyone out? But then Abelie appeared at the living-room door and greeted them.

'*Ciao*,' she said, kissing them both. But it was tense, and she didn't wear the broad smile she usually wore for Kate. She looked pale too, her pretty green eyes shadowed from lack of sleep.

'What is wrong?' Alessandro asked.

But when she replied, she lapsed into her native Italian, speaking so rapidly that Kate struggled to keep up. But Kate could make out *Mamma*, and *not good*. Alessandro asked why Abelie had not phoned him during the night to call him home (or so Kate thought), and Abelie simply looked at Kate, and then at him, and raised her eyebrows as if he had never asked anything so stupid in his life. He turned to Kate and his expression was heavy. 'We will eat later. I will take you to dinner at the trattoria.'

'Is everything OK?'

'I do not know, but Mamma will not cook today.'

They followed Abelie through to the living room. Signora Conti was sitting in a chair. This was unusual in itself – Kate had never once visited and seen her do anything but race about in an apron preparing elaborate refreshments for everyone. But today she looked pale and tired, but not in the same way that Abelie looked tired. Alessandro's mother looked utterly spent, as if a month of complete bed rest wouldn't even begin to kick-start a recovery. Alessandro threw his sister a look of alarm. Abelie merely shrugged.

'She says she is only sleepy, because she has been so busy. She says she will rest today and tomorrow she will be well.'

'It doesn't look that way to me,' Kate said, and Alessandro nodded agreement. 'Have you called a doctor?'

'She says no doctor,' Abelie said.

Alessandro repeated the request for a doctor to his mother, but she shook her head vehemently and then began to cough. Kate raced into the kitchen, filled a glass with water and ran back in with it. Signora Conti drank deep, spluttering between each swallow, but eventually she stopped coughing and gave Kate a grateful smile.

'That didn't sound healthy,' Kate said. 'I don't know much about it, but my gran once had pleurisy and it looked pretty similar to what I'm seeing here.'

'Pleurisy?' Alessandro frowned.

'Pain in the chest,' Kate clarified. 'She had a cough and fever, and was very tired. It had come from a viral illness. . .' She turned to Abelie. 'Your mother was ill on the morning of the wedding. Did she show signs of illness before that?'

Abelie shrugged. 'I do not know.'

'Has she been ill all this week since?'

'She has been tired, not running in the house as much, only little work.'

Kate was thoughtful for a moment. Signora Conti was the sort of woman who wouldn't have let them see she was ill if she could help it, so in all likelihood they wouldn't have noticed until she got so bad she could no longer cover it up. 'I think you should call the doctor anyway, just to be safe. It won't hurt to get her checked. It might turn out to be nothing, and I know she'll be grumpy about it, but it might turn out to be something serious, in which case we'll have done her a favour.'

'She will not like it,' Abelie said uncertainly, glancing at her mother, who appeared to be attempting to follow the nuances of the conversation, and even if she wasn't entirely sure what they were saying, it seemed she was getting an idea because she was frowning in disapproval.

'Probably not,' Kate agreed, trying not to look at Signora Conti's darkening expression. 'If she doesn't like it, you can blame me and tell her I insisted.' It was on the tip of her tongue to add: *She's got it in for me anyway so what difference will one more reason make?* But she managed to rein it in.

'Kate is right,' Alessandro decided. 'And we will take the blame together.'

Abelie hesitated and glanced again at her mother, who let out another loud cough, then nodded. As she hurried off to get her phone, Alessandro kneeled next to his mother's chair and stroked her hair. He spoke to her softly, and whatever he said seemed to do the trick, because her scowl now turned into a fond smile for him. She even managed a weak one for Kate.

Abelie returned a few minutes later. 'He will come in two hours,' she said.

'Is there somewhere I can buy lemons close by?' Kate asked. 'And a bottle of whisky too.'

'Mamma has lemons, but whisky. . .?' Abelie looked puzzled.

'My grandma swore by hot toddies – lemon, whisky and honey. Not exactly science but they seemed to help her feel better. I was thinking I would make one for your mother.'

Alessandro looked doubtful. 'She will not drink it.'

'What do you suggest?'

'Mamma always makes herb tea when we sneeze,' Abelie said.

'Herb tea?' Kate asked. 'What herbs?'

'Oh, we have them in the kitchen. Sage, thyme and mint. Sometimes she puts a little honey in. But she had two cups last night and...' She glanced at her mother. If there had been a significant benefit from her herb tea, then Kate would have to assume that she'd looked a whole lot worse before, and she looked pretty bad now. Abelie shrugged. 'We could try your. . . toddy?'

'Toddy, yes.' Kate smiled. 'I suppose if it didn't exactly cure her she might like the taste – I know I do. And at least the alcohol might soothe her a bit and make her feel more comfortable.'

'I will take you to the supermarket,' Abelie said, already leaving the room as she spoke. She returned a few moments later with a light jacket and a silk scarf. 'I do not know if they will sell whisky but we can try.'

Kate got the impression that Abelie would quite like the opportunity for a break and a bit of fresh air, and it seemed Alessandro guessed it too because he simply nodded agreement.

'*Va bene,*' he said. 'I will stay with Mamma.'

A brisk breeze chased high clouds across the sky, and the air was cooler than of late, but it was dry, and still much warmer than November back in England. While Abelie pulled her jacket tighter and shivered slightly, Kate was comfortable with hers flapping open as they walked to the nearby supermarket.

'Have you heard from Lucetta?' Kate asked.

Abelie nodded. 'She is having a good time. She says Venice is beautiful. Not as beautiful as Rome. . .' She shot Kate a wicked grin. 'Mamma said she should have stayed in Rome, but what would Lucetta do in Rome for her honeymoon? She would stay in her new bed with Gian for all of the day and night and we would soon have a tiny little Lucetta or Gian running around!'

Kate laughed. 'I think your mother would have been quite happy with that. I'd like to see Venice.'

'Maybe Alessandro will take you.'

'One day, perhaps. It seems like a long way off at the moment.'

'You are worried? You think you have made a mistake? Coming to Rome?'

'No, not ever!' Kate gave a smile that looked more reassuring than it felt. 'But it's harder than I thought it would be.'

'Did you think it would be easy?'

'Not easy. Just not quite such a mountainous climb.'

'You have more dress orders?'

'Just the two for Nunzia.'

'Tsshh,' Abelie hissed.

'I know how you feel about that,' Kate chuckled. 'But if one person who sees her wear them likes them enough, then they might want me to make one for them too. It grows like that, you see. At least, I think it does.' She paused. Alessandro already knew about Piccolo Castelli and she supposed he would tell his sisters, along with mentioning his opinions about it, so what did it matter if she told Abelie now? 'I might have a back-up plan too. I'm doing a trial run for a property agent.'

'Piccolo Castelli?' Abelie asked.

'How did you know?'

'Bruno heard about it and I told you. Do you remember at the wedding?'

'Oh! I was a bit tipsy! I remember getting the note from someone and found it in my bag the next day. So it was you and your on-off boyfriend all along!'

'Bruno wrote the name. He knows everybody. Property is good money – soon you will be rich and you will be able to go to Venice.'

'I don't know about that,' Kate said darkly. 'Alessandro isn't happy about it.'

'Why?'

'I'm not getting paid at first, until I learn the business.'

Abelie was silent. Kate could sense her disapproval.

'You think he's right.'

'You let too many people take from you,' Abelie replied.

'You could look at it as me taking from her, as she's giving her time to train me in what might become a very lucrative position if it works out.'

'But if she thinks you are good and clever and will sell lots of houses then she should pay.'

'I don't suppose she'll expect me to sell anything yet.'

'But if you do, she will pay you?'

'You mean while I'm training? I don't really know.'

Abelie gave a short nod. She clearly felt vindicated in her disapproval, as Alessandro did. For the first time real doubt crept into Kate's thoughts, but she pushed it out.

'It's just like making a cut-price dress for someone in the hope others will see what you're capable of so you'll get proper-priced orders,' Kate added stubbornly.

'You should not do that either. You are very good and dressmakers would ask for many more euros than you.'

'I have to start somewhere.'

'I would not have given you the name had I known they would not pay you.'

'They will pay me,' Kate insisted, trying very hard to keep the exasperation from her tone. 'Just not at first.'

'Here is the supermarket,' Abelie replied, choosing not to respond to Kate's assertion.

'Why is everyone so angry about this?' Kate stopped, laying a hand on Abelie's arm to halt her too.

'Because you are nice and kind. Not everyone in Rome is good and you have to be careful.'

'I am careful,' Kate huffed. This assumption that she couldn't look out for herself, that she was like a little girl lost in the woods, was starting to get on her nerves. She was thirty, and if she couldn't make her own decisions by now then she might as well give up.

'*Va bene*, then all will be well,' Abelie said in a way that did nothing to quell Kate's vexation. Obviously she didn't think that at all. It was easier not to push it, though. She had already agreed a trial with Shauna, and it was too late now to back out, no matter whether everyone else's hostility to the idea had set her own alarm bells ringing or not.

Abelie had expressed surprise at finding whisky at the supermarket, as had Kate, who was also pleased to see that it was quite a decent single malt. Not that it would matter once it had been mixed with lemon and honey. The smell of it as she prepared the toddy in the kitchen transported her to sickbeds where her grandma would fuss – plumping pillows and feeling foreheads while Kate grimaced as she tried to get the fiery liquid down. But as she'd grown older, she'd learned to appreciate the taste, just as her grandma had promised she would, and now, whenever she had one, she would think of her grandma, a woman who had been gone for almost as long as her father, and she would have to wipe away a private tear. But it was a happy tear, of fond memories and love once cherished. Her grandma had been very ill herself when Kate's father died, but she'd still been a rock for the girls as far as she could until the end.

Signora Conti sniffed the cup cautiously, before an encouraging smile from Kate prompted her to take a sip.

'It's good?' Kate asked. '*Delizioso?*'

Signora Conti seemed to mull over the question for a moment. But then she took another sip and it appeared she'd decided Kate wasn't trying to poison her after all.

'It smells good,' Alessandro said.

'It'll put hairs on your chest,' Kate replied. Then she caught Alessandro's look of bewilderment and she had to laugh. 'It means it'll make you strong,' she explained. 'Although I don't know if there's any scientific basis for that, or whether it'll just make her pleasantly tipsy enough to relax and not feel quite so ill.'

There was a rap at the front door. Abelie went off to get it and returned a moment later with Maria and her youngest in tow. Kate groaned inwardly. The wicked witch of the west – all she needed to take her day to a whole new level of fun.

But Maria's attention, for once, wasn't fixed on Kate. She and Abelie were conversing in low tones as they came in, and Maria went rushing straight to Signora Conti and knelt down by the side of her chair.

'She is very worried,' Abelie said, offering Kate a tense smile.

Kate's heart went out to Maria. They were far from best buddies, but she could appreciate only too well the anxiety for her ill mother. 'I can understand it.'

They watched as Maria examined Signora Conti, peering into her face and stroking a hand over her forehead. And then her attention went to the cup she was holding. Maria took it from her mother and sniffed at it, before asking what it was. Signora Conti gave a fond but weary smile and angled her head in Kate's direction.

'Hot toddy,' she said, mimicking what Kate had called it.

Maria stood and turned to face Kate, the mug still clasped in her hand. 'What is this?'

'It's harmless,' Kate said. 'Something my grandmother swore by to help with a cough and cold.'

'What is in it?'

'Just whisky, lemon—'

'Whisky?' Maria turned on Abelie now. 'Why are you letting her drink this? Mamma could have had herb tea.'

'Already she tried herb tea,' Abelie said, squirming a little under her sister's disapproving stare. 'She was no better.'

'You trusted this filth instead?' Maria squeaked, and Alessandro stepped forward.

'Enough, Maria!'

'Love is blind,' Maria scoffed, not intimidated in the slightest by his tone. 'Kate, Kate, Kate. Kate is an angel – Kate knows all. Pah! If Kate hit you over the head and stole all your money, you would still look at her like an idiot in love! She poisons your own mother and you let her!'

'It's not poison—' Kate began, but Alessandro cut across her.

'You insult Kate, and we do not do that to our guests! She has come to help, and you will take back what you have said!'

'I will never take it back,' Maria growled. 'I do not care how many times she comes to this house, she will never be a part of our family!'

'She is already a part of it,' Alessandro said. 'Everybody loves her.'

Maria threw her hands into the air. 'I do not love her! And if you think she loves you, then you are a fool! She said in this very house that she will never marry you! Are those the words of a woman who loves you?'

'Kate would not say that,' Alessandro said, looking at Kate with the utmost faith, and she felt sick. She had said it, of course, and there had been witnesses, but she had been forced into a corner. It wasn't supposed to come out like this.

'Abelie heard it too!' Maria replied, giving a look of triumph as she dragged her sister into the fray. 'Say it, Abelie!' Maria insisted. 'You heard her say she would not marry Alessandro.'

'I. . .' Abelie looked helplessly between Alessandro and Kate. 'I do not think Kate meant never.'

'But she said it!' Maria shouted.

'I didn't say never,' Kate cried. Her gaze went to Signora Conti, who was watching them, clearly struggling to follow the conversation and clearly desperate to intervene but feeling too weak. On another day and at full strength, this altercation wouldn't even be taking place in her presence – she would have stamped it out in an instant. But for all Maria's solicitude on her arrival, her mother had been forgotten at the first sniff of an opportunity to make Kate look bad.

'And what about your husband in England?' Maria folded her arms, and her look of satisfaction was supreme.

Kate's features hardened. 'I don't have a husband in England,' she said. 'I don't know who told you I did, but it's not true.'

Abelie's mouth dropped open. She stared at Kate, who felt wretched for the deceit. She and Alessandro had agreed early on that his sisters didn't need to know about her ex-husband Matt – at least not yet. It wasn't that they would never tell them, but they would pick the right moment, and it was more to spare any of them accidentally letting the secret out in front of Signora Conti than for any desire to deliberately lie to them.

Kate could only assume that Orazia was behind this particular security breach, and that she had used her paid hours as a police officer well, investigating Kate's past. Perhaps Maria had asked her to, or perhaps she'd done it for her own ends. It didn't matter now – the secret was out and the damage was done.

'Is this true?' Abelie asked. 'You have a husband?'

'No. . .' Kate replied, glancing quickly at Alessandro. 'Not any more.'

'They are divorced,' Alessandro said, almost wincing at the word. Signora Conti was silent, watchful, and it was hard to imagine that she wasn't picking at least some of this up, even just from facial expressions alone.

'You know,' Abelie said. 'Why didn't you tell us?'

'It was difficult. . .'

'So now we are a family of lies,' Maria said into the ensuing pause. She looked at Kate. 'We did not lie to each other before you came.'

'It doesn't matter, though. . .' Kate looked pleadingly at Abelie. She was a young woman, and surely she wasn't so stuck in the old ways that a divorce bothered her. 'It doesn't change the way I feel about Alessandro. . . it just means that I have a past. I wanted to forget about it, like a lot of people do. I wish I could, but I can never get away from it. It doesn't make me a different person, though.'

'I am not worried by divorce, but I am worried that you could not tell me,' Abelie said quietly. 'I thought we were friends, but perhaps not.'

Something had changed between her and Alessandro's youngest sister; Kate felt it shift in that moment, sensed everything slip out of sync. Abelie and Lucetta had been Kate's greatest allies in her time in Rome so far, and if she didn't have them, things would get a whole lot tougher. There was still Lucetta to tell, and then Kate would also have to face Signora Conti's judgement on the matter too. Things looked set to get worse before they got better, if they ever got better at all.

Kate was not to find out for some time. Signora Conti started to cough violently, a wretched sound, like someone drowning from within. They all turned to her, but the more they tried to help her stop, the worse she became, until she was gasping for breath. After ten desperate minutes, Alessandro took charge and called for an ambulance. His mother was going to hospital, whether she liked it or not.

Seven

Signora Conti had given birth to every one of her six children at home. She had never been in a hospital bed her whole life, and Kate could only imagine how her children felt seeing her lie there as they sat gathered around her sleeping form.

'She will be unhappy when she wakes,' Alessandro said. 'It may have been better for us if she was still coughing. She would not be able to complain about being in the hospital.' He turned a slight smile to Kate.

'At least she'll feel more comfortable,' Kate replied, giving his hand a quick squeeze. 'I know the doctors haven't identified her illness yet but she looked so very poorly. . . it's terrifying to think how close she might have been to real danger. If you hadn't called the emergency services when you did she might. . .'

The sentence tailed off. Perhaps it was better not to dwell on what might have been and just give thanks for what was.

Maria glanced at them, but as Kate caught her, she quickly looked away again. Her eyes were red and she sniffed loudly. It was tempting to feel that justice had been done in Maria's case, and that the guilt she obviously bore from the situation was no less than she deserved. But Kate just felt sorry for her. They all loved their mother very much, and nobody deserved to lose someone that precious, not even a scheming cow like Maria.

Isabella and Jolanda were due to arrive shortly. Lucetta had insisted on cutting short her honeymoon after receiving the phone call from Alessandro – despite his reassurance that their mother was now in the best place and getting excellent care – so she was travelling back. The nursing staff were already complaining that there were too many bodies in the room, so nobody had dared to tell them they were expecting many more. But this was a tight family, and there was no way that anyone was going to be missing when Signora Conti needed them most.

The sound of Maria's phone ringing made them all jump. Her husband had shot straight from work to collect their youngest child from Signora Conti's home while Maria accompanied Alessandro, Kate and Abelie to the hospital, and then he had picked up the others from school. It sounded like he was phoning to update Maria on the situation at home and get an update from her on what was happening at the hospital. After a quick glance at Signora Conti, Maria slipped from the room to talk to him in the corridor, leaving Alessandro, Kate and Abelie looking balefully at each other.

Kate wanted to say something, but she didn't know where to start. She owed Abelie an apology, and although Maria's absence would make that easier, she was afraid to rake it up again. It didn't really seem like the right time either, but the right time might be a long time coming as things currently stood. Alessandro was owed an explanation too, for the things that Maria had revealed, but how did she even begin to explain why she'd said it? He knew she didn't mean any of it, surely? They were OK, weren't they? He was close to her now, his hand covering hers, but perhaps that was just the emotional stress of the situation. Perhaps, in the cold light of day, he would remember it and he would demand an explanation, and anything that Kate offered was going to sound immature and trite.

'Abelie, I'm sorry you had to find out about the divorce the way you did. It wasn't my intention to hurt you or deceive you. I just. . .' She sighed. 'I have no explanation. I was scared of what your mamma would think and I didn't tell you because I thought you might think the same too.'

'I am not a fool,' Abelie said.

'Nobody thinks you are,' Kate replied.

'I know that people divorce. When I marry, it will be for the rest of my life, but I know that is not always possible for others.'

'It wasn't possible for me,' Kate said, sensing she might be getting somewhere. 'Matt walked out on me, not the other way round. If not, I suppose we would still be married now.'

Abelie turned her gaze to Alessandro. 'Maria is right — we are a family who lies now. Are there more lies to come?'

He shook his head. 'We did not tell anyone because we were afraid Mamma would discover the truth and she would be upset.'

'Did you think you would never have to tell her?' Abelie asked.

'Maybe. I do not know.' Alessandro glanced at Kate uncertainly. She had nothing to add, because that point in the future had been as vague to her as it was to him. They had tried not to think about it and enjoy what they had, believing themselves safe in their secret for as long as they chose to keep it.

'She would have discovered when you tried to marry. . . *if* you tried to marry.' Abelie threw a pointed look at Kate. 'Have you forgotten the rules? A divorced person may not marry in a Catholic church. Mamma would expect you to marry in church and she would want to know why if you did not.'

Kate spun to look at Alessandro. 'Is this true?'

'There are things that can be done—' he began, but Abelie cut him off.

'Your husband must agree to annulment before you can marry Alessandro.'

'My ex-husband,' Kate corrected. 'We're divorced.'

'But in the eyes of the church, you are still married.'

'That's ridiculous! How can that be?'

Abelie shrugged. 'It is the way of things.'

Kate let out a sigh. The situation was getting more complicated by the minute. Not only did she have a whole web of lies to untangle, it looked as if she now had to ask Matt for a favour – a huge pain-in-the-arse kind of favour that he was very likely to say no to.

'Is there another way?' she asked.

'But I thought you did not want to marry me,' Alessandro said. Kate studied him. He was deadly serious, but in his eyes was that look, the one that gently teased her, and she knew she was on safe ground.

'Maybe it wouldn't be so bad,' she said with a small smile. 'Can we marry outside the church?'

'It would be adultery to Mamma,' Abelie said. 'In her eyes you are still married to the other man, because that is what the church sees too.'

It was a bit too late to worry about adultery, because if those were the rules then she'd committed adultery, loudly and enthusiastically, with Alessandro quite a lot since she'd arrived in Rome. Did Signora Conti think they were playing Scrabble on the nights he stayed over? Did revealing her divorce make that situation even worse? 'Do you think,' she began thoughtfully, 'if I got the annulment from Matt, we could get married and your mamma would never need to know about the marriage in the first place?'

Abelie frowned. 'More lies.'

'To protect her,' Kate countered.

'Or to protect you?'

'What are you suggesting? That Alessandro and I can't be together anymore? Because that is not an option—'

'I know you love him,' Abelie said, cutting in before the tirade that Alessandro himself looked set to let loose.

'You have no idea how much,' Kate replied fervently, emotion now getting the better of her and ready for a fight. 'I have lied, and I'm sorry. But I would lie again, a thousand times a day to keep him in my life, and if I have to make enemies of everyone in Rome then I will do it, because I love him more than I have words for and I am not giving him up!'

She stopped and held Abelie in a challenging gaze, aware that her chest was tight and her heart was racing.

Abelie looked from her to Alessandro. There was a pause, and Kate wondered just what she'd unleashed. But then Abelie broke into a small smile.

'*Va bene*. We will find a way, and one day I will call you sister.'

The tension in the room seemed to dissipate with her words. Kate relaxed and allowed herself a smile in return. 'Thank you.'

'We must be honest from now,' Abelie said, and she gave a disapproving look at Alessandro, who simply nodded and grinned, looking as relieved as Kate felt.

'Please forgive us,' Kate said. 'No more secrets, I promise.'

Abelie crossed the space to hug Kate and Alessandro in turn. As she retook her seat, Maria returned. Her expression was one of suspicion for an instant, but it cleared and she smoothed her features into polite neutrality. 'Donato will come later with the children.'

'Won't it be too many people for the hospital room?' Kate asked.

Maria almost glared at her but then checked herself. 'Family must be at the bedside. I want my husband here. Jolanda and Isabella will be here soon with their husbands and children, and Orazia is coming.'

'Orazia?' Kate flicked an uncertain glance at Alessandro, but his features were unreadable.

'She is a friend of my mother's,' Maria said. 'She wants to visit.'

'I know but. . .' Kate's sentence tailed off. There was no argument for Maria's assertion that wouldn't make Kate look bad.

'Mamma is fond of Orazia,' Alessandro said mildly. 'It will make her happy to know she has come to the hospital.'

'She's too ill to know who's here at the moment,' Kate replied lamely but nobody listened.

Kate didn't have to wait long to find out what mood Orazia would bring with her, as Maria's friend arrived a few moments later. Maria must have phoned her as soon as the ambulance had been called for her to get there so quickly. As she entered, however, she barely acknowledged Kate. Instead, she began to fire a volley of questions at Maria and Abelie, an uncharacteristically soft expression colouring her features as she stared anxiously at the sleeping Signora Conti. After a brief exchange with the sisters, she turned her attention to Alessandro.

'In English please,' he reminded her in reply to a question she'd asked in their native tongue, and while Orazia sent a sharp glance Kate's way, the vexation cleared from her face and she nodded shortly. Kate was used to Alessandro reminding people to speak English in front of her, but she'd never felt more pathetic and useless about it than she did at that moment. Orazia was probably tired of hearing it, and the others must be too – they had enough to worry about without trying to frame every sentence in a language not their own. Hell, Kate would probably have felt the same in their shoes.

'It pains my heart to see her so ill,' Orazia said. 'I have told our superiors at the *Questura* and they have agreed that you do not need to work for a few days.'

'*Grazie.*' Alessandro gave a tight smile. Orazia leaned in to kiss him on the cheek, and he rubbed her back as she wrapped her arms around him. '*Grazie,* Orazia,' he repeated.

Kate's stomach lurched at the sight. He seemed to be more comforted by that one small gesture from Orazia than anything she had said or done over the past few hours. It was obvious when she thought about it, however, because Orazia understood the family better than Kate could ever hope to; she had known them for years – had worked, socialised, even shared a bed with Alessandro. Of course she'd know just what to say and do. Kate wanted to hate her but Orazia, for once, appeared sincere, her sympathy real and candid, and despite the kick of jealousy in Kate's gut, she could hardly complain. Orazia was an old friend of the family, no matter what else she was, or what trouble she caused, and it was obvious she cared a great deal for Signora Conti. And Kate found herself unexpectedly wondering whether she'd misjudged Orazia after all.

'I don't know whether I want to strangle her and finish off what the virus failed to achieve or to kiss her for still being alive,' Kate said.

Lily let out a giggle on the other end of the phone. 'Sounds like you've had one hell of a week.'

'You could say that. I'm so glad she's home, and I don't mind helping out at all – in fact, I'm mighty honoured that she's letting me nurse her when she has all those actual daughters queuing up to do it – but she isn't half hard work.'

'But do you think it's bringing you closer?'

Kate mulled over the question for a moment. There was certainly an understanding between her and Signora Conti that seemed not to have existed before she'd been rushed into hospital. Kate couldn't say what had triggered it, nor could she pinpoint at what exact juncture things had changed, but she felt they had. Perhaps it was simply that they had spent so much time together. Abelie had probably had something to do with it too, now absolutely on Kate's side, as was Lucetta after a day of sulking that was directed more at Alessandro than Kate. Perhaps Uncle Marco had put in a word on Kate's behalf, as Alessandro had asked him to. Even Maria had developed a grudging tolerance of Kate's daily presence. In the end, they'd all been so terrified they were losing Signora Conti that it had somehow pulled them together.

'I suppose it is,' she replied. 'Though she's going to hate me again when I tell her about the divorce.'

'I don't think she really hated you before,' Lily scolded. 'You have to stop assuming that people are thinking the worst of you just because they aren't singing your praises from the rooftops.'

'I know – you're right. It's just hard fitting in and pessimism is my natural default setting.'

'I don't think that's true either, or you wouldn't have taken the plunge and moved to Rome in the first place. Does she really need to know about Matt?'

'Apparently, if Alessandro and I want to marry in a Catholic church she's likely to find out because we'd have to do all this expensive and official church stuff; divorcees can't marry there unless they do. And she's pretty big on that.'

'Wow.' Lily was silent for a moment. 'Things are changing fast.'

'They are. What's new there?' she asked.

Lily's reply was delayed. 'Not a lot,' she said.

Kate frowned. It wasn't like her sister to hold back, but Kate had the distinct feeling she was doing just that.

'Everything's OK, isn't it? There's nothing I need to know about?'

'Of course everything's OK,' Lily said breezily. A bit too breezily, but Kate let it pass. If Lily had something important to say, or something that troubled her, Kate had to trust that she would reveal it when she was ready. 'Mum says Hamish is having a camera up his bum but apart from that it's very boring here.'

'I wouldn't say a camera up his bum is exciting!' Kate said. 'I'm sure Hamish doesn't think so.'

'You'd think, but Mum says he's boring everyone at the pub about it at every opportunity.'

Kate smiled. 'Just like him. It's nothing serious, though?'

'Oh I don't think so. Mum would have sounded a lot more worried than she did if the doctors were looking for anything sinister. She says they're trying to find out why he's so windy.'

'God! Please, no more details!' Kate laughed. 'I hope he doesn't wear his kilt too often if wind is a real issue!'

Lily giggled, and Kate was relieved to hear it. Perhaps she'd been wrong – perhaps there was no need to worry about her sister after all. It was only natural, she supposed, that being so far away from a sister she was so close to would make her dread the idea that she might not be there when she was needed.

'I'm glad I'm out here and away from Hamish and his wind right now and I think I'll keep well clear until it's been sorted.'

'It is still weird to think you're not coming back,' Lily said. 'Soon you'll be a regular Italian and we'll barely recognise you when we next see you.'

Not that soon if I don't get a job, Kate thought.

One other consequence of Signora Conti's illness was that Kate had postponed her estate-agent training with Shauna. Once Signora Conti had been discharged from hospital, Kate had been keen to offer support to Abelie, who was now the only daughter left at home and who had a job and commitments of her own (as all the Conti siblings did), whereas Kate had no job and very few commitments as of yet, and it seemed only fair she pitched in. To her surprise, Signora Conti was delighted with the idea, and she was happy to let Kate nurse her until someone else could take over. Kate was returning to her apartment every night exhausted but secretly rather happy with the progress they were making on a personal level. She was learning a fair amount of Italian too, not having a lot of choice when Signora Conti spoke so little English. And Alessandro told her one evening that his mother had started to call Kate her *angelo* – her angel – a fact that had apparently left Maria looking sour but made Kate swell with pride.

Shauna hadn't been quite so happy with Kate's request to postpone joining her for a couple of weeks. Kate could understand it, of course, but Shauna's attitude also strengthened the doubts that were already plaguing Kate about the decision she'd taken to accept the job, especially when everyone else still seemed to think it was a bad idea.

'It might be a little while before that happens,' Kate said to Lily now on the phone.

'Perhaps, but I think you'll get there. You always sound so optimistic and determined to make it work that I'm sure it will. I'm sorry we can't visit yet, but we're working on it. Honest.'

'How could I be anything else?' Kate replied cheerfully. 'Anyway, I have Jamie arriving this weekend and he's manic enough for ten people. I'll probably never want another visitor again!'

'I wish I could meet him; he sounds amazing.'

'He is,' Kate said. 'I wish you could meet him too, but I'm sure it'll happen one day.'

'Is he staying with you?'

'No, in a hotel. It's probably better that way – I rather like my liver and he'd be doing his best to pickle it at every opportunity if he was here at the flat. This way I get a few hours' break at least.'

Lily laughed. 'I thought it was a work trip.'

'It is. You should see him on a proper holiday!'

'You're happy, though? With your new life?'

'Getting there,' Kate said. She could lie, say everything was fantastic, but Lily would see through it, and Kate was juggling enough lies at the moment without adding more. 'It'll work out, but it needs time.'

'Like any big life decision, then.'

'Hmmm. If you could arrange for Orazia to disappear that would be a big help. And perhaps get Maria brainwashed while you're at it.'

'If only,' Lily replied. 'There are a few people I'd sort out at home first if I could do either of those things.'

'I suppose so,' Kate said. 'We all have that one person who's the bane of our existence, don't we?' Her gaze was drawn to the shadows creeping along the windowsill, stealing the colour from the room. She glanced at the clock. 'Much as I hate to cut you off, I'm supposed to be visiting the matriarch in an hour. You know, because I'm Signora Conti's *angelo* and she couldn't possibly do without me.'

'Don't let the praise go to your head.'

'No way.' Kate grinned. 'As if.'

Eight

Jamie's hug was warm and very welcome. She hadn't realised just how much she'd missed him until he was there, in front of her, for real and not just on a screen, sunlight catching the gold in his hair and his blue eyes crinkled in a warm smile.

'You look amazing!' she said, stepping back to appraise him. And he did, dressed in a soft blue shirt and jeans that showed off his slim hips. 'Nobody would guess you'd been on a plane for most of the day.'

'So do you. It's so good to see you!' He pulled her into his arms again and swung her around. She shrieked with laughter.

'So, what do you want to do first?' Kate asked as she linked her arm through his and they walked away from the glass entrance of his hotel. She felt like a kid let out to play without parental supervision for the first time; familiar places were shiny and new again and all possibilities were to be grabbed at once.

'Now, I don't believe I'm hearing this,' he said in a mock stern voice.

'What?'

'Don't you recall the first place I head to whenever I hit Rome?'

'The hotel bar? Red light district? Massage parlour?' Kate gave a coquettish wiggle of her eyebrow and he chuckled.

'Gelato!' he said.

'Oh!' Kate grinned, almost bouncing along with the pleasure his company was bringing. '*The* gelato shop! The one we visited on my first day when you tried to marry me off to some random Irish man.'

'There was nothing random about him; he had great credentials.'

'How do you know? We'd never seen him before!'

'Honey, the only credentials you needed were in front of your face. He was smoking hot!'

'I hadn't noticed. . .'

'Liar!'

'Some of us aren't as shallow as you. Pretty faces, that's all you care about.'

'Ooooh!' Jamie clutched at his chest. 'Arrow through the heart! If you're gonna keep insulting me then I'll just go right back to my hotel and sulk!'

'You can't because I wouldn't let you.'

'Couldn't stop me.'

'You'd be surprised what I could do if I put my mind to it.'

'Now that I can believe.'

'So you're taking me for gelato right now?'

'No, *you're* taking *me* for gelato – that's how this works.'

'You're paying,' Kate sang.

'OK, but just this once and only because I love you.'

'Aww, I love you too. Especially when you buy me gelato.'

The shop had been refurbished, with wrought-iron fittings, delicate ironwork tables and pink and peach walls that glowed in the sunlight filtering through pretty white shutters. Kate was pleased to note that nothing else had changed and the gelato was every bit as good as she remembered. She'd gone for a scoop of pistachio this time, coupled with their new salted-caramel flavour, which was creamy, sweet, piquant and divine. Jamie had opted for a whole three scoops, which threatened to overflow from his bowl as he carried it to a table, but he made short work of it and laughed as he patted his stomach.

'I've been thinking about this ever since I checked in at JFK.'

'I don't know how you stay so slim,' Kate said, raising her eyebrows at him, half a bowl still left in front of her.

'I'm active.'

'I'm active too but I'm sure I'd look like a bowl of gelato if I ate it like that.'

'I get a break, don't I? It's not like I can get it in New York.'

'You have gelato in New York, surely?'

'True. But it's not like it is here.'

He scraped his spoon around the edges of his bowl, eking out the last of the creamy goodness.

'You'll take the pattern off that bowl,' Kate said.

'Huh? Is this another of your sayings?'

'My gran used to say it when you were intent on getting the last of the food off your plate. You know, like you're scraping so hard the pattern will come off the china.'

'If it tastes as good as the gelato I don't care; I'll eat the pattern clean off.'

Kate giggled. 'I've missed you.'

'You've had Alessandro and his huge family to keep you company.'

'I have. But they don't make me laugh in the same way you do.'

'Even Alessandro?'

'Alessandro is good at other things. . .'

Jamie held up a hand. 'Please. . . don't torture me with the details! So,' he continued, 'tell me if I'm up to speed: Orazia is still trying to get her perfectly manicured claws into your man, Maria is on her side, everyone else *was* on your side until they found out about the divorce and now you don't know whose side they're on but you think secretly that they might be on hers, apart from Mamma Conti, who wasn't on your side, but now that she has a reason not to be on your side suddenly is. . . Does that make sense to you? Because it sure as hell doesn't to me!'

'Pretty much sums it up.' Kate licked a drip from her finger. 'It's got to the point where even I don't know what's going on anymore. I have been thinking that maybe I'm a bit wrong about Orazia though . . .'

'Oh? How so?'

'I don't know. . . but ever since Alessandro's mum got ill, she's been behaving pretty decently actually – visiting her and the family, fetching bits and pieces, being almost courteous to me. . . Maybe she's coming to terms with the fact that things have changed and that Alessandro and I are for keeps. I can't say we'll ever be best friends but. . .' She shrugged.

'Maybe, but I wouldn't let your guard down.' Jamie reached across, swivelled his spoon in Kate's bowl and pulled out a large cloud of gelato like candy floss on a stick, which he proceeded to stuff into his mouth.

'I won't,' Kate replied, frowning in her attempt to hold back a laugh. He grinned in return and went to take another spoonful, but her deepening frown must have turned into something genuinely scary because he seemed to change his mind and let his spoon drop back into his own bowl. 'But I hate thinking the worst of anyone,' Kate continued. 'I want to believe that we've turned a corner on the whole thing. I can't quite believe it yet, even though I'd like to, but the idea is a nice one.'

'And what about this job? They're all telling you not to take it. . . do you think maybe you should listen to them?'

'I think it's OK for them to tell me I'm being played for a fool because they all have a job or don't need one, and if they did need one, they'd find it much easier to come by. I have to take opportunities when I see them and they don't seem to understand that. What do you think?'

'I think you're right. After all, it's what America thrives on – seized opportunities. I say go for it and see what happens. The worst is that you'll eventually tell her to shove her unpaid training up her ass, but the best is that it turns into a real break that could make you big bucks.'

'See!' Kate smiled as she let her spoon clatter into her bowl. 'I can always rely on you to see things for exactly what they are – and to say them exactly how you see them.'

'So you want me to come and entertain Mamma Conti?' he continued.

'The problem is, if she knows you're coming she'll try and cook a banquet and I don't think she's up to it. And even if she doesn't know you're coming, when you turn up she'll be trying to cook as soon as you arrive. I'm sure she'd love to see you, though.'

'Maybe you can cook for her.'

Kate raised her eyebrows. 'Me? Cook for Alessandro's mother? Are you kidding?'

'I'd help.'

'But I can't cook anything she likes.'

'Who's been doing it so far?'

'Mostly Abelie. The others bring in stuff they've cooked at home, or they come and take over the kitchen to give Abelie a break. Nobody has even considered me cooking. I think Alessandro might have let on I'm not that great.'

'I thought he liked your cooking. You cooked for him in England, right?'

'I think he might have lied about liking it.'

'I bet Mamma Conti can lie with the best of them if she had to.'

'Thanks.' Kate gave a wry smile. 'That makes me feel so much better about it. I will do anything for that woman – take her to the toilet, bring her drinks, blanket wash, even argue with her for an hour about why she should be taking her meds when she absolutely refuses to – but not that. My cooking is too shameful; she'd probably end up back in hospital.'

'Alessandro can cook?'

'Yes, but I think even he'd baulk at the idea of putting something in front of his mum. I mean, she's the kitchen queen – nobody does gnocchi like she does. Come to think of it, nobody does anything like she does.'

Jamie leaned across the table. Kate recognised the look only too well, despite not having seen it for a good few months. It was his reckless, here-comes-a-crazy-idea look. 'Why don't *we* cook for her? You and me? She's in no position to complain if she doesn't like it!'

'Are you kidding me? She could complain if she was in a coma! That's one thing the woman does well no matter what.'

'We'll hire a chef, then.'

'What? You're crazy! Who's going to do that?'

'There are plenty of chefs in Rome. I'm sure I could find someone.'

Kate was silent for a moment. But then she gave her head a tiny shake. 'No,' she decided. 'She would absolutely hate it.' She let out a sigh. 'I mean, if you're determined I'll put the idea to Alessandro but I think he'll say the same as me. She won't want anyone in her kitchen.'

Jamie leaned back in his seat and eyed her thoughtfully. 'It doesn't have to be her kitchen. It could be yours and we could take it over to her.'

'My kitchen is deeply shit.'

'But it's a kitchen just the same. I only need an oven and a bowl to whip up a mean meatloaf. Come on – let's introduce her to some good old American food.'

'Don't forget you came to Rome to work. Don't you have actual clients to fit in? And meetings and all the other things your boss is paying you to do?'

'But I won't be doing those all the time. I can create a workable schedule for this. In fact, I'm a genius at creating a workable schedule when it comes to making room for fun.'

Kate let out a sigh. This was only going to end one way, and that was with Jamie getting what he wanted. He had a knack of persuading you to say yes without even realising you had. But maybe a day in her kitchen fooling around with Jamie was just what she needed. Despite throwing herself into every new challenge life in Rome presented, and despite loving it (when she wasn't in some state of emotional turmoil) she was tired. Some days everything just seemed like doggy-paddling against the tide, and the shore looked further and further away the harder she swam. A day with Jamie, burning stuff, splatting her kitchen walls with food and just laughing, sounded like a very appealing prospect. Jamie had no connections to anyone, no allegiances, no grudges to play out. He was just her friend, pure and simple, and that was one thing she needed right now.

* * *

'The thing about meatloaf,' Jamie began as he emptied the ingredients from a carrier bag onto Kate's kitchen counter, 'is that everyone thinks their recipe is the only one. I happen to put oatmeal in mine, but Brad's mom thinks that's the most disgusting idea since composting toilets and swears by dried breadcrumbs.'

'Well, as I've never eaten meatloaf I'm hardly equipped to judge. And I'm guessing Alessandro's mother hasn't either.'

'But,' he continued, 'it's wholesome, and comforting, and easy to make, so we can do enough to feed everyone. She's going to be a convert, I guarantee. We'll cook it here and prepare the vegetables so all we have to do is drop them in a pan when we get to Mamma Conti's house, and sprinkle some Texan love over the plates as we serve up, like my momma used to.'

'Don't you think we should stick with salt and pepper?'

Jamie threw her a grin, and then followed it with an apron.

'You bought me an apron?' Kate turned it around to take a good look. It bore the tags of the shop he'd purchased it from, and it wasn't a cheap place. 'You didn't need to do this.'

'We're going to be professional about this,' he said, pulling an identical blue-and-white striped apron from the bag for himself. 'We're a team, so we need to look like one.'

Next from the bag came a white hat. Kate rolled her eyes as he punched the inside to pop it to its full height.

'A chef's hat? A bloody chef's hat? What the hell do we want one of those for?'

'Because it's funny,' he said. 'Put it on and quit your whining.'

'What else have you got in there – Gordon Ramsay?'

'No. But I do have this excellent wine to cook with – or rather, to drink while we're cooking. And I have an iPod full of Dolly Parton. I

mean, if we're making my momma's meatloaf then we have to listen
to Dolly – it's the law.'

'Personally I'm more of a Coldplay kind of girl, but I suppose we
could give it a whirl, just this once.'

'It'll help the food taste better, trust me.'

'Hmmm, how many times have I fallen for those two words – *trust
me* – and come a cropper?'

'By *cropper* I'm assuming you mean I got you in trouble?'

'Yes.'

'Harsh.'

'But I think you'll find fair.' Rolling her eyes, Kate jammed the
chef's hat on her head and watched as Jamie did the same. She felt like
a prize turnip, but weirdly, she also felt as if some of the seriousness
had been lifted from her life, just for a moment. Jamie plugged his
iPod into the dock and clicked to start his playlist. A grin spread across
his face as the introduction to 'Jolene' kicked in, and Kate couldn't
help catching it. The music, the company, the sun slanting into the
kitchen, the smells on the air of frying onions, of mustard and sweet
ketchup, of crisp celery and fresh carrots, of fragrant mixed herbs. . .
little by little they lifted her mood until she felt that her world, just for
a moment, was perfect. Outside this bubble, she would have money
worries, job fears and secrets that would threaten to tip her life upside
down, but here with Jamie all of that seemed a million miles away.

A couple of hours later, Kate's kitchen looked as if Gordon Ramsay
had indeed climbed from Jamie's shopping bag and proceeded to have
a major tantrum with the meatloaf ingredients. Kate glanced across at
her sink and wondered how they could have made such a mountain

of washing-up in such a short space of time doing a relatively simple task. But the apartment was filled with the homely, heavenly smell of cooking meat and spices, and the dishes could wait because they were enjoying a well-earned glass of wine before they began peeling carrots and shelling peas.

A light tap at the door prompted Kate to look up at the clock and frown. 'That must be Lucetta to pick us up, but she's early.'

'Maybe she's excited to see us.'

'More likely she's come to see if we actually know what we're doing,' Kate replied as she put her wine down and went to the front door.

As Kate opened up, Lucetta clapped a hand to her mouth to stifle her laughter. 'What is this?' she asked, waving her hands up and down to indicate Kate's work attire.

'Don't ask. You'll understand when you come and see Jamie in the kitchen.'

Lucetta stepped inside and Kate was about to close the door when Alessandro appeared behind her. As he saw Kate, he broke into one of his special mocking smiles, and Kate felt herself go so hot it seemed as if her whole body was blushing.

'Very nice,' he said, nodding at the hat.

'I thought we were meeting at your place,' Kate replied, whipping it off and shoving a hand through her hair. 'We agreed there wasn't enough room in Lucetta's car with all the food.'

'I have come on my Vespa. I wanted to help.'

'You might regret that when you see the kitchen,' she replied darkly as he followed her in.

His eyebrows rose slightly, but Kate had to be impressed with his restraint. He simply ran his gaze over the chaos before greeting Jamie warmly. Lucetta had already buried herself in Jamie's arms, and she was determined not to be moved from there by anyone as she grinned out at Alessandro.

'Mine!' she said. '*Tesoro mio*.'

Jamie grinned, his chef hat now sliding to one side as he took Lucetta's waist and led her in a surprisingly light-footed dance around the kitchen to the strains of 'Islands in the Stream'.

'The wine?' Alessandro said as he shot Kate a knowing look.

'Only a little,' she replied with a sheepish smile.

'Hmm. When Jamie is here only a little wine is always a lot.'

'He's never going to change. But we still got the cooking done so that's a win for the team.'

Alessandro lifted his chin and paused for a moment, deep in thought. 'It smells good. Like meatballs.'

'You think your mamma will like it?'

'Maybe.'

'You haven't told her? It's still a surprise?'

'We have not told her. She would not rest if she knew Jamie was cooking for her; he is a guest and she would feel she wanted to cook for him.'

'That's what I thought, which is why we didn't want to tell her.' Kate began to wring her hands, a sign of nerves, a trait that had somehow crept into her personality of late and one that she recognised as coming from her mother. Quite why she was nervous wasn't entirely apparent. Signora Conti would love the sentiment even if she didn't love the food, but suddenly it really mattered what she thought of the food too. Would she be angry at being duped out of the chance to take back control of her beloved kitchen at home? Her favourite thing in the world was to feed people and see them enjoy what delights she created. Would she feel pushed out, side-lined, consigned to the scrap heap by what they were doing now? 'But Jamie was so excited about doing this, so she'd accept it with grace, right?' Kate asked uncertainly. 'As a gift from him? And she could cook for him as soon as she was well enough. . . next time he's in Rome, of course.'

Alessandro took her into his arms and planted a light kiss on her nose. 'She will show him courtesy no matter what she thinks.'

'Oh. . . but she might still be angry?'

'Not angry. Maybe a little offended, but she is soon charmed by Jamie and she will forget.'

'I hope so.'

'If you both arrive with your hats she will laugh and forget to be angry or offended.'

Kate gave him a lopsided smile. 'I suppose we do look a bit silly.'

He lowered his voice. 'Perhaps. But you also look sexy.'

That blush spread through her again, and this time the heat spread through her loins too. Something about Alessandro and the mere mention of sex never failed to affect her in the exact same way. She cleared her throat and left his arms, very deliberately pushing away the erotic images invading her thoughts.

'Lots to do,' she said. 'Better get cleaned up.'

As she walked to the sink and opened the window as wide as it would go to cool her burning face, she knew that behind her he was wearing that lazy, mocking grin. It was best not to look, just in case.

Maria and her family were curiously absent from lunch, having made some excuse about having to attend a dinner being hosted by her husband's boss.

Kate couldn't help but be relieved. Jolanda and her brood were there, though her husband had to work, Isabella came with her children, Lucetta and Gian came, both still on leave from their jobs as they were officially still on honeymoon, and Abelie had taken the afternoon off. Alessandro was on a non-shift day, so all in all there was a good turnout for Jamie's visit. Signora Conti had fussed and faffed about who was going to cook for him and how they couldn't receive a guest without a proper lunch, and Alessandro and Lucetta, both in on the secret, had assured her it was all under control and had told her very sternly that she needed to sit down and stop fretting about it immediately or they would be forced to call another ambulance to cart her off. Her reply had been to throw her hands in the air, force out some very theatrical lamentations, and then finally drop into a chair, clasping a hand over her heart. Alessandro had told Kate it was funny, but Kate wasn't so sure she would have been able to see the joke had she been there.

Signora Conti practically leapt from her invalid chair to greet Jamie as he walked in the door, only for her joy to turn to consternation as he unveiled the lunch he and Kate had prepared. In fact, she stumbled back, looking set to faint, and Alessandro ran to catch her.

'*Santa Maria,*' she murmured.

Kate grabbed a magazine to waft in front of her face as her eyes fluttered. She might have been tempted to say it was an overreaction, but anyone who knew the pride with which Giuditta Conti entertained guests would understand her response to being entertained by guests in her own home. It was all highly irregular, and as Lucetta ushered Kate and Jamie into the kitchen with their goods, Alessandro spoke to his mother in low and earnest tones.

Kate popped her head round the door five minutes later as Jamie and Lucetta got pots on to boil water for the vegetables, and Signora

Conti seemed to be more herself again. At least, as much herself as she'd been since Lucetta's wedding, which wasn't very much at all.

'Is she OK?' Kate whispered as Alessandro came to the doorway, leaving Jolanda and Isabella with his mother.

He lowered his voice to match hers. 'I have said that the dish Jamie has brought is a tradition where he comes from and it is made to honour my mother for her kindness when he visited Rome once before. I have told her that she would insult him to refuse it.'

'And she was OK with that?'

'I think so.'

'Then she must be more ill than we thought,' Kate replied, throwing a guarded glance at the back of Signora Conti's head. She looked back to see Alessandro watching her intently with a huge smile. 'What is it?' she asked, rubbing the end of her nose in case there was something on it.

'You are funny. You are also very kind. And I have not forgotten about the hat.'

For the third time that day, Kate blushed violently. Before he had a chance to make things worse, she ducked back into the kitchen and the relative safety of Jamie's company, Alessandro's chuckling still in her ears.

Once they were all seated around the table, and everyone had helped transfer the food dishes there, Signora Conti claimed control once again. Insisting on carving the meat, she stood, Jamie reaching for the dish to pull it closer for her. What had smelled so good when they were cooking it had now cooled and congealed, and resembled a huge, solid log of glistening meat, sitting in a rather unattractive pool of fat. But Signora Conti smiled graciously at Jamie, clearly recalling the fake tradition that Alessandro had dreamed up to console her, and thinking she was doing a very good and courteous thing even allowing such a culinary monstrosity into her home. Kate, however, was now less convinced. It was quite possible that she and Jamie would wipe out the entire Conti clan between them with one deadly meal. She was just relieved they hadn't made dessert as well.

As Alessandro's mother began to carve, the loaf quivered slightly, before giving up any pretence of being a stable body and disintegrating into little globules of meat and vegetables vying for freedom. It was like a weird and fascinating science experiment. Kate threw a helpless glance at Jamie, who seemed unconcerned by the event.

'Oh, sometimes it does that.'

'I thought you'd cooked this loads of times!' Kate hissed.

'Sure I have,' came the serene reply. 'And probably ninety percent of those times it turned out just like this. Tastes OK, though.'

'It's OK, Mamma. . .' Lucetta nodded encouragingly. Just to display how OK it was, she held her plate out for Signora Conti. Fighting a losing battle with a fork and long knife, eventually Abelie ran to the kitchen to get a tablespoon and Signora Conti offered an apologetic look to Jamie as she scooped up the mush instead, clearly wondering if she was insulting his lunch even further by not only making it explode but then serving it with a spoon. Jamie simply smiled brightly.

'The vegetables are probably better if I'm honest,' he commented, throwing a fond look at a bowl of carrots.

One of Jolanda's children started to cry, wailing that they wanted pasta and why did they have to eat prison food. Jolanda slapped his hand, making his cries even louder, only to be silenced by one icy look from Signora Conti, who might have been ill but was still the most terrifying person in the room. Kate wondered about the possibility of some kind of ninja-style escape through the window and a run to the nearest restaurant where she could grab an unsuspecting chef and frogmarch him back to the apartment to cook them something they could actually eat.

An excruciating ten minutes later and everyone had a plate of meat before them. Signora Conti said grace, and then they all watched and waited as she took up her fork and dug it into the meatloaf. Even Jamie looked mildly anxious at this point, realising that he was about to be judged. But to Kate's relief, as the food went in, she began to smile.

'*Che buono!*'

Kate frowned. 'Really?' She shot Jamie an apologetic glance. 'I mean. . . sorry, it's just that I'm sure my part of the cooking was really terrible. It's actually probably the reason why it all fell apart—'

'Oh, clam up!' Jamie laughed. 'Who cares what it looks like if Mamma Conti thinks it's good? Just eat the darned thing!'

Jamie didn't get everything his own way, and Signora Conti set about making a fruit salad to follow his meal, insisting that it was hardly work at all. There was nothing to do but let her, and the task, following on from her rapidly improving spirits during dinner, seemed to perk her up even more. The room was filled with laughter and gossip, Jamie's infectious humour and charm impossible to ignore, and almost everyone was a little bit in love with him in one way or another.

When Signora Conti had been discharged from the hospital, Isabella had somehow procured use of a wheelchair, adamant that her mother was to be wheeled around in it at all times until she was strong again. Signora Conti had scoffed, quite determined that it was the most ridiculous idea she'd ever heard and ordered Isabella to get rid of it. But Isabella had refused, and it now sat in the corner of the dining room quietly gathering dust.

'I've got to ask,' Jamie said as they sipped coffees. 'I keep looking at that thing in the corner – is it a wheelchair?'

'Yes,' Isabella replied, looking sheepish. 'I found it for Mamma, but—'

'Mamma would rather crawl on her knees than ride in a wheelchair,' Jolanda finished for her.

'Is that so?' Jamie said, studying the object thoughtfully. 'What are you going to do with it?'

'It is a loan, so I will take it back soon,' Isabella said. 'I was going to keep it a little longer; maybe Mamma would change her mind and use it to go out on the street.'

'Hasn't she been going out at all?' he asked.

'We've all tried,' Kate said.

'Too afraid?'

'A bit of that, and a bit of stubborn pride too, I think. She can't walk far right now, but she'd never let the neighbourhood see that. She's so used to being a little dynamo that this illness has taken the wind right out of her sails in more ways than just physical.'

Jamie leapt from his chair and bounded across the room like an overexcited puppy. Pulling the wheelchair from its forlorn station, he opened it out and patted the seat.

'Mamma Conti!' he grinned, looking up at her. 'A walk after lunch? *Fare una passeggiata?*'

She shook her head vehemently. 'No!'

'Ah, come on.' Jamie put his hands together like he was praying. '*Per favore? Vieni con me?*'

'No!'

'You won't persuade her,' Kate said, and everyone murmured agreement. Signora Conti folded her arms tight across her chest and looked so utterly formidable that it almost reduced Kate to laughter.

'A tough cookie, eh?' Jamie smiled, regarding his adversary as if weighing her up, trying to find a chink in the armour. 'Well, we have ways of making you walk. . .'

'I still can't believe you got her out,' Kate said as they shared one last coffee back in her flat before Jamie headed off to his hotel. 'There is absolutely nobody else on the planet that could have done it – not even her own kids.'

'What can I say?' Jamie replied in a lazy voice. 'I have a way with people. Moms in particular. I don't know, maybe they think I need to be nurtured or something.'

'The mummy whisperer,' Kate laughed. 'It must be that boyish charm. So what did you do?'

'What did we do?'

'When you went out? Where did you take her?'

'Just walked the block.'

'And she was happy to sit there while you pushed her around?'

'Pretty much.'

Kate shook her head slowly. 'Unbelievable.'

'She covered her face a couple of times when she saw people she knew, but they came over anyway. By the time they'd all finished telling her how much they'd missed seeing her around and were happy to know that she was getting better, she was like a queen on a walkabout – practically waving to the crowds.'

Kate giggled. 'I wish I could have seen it.'

'It was awesome. She's a local celebrity.'

'And you came back unscathed. I thought she was going to hit you over the head with her handbag or something when you first wheeled her out. She looked so annoyed that you'd beaten her into submission.'

'Don't tell people I've beaten her, especially not Alessandro. I have accommodation so I don't need a night in a jail cell.'

'I think she's in love with you. Perhaps you'll be Alessandro's new daddy.'

Jamie gave a theatrical shudder. 'Imagine that. Pretty much ticks off all the elements of my worst nightmares. Married to a woman and a really hot, out-of-bounds dude for a stepson.'

'Er. . . he is out of bounds!' Kate cried with mock affront. 'Hands off, slut!'

'OK, OK. . . I'll let you keep him!' Jamie laughed. 'Seriously, though, you two are so made for each other. I think Mamma Conti sees it too. In fact, everyone sees it – I think that's why you're having so much trouble with Orazia and Maria. They know it – they're just not ready to admit it yet.'

'You think?'

'I know it.'

'Well, I wish they'd hurry up and get it out of their systems.'

'Seems to me they already are. Maybe there's light at the end of the tunnel?'

'I think we've got a long way to go yet, but at least Signora Conti is coming round to the idea. In some ways Alessandro's mum being ill has been a blessing in disguise because it's been a good opportunity for me to get to know her.'

'It helps that you're awesome too.'

'I could be as awesome as you like but if Mamma Conti doesn't approve then I don't get into the family – simple as that. I've still got Maria to contend with too, and she's taking a lot more convincing. And not getting all the family onside makes life difficult for me and Alessandro.'

'He would never give you up. And if his sister makes him choose between his family and the love of his life then she's a bitch of the highest order.'

'That may be, but it still doesn't change the fact that family would win every time if he was pushed.'

'I wouldn't be so sure of that.' Jamie stretched and stifled a yawn. 'Would you look at that – I'm actually tired.'

'It's never been known. Must have been all that cooking.'

'I cook.'

'But probably not for so many people. That was like army cooking.'

'It went OK, though.'

'It did.' Kate smiled. 'I can't believe everyone liked it. And they weren't lying because Alessandro's mother would never lie about food – it's far too important.'

'You know what's funny?' Jamie asked, and the curious look now creeping across his face made her think that something less than funny and something more like a complete curveball was coming.

'Enlighten me.'

'Mamma Conti asked me if I was married.'

'Yes. . .'

'And I told her I was engaged.'

Kate sucked in a sharp breath. Jamie's potential for bluntness was legendary, and this was only going to play out one way. 'And?'

'She wanted to see a photo. So I showed her.'

Kate's eyes widened. 'You showed her a photo of Brad?'

'Who else was I gonna show her?'

'I know but. . . well, she's so traditional!' Kate frowned. Signora Conti had seemed strangely unruffled when they'd returned from their walk. In fact, she'd returned beaming and more affectionate towards Jamie than ever before. Could it be that she'd somehow misunderstood what Jamie had told her? Or had she actually been OK with it? 'She got it? That you're engaged to a man?'

He nodded. 'I told her right out that I'm gay.'

'What did she say?'

'She said she thought it was a sin to be with another man.'

'But she was OK when you got back. She was happy.'

'Yeah, she was cool with it.'

'She was?' If Kate's eyes could have gone any bigger, they would have taken over her face. 'But she said it was a sin.'

'Sure. But I said that if God made everything then he made me and he made me gay for a good reason, because surely God didn't mess up.'

'Wow – that's telling her!'

'But there was no animosity. She was cool – started to laugh. She said that God might mess up and being gay was still a sin, but God loved everyone the same, even sinners, and so she would still love me too, even though I was a huge fuck-up.'

'She said that?'

'Not the fuck-up bit. But pretty much the rest.'

Kate shrieked with laughter. 'Oh my God! I cannot believe you had that conversation with her! And you came out unscathed!'

'What was she gonna do, have me shot? And I was the one with the wheelchair at my fingertips. Maybe I'd have tipped her out onto the road if she'd given me a hard time.'

Kate shook her head, staring at Jamie in wonderment. 'You're bloody amazing, do you know that? Truly one of a kind.'

'You haven't heard all of it yet. I asked her what else she thought was sinful. I figured, while we were on the subject of theology, it might be fun to set the fox on the henhouse.'

'You had a complex theological debate with your rudimentary Italian and her three English words? This I have got to hear.'

'Hey, enough of the rudimentary! My Italian is better than yours.'

'Which is crap, so that's no recommendation. You know what I mean. Continue.'

'I wouldn't say it was complex, but we got by OK and we understood each other. I know one thing that'll wipe the smile off your face.'

And it died, Kate suddenly serious. What the hell had Jamie said now?

'She knows about your divorce.'

A silence descended on the room, all the more palpable in contrast to the laughter of previous moments, as Jamie let this information sink in and Kate could find no reply for it.

'Who told her?' Kate finally managed to croak. As if she needed to ask, but it seemed like the natural first response, the only response she could give.

'Nobody. At least she says so. But she sees and understands more than you think and maybe it would be wise to remember that.'

'So nobody told her? She just worked it out? I find that hard to believe.'

'That's what she says.'

'Was she angry?'

Jamie gave her a warm smile. 'Stop worrying. She was cool about it.'

'She was? Are you sure you didn't accidentally swap her wheelchair for one containing a woman who lives in the twenty-first century and have this conversation with her instead?'

'No!' Jamie laughed. 'She loves you, so why wouldn't she be cool with it?'

'But I thought it was a sin. Maria said the church thought it was adultery, having it off with a divorcee who wasn't annulled or something or other.'

'I think it is.'

'Then she doesn't mind us sinning? I mean, me making her son sin. Oh, God; that sounds so weird! I sound like a Satan worshipper or something!'

'She says it's OK because she knows you're not sleeping together yet. I think she's hanging on to see if. . . well, basically, to see if you stick around. Then she's going to see the priest about getting your annulment sorted.'

'She told you this? She's going to just toddle off, no consultation, and see if the priest can make me pure again? Bit presumptuous.'

Jamie chuckled. 'Don't look so riled. I'm sure she'd have mentioned it to you first. But if you'd said no, then you might have found yourself in hot water.'

'What about Alessandro? Does he know about any of this?'

'I guess you'd have to ask him that.'

Kate shook her head. It was hard to take it all in. 'I can't believe she thinks we're not sleeping together. I mean, who would think that?'

'Maybe she thinks Alessandro is a good Catholic boy.' Jamie raised his eyebrows. 'Clearly not as good as Mamma would like him to be. Or maybe she just doesn't want to acknowledge the possibility. But I say what she don't know won't hurt her; she's happy believing that, so why don't you two just keep it between yourselves?'

'Do you think she was angry? Because we didn't tell her?'

'I guess she realised you were too scared to. She's a smart cookie, and maybe her kids should give her more credit. She's more open to change than anyone realises, and she may seem like a Victorian but she's got eyes and ears and she knows that the world is changing pretty quickly. She may worry about the moral welfare of her kids, and she may want them to be good Catholics, but she also knows that she has to shift her attitudes to fit in with what life is like now.'

Kate cradled her coffee mug, thoughtful as she breathed the aroma in. In light of all this, she was almost more uncertain of herself around Signora Conti now than she had been before. Far from being reassured by the news, as she suspected Jamie had hoped she would be, she was more worried and perplexed than ever.

Nine

Kate placed a mug on the table next to Signora Conti, who looked up from her seat with an affectionate smile. In the mug floated a wedge of lemon; the sharpness of the fruit with the sweetness of honey and the peaty aroma of whisky fragrancing the steam that curled into the air from its depths. Signora Conti smacked her lips appreciatively as she lifted the cup to breathe it in. Kate suspected that she was well and truly on the mend now, but since returning from hospital, she'd taken quite a fancy to Kate's hot toddies and despite Maria's disapproval had asked for one almost every day. The Conti home was strangely peaceful, with just her and Signora Conti in – everyone else either at work or doing family duties. Kate liked the banter and good-humoured chaos of their huge family but rather liked it this way too.

'*Grazie.*'

'*Prego,*' Kate replied.

Whatever had been said and whatever it had meant on the day she and Jamie had come to a new understanding of the world during their unexpectedly philosophical walk together, Signora Conti had been nothing but lovely to Kate. Lovelier, perhaps, than she had been before, though she'd always shown generosity and courtesy despite her initial doubts about Kate's relationship with Alessandro. Kate had pulled herself together and decided on the more pragmatic approach of continuing to visit and nurse Signora Conti as if nothing had happened, counting on the fact that her almost-mother-in-law would do the same. If she'd gone this long without mentioning the divorce, then perhaps it really didn't bother her as much as everyone thought it would.

Kate had spoken to Alessandro about it too, as Jamie had suggested she should, but he had been at as much of a loss as she was. He'd had no idea that his mother had guessed and was even more confused by her non-reaction. But where Kate had fretted, he had taken it as a good omen that meant positive things for their relationship.

Kate glanced at the clock. It had just gone eleven in the morning, and Alessandro would be home from his night shift soon. Her heart still picked up speed when she thought about seeing him, and she wondered if that would ever stop. She had certainly never waited for Matt's return from work with such anticipation so she had no frame of reference to gauge it. But then she hadn't detested Matt's job quite so much. She was proud of Alessandro, of course, but she hated the unsociable hours, the constant worry that something bad would happen to him, the days when he would come home after something bad had happened to someone else that had shaken him to the core – not often, but she was beginning to get used to the fact that they were a reality – when he would seem so pained and so vulnerable that she wished she could wrap him in her arms and keep him safe until the world had stopped hurting him. He saw the good side of Rome, but he often saw the dirty underbelly too, and Kate wondered some days just how he stayed so positive and forgiving in the face of it all.

The next moment the key sounded in the lock and he appeared before them. Often, he changed from his uniform and came home as a civilian, but today he was still wearing it, and so Kate guessed that the night hadn't gone well and something had him running late. But though he looked weary, there was still a warm, sexy smile for Kate, and then he made a beeline for his mother, whom he greeted far more affectionately with a kiss and a hug and words of solicitude. Kate knew why he had done that and she didn't mind; it was like having a toddler and then a new baby arriving – far more important to reassure the former that the arrival of the latter would not diminish their parents' love for them than to plant a seed of jealousy that could grow into one hell of a weed.

When he eventually stood up he turned to Kate and gave her a chaste kiss on the cheek. Their relationship had changed – in front of Signora Conti at least – and if his mother wanted to believe that they had still yet to know each other in the biblical sense then they had decided to encourage the belief by appearing that way around her. It seemed pointless to rock a boat that was lovely and stable just as it was. And if Signora Conti didn't believe it, they certainly didn't want to annoy her into doing something about it by pushing their luck.

'It was a hard night?' Kate asked.

'An arrest, very late in the shift. . . much paperwork.' He dragged a hand through his hair and let out a ragged sigh. 'It is nothing; I am only tired. How is Mamma?'

'She seems really well today,' Kate said. 'Abelie was going to study at home, but she wouldn't have got much done so I told her I'd be able to manage if she wanted to go to her friend's house.'

'She has her whisky,' Alessandro said, looking over at Signora Conti with a fond smile. 'I think she will never stop drinking that now.'

'I don't think one every now and again will harm,' Kate said. 'My gran swore by them. After all, there's vitamin C in the lemon, hydration from the hot water, anti-inflammatories in the honey and the whisky helps to thin your blood. Which is a good thing apparently,' she added in reply to his questioning frown.

'I believe you, little nurse.' He smiled. 'I am sorry – I will have to sleep soon.'

'It's OK. I didn't expect anything else. When Abelie is back this afternoon I'm going to see Shauna Davies. . . at Piccolo Castelli.'

His expression darkened.

'I know how you feel about that,' Kate said. 'I still think it's worth taking a chance on. I have to try at least, and she's been very patient waiting for me to start when she could have just employed someone else who could've started sooner so I owe her the courtesy of turning up when I said I would. I promise I won't let the training go on for too long before I press her for a final decision on employing me. Besides, the more I think about it, the more I feel it's something I really want to try. I think I might quite like showing people around houses for a living, and I think I might be good at it.'

His features softened into a faint smile. 'You are thinking about this a lot.'

'Yes. I can't keep dipping into a pot of money borrowed from my sister, and I don't want to. I'll keep my eye open for other job opportunities, of course, but your mother is almost well again, and apart from the odd sewing job there's no excuse for me to be sitting around in my apartment waiting for work to come to me. I need to be out doing something. If nothing else, sitting around will drive me mad before too long.'

'If your days are full of work, how will I see you?'

'You don't work every night. It'll be horrible for me too, but we knew this would happen. We'll just have to make the best of what time we do get together.'

There was a pause. 'I see you will not be stopped.'

'No. Even though that makes me sound like an evil overlord trying to take over the world.' He gave a confused frown and she laughed. 'Never mind. Thank you. It means a lot to me that you're agreeing to this.'

'I did not need to agree – you would have gone anyway.'

'I would, but I'm happier doing it this way.'

'Will you return before I work tonight?'

'If you want me to. I only need an hour or so to go through some arrangements with Shauna to start next week. I was planning to see Jamie for dinner later this evening but that will be after you've gone to work.'

'*Va bene.* I will sleep now and we will talk later.'

Kate threw a cautious glance at Signora Conti, who had turned her attention to the newspaper and was making a very good pretence of not listening to them. After Jamie's revelations, she no longer trusted just how much Alessandro's mother was taking in. 'Here or at mine?' she asked, lowering her voice and then instantly realising that it would just encourage his mother to listen harder.

'I will come to you,' he said. 'For a little while and then I will have to go to work.'

For the first time since she'd known him, Kate got the distinct feeling that the prospect of going to work made him sad. Even on days when he'd been less than enthusiastic, he faced it with a stoic positivity, a necessary evil that it was pointless complaining about, a job that needed to be done and one that he was proud to do.

'Are you sure everything's OK?'

He nodded. 'I will see you later.'

There was no more talk. Kate watched as he trudged away to his bedroom.

It was half an hour after he'd gone to bed that Kate opened the door to find Orazia on the step.

'I have come to see Signora Conti,' she said stiffly.

Despite their forced courtesy of late, Kate would still have very much liked to slam the door in Orazia's face. But she stepped back to admit her. 'She's in her chair,' she said, flinging her arm out to indicate that Orazia would find Signora Conti in her favourite seat by the living-room window. Perhaps pointless, as Orazia and anyone else who knew Signora Conti well would have known where her favourite chair was.

Kate followed Orazia down the hallway and watched at the living-room door as Orazia bent to kiss Alessandro's mother, swapping pleasantries and bestowing a large fruit loaf of some kind on her. Whatever it was, Signora Conti uttered a squeal of delight and told Orazia that they must cut into it immediately. She made to get up but Kate stepped forward.

'I'll do it,' she said, holding her hands out for the loaf.

'I will take it to the kitchen,' Orazia said. 'We will have coffee with it. Would you like to try some, Kate? I can make three coffees.'

Kate blinked, taken aback by the offer. It was coming from Orazia but it seemed genuine enough. It was unfortunate that this was the one time she couldn't stay to take her up on it, because this might have marked a turning point for Kate and Orazia, and she felt keenly the missed opportunity. But she'd already arranged to meet Shauna and she couldn't stay.

'I would have loved to,' she began, 'but I have to be somewhere in an hour. In fact I was just getting ready to leave when you turned up.'

'Ah, then it is lucky I am here to keep Signora Conti company.'

'Oh, but Alessandro—' Kate stopped, a sudden realisation hitting her. Alessandro was the only other person in the house. He was in bed right now, but he would be up in a few hours. Abelie wasn't due back for ages. Did Orazia know this? Was it why she'd turned up at this particular moment?

Kate shook herself. Stupid and paranoid – this situation was getting more ridiculous by the day. Here was Orazia, offering the olive branch, and Kate was still suspicious. She might be here with Alessandro home and Kate missing, but Signora Conti was there too, and what on earth were they going to do with such a formidable chaperone in situ, even if Alessandro was tempted?

'Alessandro is in bed,' she said, forcing herself to be mature and rational about the whole thing. 'He's just finished his shift.'

'I know this,' Orazia replied sweetly. 'I saw him leave the *Questura*.'

'But I suppose he'll sleep for a few hours.'

'This I know too,' Orazia said. 'I will not wake him. I will stay here with Signora Conti and we will talk and eat and take coffee. Do not worry. Go to your meeting and all will be OK with us.'

Kate looked from a beaming Signora Conti to a smiling Orazia. Perhaps she wouldn't wake Alessandro, but he would wake in a few hours and Orazia would be there while Kate was not. But there was little Kate could do about it. She had no choice but to stick with their plans. Orazia would likely wait to see him when he woke, before he got to Kate, but there was nothing Kate could do but put up with it. The best she could hope for was that she wasn't driven mad with jealousy thinking about it.

'I sure do miss the seafood at Trattoria da Luigi,' Jamie said, giving his meal a critical once-over.

'This is lovely,' Kate replied through a mouthful of spicy chicken. 'What's wrong with it?'

Jamie glanced around the cosy restaurant. Decorated in claret and gold with murals on the walls depicting ancient Roman scenes and candles in wine bottles at every table, it was charming and very Roman. Perfect for a low-key dinner catching up with old friends. But Jamie's expression was uncharacteristically melancholy. 'Nothing,' he said. 'I just miss it.'

'What's eating you? You look like someone just stole a thousand dollars from you and threw you ten back.'

'I'm sorry. Brad called earlier today. He's been doing some research and, although we can have a pretend marriage ceremony in lots of places in Rome, the Italian authorities don't recognise same-sex weddings so we wouldn't actually be married.'

'That's a real shame,' Kate agreed. 'Brad is disappointed too?'

'Yeah. We're both real disappointed.' He took a sip of his wine. 'It's not even about the wedding, it's the attitude that makes me sad, y'know?'

'I suppose so. It's just the way the world is, but things are changing all the time, so never say never. Maybe the law will change soon. It has done in lots of other places. Can't you hang on? Or you could get married elsewhere and still have a celebration ceremony here. Someone was having one of those the following night in the villa where Lucetta had her wedding reception, so that must be an option.'

'I guess.'

He looked like a little boy who'd just had his favourite toy stolen. Kate couldn't help but smile. 'Oi!' she said, giving him a gentle kick under the table. 'This is not like you. I thought I was the pessimist.'

'I'm allowed to indulge sometimes.'

'It seems to be catching today. Must be something in the air.'

'Why do you say that?'

Kate shrugged. 'Alessandro wasn't himself at all earlier. He was tired after work – excusable if he's had a hard night, I know, but he wasn't much cheerier when he called in to see me at home before he went back on shift.'

'And he didn't tell you what was wrong?'

'No.'

'I guess he's occupying his man cave right now. Don't worry about it.'

'I suppose that must be it. I'm just not used to seeing it. And if something has happened at work, I want him to be able to share it with me so I can support him. I shouldn't have to spell that out, though, should I? We're a couple now and that's what couples do.'

'Maybe he wants to spare you from something really horrible. His job must be tough at times, and he loves you. Maybe there are some things he thinks are just too awful to burden you with.'

'I suppose so. I just hope he's OK. He talks to me when he's happy, but when things are bad he clams up. I can't support him if I don't know what's going on and that makes me sad and anxious too. Matt and I were like that and it's not healthy.'

'He's not Matt.'

'I know. What's worse is Orazia was there when he woke up.'

'She was?'

'Spending some time with Mamma Conti. Which is OK, I suppose, as they're good friends, but there was just her and Alessandro's mum and Alessandro in the flat. I know it's paranoid, but I couldn't stop thinking about it. I mean, Orazia was really nice today too so I don't have any reason to be stressed about it.'

'Maybe she was being nice because she was feeling a little smug about the situation. You being out of the frame while she got cosy with the Contis.'

'Maybe, but she seemed genuine enough. Even offered to make me coffee. I suppose she could have known they'd be in the flat alone, but I'm starting to wish I could trust her and Alessandro a little more. I'm starting to sound like the nutter and Orazia is looking perfectly reasonable.'

'I do think you ought to trust Alessandro more,' Jamie agreed as he wagged a finger at her. 'She might be up to no good but he wouldn't go for it.'

'But he can offload to her in a way he can't to me. About work, I mean. And she'd understand what he's going through in a way that I could never do. I can see why that would bring them close – as friends, I mean. And then it's only a hop, skip and a jump to something more than friends, isn't it?'

'In some cases I might say yes, but I think you need to sit back and see how it pans out.'

'It's Orazia, though.'

'You just said you were being paranoid about her.'

'But what if she's the thing making him stressed at work? What if he still has a little nugget of feeling for her? Or he feels sorry for her because she's alone and she has nobody to love her and he's got me? He's known her for years and he's always saying she's his friend and he doesn't like to see her unhappy even when she's being a pain.'

'Now who's being pessimistic?'

Kate forced a smile. 'I know; I'm going to shut up about it now. But that's my role in this friendship don't forget. I'm the neurotic one with an overdeveloped sense of propriety and you're the fluffy, gregarious tart. That's how it works. Tamper with the order of things and the world might just come to an end.'

Jamie raised his eyebrows. '*Fluffy, gregarious tart?*'

'It was the best I could do off the cuff. How about empty-headed socially forward slapper?'

'I don't know what any of that means but I think you might have just insulted me.'

'Probably. Do you care?'

'I should whip your skinny ass.'

'But you won't because you love me.'

'Unconditionally.'

Kate grinned broadly. 'See, we both feel better with that out of the way.'

Jamie returned the grin as he scooped up a forkful of pasta. 'I do kinda feel better. Who knew that being insulted could be so good for the soul?'

'Maybe we'll just save it for private moments, though. Our dirty little secret.'

'So, how did it go with the lady from real-estate company? You met with her today, right?' Jamie asked, changing the subject.

'Shauna? I did. It went well. I was worried that she wouldn't want me back after I'd had to put her off for a week, but she was pleased to see me and completely lovely. We've agreed that I'll join her on a viewing next Monday. I can't wait, actually. I think it's going to be great.'

'It's a pity I'll be back in the States by then – we could have celebrated in style when you nail it.'

'We haven't even got to the appointment yet, let alone nailing anything. Let's not get ahead of ourselves.'

'You're clever, funny, sweet, polite. . . people will love you. What could go wrong?'

'Quite a lot in my case,' Kate replied darkly.

Rome seemed somehow greyer with the departure of Jamie the day before, but Kate had no time to dwell on his absence while she was so consumed by nerves for her first day with Shauna. At least Alessandro had seemed brighter that morning when he phoned. He wished her well for her first day, which was something considering his disapproval of the idea, told her he loved her and that he would try to see her before he went back to work that evening, even if it was only for a few snatched moments. Kate was aware that their working hours might present a problem sooner rather than later, and that time together was going to be scarce and precious, and perhaps that was why he was putting his doubts about the job aside to make their time together as good as it could be. Whatever the reason for his change of heart, she was happy to hear it, and if the work schedule proved to be a problem for their relationship, then they would have to address it. For now, she had other things to think about – mainly the stomach ache that had her rushing to the toilet every time she thought about the day ahead.

The second dilemma of the day had been what to wear, and after putting it on and taking it off a few times, the new dress she had made from the gorgeous fabric Nunzia had bought for her was back on again. She'd finished sewing and pressing it the night before, desperate for a task to take her mind off the coming week and hoping it would tire her enough to send her to sleep when she finally retired. It didn't, but at least Kate had something to show for her bleary-eyed tumble out of bed when the alarm went off the following morning.

She stood in front of the mirror and frowned, critically appraising herself. 'It's not coming off again,' she said sternly to her reflection, which looked just as sternly back at her.

A tailored suit jacket wasn't something she owned. In fact, it wasn't something she'd ever owned; she just wasn't a suit kind of woman, and her former job in the offices of a scruffy pet-supply warehouse hadn't really demanded a power suit and killer heels. Lucetta had offered to loan her a black one which coordinated well with the grey-and-black dress, but Kate had decided against it and hoped that being completely herself would be enough. So she'd teamed the dress with a fine-knit cardigan and black court shoes and decided she looked just the right side of cute to be presentable with it.

Feeling as though someone had loosened the screws in all her joints, her heart thumping like mad, Kate locked up the flat and went to catch the bus for her first day at work in Rome.

Ten

Like so many stock phrases, a fish out of water was so overused that it had almost lost its true meaning. But Kate felt keenly what it meant right now as she stood in the middle of the busy front office, agents at desks jabbering away on phones in Italian, German, French, English and one other language that sounded like nothing she'd ever heard before. This was a world away from the sleepy starts at Mr Woofy. Kate, arriving at Piccolo Castelli, was completely and utterly out of her comfort zone as she waited for Shauna to finish a phone call.

One or two people smiled brightly at her and bid her good morning. Presumably they had at first thought she might be a customer, because as soon as she explained that she was waiting for Shauna in order to start work they quickly lost interest. Shauna glanced up, indicated to Kate that she would be with her shortly, and then returned to her call, and Kate was reduced to fiddling with the hem of her cardigan as she paid an unnatural amount of attention to a huge map of Rome taking up the entire wall behind Shauna's desk in a bid to look like she wasn't nervous. Which any spectator with an ounce of perception would have instantly seen wasn't true at all.

'There's no need to look like a startled rabbit,' Shauna smiled as she eventually ended the call and left her desk to greet Kate.

'Sorry. It's just. . . it's been a long time since I had a first day at a job.'

'A week in and it'll feel as if you've been here forever. We're a friendly bunch – at least we usually are. You've probably caught us at a bad time for a first impression as Monday mornings are when all the clients have had the weekend to think about complaints they want to make but nobody in the office to phone about them. It's like floodgates opening on the Hoover Dam come nine o'clock. Step back in on a Friday afternoon and we're a very different office.'

'But you work Saturdays?' Kate asked. 'I thought you said you did.'

'I don't know why but there's a very different feel to Saturdays. Perhaps because it's all viewings at lovely locations and no phone work in the office. I tend to save all my rural appointments for Saturdays if I can – gives me an excuse for a trip out somewhere nice. Sometimes it feels like I'm not working at all.'

'Well, that can't be bad,' Kate said with a self-conscious laugh.

'It's not. Would you like to grab a coffee with me while we go through today's schedule? Then we'll hit the road.'

Kate nodded. She would have asked if she could get that laced with brandy, but getting pissed on your first day was probably a tad frowned upon.

'We've got some lovely viewings today,' Shauna said as Kate followed her to her desk, where she pulled a jacket from the back of her chair and grabbed her handbag.

Kate frowned. 'I thought we were getting coffee before we went.'

'Oh, we are. There's a fantastic little place around the corner – gorgeous coffee, the best biscotti in Rome and a new barista hot enough to steam the cappuccino milk without a machine. Far too young for me, of course, but easy on the eye and good for a midnight fantasy or two, if you know what I mean.' Shauna held the door open, allowing

Kate to step out onto the street before following. 'I find that coffee-shop meetings are far more productive than the ones held in a stuffy office,' she continued.

'I wouldn't know much about that,' Kate said, falling into step alongside her as she began to walk. 'The closest we got to coffee shop meetings in my last job was a bacon sandwich at the desk as we complained about the vending machine in the lobby.'

Shauna threw back her head and laughed, and Kate was taken by surprise to see that it was genuine amusement. 'That's priceless! A sense of humour goes a long way in this business.'

Kate wasn't trying to be funny, but if Shauna wanted to believe she was then perhaps it was easier to let it go.

'I've got to say that's a gorgeous dress, by the way,' Shauna added. 'Fits you beautifully.'

'Thank you.' Kate looked to her side to see that Shauna was looking her up and down with approval. What would she think if Kate told her she'd made it herself? Would it make her look talented, with a worthwhile hobby, or a county bumpkin who turned up for work in homemade clothes?

'Where did you get it?' Shauna asked before Kate had worked out her strategy.

'Nowhere in Rome.'

'Oh, back home in England?' Shauna said. She almost sounded disappointed.

'Well. . . actually I made it. The fabric was from a shop in Rome, but I designed it and made it myself.'

Shauna broke into a broad smile. 'Really? Wow, I'm envious. I'm absolutely useless with my hands. I can't even sew a button on. Does it take you long?'

'It depends on what I'm making but this wasn't too bad. I was a bit worried this morning that it wouldn't be formal enough but I haven't worn it yet so my inner child got the better of me and I put it on.'

'I think your inner child has excellent taste. It's just right. Too formal can sometimes be off-putting for clients as much as too scruffy is. Thank goodness we've lost all those huge shoulder pads that were in fashion when I started out during the eighties.' She threw a sideways glance at Kate. 'But I suppose you're a bit too young to have been wearing suits in the eighties.'

'Sorry, but yes. I was more likely wearing nappies.'

'Ugh, it makes me shudder when I hear some people can't even remember Wham! breaking into the charts. I was working at my first job at the time; I remember going to Woolies to buy "Young Guns" in my lunch break. God, I feel old. You probably weren't even born. I bet you don't even know who they are!'

Kate smiled. 'I know who they are. But I don't know much about them to be truthful.'

'Well,' Shauna continued cheerfully, 'you'll be this old one day and there's only one alternative to that, which I really don't fancy much so there's no point in complaining.'

'I think you look fantastic,' Kate said. 'If I look like you, I won't mind at all.'

'Well, the bodywork is OK I suppose, but what's under the bonnet – that's a different story. Not one I'm going to bore you with now. Ah, here we are.' She stopped in front of a sandstone frontage, clad in thick ivy. Even this early Kate could smell coffee on the air. A tall and ridiculously handsome man was arranging tables and chairs outside. Kate couldn't help but stare at him. If this wasn't the barista Shauna had been referring to, then the place must also be doubling up as some secret lab where they were genetically engineering perfect specimens of manhood.

'*Ciao*, Luca,' Shauna greeted, and the man turned with a broad smile.

'*Buongiorno*, Shauna! How are you today?'

'Tired,' she said, 'but nothing that a cup of your divine macchiato won't cure.'

'*Sì* . . . you are too kind. And for your friend?' He turned a full-beam, sexually charged smile on Kate, and suddenly the world around her melted away. God he was hot. Forcing herself to remember that she already had a very hot Italian of her own, and that two was greedy in anyone's book, she smiled back.

'Macchiato sounds good. I'll have one of those too.'

'*Certamente. Un momento.*'

'I was right, wasn't I?' Shauna whispered as they followed him inside. 'Sex on legs. Curse the fact that I can remember Wham!'s first single, because he can barely even remember the Take That reunion, and I was old enough to have ditched two no-good husbands by then.'

'Some men like more experienced women,' Kate replied.

'I love how diplomatically you just told me I was old,' Shauna laughed. 'With tact like that, I can see we're going to get along famously!'

Kate shot her a broad smile. She already liked Shauna a lot too. She liked her irreverent humour, the way she didn't take herself too seriously, and Kate suspected she had a wild side she reserved for when she was off duty that would make for some fun office parties. For sure, Kate was beginning to harbour high hopes for this job. In which case, she had to do her best to impress over the coming weeks to make sure it became hers for good.

* * *

They enjoyed a leisurely hour with coffee while Shauna told Kate more about her business and advised her on some basic dos and don'ts of property management, as well as the more complicated dos and don'ts of looking after clients from all walks of life and all parts of the globe. Their business was mostly with foreign buyers – people who wanted buy-to-lets for holidaymakers, those who wanted holiday homes of their own and some – like Kate – who wanted to relocate for good. Most of their vendors were Italian, but a good many were foreigners who had previously bought houses in Rome and the surrounding area but now, for one reason or another, needed to get rid of them. It all sounded hellishly complex to Kate – the obscure laws to watch out for, people who thought they could con the system for a fast buck, the sad cases of bankruptcy that forced people to sell much-loved homes and the animosity that could come from that. There was so much to learn and remember that her head was spinning with it all. But Shauna had told her not to worry for now, and that the point of shadowing for the first couple of weeks was to do just that – stand quietly behind Shauna and take note of how she worked. After that the plan was for Kate to do some of the talking, with Shauna's support and input, then for the tables to turn as Kate got more confident so that she would conduct the appointments and Shauna would shadow, keeping a close eye on things, ready to step in should the appointment go awry. If they were both happy at that point, and Shauna thought Kate was up to it, Kate would start to get clients of her own.

It sounded like a good, solid plan and when Kate had expressed her contentment with the arrangement, they finished their coffees, Shauna throwing one last hungry glance at Luca as he polished the shop counter, and then walked back to the office to pick up Shauna's car.

'Mr Richards is our buyer,' Shauna said as she unclipped her seat belt. 'Not Keith or Cliff, I'm afraid – I think he's an investment banker. The vendor is in America at the moment and can't get away to come and show the property herself, but that's what we're here for anyway.'

Kate stared up at the house as she climbed from the passenger side of the car. 'Wow!'

It was smaller than the villa Lucetta had held her wedding reception in, and the classical architecture boasting ivory stone and wedding cake columns had been interspersed by huge panes of glass that almost formed walls themselves. Steps led up to the main house from the road, and a gated driveway to the left swept around to what Kate presumed was the back of the house. As Shauna had parked outside the main entrance instead of taking this road, Kate had to guess that the gates were locked.

'It's rather lovely, isn't it?' Shauna agreed. She rifled in her handbag and produced a vast set of keys. 'Now then,' she murmured, examining each one in turn. They all had tiny white labels on them bearing letters of the alphabet. 'Aha!' Shauna said, singling out one that bore the mark *FD*. 'Front door. Ingenious, eh?'

Kate smiled. 'Simple and effective.'

'It's simple alright. I'm not sure kindly labelling the keys for a potential burglar is a good idea, but I suppose the vendor thought I'd be the only person who would have possession of them.' She raised her eyebrows. 'So let's hope we don't lose them, eh?'

'Are we leaving the car here?' Kate asked.

'For now. I don't want to unlock too many doors and gates if I can help it – it's asking for trouble as I'm likely to forget to fasten them up again and you never know who might be snooping around, ready to take advantage while we're showing the client around. Best to keep it simple if we can.'

'See, I'm learning already. I'd have opened up the gate and driven the car right in.'

'It's experience, darling. Nothing more and nothing less. You'll get there eventually.'

Kate followed as Shauna made her way up the steps. 'It's been empty for a little while now. I like to come in and air the place before a viewing, make it nice and fresh.'

'Has it been on the market long then?' Kate asked, surprised that such a beautiful house hadn't been snapped up as soon as it went up for sale.

'Six months. If you're going to spend a million plus euros for a house, you're going to make damn sure it's perfect for you. It's like choosing someone to marry – you have to fall completely and utterly in love before you commit. We've had a few viewings and most flirted with it, some even went as far as a kiss and a cuddle, but nobody has fallen for it yet.'

Kate laughed at the analogy. 'That's an interesting way of looking at it. I won't forget that advice in a hurry.'

Shauna unlocked a front door of heavy honey-toned wood with delicate wrought-iron panels inlaid upon frosted glass. It swung open to reveal a vast lobby, the floor tiled with rose-gold stone, simple cream walls and a sweeping staircase of wood and black iron. Three of the walls had wooden doors leading to various other rooms, apart from one, which was almost entirely glass, allowing sunlight to flood the space. There was a slight odour – that peculiar, unnameable smell of somewhere unlived-in – but considering it had been empty for some time, it wasn't as musty as Kate would have expected.

They set about opening doors into each room, making a quick check of the contents, opening blinds and curtains and letting the air in. Shauna swept her finger along the surfaces to make sure that the maid the owner had employed to come in and clean once a week was doing her job.

Each room was the epitome of taste and wealth. The living room was dressed in sumptuous creams and slick Italian leather, with vast windows overlooking perfectly manicured lawns that stretched the length of at least two football pitches. Not that Kate had much idea what size a football pitch was, but it seemed to be a go-to unit of measurement on any news report she'd ever read that included the size of some grounds or other. The kitchen was gloss white and chrome, the look sharpened by the addition of slate-grey walls, and it was bigger than her entire flat. Every bedroom had an en suite (and there were six), each beautifully finished. From the window of the master bedroom, Kate looked across the grounds to see that beyond the lawns and immaculate flower beds was a grove of olive trees. Kate had only ever seen houses like this on TV or in magazines, and she could barely imagine the sort of person who could afford this. He'd be someone debonair and handsome for sure – a self-made millionaire with a sharp suit and an even sharper intellect. He'd look right through you, a piercing flinty gaze, and he'd have the measure of you in an instant. She almost fancied their buyer would look like Daniel Craig or some other rugged film star. She couldn't wait for him to arrive to find out more.

Shauna called from the bottom of the stairs. 'All good to go up there? Our client is here; I've just seen the car pull up!'

'Yes, all fine!' she called back, racing from the bedroom and down the stairs. At the bottom she stopped, straightened her dress and smoothed her expression into something she thought looked reserved and professional, even though she was bursting with curiosity about the man who was coming to view the house.

'I'll go and get him,' Shauna said. 'Wait here for a minute.'

Kate nodded and watched as she strode out of the front door. A moment later she returned with Mr Richards. If Kate had been expecting a suave, handsome playboy, she couldn't have been more wrong. Mr Richards would have struggled to reach her shoulder. He was almost as round as he was tall, with a head like a boiled egg but he had a quick, shrewd expression that made Kate think he might be a bit of a wizard in the boardroom. If he'd made enough money to buy this house, she'd bet he'd made it with his wits.

'This is my colleague, Kate,' Shauna announced. Kate stepped forward to shake his hand.

'Pleased to meet you.'

His grip was firm and he broke into a good-humoured smile. 'The two-pronged attack, eh? Two lovely ladies trying to persuade me this is the house for me.'

'Kate has just joined us,' Shauna said. 'In fact, today is her first day, so she's with me to get a feel for the job.'

'I recently moved to Rome,' Kate said. 'From Manchester.'

'You're planning to stay permanently?'

Kate smiled. 'That's the idea.'

'And you like it?'

'I love it.'

'Well, that's a recommendation,' he replied approvingly. 'My wife isn't really sure about this and she kicked up a stink about coming over to view – hence the fact I'm flying solo today.' He let out a phlegmy chortle. 'I have a feeling at some point we'll end up back in England and renting this out, but I wouldn't mind a change of scenery for a year or two.'

Kate wondered why he was here viewing the house if his wife hadn't wanted to come. Did it make him arrogant enough to assume that she'd fall into step with his wishes? Or did it make him a bully who would force her to move? Or perhaps they would simply work out an agreement that suited them both. She had a feeling that this sort of puzzle would probably present itself quite a bit as she got to know more clients, and it was something that would drive her mad with curiosity. But she would have to be curious for now in the case of Mr Richards – at least if he didn't volunteer the information – because it was a question that she definitely couldn't ask.

His gaze turned to the stairs, and as he examined them, looking equally impressed with the entrance hall, Shauna gave a surreptitious thumbs-up to Kate.

'Would you like to begin the tour?' Shauna asked him.

'Very much so,' he replied, turning and fixing his gaze on Kate. 'And Kate here can tell me all about how she's settling in to life in Italy.'

'I'm sure she'd love to,' Shauna smiled. 'Wouldn't you, Kate?'

'Um. . . of course.'

Mr Richards regarded Kate with that same shrewd look he had worn when he first arrived, and it was somehow as if he was x-raying her soul. Guessing at the details of his personal life was one thing, but sharing the details of her own with him was quite another. It was going to take some careful editing if her private life was going to stay just that.

* * *

'Three very good viewings today, I think,' Shauna announced with a tone of deep satisfaction as she pored over her diary. They were back at the same coffee shop they'd visited that morning, sitting outside even though the sun was low in the sky, the approaching evening bringing a distinct frost to the air. Shauna had been disappointed to see that her favourite barista was not on duty and had decided to catch the last of the day instead, not really giving Kate a choice on the matter.

Kate reached for her coffee cup and took a sip, her gaze distracted by two women who had just arrived. One of them looked eerily like Orazia, though she had gone through to the main shop before Kate had a chance to look properly. She was beginning to think she might need professional help to address the unhealthy paranoia she was developing about that woman. Shauna looked up as Kate failed to reply.

'You've enjoyed today?' she asked.

'Oh, yes,' Kate said. 'It's been brilliant.'

'You think it's something you might get on with? The clients certainly seemed to warm to you. I think you're quite a natural and open person, and that's good, because most of them can see right through bullshit. As far as Mr Richards goes, I think his decision to buy definitely had a lot to do with hearing how you'd settled in Rome – so bravo to you. Pretty much your first sale – although you know I won't be able to pay you commission on that as you're not technically employed by us yet,' she added by way of half apology, half warning to Kate not to expect a share of the commission no matter how instrumental she might have been in securing the sale.

The comment passed her by, however, and Kate was more occupied by the recollection of how keenly Mr Richards had questioned her on the particulars of her moving to Rome. She had tried to be sparing with them, but he'd had a way of getting information from her that she hadn't wanted to give. Shauna was uncannily accurate in her observation of Kate's character, but openness was one trait that she perhaps ought to work on putting away while she was showing prospective buyers around. Or anyone else, for that matter.

'Yes,' she said slowly. 'I think I'm going to like working with you.'

'Brilliant!' Shauna took a slurp of her coffee. The cup went back into the saucer with a clatter and she slammed the diary shut. 'Well, I have a hot date with a meat and potato pie. You can rave about the food here as much as you like – and nobody loves it more than I do – but sometimes a bit of British stodge is what you need after a long day. I have to make the damn things myself, of course, but once you get used to making them it's like second nature. You'll be OK to get home from here?'

Kate nodded.

'So I'll see you at the office tomorrow morning then? Same time as today?'

'Yes.'

Gathering up her diary, pen and phone and stuffing them into her handbag, Shauna gave Kate a bright smile before marching off. Kate watched her go. There was a woman who knew who she was and where she was going in life – who was comfortable in her own skin and confident in her abilities. If only Kate could steal a little of that from her right now, because she felt none of those things. Where Shauna had been pleased with Kate, Kate had sometimes felt awkward and conspicuously like a spare part, following Shauna and her clients around with nothing much to say apart from answering questions about her own meagre experience of living in the city when asked. She hadn't lied to Shauna about enjoying the day, but she couldn't yet say whether the job was a long-term prospect for her.

She looked at her watch. She'd finished much later than she'd anticipated, and she'd had to ignore a call from Alessandro, sending a brief apologetic text that she couldn't talk as she was still working and would phone back when she could. But by now he would be on his way to work and wouldn't be able to talk either – at least not for a few hours. The idea made her feel strangely empty. Over the months she had come to rely on his counsel and opinions more and more, and he was a good listener. Not today, though.

Draining the last of her coffee, she collected her bag and began to make her way home. She recalled seeing a bus stop a few blocks away, and hopefully she'd be able to work out a route from the timetable, or someone at the stop would be able to help. The idea of trying to communicate her needs with her very rudimentary Italian wasn't a thrilling one, but sometimes it was necessary and, as Alessandro kept reminding her, doing it regularly would build her confidence, which, in his opinion, was really her biggest barrier to learning the language. She had a feeling he was right, though it was difficult to admit.

She had barely got to the corner of the road when she caught her phone ringing from within her bag. A smile lit her face as she saw Lucetta's name on the screen.

'*Ciao*, Kate!' she greeted airily. 'What are you doing?'

'Right now? Walking!'

'Why are you walking?' Lucetta asked, and she sounded so genuinely mystified that Kate had to laugh.

'Because I still can't afford a car and I need to get home.'

'Mamma is cooking dinner. She wants you to come.'

'She's cooking?' Kate frowned. Signora Conti's idea of cooking dinner was three hours' hard graft in a steamy kitchen, unlike Kate, who considered making beans on toast a culinary feat. 'Are you sure that's a good idea? She's only just got back on her feet from her illness and I don't think she should overdo it.'

'You should try to tell her that. She will not listen to us.'

'I might be a while yet, but I will come if only to tell her off,' Kate said, secretly happy to have been invited. Sometimes she was content to sit quietly in her flat alone in the evening, but sometimes it felt very big and empty. She had a feeling that tonight would be one of those nights, and if she couldn't have Alessandro, at least she could have the next best thing. 'Will Maria be there?'

'No,' Lucetta laughed. 'Not tonight. She is going to her husband's mother for dinner. We will hear about it tomorrow because she hates her. So you have no need to worry.'

It wasn't a huge leap of the imagination to see that could well be true of most people in Maria's case. 'Sorry,' Kate said sheepishly. 'She just makes me feel a bit. . . well, you know, it can be awkward trying to talk to someone who doesn't like you much.'

'Kate. . . she does like you.'

Kate raised her eyebrows. 'She has a funny way of showing it.'

'You will see one day soon. She likes you as well as we all do. But she is stubborn.'

Stubborn hardly begins to cover it, Kate mused.

'When will you come?' Lucetta added.

'It depends on the buses. I don't suppose you'd know much about which ones to catch?'

'Pah! I never take the bus!' Lucetta snorted, and Kate could just picture the look of absolute derision on her face. 'They smell terrible, and they are too slow! Tell me where you are and I will come for you in my car.'

Kate could have put up all sorts of arguments for independence, but she was just too tired and grateful for Lucetta's offer. If she was honest, she was quite looking forward to one of Signora Conti's divine meals too, despite her misgivings about the old lady's fitness levels.

'You're a star!' she smiled.

'I know,' Lucetta replied.

Talking through a mouthful of artichoke should have been incredibly unattractive, but the way Gian looked at his new wife as she did this, fork waving in the air as she gesticulated crazily at Kate, anyone would have thought she was bathing delicately in asses' milk. Clearly, the honeymoon phase was far from over, and he was just as enamoured with her as his wife as he had been with her as a girlfriend. Kate had wondered whether Lucetta had saved herself until marriage, as their mother would have wanted her to, but, of course, it had been a question too delicate to ask. If she had, then perhaps it was all the rampant sex they would be enjoying now that God was giving them free rein that was making him look so soppily at her.

'Your dress is beautiful,' Lucetta said. 'Did you make it?'

'I did,' Kate said. 'I had a few compliments today actually.'

'I can see why,' Lucetta said, eyeing it appreciatively. 'If I could pay you I would ask you to make new dresses for me every day.'

'You know I would make new dresses for you anyway – you only have to ask.'

'Yes.' She looked at Kate from beneath a frown. 'You are too kind. You give to people all the time but they do not always give back.'

'Yes, but you're family. I mean . . .' Kate continued, blushing, 'practically. I always help family.'

'You must value your skills more,' Lucetta continued. 'You could make lots of money from your dresses but instead you make them for free for everybody in Rome.'

'They're not free—' Kate began, but Abelie joined in.

'Your landlord pays you so little for them they are almost free.'

'Salvatore wants dresses?' Gian cut in.

'His wife wants dresses,' Kate corrected. 'Only two.'

'And before that,' Abelie reminded her.

'Yes. . .' Kate said.

'Yes!' Abelie chastised. 'Do not pretend you have forgotten!'

'If you sold them for a good price you would make money and you would not have to work for Piccolo Castelli for free,' Lucetta chimed in.

Kate was beginning to feel distinctly harried. 'It's hard to get it up and running,' she said. 'It's not like I can open up and instantly have customers.'

'Why not?' Lucetta demanded. 'Once people find you they will give you work. But they must find you first. Have you made your business known?'

'Bruno made cards to give to people,' Abelie put in, looking very pleased with her part in the venture.

'He did,' Kate replied carefully. 'And it was very kind of him, but I have to meet people first in order to give them a business card, and even then I can't just hand them one out of the blue. They have to go to the right people; there's no point in giving them out willy nilly.'

Abelie frowned. '*Willy nilly?*'

'I can't give a card for dressmaking to a male construction worker or a priest,' Kate clarified. 'They have to go to people who are likely to buy my dresses and, as yet, I haven't really met many of those.'

'Perhaps you can give them to the ladies who come to see houses,' Abelie mused.

'I'm not sure Shauna would be happy about that. I'm supposed to sell them houses, not clothes.'

'People need both,' Lucetta said carelessly, licking some tomato sauce from her finger and almost sending Gian into raptures at the sight.

'I still don't think it would be appropriate,' Kate replied. 'Besides, the people who come to see these properties are mostly so rich they would be able to get handmade clothes from Stella McCartney herself so they wouldn't want to bother with mine.'

'They are exactly the people you need,' Lucetta said.

'No.' Kate gave an emphatic shake of her head. 'It's just not going to happen.'

'I think you are afraid,' Lucetta said.

'I'm afraid?'

'*Si.*'

'I don't know why you think that.'

'You feel you will fail, so you do not try. That way, you do not fail. You can say I do not have time, or I do not have customers, but you do not have the courage – that is the truth.'

Kate stared at her. 'You're joking?'

Abelie nodded at her sister. 'Lucetta is right. All this time you have only sewn for friends or favours. You are afraid that what you have is not valuable and so you do not ask for money. You must understand that it is valuable. You must tell everyone it is valuable and they will start to believe you. Then you can make money.'

'How can you be so sure? It's not that easy.'

'It is not easy,' Lucetta agreed. 'That does not make it impossible. It is your dream, yes?'

'Sort of,' Kate said.

'What is sort of? When I first met you it was so. Has your dream changed?'

Kate shook her head slowly. With all that was going on, she hadn't really thought about that question for a long time. Life had been about getting immediate work, keeping a roof over her head and settling into a routine in Italy. There had been love rivals, and a disgruntled mother-in-law and leaky taps to worry about. Her hopes and ambitions for the business had gone into storage, and the less she'd taken them out to look at them, to love and cherish them, the duller they'd become. One day, perhaps, if the times they came out of the box became fewer and fewer, she might forget where the box was kept and never find them again. But she hadn't really seen that clearly until now.

'Nothing has changed,' she said. 'I've been busy, though. With everything else.'

'You can do one thing only?' Lucetta said, arching an eyebrow at her.

'For now, yes. It's difficult. . .'

'Then you will never have your business.'

Kate took a gulp of water. 'If this is some reverse psychology, meant to goad me into action, then it won't work,' she said slowly. 'I appreciate that you're saying all this out of kindness, but I have to walk before I can run – I mean I have to get the basics of life here sorted before I complicate things,' she added in answer to Lucetta's look of confusion. 'I will carry on making bits and bobs for people for now, and that's all I can do. I know you think it's a cop-out and you don't approve, but that's what I've decided to do.'

Lucetta gave a short nod. Kate's gaze went to Abelie, who shrugged.

Then Gian nudged Lucetta and smiled. 'Mamma is sleeping,' he whispered, nodding towards Signora Conti who was slumped in her chair, eyes closed and snoring softly.

Abelie stifled a laugh, while Lucetta broke into a broad grin.

Kate frowned. 'She must have exhausted herself making dinner. I said she wasn't up to it.'

'I will take her to bed,' Abelie said, getting up and making her way around the table to rouse her mother. Kate watched, giving silent thanks for the distraction and somehow feeling as if she'd just done a taxing stint on a psychiatrist's couch.

Eleven

There were five team members in all, including Shauna, at Piccolo Castelli. Charles had arrived in Italy on a gap year in his law course in 2009 which had turned into two gap years and then three and then he had lost count. He cheerfully announced to Kate that he loved Italy so much he had yet to return home and his university tutor had given up asking about his plans to resume studying sometime around 2013. Kate would later learn that he'd trained with Shauna in very much the same way as she was doing before he'd got his work permits and been allowed to stay as a fully-fledged team member, a fact that buoyed Kate no end. His client base was mostly English and English-speaking customers, though he could manage Italian and a smattering of Polish when he needed to.

Then there was Giselle, who handled the French and German clients, being a Frenchwoman fluent in German too, though on chatting to her Kate was rather ashamed when she noted that, even as Giselle apologised for her English, it was pretty much perfect too.

Nonna Rossi worked on reception. She was a dough-faced lady, close to retirement, who smiled so much and so widely it looked like she was being tickled at all times. Her real name wasn't Nonna, although everyone called her that on account of her matronly virtues and the sweets and candies she showered on her little flock of workers every day. Shauna said that while she owned the business, Nonna was the beating heart of the organisation and the one member of the team they couldn't do without.

That left Elizabeth – half Chinese and half Scottish and uncommonly pretty for it. She took care of most of the Far Eastern clients. Any Italian clients that walked through the door went to whoever was free and could speak decent Italian, but their business had been built largely with rich foreign buyers or well-heeled Italian sellers as their customer base, dealing in properties that were beyond the means of most ordinary Roman residents, which meant most of them actually spoke excellent English. A lot of their work was done online or over the telephone, but when it came to the actual nitty gritty, there was no substitute for face-to-face. It made sense to Kate – there weren't many people, no matter how rich, who would want to buy a house they'd never seen in real life.

Her second morning was a world away from her first – far more relaxed with time to talk and get to know the people she hoped would be her new colleagues.

'It's always calmer on Tuesdays,' Elizabeth said. 'And you caught us on an especially bad Monday yesterday too.'

'So . . .' Charles called over from his desk, 'you've just moved to Rome?'

'Yes,' Kate said. 'A few months ago.'

'And how's that working out for you?'

'Good,' she said, trying to maintain a neutral tone but guessing that something of an inquisition was coming her way.

'Come to live with a bloke?' he asked. And there it was.

'No, not exactly . . .'

Charles waggled his eyebrows suggestively. 'Do you want a bloke?'

'Oh shut up!' Giselle shouted, throwing an eraser at him. He laughed loudly as it missed and skittered across his desk; then he scooped it up and tossed it back. 'Don't listen to him,' she added, smoothing her frown into a smile for Kate. 'He is an idiot – that is why no woman will have him.'

Nonna crossed the room and gave Kate a warm hug. 'Welcome,' she said, and Kate did feel very welcomed by the gesture. She could see why everyone called her Nonna, the Italian word for grandma. She was also relieved that Nonna knew exactly how to deflect the interrogation that was coming by taking her off to show her how the branch phone system worked.

'Your dress is very beautiful,' Nonna said, giving Kate an appreciative once-over.

'Thank you,' Kate said, brushing a self-conscious hand down the forest-green shift she was wearing.

'Did you make it?'

'Um, actually I did. How did you. . .?'

'Shauna said the beautiful dress you wore yesterday was one you made. Everybody here admired it.'

'Really?' Kate glanced around the room. The women here looked far too sophisticated and stylish to be impressed by her little old home-mades.

'Oh yes!' Nonna nodded enthusiastically. 'Now then,' she continued, 'would you like me to show you where we keep the office supplies?'

'That would be lovely,' Kate said and smiled, her confidence growing by the second. If the office of Piccolo Castelli was half as nice to work in as it seemed today, she was going to be very happy here indeed.

* * *

It was Sunday and Alessandro was sulking. Not sulking, exactly, but as close as Kate had ever seen. She might have found it annoying if it hadn't been so funny.

'I have to get these finished,' she said, feeling like a mum chastising her impatient toddler. 'We can go out later.'

'Later will be cold and dark,' he replied from the sofa, where he lay stretched out with his back to her as she sat at her sewing table. He put the book he was holding but clearly hadn't been reading at all back to his face with a heavy sigh. 'We will not be able to walk far.'

Kate snorted. 'You're being ridiculous. If you want to see what cold and dark really looks like, come and spend a winter in England.'

'I have barely seen you all of the week,' he said, lowering the book again. 'And now when I am here you sew.'

'That's because we've both been working. If you had a job with normal hours it wouldn't be a problem. And I have to sew, because Nunzia is expecting these and she needs to be able to try them on well in advance of her party in case they need to be altered.' The sewing machine whirred as she raced a line of stitching along a hem. 'I can't very well sew them while I'm at work so I have to do them today and the more you complain and distract me the longer it will take. The longer it takes, the longer you'll have to wait before we can go out. So why don't you carry on reading quietly and I'll tell you when I'm ready.'

He let out another sigh. 'The job for no money. It makes me unhappy in every way.'

'Please don't let's start that again. I've really enjoyed this week, and I told you that Charles started in the same way and he's been working there – with pay – for years now. It's going to be fine. You want me to be able to stay in Rome, don't you?'

'Of course.'

Alessandro added nothing more, and Kate resumed her task. There was silence, apart from the steady thrum of the machine as she pushed the fabric through, stopping every so often to check her work. Alessandro had the book to his face, but Kate hadn't noticed him turn a page for at least ten minutes. She could be a slow reader, but nobody was that bad.

'What's really wrong?' she asked, halting for a moment.

He put the book down again, but his gaze was still trained on the opposite wall. 'Nothing is wrong.'

'You're making all this fuss about us going out. You don't usually mind so much if we're in and if we're sometimes doing our own thing. Something else is bothering you.'

'I have missed you,' he said.

Kate snipped a line of thread and pulled the dress free from the machine to inspect it. She paused, lowered the dress and stared at the back of his head. 'Is there something else going on? Something you need to tell me about?'

He swung his legs off the edge of the sofa and swivelled round to face her. 'I do not know what you are talking about.'

Kate didn't even know what it was herself, but something niggled. Things were looking up, going well for once, but that only made her suspicious that disaster was waiting around the corner. She almost sensed that Alessandro felt it too. 'Never mind,' she said, shaking herself.

'Do you think we will marry?' he asked suddenly.

'I expect so,' Kate replied, ruffled, forced into an automatic response that she wasn't even certain of herself. 'I mean, I suppose it
depends on Matt but—'

'He will help?' Alessandro asked. And it felt to Kate that he seemed
more desperate and hopeless of the prospect than he'd ever done before. This uncertainty just wasn't like him.

'If I catch him at the right moment and he's in a good mood, I
think he'll agree. I'm sure we can work it out.'

Alessandro said nothing, but he seemed satisfied with her reply,
relaxing back onto the sofa and putting the book back to his face.
'Sew,' he said. 'Then we will go out.'

Sunday began a three-day stretch of Alessandro being off-shift. He'd
come straight from work on Saturday night and stayed over, and after their heart-to-heart about the past and the future, both of them
feeling sombre and introspective, they'd stayed home to eat instead
of going out, Alessandro rustling up a meal with the few bits left in
Kate's fridge that she would never have imagined could be made from
them. They had spent the rest of the night lying in each other's arms
on the sofa – listening to music, watching the news – but mostly talking. Kate had loved it – the closeness, the feeling of intimacy that,
for once, didn't come from sex. This was something much deeper, a
new understanding of each other, a feeling of oneness that had somehow grown from laying bare their insecurities and sharing them. They
discussed marriage again, as they often did, but whereas he usually
talked about it in terms that made it seem like a distant prospect, this
time he was talking about it as something that could be an imminent
reality. The problem was in Kate's divorce, and she understood that it

was difficult for him to ask her the question with any real intent with that barrier in their way. If things had been different, if they were free to marry and he proposed, would she have said yes? Perhaps a month ago the answer to that would have been uncertain, but as she lay in his arms, she was beginning to think that it wouldn't be such a difficult decision after all. This was what she had always wanted – the romance and the sex were amazing of course – but this quiet understanding, two souls in complete harmony – this was a feeling she could cherish forever.

On Monday morning he lay in bed watching her dress as the early sun washed the room in the colours of an old photo.

'You're putting me off,' Kate smiled as she slipped into her skirt and zipped it up.

'I like to watch you move around.'

'I have no idea why.'

'Because I find it beautiful.'

Kate blushed. Even now, as well as they were beginning to know each other, he still had the power to make her burn up with the slightest look, the most innocent sentence. She wondered if that would ever fade. She hoped not.

'Come and kiss me,' he said.

Kate shot him a sideways look. 'Not likely. I'll be late for work.'

His lip curled slightly, and then he straightened his face again, but not before Kate saw it. They had agreed now that she would do what she felt best in terms of building her new life and he wouldn't interfere when it came to personal choices such as her career. She could tell he was dying to give an opinion and she had to admire his willpower for keeping it in.

'I will drive you,' he said.

She turned to him and planted her hands on her hips. 'On your scooter? I might as well not bother brushing my hair then.' Fastening her blouse she shook her head. 'I'll get the bus. You can stay in bed and get some rest – you need it after the week you had at work.'

He stretched and flipped himself onto his back, rubbing a hand through his thick hair. 'I cannot stay in bed. I must see Mamma today.'

'I wish I could come.'

He turned to her. 'I will tell her she is in your thoughts.'

'She's in my thoughts a lot,' Kate said. 'I'm so glad she's starting to get better. I was seriously worried about her for a while.'

'She is strong.'

'Like her children.'

'Yes.' He grinned. Then he was serious again. 'I am going to talk to her about seeing the priest for your annulment.'

Kate stopped, hand mid-air as she gripped the hairbrush. 'Do you think that's wise? I mean, do we have to involve her at this stage?'

'Yes. If there are no secrets between us then there must be no secrets with Mamma. The same for everyone. She will help. She loves you; she will be happy for this.'

'But it means we have to acknowledge our lies to her in the past.'

He nodded slowly. 'Now is the time.' He shrugged. 'Two years, three years, we don't say anything. . . that is far worse. We say it now.'

'I suppose so,' Kate replied thoughtfully. 'And she does actually already know – she just hasn't heard it from us, so I suppose it won't be a shock.'

'*Va bene*. So I will talk to her.'

Kate couldn't say she was entirely comfortable with the idea, and even less thrilled about not being able to go with him. 'Do you think we should wait?' she asked. 'Just until I've finished work so I can go with you. Perhaps we should tell her together?'

'I will go home but I will wait. When you are ready, we will talk to her together.'

'Tonight?'

'Yes.'

Kate paused. This was really, actually happening. What did this mean for their relationship? Whatever it was, it felt huge. 'OK. Tonight.'

The promise of a little extra time with Alessandro had been too much to resist, and so Kate had forsaken her plan to catch a bus to work and was now heading downstairs to get a lift on his scooter. Slightly annoyed with herself for being so easy to persuade, she turned the key in the front door and gave it a tug to make sure it was secure before turning to Alessandro, who was waiting in the corridor.

'I don't know why I let you talk me into this,' she said. He raised his eyebrows, that mocking smile twitching at his lips.

'It will wake you up.'

'It'll do that alright. God knows what state my hair and clothes will be in by the time we get there.'

'Always worrying.' He shook his head solemnly, but that smile was struggling to stay under control. Kate found herself returning it.

As they got to the stairs, they met Salvatore coming up, his chest of stolen war medals clanking together like a strange kind of percussion section in an orchestra. He greeted them airily, grabbing a quick word with Alessandro in Italian, asking about his mother's health, which Alessandro replied to in English with a meaningful glance at

Kate. They had already discussed Alessandro's belief that Salvatore pretended his English was a lot worse than it actually was so that Kate would be put off making any complaints about the apartment. Obviously Alessandro was determined to stick with his theory, and whenever he was speaking with someone in front of Kate, he always tried to conduct the conversation in English when he could. Kate needed to practise her Italian, as she kept reminding him, but secretly it pleased her that he showed such consideration for her.

Salvatore turned to Kate. 'Nunzia's dresses?' he asked. 'Ready?'

'Almost,' Kate assured him. 'She can come by this evening if she likes to try them on. It's better if she does that before I finish everything off; it will be easier to alter them at this point if I need to.'

Alessandro turned sharply to Kate.

'Oh, I'm sorry!' she said. 'I forgot! We had plans.'

'It does not matter,' Alessandro said, his features relaxing. 'It can wait a little longer.'

'Are you sure?' Kate asked, looking from one to the other. 'I mean, I suppose Nunzia is waiting for her dresses. . .'

Salvatore nodded eagerly.

'You can see her this evening, and we will see Mamma tomorrow.'

'So Nunzia can come this evening,' Kate said to Salvatore.

'This evening?' he repeated.

'*Stasera*,' Alessandro clarified, doing a terrible job of hiding the crease in his forehead that said he didn't believe the act for a moment.

'*Sì!*' Salvatore nodded enthusiastically. He turned to Kate and grabbed her hand, jogging it around in a way that was not quite a handshake and almost an assisted hand jive. '*Grazie mille!*'

'Wait!' Alessandro called as he turned to go. Salvatore turned back with a silent question. Alessandro shot a glance at Kate, and then took the landlord to one side. Kate held in a groan. Alessandro couldn't help himself when it came to what he perceived as his duty to protect her, and that meant interfering in her affairs with the landlord. He was obviously providing Salvatore with a long list of faults in the apartment, though he spoke so quickly and in such low tones that Kate could barely tell anything he said, and as he finished he clapped Salvatore on the back with a nod that looked far less friendly than it did grim.

Salvatore tottered away, medals clattering against each other and echoing down the stairs as he went.

'Please tell me you didn't shout at him about the jobs that need doing in the apartment,' Kate said.

Alessandro put on the least convincing innocent expression that Kate had ever seen. 'I would not,' he said, a hand on his chest. 'You did not want me to talk about it. And my voice was very quiet.'

She folded her arms across her chest. 'So what did you just discuss?'

He shrugged. 'Police business,' he said.

Kate sighed. She didn't believe that for a minute, but what was the point in pushing it any further? At least the jobs would get done now, she supposed.

Kate had accompanied Shauna to a luxury penthouse to show an Australian cosmetics mogul around in the morning, and in the afternoon had been to measure up a holiday home being sold by a family who lived in the north of Italy and were swapping it for one closer to Naples. The rest of the time had been filled helping with filing, data input and webpage updates, along with getting to know her colleagues a little more, and although she'd arrived home tired, she was happy. Shauna had been pleased with the field visits, and had intimated to Kate that she felt she might be ready to conduct a viewing or two herself the following week, which also meant she would be putting her on the payroll. She was currently explaining all this Anna, who had phoned for a quick catch-up before she went out to the cinema with her husband, Christian.

'I'm so happy for you,' Anna said. 'A bit sad, but happy too.'

'Why sad?'

Anna laughed lightly. 'Sad for us. If you've got a job and you're doing well, you won't come home.'

'This is home now,' Kate said. 'And I was never coming back anyway.'

'I know that, but if you couldn't get going there then. . . It was a bit of a selfish hope on my part, you know? I can't help it.'

'I know. I miss you too. In fact, I'm still waiting for my visit.'

'I want to come; things are just so bloody busy here right now. And I don't want to come without Lily because that doesn't seem fair, and she's got stuff going on too.'

'Stuff?'

'I don't know – something to do with work I think. She's been a bit vague about the whole thing really. But there seems to be a lot of dealing with HR, according to what Joel has told Christian. I wonder whether she's applying for a promotion or something, and you know how cagey she is when she's uncertain about the outcome of something she's trying to do – doesn't want to jinx it by talking about it beforehand.'

'Oh. Did Joel tell Christian this at football training? It seems those blokes gossip more than they think we women do.'

'I know. Something else Christian heard at footie—' Anna paused, and Kate knew this was going to be something about her ex-husband, Matt.

'Let me guess – Matt's marrying his girlfriend.'

'It didn't take much working out, I suppose.'

'No, but I am surprised, considering the last time I saw him he told me he didn't love her.'

'I suppose he's finally grown up and accepted his responsibilities. After all, there's a baby to think of. And maybe he does love her after all. Sometimes it sneaks up and takes us by surprise, doesn't it?'

'That old devil called love?' Kate smiled ruefully. 'It certainly does, and it never wants to make things easy for us.'

'That sounds to me like everything is no longer rosy in the garden with Alessandro.'

'It's not us,' Kate said quickly. 'It just seems everyone else is out to make things as difficult as possible. Orazia for a start, although I'm beginning to think that might be in my head; she's being sweet at the moment but I just can't bring myself to trust her. And Maria isn't improving as much as I was hoping. They only need to find one more member of the team and they could be giving out career advice to Macbeth. Then there's this bloody marriage business. . .'

'That bad?' Anna laughed. 'And I thought Christian's mum was hard work. You sound like you need a hug.'

'I do. You two are the cruellest sisters there ever were not being here for hugs when I need you.'

'You could hop on a plane and come to England and I'd hug you to death.'

'Not bloody likely on my current income.'

'But you're managing on the money you borrowed from us?' Anna's tone was serious now. 'Because if you need more then I can—'

'It's fine,' Kate cut in. 'Please don't worry. With a bit of luck I'll be earning from next week, commission on top of that, and perhaps taking in more sewing jobs in the evening. I'll be able to live comfortably and pay you what I owe you.'

'I've told you I don't care about that.'

'But I do. I want you to have it back as soon as I can manage.'

'Don't leave yourself short.'

'I won't.'

'And you can get a flight over here before you think about paying anything back, so that we can hug you.'

Kate was silent for a moment. 'So you're not going to make it over for Christmas? I know it's only three weeks away but I was sort of hoping. . .'

'I'm sorry,' Anna said quietly. 'I know we talked about it, but I just can't ask Christian to spend Christmas away from home and his family, and Lily feels the same about Joel. Then there's Mum.'

'She's not coming either?'

'Hamish isn't well, which I know Lily told you about, and she says it's too far for him. She won't leave him, you know, not after what happened to Dad—'

'I know, I get that. And I want to stay with Alessandro, and there's no way he's leaving his family at Christmas; they'd never forgive him.'

'So that's sort of scuppered it.'

'Sort of.'

'It's going to be weird, isn't it?'

'Our first year apart. It will be.'

'But we can do something afterwards for sure,' Anna said brightly. Kate knew that the optimism in her voice was just for her benefit and not what she really felt. It seemed only fair to continue the charade for her sister's sake.

'Of course we can,' she replied. 'Spring in Rome is gorgeous, or so everyone keeps telling me. How about Easter?'

'I'm sure we can do Easter, if not before. I really am sorry, Kate, I feel just awful about Christmas.'

'Don't be,' Kate said, doing her best to sound cheerful. 'It'll soon be here and gone again and then I'll see you, right?'

'Right,' Anna said. 'Just try and keep me away.'

Kate glanced up at the clock. Suddenly, she wanted to cry. But Nunzia had arranged to come and try her dresses and no matter how melancholy Kate now found herself, she was going to have to keep a lid on it for a while.

'I'm sorry, I have to go; I'm expecting someone any minute.'

'Oh. Is Alessandro coming over?'

'No, my landlord's wife. I've made dresses for her and she's coming to try them on.'

'And she's paying for them?'

'Yes,' Kate said, deciding to leave it at that.

'But that's brilliant! You never said! Didn't she have one a few weeks ago too?'

Kate smiled. 'She did.'

'See,' Anna said in a voice full of satisfaction. 'I told you that global fashion giant of yours wouldn't take long to get started.'

'Global fashion giant?' Kate laughed.

'Hey, Vivienne Westwood started off making jumble for punks and now look at her. Small beginnings, sis, remember that!'

Kate smiled, buoyed by her sister's faith in her abilities, even if it was a little misplaced. 'I'll try,' she said.

'Good. Then I'll let you get on. Phone me at the weekend, OK?'

'I will. Love you.'

'Love you too.'

Kate ended the call and let the phone drop onto the sofa next to her. Most of the time she felt strong and independent and completely able to cope with her new life. But sometimes, just the voice of a family member or old friend would overwhelm her with homesickness and the urge to pack up and go back would take her.

There was time to pull herself together and perhaps make a quick coffee before Nunzia arrived. Kate took herself to the tiny kitchen, rubbing at her eyes as she flicked the kettle on. Things were getting better, and they were getting easier, weren't they? She could speak more of the language than she could when she arrived, she had all the paperwork she might need sorted, a decent apartment, a gorgeous boyfriend and family, was making new friends and almost had a fantastic job. So why didn't it feel that way?

Twelve

'Are you sure it's not a bit tight?' Kate asked, stepping back to give the dress Nunzia was wearing a critical once-over.

Nunzia looked blankly at her.

'Tight?' Kate asked again, puckering her lips, half cross-eyed, and squeezing her arms around her body to indicate that something was squashing her.

Nunzia giggled. 'Your . . .' She pointed at her own lips. '*Bocca!*' she announced.

Kate supposed that her face probably did look a bit funny and she had to laugh too. Half an hour in Nunzia's pleasant company and homesickness was banished, at least for a short while.

'It's OK? *Bene?*' Kate pressed after she had finished laughing.

'*Sì.*'

Kate shook her head. 'I still think it looks a bit snug,' she said, more to herself than Nunzia, who had tottered over to the full-length mirror to take a proper look and was now admiring her reflection. 'I could let it out a little,' she added, louder for Nunzia to hear. Nunzia turned to her. 'Make it bigger,' Kate clarified, miming the action of the dress expanding around her waist.

'No bigger,' Nunzia said, a forceful shake of the head accompanying her statement. 'I like.' She broke into a grin. 'Salvatore like!'

Kate smiled 'Well, it certainly shows your curves. I'm sure Salvatore would like it but you might find one forkful of pasta at your party will mean you can't sit down in it.'

Nunzia looked confused, and Kate knew that she had probably caught very little of what she'd just been told.

'Please,' Nunzia said, waddling back over to Kate and turning around for her to unzip. 'Two dress.'

'Dress number two coming up,' Kate said, freeing Nunzia from dress number one. She grabbed the second one from the hanger and hoisted it over Nunzia's head. Nunzia twisted round so Kate could fasten it then turned back. Kate gave a grunt of satisfaction.

'Much better,' she said. 'Fits where it should. You like it? Happy?'

'I like!' Nunzia beamed. '*Grazie mille!*'

'That's OK,' Kate smiled. 'It's what I like doing.'

Nunzia grabbed her in a fleshy hug, and Kate laughed, taken aback by the strength of the affection.

'It was really nothing,' she insisted. 'But I'm glad you're happy.'

'*Sì*, happy, happy!'

Nunzia toddled to where she had left her handbag and pulled out a wad of notes. 'For you.'

Kate frowned. There looked like a lot there, certainly more than she'd agreed with Salvatore. She quickly thumbed through to count. 'There's too much,' she said, holding some out for Nunzia to take back. But Nunzia shook her head and pushed Kate's hand and the money back towards her.

'You take! Good job, very happy.'

'No, I—'

'You take,' Nunzia insisted and reached to give Kate a kiss on the cheek.

Kate blinked at her. Everyone, including herself a little, had been complaining she wasn't being reimbursed adequately for this favour, but now she'd earned more than she'd asked for and had been gifted the fabric for a new dress. By anyone's standards it had turned into a good deal.

Nunzia made her way to the mirror and began to examine her backside with a big smile. 'I like,' she said.

'Good,' Kate said, glancing down at the money in her hand with a bemused smile. 'I like that you like.'

Alessandro was waiting for her when she left the office at the end of the day – leaning against the wall, hands in his pockets and his face turned to the sun. As she approached, he pulled off his sunglasses and gave her a sheepish smile.

'I told you I would get the bus,' she said.

'I wanted to come for you.'

Kate raised her eyebrows. 'So you could check I was leaving on time?' She'd made no secret of the fact she'd stayed past working hours with Shauna a couple of nights during the previous week – keen to learn and make a good impression – and he'd made no secret of the fact that he was not happy with that arrangement, particularly as she was still training.

'Of course not,' he said, his face the picture of innocence.

'Well,' Kate said, following him to the scooter parked at the kerb, 'I'm here bang on time so you can't complain, can you?'

'Mamma is waiting. She will cook tonight.'

Kate could have argued that she wanted to go home and get changed first, but there didn't seem any point. Alessandro had a habit of making arrangements without consultation and expecting her to simply go along with them so she was used to this, and, besides, they needed to speak to Signora Conti tonight about their plans for the future, so what was the point in putting it off? Waiting would only make her nerves worse. 'You shouldn't have let her cook,' she said instead. 'She's still recovering from her illness and all this work is hardly going to help.'

'The work makes her feel better,' he said, kicking the engine into life. 'She is bored and she cannot sleep at night because she is sitting all of the day.'

Kate hitched up her skirt and climbed on behind him, wrapping her arms around his torso. Riding pillion on his scooter never got any less scary.

Roasted tomatoes, basil and garlic scented the air of Signora Conti's home. Kate hadn't realised just how hungry she was until they let themselves in at the front door and the smell set her stomach growling. It was so loud that Alessandro stared at her before throwing his head back with laughter.

'A food emergency,' he said once he'd stopped. 'I will tell Mamma we need to give you plenty.'

'It's been a long day,' Kate grumbled, mortified by the betrayal of her own body. How was she supposed to look sexy, sophisticated and desirable at all times when her stomach insisted on making her sound like a pig hunting truffles?

Signora Conti rushed in from the kitchen, the trademark padded headband that always held her bobbed hair neatly in place sliding back and letting steel-grey ropes free from its confines. There were smears of tomato sauce down her apron and her cheeks were ruddy, but her eyes were bright with pleasure. If Kate had worried about her being up and about again, she needn't have. Signora Conti looked as fit and well as Kate had ever seen her, and even happier to be back in her beloved kitchen, hands on with the cooking and totally in charge again.

'*Ciao!*' She kissed and hugged Kate, and then Alessandro, even though she'd probably only seen him an hour or so before.

Abelie wandered in from a door off the main room, giving Kate a warm smile and greeting her too. 'Are you well?' she asked. 'We never see you now.'

Kate laughed. 'You saw me a few days ago.'

'It feels like a long time,' Abelie said. 'Lucetta is coming with Gian. Isabella and Jolanda cannot. Maria will come with her husband and little ones in one hour.'

Kate shot a glance at Alessandro, but the significance of that last sentence seemed lost on him and he merely nodded to acknowledge the information. Maria being there would make it a lot more difficult to have the discussion with Signora Conti that they'd wanted to have. In fact, so would Isabella and Lucetta, if only because the more people that were there, the more awkward she would feel. And this family didn't do secrets (as a rule anyway) so there was no taking Alessandro's mother to one side to discuss it in private. If they had anything to say, they would be saying it in front of everyone. She was beginning to wish she'd put Nunzia off the previous evening and come when it was likely to have been quieter.

'Kate is very hungry,' Alessandro said, grinning at her as he did. 'We must give her food now before she dies.'

'Very funny,' Kate said, giving his arm a slap. It only made his grin wider.

His reply, witty as Kate suspected it would have been, was cut short by the arrival of Lucetta and Gian. Signora Conti rushed to embrace them both, chatting away and stroking their faces as if they'd just been reunited on one of those lost relative TV shows. But Lucetta looked equally as pleased to see her mother, and Kate guessed that had a lot to do with how much Signora Conti's health had improved over the last few days. The drugs that Kate had cajoled, begged and bullied her to take were working their magic, and it seemed that the hot toddies she'd taken to indulging in every night weren't doing too much harm either.

'Kate!' Lucetta exclaimed, kissing her. 'Are you well?'

'Brilliant.' Kate smiled. 'A bit tired but happy. You look fantastic; being married must suit you.'

'But of course!' She threw a fond smile back at Gian, who was busy having his hair examined by Signora Conti. Lucetta's mamma had apparently decided it needed a cut and was threatening to fetch some scissors there and then. He returned it with a look that pleaded for help, but Lucetta only laughed and turned back to Kate. 'Your job is going well?'

'I'm loving it.' Kate glanced at Alessandro, a sly smile on her lips. She hadn't yet told them about Shauna's plans to put her on the pay-roll and, thus, make her an official member of staff the next week if all went well – mostly because the opportunity hadn't presented itself. But now seemed like a good time. 'And. . . it's going so well that if this week continues to be good, next week I'll be a paid part of the team.'

'*Fantastico!*' Lucetta squeaked and pulled Kate into another hug.

Kate blushed and glanced at Alessandro to see that he was smiling at her, a curious look on his face. Was he ever so slightly annoyed to be proved wrong about Shauna? But he leaned to kiss her anyway and whispered in her ear, 'This makes me happy.'

'Me too,' Kate replied, but she barely had time for anything else, as Lucetta had explained to Signora Conti and Abelie and they had both rushed to congratulate her too.

She gave a bemused smile as hugs and kisses and compliments were thrown in her direction – of how clever, how kind, how lovely she was. If they were this excited at the mere possibility, then she had better get that job now for sure or they were going to be devastated. Would failure work the other way and make her instantly detestable?

Then Abelie looked around at the sound of the front door slamming, and Kate followed the direction of her gaze to see Maria storm in, no husband, and her four children looking somewhat terrified in her wake. By the look on Maria's face, Kate could see why that might be. Instantly, everyone guessed the same – something or someone had made her very angry, and being on the receiving end of Maria's anger – whether directly or indirectly – wasn't a place you wanted to be.

Without a word of greeting, she launched into a tirade, hands flying all over the place, making gestures Kate had never seen before (and she'd seen quite a few on the streets of Rome since she arrived, many of which Alessandro had laughed about as he explained their less than complimentary meanings) and shouting in rapid Italian, her voice getting louder, swinging from anger to exasperation to tears and then anger again in a terrifying cycle. Her younger children had made their way to Abelie and stood at her skirts as she hugged them, while the oldest, a boy of fourteen, simply looked on in mortified horror, as what Kate, even with her rudimentary grasp of the language, was beginning to work out were passionate threats concerning her husband and the various bits of his anatomy she wanted to remove with sharp and not very sanitary instruments. Signora Conti was doing her best to calm the situation and took Maria to sit down as she began to cry, while Lucetta went to assist, leaving Alessandro, Gian, Kate and Maria's oldest son to stare dolefully at each other.

'What's happening?' Kate asked in a whisper.

Alessandro turned to her, his expression darkening by the second. 'Maria thinks her husband has been unfaithful to her. She has found . . .' He glanced quickly at his nephew, before taking Kate to one side and lowering his voice until it was barely audible. 'She has found hair in their bed. She says it is not hers.'

'And she's concluded he's having an affair just from that? Could she be mistaken? Could it be hers after all?'

Alessandro shook his head. 'I do not think so. You would know if another woman's hair was in your bed?'

'Well, yes, I suppose so. But there might be an innocent explanation for it. They have a cleaner or something?'

Alessandro shook his head. 'No cleaner. He has done this before. Maria forgave him. This time she wants to divorce him.'

Kate turned her gaze to Maria, who was now being comforted by her sisters while Signora Conti dabbed away her tears. 'She sounded like she wanted to do a lot more than just divorce him.'

Alessandro had a smile twitching at the corners of his mouth. 'It is her way – full of fire. Inside, she is dying. She loves him and she knows that divorce will bring shame to Mamma. So she does not say this lightly.'

It was not often Kate had felt the urge to pity Maria; in fact, she never imagined she'd see the day. But looking at her now, the pity welling up inside was genuine, and she wished they were on better terms, just so she could try to offer some comfort. But, she supposed, Maria had enough family there to do that. One thing was certain, the night now belonged to Maria and her woes, and any discussion of anything else would have to wait.

Thirteen

'Kate, can I have a quick word?' Shauna beckoned her over. It was Friday afternoon, and the office was quieter than it had been all week.

Kate nodded. Putting the pile of glossy sales sheets to one side, she left the desk she was sharing with Nonna Rossi and made her way over.

'I don't want to keep you in suspense any longer,' Shauna said. 'I know you've been patient and you've done a sterling job. And I'm sure it's not easy sharing a desk, even if that is with Nonna. So I was wondering how you'd feel about me ordering a new one for you? We could put it, say. . .' her eyes raked the room, 'in that corner next to Elizabeth? What do you think?' Her gaze turned back to Kate, a smile loitering at her lips.

'Um, I suppose that would be nice.'

'And I'm going to need some paperwork from you – tax and proof of residential status and that sort of thing.'

Kate broke into a smile of her own.

Shauna laughed. 'Finally she gets it!'

'I have the job?'

'You have the job. It's been an absolute pleasure to work with you these last couple of weeks and I'm more than happy to take you on officially. If you're happy with that, of course.'

'Happy? I'm thrilled!'

'Good. Then all that remains for me to do is welcome you aboard and deliver the good news to the rest of the team. I think everyone will be happy to have you with us – it'll certainly take some of the pressures of the workload off so for that reason if no other.'

Kate didn't care about the pressures of the workload, or whether the others wanted her or not. She had a job, and she could earn, and finally that dream of making a real, concrete, forever life in Italy was becoming a reality that she could see in clearer detail than ever before. It was there, in front of her, and all she had to do now was take it.

Alessandro reached for her hand and gave it a squeeze as they walked along the wide pavements of the city centre. The skies were smoky grey, a chill breeze finding its way through the fabric of her light jacket, and for the first time since she'd moved to Italy she felt cold.

'You are hungry?' he asked.

'I've been hungry since ten o'clock,' Kate said. 'I don't know why we have to make all this fuss. I'd have been happy enough eating at my apartment.' She also thought it was slightly strange that Alessandro had a Saturday off but they weren't eating at his mother's, as they would normally do whenever they had the time. She loved that he wanted to celebrate her new job, but his mother wasn't a woman you refused easily. Aside from this, she had a mountain of chores at the apartment that needed doing, and although she was now finally earning, this was still an unnecessary expense. Alessandro would insist on paying, of course, but that wasn't really the point.

'Is this the place?' Kate asked as they halted outside the building. She looked it up and down, and then turned to him, confusion written across her features. 'But this is the hotel where I stayed on my first trip to Rome. Why would we be eating here?'

'You will find out,' he said, a strange look that Kate couldn't fathom on his face.

'What's going on?'

'You will find out!' he repeated, laughing as he tugged at her hand to lead her inside.

The lobby was just as she remembered it – sumptuous clarets and golds and far more luxurious than she had been able to afford. Her credit card had remembered it more forcefully than she had for a great deal of time afterwards. The smell of brass polish and cut flowers assailed her, transporting her back to the exact moment she had first stepped inside. So much had happened since then, and yet it seemed like no time at all. She turned to Alessandro with a questioning look. Was there some sort of anniversary she'd forgotten? Some significance to this hotel, on this day, that she ought to know? He smiled down at her and then looked ahead. Kate followed the direction of his gaze and this time, from across the lobby, saw four figures rushing towards them.

'Oh my God!' she squealed.

Anna and Lily threw their arms around her.

'I can't believe you're here!' Kate cried.

They were huddled together, the three of them all crying and laughing and talking at the same time.

'You absolute cows!' Kate laughed, wiping tears from her eyes as they finally broke apart. 'You told me you couldn't come until next year!'

'We couldn't,' Anna said. 'Not really.'

'But I had some news,' Lily added, 'and I wanted to tell you in person. It also means that I won't be able to fly in a few months.'

Kate stared at her. 'You're not. . .'

'Yes!' Lily nodded, beaming. 'I'm pregnant.'

'Oh,' Kate faltered. It had only been a few months since Lily's first pregnancy had ended in tragedy. Kate wanted to congratulate her, of course, but there was a small voice of caution holding her back.

'I know what you're thinking, and we're being cautious too.' Lily turned to Joel, who was standing with Christian and Alessandro as they waited for the women in their lives to remember they were actually there too. 'But we're cautiously happy, and I'm going to do everything I can to make sure it goes OK this time.'

'You're OK now?' Kate asked. 'Should you have been flying at all?'

Lily smiled. 'I'm fine. I wanted to come.'

'It was now or never, really,' Joel put in. 'Well, not never, of course, but you get the idea. If we hadn't come now, it might have been a very long time before we did.'

'How far gone are you?'

'Five, maybe six weeks. Early days yet. I've got an appointment with the midwife next week so she might be able to date it more accurately.'

'Next week?' Kate asked. 'So how long are you staying for?'

'Only a couple of days. It's all any of us could get off work.'

'I know. It's OK. I have work myself on Monday so you would have been entertaining yourselves anyway.'

'We'll just have to make the most of the weekend. Pack in as many sights and ice-creams as we can.'

'It's gelato here, not ice-cream. Let me tell you there's a huge difference.'

'Oh, look,' Anna laughed, 'she's gone native already!'

Lily giggled. 'I think I could eat quite a lot of gelato or ice-cream, and I wouldn't care which it was, especially as I'm eating for two now.'

'But take it easy,' Kate warned. 'Don't overdo it.'

'Yes, Miss,' Lily said, saluting her.

'You know what I mean,' Kate said.

'I do. I'm just kidding.'

'It's fantastic news, really it is,' Kate smiled. 'I'm so happy for you both.'

'Don't worry, we don't have anything that exciting to tell you,' Anna said. She looked at Christian, who simply grinned. 'The only new addition to our family is the *Game of Thrones* box set.'

'Don't tell me anything that's going on!' Kate cried. 'I haven't been able to see the new series anywhere!'

Christian laughed. 'Well, if that's all you've had to worry about while you've been here then it sounds as if you've had a blast.'

'You say that like *Game of Thrones* isn't important!' Kate squeaked.

Alessandro slipped an arm around her. 'I am glad you could all come,' he said to the others. Kate looked up at him.

'Is this anything to do with you?'

'We told him we were coming,' Anna said, 'and we asked Alessandro to keep it a secret because we wanted to surprise you.'

'Well, it was certainly a surprise,' Kate said. 'I didn't have a clue! At least I know now that if I ask him to keep something a secret it will go to his grave.'

Alessandro chuckled. 'Come, we will eat and talk more at the table.'

By the time Kate and Alessandro left the hotel bar it was two in the morning. They'd eaten, drank, talked and talked, and every drink had been followed by another one. Plans to go out into Rome had been shelved – everyone was just too comfortable where they were and happy to be reunited. Lily, forced to be teetotal, had fallen asleep eventually on Joel's shoulder as they lounged in the plush armchairs of the bar area, their high spirits and lively conversation sometimes drawing a little too much attention, and at this point they'd finally conceded defeat with promises to meet up again first thing so that Kate and Alessandro could give them a whistle-stop tour of some of the tourist favourites of the city, followed by a quick stop at Alessandro's home to meet his family. Monday morning would see them going home, and Kate tried not to think about how close that day was as she dressed the next morning.

'You are sad?' Alessandro asked, kissing her neck as she fastened her blouse.

'What makes you say that?'

'You are quiet. Your eyes. . .'

'I'm just thinking about how much I'll miss Lily and Anna when they've gone back. It feels like years since I've seen them. And now Lily is pregnant again, I'm worried about her. If it ends badly, like last time, I don't know how she'll cope.'

'You cannot keep an unborn baby completely safe, no matter how you try.'

'I know that. But I can be there for her. Help and support her if it goes wrong. She'll need someone to cry with, to hold her, tell her everything will be OK. I know she has Anna, and she has Mum and Joel, but I feel guilty that I should leave all that to them. It doesn't seem right, somehow.'

'It may be well this time.'

'I know. And it probably will, so I'm getting worked up over nothing.' She stifled a sigh. A conversation like this would only worry

Alessandro and perhaps it was best not to have it. But then he aired exactly the fear she'd guessed he might have.

'You wish to go back?'

She turned to him. 'To England?'

'Yes.'

'Sometimes,' she admitted. 'But never enough to make me leave you.'

'I would be sad if you were unhappy here. I do not want you to be unhappy, even for our love.'

'Well that makes two of us, but you would be sad if you lived in England, and probably sadder than me here, so I guess that makes the best option me staying here. Besides, I like it. But sometimes I will miss home and that's only natural. It's not for you to worry about.'

'You call it home. You always call England home, but you live in Rome. If you truly felt you belonged, you would call Italy home. The truth is in the things you do not know you are saying. That is why I worry.'

Kate paused. It suddenly occurred to her that she did do that a lot. It was unconscious, something that just came out. 'It doesn't mean anything; it's just a habit. You shouldn't worry.'

'This is the truth?'

She wrapped her arms around his waist and smiled up at him. 'This is the truth. Home is with you, no matter what I call it.' She reached up to kiss him. 'I never said thank you, by the way.'

'For what?'

'For my surprise. It was lovely. I'll miss my sisters like crazy when they've gone but it will have been worth it to spend some time with them.'

'It was nothing.'

'It was very thoughtful.'

'It was not all me. Anna emailed me; she thought it would be funny, so we planned it together.'

'Well, I love it.'

'How much?' he asked, moving in for another kiss, his hand travelling the length of her back to pull her closer.

'Not that much,' she said, smiling as she pulled away. Ignoring the tingle in her loins, she disentangled herself from his embrace. 'If we don't get ready, they'll give up waiting for us and go exploring on their own, and that will make me about as popular as a dose of the flu. Besides, if we're late out to sightsee, we'll be late for dinner with your mamma and she won't like that at all.'

'She is very excited to meet your sisters. She has talked about it all of the time since she knew.'

'I'm surprised she managed to keep it a secret,' Kate mused. She had learned that Alessandro's mother had been the only other person in on the surprise, and that was purely because she would have been hell on toast had she not known they were coming and been unable to prepare a sumptuous feast – and because had they been in Rome and Alessandro not taken them to meet her, he would very likely have had his pants pulled down and his bottom smacked in a way that hadn't happened since he was five once his subterfuge had been discovered.

'She is wiser with secrets than you think,' he said, and his words brought to mind Jamie's, who had more or less said the same thing. Kate didn't doubt that for a moment.

'One thing,' she asked, knowing that it was a sticky subject but one she would have to broach if they were all going to be on the same page, 'do I have to tell my sisters not to mention Matt or the divorce? I mean, Jamie says that your mamma already guessed it, but as we haven't really had a chance to discuss any of it properly with her yet, do you think I ought to?'

'Perhaps, for now,' he said thoughtfully. 'She is so worried about Maria that she might not want to think about so much divorce. She will start to feel it is everywhere she looks.'

'It sort of is,' Kate said. 'I know she doesn't like it but it's a part of life nowadays that's hard to ignore.'

'Not in Mamma's family.'

'Apart from Uncle Marco.'

'*Sì*. But he is only one, and he is Papa's brother not Mamma's.'

Kate turned to the mirror and fastened an earring. 'Do you really think Maria will divorce? That she'll actually go through with it?'

'I do not know. But she is very angry.'

'A lot of couples get angry with each other but they don't divorce. Divorce is more than just getting angry, it's something far more fundamental; it's something in your marriage that's so broken it's gone past fixing. It's huge and not a decision to be taken lightly, and I know this better than most.'

'You do not think adultery is enough to break a marriage?' Alessandro said, holding her in an unnervingly frank gaze. 'I think so.'

'Yes,' she said quietly. 'I suppose it is.'

'If Maria wants to divorce, then I will help to persuade Mamma that it is a good thing. If you know that divorce is a big decision, then you must also know that divorce can bring happiness. We are happy now, and my sister can be happy too.'

There was no argument for that. No matter how Maria had vexed Kate in the past, no matter how instrumental she'd been in Orazia's bid to oust her from Alessandro's life, she was still his sister, and what mattered to him had to matter to Kate too. So she'd offer her support, even if it did stick in her throat.

The dank grey of the skies had cleared overnight, and the morning was bright and fresh as Kate and Alessandro greeted the others outside their hotel. Despite the lateness of their retiring, everyone had agreed to meet early in order to make the most of the day they had left in Rome, but it meant a few bleary-eyed smiles and stifled yawns as they drew up their plan of action. As they didn't have a lot of time to fit in rather a lot of sights, Alessandro suggested a hop-on-hop-off bus tour. Kate giggled at the idea of him, a fully-fledged Roman, doing about the most cheesy, touristy thing to do in Rome, and though he laughingly admitted that he may have to board the bus in heavy disguise, everyone agreed that it would be fun and fast and would allow them time to linger where they wanted to, while still being done in time to get to Alessandro's home for dinner. And although nobody said it, the thought of Lily doing so much walking was a worry to them all. Kate breathed a silent sigh of relief when they all agreed to Alessandro's plan without drawing attention to that fact and dampening Lily's spirits by making her fret or feel like a burden.

Over the past week Kate had noticed the temperature dropping sharply in the city, so that even she, a hardened Mancunian used to regular frosts and icy rain, felt the need to pull on a woolly sweater beneath her coat on venturing out. Everyone else in the party had taken advice from Alessandro and brought plenty of warm clothing with them, though Christian was removing layers as they sat down on the top deck of the bus and Joel's coat flapped open. Kate wondered how they weren't shivering; perhaps she was becoming acclimatised to the weather in Rome much quicker than she had realised, because there was no way her coat was coming off, while Alessandro blew into his hands to thaw them out.

'I can't believe it's so quiet,' Anna said, grabbing the guard rail of the open bus top to peer down onto the streets like an excited child. 'I imagined it was always crazy.'

'Not always,' Alessandro said. 'December is a good time to come – the tourists have gone home and it is easy to see everything.'

'No queues for attractions and no waiting for tables at restaurants either,' Kate added. 'That was the biggest pain when I first came here; it used to drive me mad. And even though it's cold here now it's still beautiful.'

'It's nowhere near as cold as home,' Lily said. 'We've just left forecasts of minus five. I'm happy to be out of that, even if I'm not exactly slapping on the sun lotion here.'

Anna let out a squeak that had Kate and Lily in fits of giggles as the bus started to pull away from the kerb. 'We're off!'

Kate laughed. 'How old are you? You're supposed to be the sensible one.'

'I'm the oldest but I don't always have to be the most sensible,' Anna replied, poking her tongue out at Kate before turning her attention back to the streets trundling past them. 'What's the first stop on the map?' she asked Christian, flipping around again to get a look at the bus route spread across his knee.

'The Piazza Venezia, I think,' Christian said, poring over the page. As Anna bowed her head close to help him work it out, Kate glanced across at Alessandro with a bright smile.

'Thank you,' she mouthed. It wasn't quite Christmas, but she had a feeling that spending this time with her sisters was the best gift she was going to get.

As the bus wove up and down the streets of the city, Kate watched her sisters – gasps of approval, awestruck faces, enthusiasm for each new sight – and for the first time she began to understand the pride Alessandro displayed in his city. It was her city now too: beautiful and incredible – like nowhere else on Earth – and everyone should surely love it as she now loved it. Her heart swelled at every tiny reaction, and what little knowledge she had gleaned during her time there she was happy to impart. They would understand now just what had drawn her to this incredible place, and why she wanted to make a new life there. After all, who could visit and fail to dream a little about what it might be like to wake to these sights every day, to lay claim to them as their own, as the other lovers of Rome did? The Parthenon with its statuesque columns, the mighty Colosseum, the majesty and romance of the Trevi Fountain, the bustle and vibrancy of the Piazza Navona, now festooned with decorations for Christmas and lined with bright, fragrant stalls of the yearly market to honour that season – all these and many other treasures belonged to Kate now. Alessandro had worried that Manchester would always be her home, and perhaps it would, but Rome had captured her heart and soul.

Daylight had been chased through to twilight by the time the party set off in a cab to see Signora Conti, and as the city's lights began to flicker into life, piercing the gloom like brilliant jewels on black velvet, Rome went from natural beauty to sexy siren, more stunning than ever.

'I can see why you love it here,' Lily said dreamily, gazing out of the window, the warm glow of the streetlamps reflected in her eyes. She turned to Kate with a smile. 'It's amazing.'

'Tempted to move?' Kate asked.

Lily laughed. 'Tempted to try and persuade me?'

'A little.'

'It's gorgeous but. . .' She glanced at Joel, who was deep in conversation with Alessandro, sharing his thoughts on the differences between British and Italian football, and then back at Kate again.

'I know. It's not home.' Kate reached across and squeezed her hand. 'It was a bit of a vain hope. You know life would be perfect for me if you and Anna were here, but that's not perfect for you, is it?'

'Things are different for us,' Anna cut in. 'You had nothing to leave behind – not really.'

'I know. I was just thinking out loud.'

'But we'll be here so often you'll think we've moved over,' Lily said.

'Don't forget you've got a baby coming,' Kate said. 'That might make visiting a bit trickier.'

'For a short while. But I'm sure we'll work around it,' Lily replied cheerfully, but in her voice Kate heard fear. Nobody had said it, but everyone was scared that she would lose a second baby and what that would do to her mental state. She'd almost had a nervous breakdown losing her first. But for now, at least, she'd trusted them with the news that she had probably thought about keeping to herself for a while, and they had to repay that trust by not letting their own fears get the better of them, because that was no help to Lily at all. She'd told them because they were a family who didn't keep secrets, but she'd also told them because she needed their strength and support to stop her spiralling into a negative storm of self-doubt and fear. She needed them to help her believe that this time she could get through the pregnancy, that she had to put the past behind her and try to cherish each precious moment of it, and if they couldn't do that for her, then both Kate and Anna had failed her as sisters. Kate understood this without the need for one word from Lily, because she understood her sisters almost as well as she understood herself.

Just under twenty minutes later, Signora Conti had Lily in such a crushing hug that Kate was seriously worried about what damage it might be causing that little peanut of life she had growing inside her. It was tempting to rush between them and drag Lily from harm's way, and it was only Alessandro's reassured, relaxed smile as he watched them that slapped some sense back into her.

'Mamma is very happy to meet you,' he said as Lily was finally freed. Anna was then subjected to the same, quickly followed by a slightly shell-shocked Joel and then Christian. 'She has been very excited all of the day.'

'We're happy to meet you too,' Anna said to Alessandro's mother, who nodded and smiled broadly as Alessandro translated for her.

Once Abelie had been introduced, they chatted pleasantly while the inevitable troupe of the rest of the Conti family arrived. Not one of them would ever miss an opportunity to inspect a potential new family member or even just a friend, and true to form, they arrived in shifts: Isabella and her family first, then Jolanda and hers, Lucetta and Gian, and finally even Maria, joined by her children, the absence of her husband a notable feature of her attendance – all laden with dishes they had brought to contribute to the meal. With warmth and good grace, each of them greeted Kate's family, and once again, Kate couldn't help but note that even Maria was making an effort to be friendly. Perhaps her own family woes had taught her some valuable lessons, but whatever it was, she certainly seemed humbler and less judgemental than she had before.

'Come, come,' Signora Conti urged everyone to the table in the best English she could muster, and then with Abelie and Jolanda assisting, she scurried out to the kitchen to begin plating up the various delights she'd prepared for dinner.

'Brace yourself,' Kate whispered to Anna with a grin. 'It looks as though Alessandro's mother has swapped their far bigger lunch for dinner so that she can welcome you properly. She did it when I first came over and my stomach took days to recover! I hope you're hungry because after today you might never be hungry again.'

'I am,' Anna said. 'Starving! And it smells amazing.'

'Mamma Conti's dinners *are* amazing,' Kate agreed. 'But she makes way too much. God only knows how she affords all the food.'

'Oh.' Anna suddenly looked troubled. 'Do you think we ought to have offered to contribute?'

'God no!' Kate laughed. 'She'd be seriously offended! She'd give you her last bowl of pasta and if you tried to repay it with so much as a bean she'd feel she'd failed in her task as hostess. No, enjoy it and thank her and that will be enough.'

Alessandro's mother put her head around the kitchen door, and a single look was enough to send the oldest grandchildren to her aid, while Maria and Isabella kept control of the youngest ones. Then, moments later the dishes started to arrive at the table: cured meats, preserved vegetables, green salad, bread, olives and salted fish.

'Wow,' Lily said with an approving sweep of the table. 'This looks wonderful; we won't be able to move after all this.'

'This is only the first course,' Kate said, shooting a conspiratorial smile at Alessandro who grinned in return. 'You just wait – you really won't be able to move by the time all the courses have been served, and you have to try each one because they're just too good to leave, no matter how full you are.'

At this, Lily almost seemed to pale, and Alessandro threw back his head and laughed. 'You are in Italy! What we do know is food!'

As promised, the antipasti was followed by the *primo* course, for which Signora Conti had made a divine pea risotto, then the *secondo*, which consisted of a choice of spicy sausage or salmon, with the *contorno* or side dish of crisp seasonal vegetables. Then came the *insalata* (another garden salad), which was followed by the cheese course. To make certain everyone had groaning stomachs, the dessert came hot on the heels of all the savoury courses, but thankfully this was a panna cotta so creamy and light that, apart from the sublime taste, its presence barely registered on the digestive system at all. Lastly came coffee, and then limoncello (though Lily, as soon as a delighted Signora Conti discovered the pregnancy, was served a tasty herbal brew that she failed to catch the name of). All the while spirits were high and conversation flowed freely as everyone got to know each other, and Kate was happier than she could say to see everyone getting along. It was all she had hoped for but at times had dared not. Even Maria seemed cheered by her exchanges with Kate's sisters – finding common ground with Anna in particular, who, when Kate really thought about it, probably had a similar temperament. Signora Conti beamed at every new compliment to her home, cooking and family. At one point she even went so far as to reach over and pinch Joel's cheeks, which caused a gale of laughter from Lily, who said that if he was going to go around looking like a twelve-year-old with a beard that was barely bum fluff then he should expect people to treat him like one. Christian would have laughed too, but it seemed he was wiser than to think he wouldn't be next on Signora Conti's maternal radar, and so he allowed Joel one last bastion of dignity by shooting him a sympathetic look. Alessandro patted Joel on the back and reminded him that he'd suffered thirty years of such fussing, at which point Lucetta reminded him that he was an ungrateful brat and if he'd been her son she'd have turfed him out onto the streets. Everyone laughed, even Signora Conti, who probably didn't have much of a clue what Lucetta was saying as it was in English, and who then lit up with pride as Alessandro nipped around the table to give her a kiss and a hug and tell her she was truly the best mamma in the entire world.

More drinks followed dinner, and Signora Conti proudly showed Anna and Lily, accompanied by Kate and Lucetta, the view from her balcony, where the distant lights of Rome were scattered through the darkness, as the others chatted inside. It was chilly out there, a frost snapping at their noses and fingertips, but it was a welcome relief from a dining room that had become too hot with the number of bodies crammed into it.

'I really can see why you love it here,' Lily said to Kate as she stood and stared at the view, her breath curling into the air. It was one that Kate, already, was beginning to take for granted, but as she gazed at it with her sisters, her belly full of fabulous food, a room full of happiness and good feeling, she saw it as if for the first time and fell in love all over again.

'I really do,' she said, turning to her with a smile. 'I can't imagine ever leaving now.'

'And we love Kate,' Lucetta said. 'You do not need to worry that she is far away from family, because she has a new family here and we will take good care of her for you.'

'We can see that,' Anna said. 'And we're grateful she has such wonderful people to look out for her. I must admit that when she first came over we thought she'd want to come back after a couple of weeks, but. . .' she turned to Kate, 'you've really made it work. A job that's going well, a flat, good friends, an adopted family, a caring boyfriend – it seems you've got everything you could wish for.'

'I could wish for a much posher flat and a lot more money,' Kate laughed. 'But the rest. . . yeah, it's more or less perfect; I'm pretty happy right now.'

And even as she said it, Kate suddenly shivered. The night air had a bite to it, but she couldn't help feeling there was more to it than that.

Fourteen

The weekend had come and gone too quickly, and with it Kate's visitors. Though she'd been happy to see them, her sisters being in Rome had inevitably stirred up feelings of regret that she would have to lose them again. It was silly, of course, because they were only a matter of hours away and come the new year she hoped to have earned enough money to go and visit them even if they couldn't get back to Rome so easily. But still, watching them go through to the departure lounge of the airport left a hole that was so big, she almost wished they hadn't come in the first place. Alessandro had pulled her close, seeming to understand her pain, and they had lingered until they could wait no more, knowing that the flight had gone and that Anna and Lily had gone with it.

The following day had brought a new week at work and little time to miss her sisters. A hectic start had meant she was too busy to think about much at all. There was certainly no danger of being bored and unmotivated at Piccolo Castelli, and a morning doing administration under the watchful eye of Nonna Rossi flew by so fast she almost fell off her chair in the most comical way as she looked up at the clock to see lunchtime had completely passed her by. Nonna Rossi came over to her desk with a stern rebuke.

'Lunch is very important,' she said. 'You must not forget to eat.'

Kate hadn't noticed Nonna herself go out for lunch, but perhaps it was better not to mention it. She hadn't noticed anyone else get lunch either, but some had the leftovers of theirs littering their desks, or else were talking about what they'd just eaten, so she had to assume that she really had been that wrapped up in her work.

Shauna had been happy enough with Kate at the end of the day but didn't have any visits out of the office for her to undertake alone just yet. All in good time, she'd said, and Kate had to be content with that, even though she was aware that the sooner she got onto the sales sheet proper, the sooner she could start supplementing what was really quite a meagre basic wage with some commission. She was not a natural sales person, and though that aspect of the job might not be her strongest, she was desperate and willing to do what it took, hoping that, above all, a natural rapport with her clients would be enough without having to resort to pressured sales tactics.

All in all, it had been a good day despite a humble workload, and with Alessandro back on his own night shifts, she was ready for a quiet evening: shower, supper and bed.

But the universe had other plans, and as she turned the corner, she spotted Salvatore outside her building, his car at the kerb and his back to her as he paced up and down. As she drew closer, she could see that he was on his phone, deep in conversation.

Kate stopped, a groan forming in her throat. While she liked him, she wasn't in the mood to make small talk, and especially small talk with a language barrier that made it harder work than usual. And while Alessandro kept telling her that Salvatore's English was better than he let on, he still wasn't letting on, not for Kate at least. Could she somehow slip past him and into the building undetected?

Kate would never get to put her theory to the test. There was a squeal of delight from his car and the door flew open. Nunzia clambered out, tottering towards Kate with a huge smile on her face.

'*Ciao*, Kate!' she cried. 'Hello!'

She pulled Kate into a hug, and as she did, Kate caught the slightly sheepish smile on Salvatore's face.

'Hi Nunzia,' Kate said with a smile. '*Come sta?*'

'*Bene, grazie!*' Nunzia replied. 'My dress,' she continued, grasping Kate's hands affectionately. 'My dress. . . very beautiful. Many admire!'

'She is very happy,' Salvatore put in, now making his way over. 'All of the friends, they love her dress – *bellissimo!*'

'I'm glad you like it,' Kate said. 'And it's lovely of you to come over and tell me. I'm assuming you didn't want me for anything else?'

Nunzia scuttled off to the car and reappeared a few seconds later with a paper bag. From it she pulled a roll of fabric.

'You want another dress?' Kate said, trying hard to hold back a frown. It wasn't that she minded sewing another for Nunzia, but she would have preferred to help choose the fabric, if only to ensure that what they purchased was the appropriate weight and weave to suit whatever style of dress Nunzia had chosen.

'*Sì*, please!' Nunzia said.

'Her friend would like a dress too,' Salvatore put in. 'If you could.'

'Her friend?' Kate repeated, realising just how stupid she was sounding right now.

'*Sì!*' Nunzia beamed. 'Loretta. She like very much. She pay plenty money, very rich.'

'I'd need to measure her up,' Kate replied uncertainly. 'Could she come here?'

Would she want to come here was the question Kate really wanted to ask, particularly if she was very rich, but as Salvatore was standing right there, perhaps she shouldn't insult his building.

'I take you,' Nunzia replied. 'Four days. *Si?*'

'At the weekend?' Kate asked. She didn't have much else to do so perhaps it wouldn't be a bad idea. And what she was really trying to do was stop herself from getting too excited by the prospect of a real and proper customer.

'Yes, the weekend,' Salvatore confirmed. 'She lives outside Roma. Nunzia can drive you. She will want many dresses, I think.'

'She will?'

'*Si*,' Nunzia said. 'Many dresses!'

'OK, well. . . she won't want them for Christmas, will she? Only that doesn't leave a lot of time and I'm working now in the week.'

Salvatore waved his hands to calm her. 'It's no problem. You tell her, not before Christmas. If she wants dress for Christmas, she must go shopping.'

Kate turned to Nunzia. 'Do you want yours before Christmas? I could probably manage it but there isn't a lot of time.'

'Nunzia has plenty dresses,' Salvatore said, but that didn't stop Kate feeling somewhat obliged to pull a special favour for her. And it wasn't as if her evenings were packed while Alessandro was working.

'Well,' she began thoughtfully, 'I do already have Nunzia's measurements, and we have the fabric.' She looked at Nunzia again. 'If you want to choose a style now then I suppose I could try to make it before Christmas. I don't mind, though I can't promise.'

Nunzia squished Kate's cheeks and then pulled her into a hug. '*Grazie mille, Kate! Siete una piccola stella!*'

* * *

It transpired that Nunzia had chosen her fabric well, and the dress that she had asked Kate to make for her suited its handling perfectly. Kate had been glad of the nightly distraction too. And yet in her own apartment, with plenty of time to think, she found that instead of dwelling on the positives of her new job and possible new sewing clients, her mind kept taunting her, going back to the idea that Orazia was working side by side with Alessandro – these days probably seeing more of him than she herself did.

Nunzia duly turned up on Friday night to collect her dress.

'Beautiful!' she trilled as she studied her reflection, running a hand up and down between her waistline and her hips to admire the fit.

'I'm glad you like it,' Kate said. '*Prego.*'

Nunzia hurried over to a little clutch bag she'd left on the dining table. Taking a wad of notes from her purse she pressed them into Kate's palm with a broad smile. Kate flicked through it and quickly concluded that it was too much again. She separated the money and offered the extra back to Nunzia, but the landlord's wife simply gave a firm shake of her head. 'For you,' she said. 'My friend Kate.'

Kate stood awkwardly with the notes in an extended hand. She didn't want to keep taking more than Salvatore had agreed but she didn't want to offend Nunzia by refusing her kindness. But then Nunzia fastened her handbag as if to indicate that the matter was closed and she would hear no argument, and Kate curled her hand around the money, shoving it guiltily into the pocket of her dress.

'We have party,' Nunzia said, going back to the mirror to check her reflection again. '*Natale . . .*'

Kate frowned slightly. 'Christmas party?'

'*Sì*. You come?'

'It's *your* Christmas party?' Kate asked.

'*Sì*. My house.'

Lovely as Nunzia was, the last thing Kate wanted to do was go to her Christmas party, mostly because she knew that Salvatore wouldn't be happy about it. She felt quite certain that he'd rather chew his own arm off than have one of his poorer and less socially impressive tenants at his own private function. A friendly word whilst collecting her rent was one thing, but having her over for dinner was quite another.

'It sounds lovely,' Kate began slowly, 'but. . . well, my Italian is not good and I would find it difficult to talk to the other guests. You understand?'

'You come,' Nunzia insisted. Kate wasn't sure whether she hadn't taken in her argument or whether she simply didn't care.

'When is it?'

Nunzia hesitated, working it out silently on her fingers. 'Ten days.'

'I'll try,' Kate said. 'I'm not sure whether we have family commitments coming up but I'll check with Alessandro and let you know.'

Nunzia gave a satisfied grunt and turned her attention to a stray hair. Kate was pretty sure she'd discover something in the diary for ten days' time, even if it was a little white lie she had to pencil in herself.

'You see my friend for dresses?' Nunzia asked, breaking into Kate's thoughts.

'Loretta? When does she want me?'

'*Sì*, Loretta. I ask. I call you.'

'Before Christmas?'

Nunzia tilted her head this way and that.

'*Natale?*' Kate corrected. 'She wants her dress before *Natale?*'

Nunzia held her hands up in an exaggerated shrug. 'I telephone and I tell you when.'

Kate held in a sigh. Not exactly the kind of scheduling she found useful, but it looked as though it was the best she was going to get for now. Forcing a smile, she began to unzip Nunzia's dress. 'I'll get this packed for you and then I'll make us a coffee.'

Saturday evening saw Alessandro off shift again, and he was sitting with his arms curled around Kate on the sofa as they shared a bottle of wine.

'Christmas is almost upon us,' he said slowly, 'and Maria will have to decide what to do.'

'So you think Christmas may persuade her to take her husband back?' Kate asked.

'No. She has made her mind up about that. She will have to decide where she will live. Her husband owns the house, and he will want to sell it; Maria will have nothing.'

'She must be entitled to things – half of the property and money for the children?'

'Perhaps. But she will find life hard by herself.'

'Will your mother take her back – to live with her, I mean?'

'Yes, always. Mamma says there is always a home with her to all of us when we leave, no matter what. But there is not much room for Maria and all of her children all of the time, and Mamma is not so strong these days.'

'There would be more space for Maria if you moved out,' Kate said, and she shot him a sideways glance as she reached for her wine glass. 'A noble sacrifice, I think.' The idea had struck suddenly, but perhaps, for once, Maria would be doing Kate a favour, even if she didn't know it.

'You mean I should live here? With you?'

'Would your mother be very upset by the idea? After all, she's getting used to a lot of new ideas these days, with Maria getting divorced and you dating me. Perhaps she'd be more open to the possibility than we think. It would help everyone out and I'd love it.'

'It would be too much for Mamma. She must get used to Maria's divorce first, and then perhaps we will try it.'

Kate smiled. 'You'd move into this apartment with me? I mean, sometime soon?'

'Maybe. I would sooner marry you.'

'But we can't, remember? There's too much to sort out first, and if I'm honest, I don't know if I can be bothered with all that annulment business. Can't we just live over the brush and have done with it?'

He frowned. 'What is over the brush?'

Kate laughed. 'My gran used to say it. For years I had no idea what it meant, but she always said it in a very disapproving voice about couples she thought were quite filthy. It means living together without being married.'

'Mamma would disapprove too. I do not think it is such a good idea.'

'But people do it all the time now. Nobody cares.'

'Mamma does.'

Kate was silent for a moment. God, his family, as much as she loved them, could be so bloody infuriating. While their delightful old-fashionedness was reassuring and endearing, it also drove her mad. It wasn't that she was against the idea of marrying Alessandro, and even this early in their relationship she felt in her heart she would be happy with him, but she railed against the idea of having no other option. Other couples happily spent a year or two living together before they committed, but if she wanted him there full time, it looked as if she was going to have to dive into another marriage. Not only that, but it sounded like a lot of hassle, stress and expense to get to the stage where they would be in a position to marry because they had to jump through a ton of religious hoops so that they could wed in the church, where Signora Conti wanted them to marry, when a civil service would have suited Kate just as well.

'I could buy an apartment of my own,' he said. 'If Mamma is happy for that.'

'There doesn't seem a lot of point when I have this one here. Why pay out for another; it seems like a waste of money that you could be saving towards a better place in the long run. That's why it makes sense for you to come and live with me. I mean, you spend quite a lot of time here anyway so it wouldn't be that different if you moved in completely.'

'It would be different for Mamma.'

Kate bit back the irritated sigh she so wanted to let out. 'So Maria will come to live with you and you'll all be squashed in like sardines?'

'Yes.'

'She'll move back in with your mother before Christmas?'

'Perhaps this week. Today we will know what she has decided.'

Kate was quiet again. She'd been looking forward to her first Christmas in Rome with the Conti family, especially now she'd been able to meet up with her sisters for an early celebration of their own, but now she wasn't so sure.

* * *

Try as she might to concentrate, it was hard. Sitting at her desk, knowing that Alessandro was helping to move Maria back into their childhood home along with her four children was driving Kate to distraction. On top of that Christmas was coming, and although Maria would have been present at their celebrations (as everyone always was despite the lack of room), the finality of her situation would lend the atmosphere a new heaviness that would be hard for them all to ignore. Strangely, the one positive to come from the situation was that Maria's new circumstances had somehow softened her towards Kate. Perhaps in Kate she now recognised a kindred spirit, an inspiration, a template to show that life could and did get better, even after an unwanted and unexpected divorce. She'd moved in bit by bit, a little more each day, but today Alessandro was helping her with the final belongings. What was going to happen to her house once she left was a matter Maria seemed reluctant to discuss, even when Kate had offered the services of Piccolo Castelli if they wanted to sell it. But Kate hadn't pushed, guessing that Maria was still in some kind of denial and didn't want to think about it. She had simply shrugged and said that her husband could clean up his own mess, and left it at that.

She'd read the same paragraph of the particulars of a villa in Umbria three times when Shauna came over to her desk.

'How's it going?' she asked, perching herself on the edge and crossing her long legs. 'Still happy?'

'Yes, it's brilliant,' Kate lied. 'I'm very happy.'

It wasn't brilliant lately. Her colleagues were lovely, the job was interesting enough, but Kate felt the absence of something that she couldn't quite put her finger on. Was it, perhaps, inspiration? Passion? It was a job, and she needed it, but she was beginning to feel that it wasn't all she'd hoped it would be. In ten years, would she be sitting here and wishing she'd followed her heart rather than her head? First Mr Woofy back in England and now this. Would she feel she'd wasted her working life doing jobs that didn't seem to matter? She shook the notion. Beggars couldn't be choosers, as Matt had so often reminded her when she'd complained about Mr Woofy, and the fact of the matter was she'd made the decision to come to Rome knowing that things wouldn't be perfect at first, and that she would just have to dig in and get on with it if she was going to make the move work. At least she had work, and it was better than some of the jobs she'd been prepared to take – probably better than her woeful qualifications deserved.

'You're settling in well,' Shauna continued, 'and you've impressed everyone with how hard you work and how on the ball you are. I realise that you've been desk-bound since you joined us properly, and that might be frustrating for you. Christmas is coming, so it's pointless moving anything along now, but I thought after the break you might want to take on a client base of your own and go out to do viewings.'

'I'd like that,' Kate said, mustering a bright smile. 'That would be great.'

It will *be great*, she told herself sternly. *It* will *be great, so just shut up and get on with it.*

If Kate had thought Signora Conti went overboard with food at any other time of the year, at Christmas she took it to a whole new level. Kate was quite sure she'd need to have her stomach pumped come Boxing Day evening, and Alessandro had laughed at her as she rolled around their sofa complaining about it. Christmas Eve kicked them off: fish and vegetables for *giorno di magro*, or eating lean, as Alessandro explained it, to save themselves for the main event the next day. But after the nine courses of fish, vegetables and pasta that his mother had prepared and cooked were done, Kate couldn't see where on earth the lean bit came in, but she did think someone had a very strange notion of what it was to abstain from indulgence.

Christmas Day had featured large amounts of turkey, which Alessandro said some families in Rome ate and some didn't, but Signora Conti had got one especially for Kate, and the kindness of the gesture almost reduced Kate to tears. Signora Conti had hugged her, and then everyone else had hugged her, including Maria and her four children, at which point Kate really did start to cry, prompting them to hug her some more.

The one low point was the arrival of Orazia on Boxing Day. Ostensibly coming to see how Maria was, she paid rather a lot of attention to Alessandro, going out of her way to laugh at his every joke, sit as close as she could possibly get and generally make Kate more paranoid than ever. But nobody else seemed fazed in the slightest, and even Alessandro laughed and joked with her as he would with any old friend. Kate just couldn't work the woman out and she was fast becoming convinced that the problem was all with her and not Orazia at all. Perhaps it was entirely down to high spirits and large amounts of wine, but if everyone else was happy to have her around and didn't see any danger, why did Kate need to feel so nervous? As was her way, Signora Conti graciously extended her hospitality to Orazia and insisted she stay as long as she liked, and so the wasp in Kate's gelato stayed for dinner and late into the evening as well. The one blessing was that she barely paid Kate any heed at all – at least not until the conversation turned to Kate's job.

'You have work now?' Orazia said, smiling. Kate suspected that her having a job was no surprise to Orazia, who usually made it her business to find out everything that Kate was up to. 'That is very good.'

'Thank you,' Kate offered as a neutral reply.

'Soon she will be the boss!' a drunken Lucetta cried, waving her fork in the air.

'We are very proud of her,' Alessandro said, shooting a fond glance at Kate. 'She will be able to stay in Rome now that she has work.'

From the corner of her eye, Kate noted Orazia's demeanour change in an instant. It was subtle enough, and perhaps anyone not paying as much attention would have missed it, but Kate didn't.

'That is good,' Orazia said, ramming a forkful of pasta into her mouth and chewing as if she was eating tree bark.

'It is more than good,' Alessandro said. 'It is the most wonderful news.'

'It pays well?' Orazia asked.

'It's OK,' Kate said.

'It will pay well soon,' Alessandro said. 'Kate will sell plenty houses and she will make enough to buy a nicer apartment than the one she rents from Salvatore.'

Kate waved the praise away. 'I don't think that'll happen any time soon.'

'You are clever,' Lucetta said. 'You make the worst of life good. And if you do not sell lots of houses you will sell many dresses and you will be rich.'

'Don't be daft,' Kate replied, shooting a cautious glance at Orazia, whose expression was unreadable. But she saw a flicker of emotion as Maria spoke, though she couldn't quite work out what it was.

'I admire your strength,' Maria said earnestly. Kate turned to her, aware she was staring but unable to help it. 'You come to Rome with nothing and you make a home. You have great sadness in your life and you make it happy. That is strong. I wish I was strong like that. . .' Her voice wobbled, and Abelie leapt up to throw an arm around her while Kate felt the heat spread to her face. What had just happened? Was that a compliment from the stony-hearted Maria?

'Maria is right,' Alessandro said, beaming with pride at Kate. 'We are all happy you have come to Rome.'

Kate forced a smile for Alessandro as he leaned in to kiss her lightly. But her gaze was drawn to Orazia, who was now concentrating a bit too hard on the plate in front of her and holding her fork in a grip that suggested she was anything but relaxed. Kate tried not to dwell on it. While she didn't want to see trouble around every corner, that didn't mean it wasn't there, just the same.

Fifteen

Her stomach needed to behave. After a brief morning meeting at their favourite coffee shop, a quick trip back to the office to gen up on the particulars of her first visit and collect any paperwork she might need, Kate found herself in a car borrowed from Shauna and out on the roads, driving in Italy for the first time since she'd arrived. Not the best, perhaps, but a competent enough driver at home, even on the sometimes complicated one-way systems of Manchester, this was a whole new level of scary. She was desperately wishing she'd chosen a better moment to take her first solo trip, but as she hadn't needed to drive before, she'd kept putting it off. Now she was reaping the rewards of that decision. Not only was she coping with the steering wheel and gears being very unhelpfully on the wrong side of the car, and having to remember to stay on the right side of the road, but just about every other driver in Rome seemed determined to get in her way. Horns sounded so often that she couldn't tell whether they were directed at her, at someone else or just for the hell of it. In the corners of her vision, cars flashed by so close to hers that she could see in crisp detail the gashes and scrapes down their bodywork (which almost all seemed to have) and what made things even worse was the knowledge that this wasn't her car to trash, though trashing did seem to be the inevitable fate of it, no matter how hard she tried to stay out of everyone's way. The road signs didn't help, nor did the fact that she had no idea where she was going and the satnav Shauna had set up for her had decided it would rather be doing something else and had stopped making sense almost as soon as she'd left the office. Even time itself seemed out to get her, and the clock on the dashboard mocked her as the minutes raced towards the appointment slot – unlike her car, which seemed to be racing around and around in circles, caught up in the speedway track that was otherwise known as Rome's highways. She'd wanted to arrive early, and had set out in plenty of time to be there, cool and calm before her client arrived. At this rate, the client was going to be placing a very angry call to the office to demand an explanation for where she was.

Half an hour later, her blouse damp with perspiration and her heart beating at twice its normal rate, she pulled up outside a cream-stone frontage. It contained the rather small, averagely priced apartment that was Kate's first solo outing as an actual estate agent. The street outside was empty, and although Kate herself was a couple of minutes late, she had to assume that the prospective buyer was late too.

'Thank you,' she mouthed to the heavens as she clambered from the car and clicked the fob to lock it. Taking a deep breath and a moment to straighten herself out, she fished in her bag for the apartment keys. But she stopped at the doors, hesitant. Shauna always liked to get there early and give the property a cursory once-over so there would be no nasty surprises when the buyers were shown around. But if Kate did that now, she ran the risk of not being there to greet them outside the building when they arrived.

Eventually, she decided to wait.

She waited.

And waited some more.

Kate glanced at her watch. Ten minutes had passed. It wasn't so late, considering the trouble she'd had getting there, and perhaps the client was stuck in traffic or lost too. She was just about to call the office to see if they knew anything when her own phone started to ring.

'Kate.' Shauna's tone was uncharacteristically abrupt at the other end of the line. 'Where are you?'

'I'm at Via di San Francesco. That's where I'm supposed to be, isn't it?' she added, her stomach suddenly lurching at the thought she might have made a mistake.

'If you're there, how come the client is phoning me telling me you're not?'

'They are? But I'm standing outside the building and there's nobody here. In fact, the road is pretty much empty so they're not anywhere nearby.'

'Well, they're telling me they're there and you're not, so you'd better go and look for them.'

'I will, I'm—'

The apology on Kate's lips was cut short by Shauna slamming down the phone.

'Great job, Kate,' she muttered as she scanned the street once again, though quite where she was expecting her client to leap out from was a mystery. There was definitely nobody else here. With no clue of what else to do, she rattled the huge iron key in the lock of the main doors and let herself into the building. If she'd had to unlock the door, then she didn't really see how her keyless buyer could be in there, but she couldn't think where else to look and standing on the front steps like a prune wasn't going to find them.

The apartment was on the second floor. Rather than wait for the cranky old lift, Kate dashed up the stairs. At the top, she glanced along the landing to see a statuesque blonde leaning on the wall outside the apartment she was meant to be showing. Her prospective buyer, she presumed, though Kate didn't have a clue how she'd got into the building.

'Miss Collins?' she asked uncertainly. The woman turned to her, gave her a cursory glance up and down and then nodded.

'I thought the appointment was for eleven.'

'It is. I was here,' Kate said, trying not to be flustered by the woman's manner. She couldn't be more than twenty, but she was tall and attractive, with a posh accent, immaculate clothes and make-up. This was an apartment at the cheaper end of the property ladder, but Kate was still taken by vague surprise that such a young woman could afford it, and by the way Miss Collins spoke to her. 'I was outside waiting. I'd assumed you wouldn't be able to access the building without me so I wasn't expecting to find you in here.'

At this the woman's attitude seemed to soften. 'One of the residents was coming in and when I told them I might be buying here they asked if I wanted to get a look inside.' She shrugged. 'And you weren't here so I thought, what the hell?'

Helpful, Kate thought. *Bloody brilliant.* She wanted to mention how helpful calling the office to drop her in it had been too, but perhaps that would be pushing it. 'I'm sorry you've had to wait,' she said instead. 'Pesky misunderstanding but I'm here now, so we can go into the apartment if you like.'

As the front door opened, a mouse scurried across the floor. Kate's groan was audible, and there was no point trying to hide it because there was no way her client had failed to see it too.

'I think it's been empty for a while,' Kate offered by way of a lame explanation.

'I think it's in need of pest control,' Miss Collins said crisply, stepping over the threshold.

The curtains were closed, and Kate almost wondered whether it would be better to leave the place in gloom, dreading what else the daylight might show up. But she crossed the room and threw them open anyway, a cloud of dust issuing forth as she did and revealing a scattering of bluebottle corpses along the windowsill. Next time she did a viewing, she was going to get there an hour before with some cleaning supplies to make sure the place was spotless, because this was simply embarrassing. If she hadn't known better, she'd have sworn that this was some kind of induction prank pulled by her colleagues to welcome the newbie.

'I take it you haven't been able to sell this place,' Miss Collins asked with a grimace as she took in the room. 'No wonder it wasn't on the website. Next time one of your office monkeys "recommends" a place in my price range, I might think twice about trusting their recommendation.'

Kate tried not to scowl. So it needed a good clean and a lick of paint – perhaps some sturdy body armour to protect from the bugs and rodents. It had been empty for a while, but then many properties had and, if nobody was going in, how could it be pristine? What was this girl expecting?

'I know it's hard to see past the grime, but you must remember that we're in a prime location here,' she said. The sale had already gone, so what was the point in pussyfooting around? 'This is Rome, after all, and you're going to spend a lot of money on a shed here. This apartment is catering for a more modest budget. If you want to look at something more expensive, we have other properties on our books that require no work at all to move in.'

'This is in my budget,' the girl said quickly, her arrogance suddenly gone.

'And I suppose there wasn't a lot else on our books?' Kate replied. 'I've only recently moved to Rome myself, and I know exactly how hard it is to find a good property on a budget. May I enquire why you're buying and not renting?'

'It was meant to be an investment,' she said. 'My Italian grandmother recently died, and she left me some money, on the proviso that I maintain some link with Italy. So I thought it seemed like a good idea to buy a place here. My boyfriend reckoned I'd make a killing renting it out as a holiday let. I had wondered whether I might even live in it myself, but looking around now, I guess I overestimated what my money would buy me.'

'It's not as bad as it looks,' Kate said. 'My apartment was way worse than this when I moved in, but it's quite cosy now and it didn't take as much work as you'd think. If you let me show you around, I can give you lots of cheap ideas about what you could do in here, and maybe you would be tempted to move in yourself, but at the very least you'd have something good to rent out. There are a lot worse places to be in the world than here and people like me, who are just starting out, would snap your hand off to take a flat in this neighbourhood. It's a bit out of the centre for most holidaymakers, perhaps, if I'm being completely honest with you, but then again, some like that because it's more peaceful at night. I think either way, even if you didn't make a killing, you'd make enough to cover your initial outlay and some to put away for a rainy day, and when you come to sell on – if you can ever bear to sell on – you should make a tidy profit for the effort you've put into making the place habitable.'

Miss Collins blinked at her. And then nodded. 'Thanks. Um. . . sorry, what was your name?'

'Kate.'

'I'm Verity.'

Kate extended her hand, a subconscious signal that they should start their meeting again on a better footing, and Verity shook. 'Pleased to meet you, Verity,' she said and smiled. 'So, shall we go and see if we can find out just how many mice you might need to collect rent from if you do buy this place?'

'It's impressive,' Charles said carelessly. At least, it sounded a bit like that, but the mouthful of boiled sweets he was talking through made it difficult for Kate to understand.

'It is,' Elizabeth agreed, sans the chomping and, therefore, much easier to understand. 'Nonna hasn't been able to get anyone to look at that place for months, but the first person you get through the door puts an offer in. What kind of bribes did you have to employ?'

'We just chatted about what she wanted, and the possibilities for the place, and eventually she saw it the way I did. I just said what I thought, really.'

'Wow, who knew giving your honest opinion actually worked,' Charles said, staring down at his phone. 'That's a new one.'

'We don't lie,' Shauna scolded.

'No, but we sometimes keep the truth to ourselves,' Charles replied, rooting in the bag on his desk for another sweet.

'That's just you,' Elizabeth said. 'Some of us have morals.'

'It's just you with the morals, which is why you barely sell anything,' Charles said.

Elizabeth's brow creased, but then she smoothed her face into a smile for Kate. 'I think it's brilliant. Well done to you. Do you feel like a real estate agent now?'

'Not exactly,' Kate said. 'But I do feel slightly less useless than I did at nine this morning.'

'In that case,' Shauna said, making her way over to Kate's desk and dropping a sheaf of paperwork onto it, 'there's a couple of nice viewings tomorrow if you fancy having a crack at them. No pressure, but if you can work some more of whatever magic you worked today, you and I will be getting along famously.'

Kate glanced around the office, where her colleagues eyed her keenly, apart from Charles, who was doing his best to appear disinterested as he fiddled with his phone. 'Of course,' she said, 'I'll do my best.'

Charles let out a yawn as he reached for another handful of sweets. 'Let's see how far your beginner's luck will stretch,' he said before stuffing them in.

There were no more instant sales, but the week went as well as Kate could have hoped for. Driving around the city became slightly less terrifying, though still scary enough for the danger of a stomach ulcer from the constant stress to be a distinct one, but she'd mastered the satnav, and the art of arriving at her destination in plenty of time to make sure she knew what was coming when she opened the front door of the property. So far it had been simple viewings for prospective buyers, but Friday came, and Shauna took her to one side.

'Elizabeth has called in sick and everyone else is a bit tied up this morning. Do you think you could handle a valuation?'

'Me? Value a property?' Kate asked doubtfully. 'I don't know.'

'You wouldn't have to actually quote anything,' Shauna replied. 'Just go along, measure up, take photos, generally look the part, then email all the particulars to the office and we'll send you the price right back. You give the vendor the figures and nobody's any the wiser. What do you think?'

She didn't see that she had a lot of choice. This was her job, after all. 'I can do that.'

'Fantastic. I knew I could rely on you. I'll email the particulars over to you now and you can go through them before you leave. They're expecting you at ten thirty.'

The house was in a pretty suburb of neat gardens, elaborate iron gates and charming piazzas with marble fountains at every turn. Even if Kate worked non-stop for a thousand years she could never hope to afford a place like this, and she certainly couldn't imagine wanting to sell it. In fact, it was so lovely that Kate almost let out a wistful sigh of longing as she rang the bell to meet the vendor.

Moments later she was greeted by a mountain of a man, dark-featured, perhaps in his mid to late forties. 'Kate?' he asked, but though he gave her a stiff smile, his eyes were hard and the tone of his voice anything but friendly. His English was good but immediately she recognised that he was a native. She hadn't really been warned what to expect or who was selling the place, and she wasn't really sure why the fact that he was Italian should surprise her, but she'd dealt with so many expats and prospective expats this week, she'd almost forgotten that Italians had properties to sell too.

'Yes, I'm Kate. Nice to meet you.' She put her hand out for him to shake, but he simply stared at it until she was forced to drop it to her side again.

'This way,' he said, and Kate followed him in.

The house was pristine and as grand as the outside promised, though it was cold and soulless, and Kate almost thought she'd prefer to live in the run-down flat she'd sold at the start of the week than this clinical, marble-floored show home. As Kate trailed the man from room to room, he pointed out pertinent features in sentences that were bordering on monosyllabic. Kate took photos and scribbled down hasty details, all the while her desire to get the job done and get out growing stronger and stronger.

'How much?' he asked as they finished up back in the entrance hall.

'I'll need to do some calculations,' Kate replied, repeating what Shauna had told her to say. 'I'll have to pop to the car and work it out, then I'll come back to talk to you about it.'

'You cannot tell me now?'

'Well, I can, but in a moment.'

'A moment is not now.'

Kate forced a smile. 'Please, give me a minute. I will go to the car and be back shortly, then we will talk over the price.'

His mouth was set in a hard line, but he nodded and as Kate left to go back to her car the door slammed behind her.

'Charmed, I'm sure,' she muttered. If he had a partner, they were either more miserable than him or a saint.

Safely in the car and out of earshot, she dialled the office number.

'Hey, Charles, it's Kate. Are you free to give me some figures on the valuation if I email the details to you now?'

'Me?'

'Shauna said somebody would do it for me,' Kate replied, slightly taken aback by his attitude. 'It doesn't matter who but you answered the phone.'

'Yeah, well, Nonna's on a break so I picked it up. Can it wait?'

'Not really. I'm at the seller's house and he wants to know how much we're planning to market his place for. He wants to know right now, and Shauna said—'

'Yeah, yeah. . . Shauna would, and she's gone out too.' He let out an impatient sigh. 'If she's going to send you out to do valuations then you should be doing them. So now the rest of us have to carry you because you can't.'

The question of why Shauna hadn't sent Charles to do it instead of the rookie was on Kate's lips, but judging by the way he was speaking to Kate in his boss's absence, perhaps the question didn't really need asking. She was annoyed, however, that she'd been asked to do this job on the proviso that support would be on hand and now, when she needed it, that support was nowhere to be seen.

'She's well aware that I don't have enough experience to put a price on a property yet, but if I don't come out into the field I'll never get that experience. So if you could see your way to helping me out that would be much appreciated.'

'Ah, well. . . the blue-eyed girl not quite such a superstar after all, eh?'

Kate's mouth fell open. Where had this come from? He'd been lax, and he'd sometimes lacked a little professionalism in the office, but Kate hadn't pegged him as the jealous type. Did he somehow feel threatened by her? She couldn't think of any instances where she might have caused that.

'I'll dig you out of your hole,' he drawled, and Kate thought she heard him rustle in the sweet bag that was a constant feature of his desk. 'But you owe me big time.'

'I owe you because you're doing your job?' Kate bristled. 'If you say so. I'm sending everything through now and I'm waiting with my phone for a reply – which I do need right away if you could possibly manage it.'

Without waiting for his response, Kate ended the call then began to stab an email out on her phone with her photos and measurements attached. *Jumped-up little shit. What have I ever done to him, other than be nice?* It would serve him right if she told Shauna just how unhelpful he'd been, but Kate's sense of fair play would never allow her to do that.

She pressed send and then locked the screen while she waited. Through her rear-view mirror, she could see the owner of the house at the curtains, watching her car. If all valuations were going to be like this, she might just be tempted to ask Nonna if she fancied swapping jobs with her. Reception didn't pay commission, but it didn't mean dealing with this kind of crap either.

Fifteen minutes later (a fifteen minutes that Kate was sure Charles hadn't really needed to do what was a simple task for someone of his experience) Kate had her price – a curt one-line email with no pre-amble. Whatever, it didn't matter as long as she got the information, and it was something she'd have to discuss with Charles himself if it happened again. Perhaps he'd been having a bad day, or something else had pissed him off right at the moment Kate had needed him. She'd give him the benefit of the doubt for now – all that mattered was getting back to her client.

'I thought you had gone,' the man said as he opened the front door to readmit Kate.

'Sorry,' she replied, although they both knew he'd been watching her car the whole time and thought no such thing. 'I have some figures for you now, and if we can sit somewhere we can go through them.'

'This way,' he said, his tone brusque as he led her back to a sun-drenched study. Kate swallowed back a sigh. If she got this property, it would be a bloody miracle.

'You got the property?' Shauna beamed as Kate handed her the completed paperwork.

'Signature's right there,' Kate said. 'Although I have to say,' she added, looking very deliberately at Charles, who sat at his desk with his arms folded, watching the conversation, 'Charles was brilliant. So very helpful.'

'I'm glad to hear it,' Shauna said looking vaguely surprised. 'I knew I could rely on my team.'

'Absolutely. And Charles especially. Couldn't do enough for me when I rang in for help with the valuation; falling over himself to get the details over as soon as he could. Like, literally, the speed of light.' She smiled sweetly at him. If he wanted a battle, Kate was going to make sure she dampened his powder first.

'Aww.' Shauna gave an indulgent smile, like a mother with a wayward toddler who'd just done something very clever. 'It's great to see you two making such a formidable team. I'll have to buddy you up more often.'

'I'd love that,' Kate gushed.

'Of course,' Shauna said. She scooped up the paperwork and gave it back to Kate. 'Pop this in Nonna's in-tray, would you? And if you're happy, I'm going to give you some more valuations to go out to. Might as well get the experience in so you'll be up and running as a solo agent that much faster, eh? And we can work on your knowledge before you go, so that eventually you'll be able to work the value out for yourself.'

'Oh, yes. As long as I can always have Charles on the other end of the phone, I think that's a brilliant idea.'

As she sashayed past his desk on her way to give Nonna the paperwork, Charles shot Kate a surreptitious grimace, but she didn't react. She needed this job, probably a lot more than he needed his, and there was no way his sulky face was going to drive her out, so if he didn't like working with her, he was going to have to do the leaving.

The sound of grinding metal made Kate jump again. Nunzia's car kept slipping out of gear – a problem Kate suspected was down to her driving rather than a fault on the brand-new Fiat – and she was jittery enough without the jarring noise.

'New car,' Nunzia tutted, as if that explanation was enough. 'Different.'

'You're not used to it, I suppose.'

'Very bad,' Nunzia said.

'Yes, it can be difficult driving a car you don't know very well,' Kate agreed, though it wasn't a problem she was likely to encounter for a long time, mostly because it was going to be a long time before she could afford a new car. And after her experiences in Shauna's borrowed car, she was just fine with that. 'But it is lovely,' she added. 'Very bright.'

'*Sì*. Very nice.'

Kate turned her attention to the countryside speeding past her window, anxious not to distract Nunzia too much from her driving. Fields of ochre and green rolled away from the road, reaching for the heather-hued hills beyond, clear blue skies framing the picture. There were lone cypress trees and sleeping vineyards, rocky outcrops and juniper-clad slopes. Above them, a noisy cloud of starlings raced into view, a mass of twisting and turning bodies that moved so effortlessly in sync as they switched directions that they became one huge, undulating shape.

Rome was stunning but it could be intense; the landscape it gave way to as one left the city was a different kind of beautiful: serene and charming, a place Kate could imagine retiring to one day with Alessandro, where they would sit on a porch and watch the sun sink below the hills as they sipped wine from their own vineyard and listened to the delighted squeals of their grandchildren at play.

She shook herself. It was a wonderful dream, but right now a dream was all it could be. When she'd seen him briefly the day before, Alessandro had been distracted again. She'd tried to prise the reasons from him, but he'd been vague at best, and she'd found the conversation frustrating and taxing.

Then their discussion, such as it was, had been interrupted by a phone call from Signora Conti, who'd needed his help at home, and he'd left Kate with promises that they would talk more when they had the opportunity, though she suspected he was hoping she'd forget. It was probably something at work again, and more than ever she wished she could understand his job a little better. It didn't help that she was fully aware of a woman not too far away who did and would have been only too willing to offer him a shoulder (or something fleshier) to cry on.

'Here!' Nunzia said, breaking into Kate's thoughts. She stepped on her brakes so hard that Kate had to throw her hands out and steady herself on the dashboard. She had a seatbelt on but still felt as if she might hurtle through the windscreen. Nunzia looked across with a sheepish smile.

Kate gave her a vague smile in acknowledgement, surprised to find they'd stopped outside a house that had been so well hidden from the road by an incline and a grove of trees that she hadn't even realised it was there at all.

'This is where Loretta lives?' Kate asked as she looked back at the house.

'*Sì*,' Nunzia said, collecting her handbag from the back seat.

'It's gorgeous,' Kate said.

The building was set in informal gardens, with fragrant olive and cypress trees shading the main dirt road that ran up to a paved loggia hugging the front aspect. It was built from rustic, honey-coloured stone, chunky terracotta tiles on the low roof, and to the left side of the property Kate could just make out the corner of a swimming pool, covered for the winter, or so she presumed. She had seen a lot of properties in the last few weeks for work, but unlike many of those, this felt instantly homey. Loretta had plenty of money, or so Nunzia had said, but if this was her choice of home then Kate felt she would be down to earth and approachable too. This was exactly the sort of house that featured in the dream Kate had, of her and Alessandro retiring to a cosy retreat in the countryside to end their days in blissful peace and quiet.

The front door opened and a lady around Nunzia's age, dark hair cropped short and threaded with grey, rushed out to greet them. After throwing her arms around Nunzia, she turned to Kate.

'Welcome!' she beamed. 'You are Kate?'

'I am.'

'Nunzia speaks of you all of the time! Your dresses. . .' She kissed her fingers. 'You make me plenty dresses?'

'If you want me to,' Kate replied, feeling slightly overwhelmed by Loretta's enthusiasm. 'Each one takes a little while, though, so if you needed them for an occasion I'd need some notice.'

'Of course,' she said, taking Kate's hand and leading her to the house. 'First, we drink, eh? A little lunch? You like chicken?'

'Well, that sounds lovely but—'

'Come, come,' Loretta urged, pulling Kate's hand. 'Full belly, then we will talk business!'

Despite being convinced that she wouldn't after the tense conversations with Alessandro the day before, Kate had thoroughly enjoyed her visit to Loretta's house. Not only did they make arrangements for Kate to accompany both her and Nunzia on a trip to the fantastic haberdasher's in Rome that Kate had fallen in love with, but Kate also felt like she'd made another new friend. Lunch had been a riotous affair, and before she'd finished her first glass of red Kate was snorting at jokes Loretta was making about her poor unfortunate (and thankfully absent) husband. She'd almost swooned when Nunzia had persuaded Kate to share a photo of Alessandro with them and had jokingly offered Kate vast amounts of money to swap for a night before erupting into fresh giggles with Nunzia. They'd parted on good terms; Kate looked forward to seeing her again, and to seeing what business her new friend might be able to bring her way.

But Monday morning followed all too quickly, bringing a return to reality, and a return to the sensible world of estate agency.

Sixteen

As Kate walked in to a breezy greeting from Nonna, she couldn't help but notice that although she had arrived ten minutes early, Charles and Shauna were already deep in conversation at Shauna's desk. And Charles, for one, didn't look happy. Gone was the cocky grin that normally accompanied him opening his mouth; instead, he looked sober, repentant, but also a little belligerent with it. Their voices were low, and, as a result, everyone else in the office seemed to have turned down the volume too, so that it was like a doctor's waiting room, where the quieter everything got, the quieter everyone became, and even the tiniest whisper was loud enough for everyone to hear as a result.

Kate caught something about complacency, and how Charles would have to step up to the plate like others were doing, difficult economic times, can't afford to carry lazy team members, and some other generally uncomplimentary stuff. She didn't want to hear this and concentrated very hard on booting up her computer and checking her diary, but it was difficult not to catch significant amounts of the conversation. If conversation was what it was, as it all seemed to be one-sided, with Shauna talking and Charles silently sulking. It would have been more appropriate to have taken him to one side, somewhere away from the office where his colleagues sat. It would have been kinder, and despite her disagreements with Charles, Kate felt the unfairness of his public dressing-down. But perhaps Shauna was making a point, trying to shame him into improving his apparently lagging performance.

After ten minutes or so, the sound of a chair scraping the floor made Kate turn to see him shuffle back to his desk. He had come to Rome as a gap year student who'd never returned to his studies, and he had never looked more like the archetypal student stereotype than he did at that moment. She shot him an uncertain smile, but he simply glowered in return.

So much for making friends and offering support.

It was dingier than the properties she'd dealt with so far, and the neighbourhood looked so seedy that Kate was beginning to wish she'd asked someone to come with her. But when Nonna had expressed some concerns about the address, Kate had blithely assured her that she was perfectly capable of holding her own and if the client was expecting her, she didn't see what trouble she could get into. Kate hadn't seen all the suburbs of Rome, and she didn't expect any of them could look anything less than pristine, so the guttering hanging from the roof of the apartment building, the missing slates and the peeling paint on the main doors was a shock. But she supposed that not everybody could afford to live in luxury, and a commission was a commission, wherever it came from. The matter of Charles's impromptu dressing-down that morning had put everyone on edge, even though the fact remained unspoken, and Kate had to get on with her job whether she liked it or not if she wasn't going to find herself on the receiving end of a disciplinary of her own.

Taking care to make sure the car was locked, she checked the address in her notebook again. This was it. A deep breath, a painted-on smile and she made her way up the steps to the buzzer to be let in.

Moments later she found herself at the door of a first-floor apartment. It was opened by a young man, dressed casually in jeans and a hooded top. His eyes suggested a lack of sleep, and he couldn't have been more than twenty-five, but Kate resisted the temptation to judge him for that, recalling her very first solo mission when she'd met a young woman and assumed, wrongly, that her age meant she was in no position to do business.

'I'm Kate,' she said brightly. 'From Piccolo Castelli.'

'*Sì.*' He opened the door wider for her and turned to go back into the apartment. Assuming it was an invitation in, she followed and closed the door softly behind her.

The front door led directly into the living space, where a TV was set slap bang at the centre of the room, two armchairs in front of it – one of them filled with another young man. He looked up, grunted at Kate and then went back to the computer game he was playing, growling at the television as he shot at a pixelated zombie.

The first man dropped into the vacant armchair and waved a hand carelessly at the room.

'You look,' he said.

There was a frown fighting to crease her brow, but she held onto her smile. 'You want me to measure up? I can do that. This is the kitchen, through here?'

'You will see,' he said, taking up a spare controller and joining in his friend's game.

Seeing no point in trying to engage him further, Kate took herself into the kitchen. She didn't have anything down about this being a rented property being sold by a landlord, but perhaps it was. If the two men 'showing' her around now were tenants rather than the owner, it would explain their complete lack of interest in the proceedings. It would also explain the pong in the kitchen, she reflected as she walked in and the smell hit her from the pile of washing-up in the filthy sink. She wouldn't need a call to the office to value this dump – it was worth the price of a good cleaner and not much more. She'd seen more desirable skips at the back of Manchester's Arndale Centre.

Measuring up anyway, she then found her own way to the bedroom (not that it was difficult as, apart from the bathroom, it was the only other room in the flat), to find more squalor, and then finally rushed in and out of the bathroom as quickly as she could before the E. coli, which must have been advanced enough in this place to have grown legs, caught up with her.

'I'll have to go to the car to work out the price, then I'll come and talk you through it,' she said, as she had done with all her other valuations the week before.

'Write,' the first youth said, miming scribbling on a sheet of paper. 'Give to me. That is all.'

Instead of going to the car, Kate took herself onto the landing and phoned the office, relieved to get Giselle instead of Charles, who would have made things as awkward as possible, or Shauna, because Kate didn't want to sound as if she couldn't or didn't want to handle this visit, and she was fast beginning to think that she couldn't. She could certainly think of many other things she'd rather be doing.

'I don't know who these two men are,' Kate said in a low voice as she paced the landing, 'but I don't think they're the owners. Anyway, they don't seem keen on selling either way.'

'But if we've got them down for a valuation we have to give them a price,' Giselle said. 'Let me have your details and I'll work it out.'

Kate went over her measurements and a quick (as diplomatic as she could manage) description of the state the place was in, and Giselle gave her a figure, which she scribbled down on a compliment slip. Not wanting to go back in at all, she steeled herself and knocked at the apartment door again. It was opened by the first youth, who looked at her, then at the piece of paper in her hand, before taking it from her and shutting the door.

Kate turned away, this time her brow creased in intense puzzlement. This had to be the weirdest valuation anyone had been on, not just her. Although, she had to be thankful that they hadn't invited her back in, because she hadn't really wanted to go back in. She didn't imagine for a minute that they would enlist the services of Piccolo Castelli to sell the flat and, if she was honest, that would make her very happy. It wasn't a place she wanted to rush back to.

'Can you stay behind for ten minutes tonight?' Shauna said, bending over Kate's desk and speaking low into her ear.

Kate spun around, surprised to find her there. She'd snuck up so quickly and Kate had been so engrossed in what she was doing that she hadn't heard her approach. There had been a lot of work waiting on her desk on return from her strange viewing, and she was trying valiantly to catch up. 'You need me to work over?'

'I need to talk to you.'

'Um. . . OK.' There was more than a little of the *see me after class* about it, and although she'd agreed straightaway, the request had rattled her.

Shauna gave a terse nod and then went back to her desk. Kate glanced up at the clock. It was late anyway, and although they tended not to have a set-in-stone closing time, most of them packed up around five unless there was something in particular they needed to finish. Shauna herself often stayed much later, but it was her business and it was understood that was her prerogative. Kate didn't suppose she'd have to wait too much longer to find out what her boss wanted, but her concentration was shot now and though she messed around, ostensibly tying up loose ends, the final few minutes of the day were such a waste she might as well have not been there at all.

Shauna locked the door once she'd seen everyone out and turned to Kate. She looked pained, and not at all like the determined, steely Shauna that had been chastising Charles that morning.

'Is everything OK?' Kate asked, certain that it wasn't.

'I feel certain there's been some sort of mix-up – at least, I want to believe that. Kate, tell me I haven't gravely misjudged you.'

'I don't understand—'

'We got a call from the apartment on Via del Francese an hour or so after you'd visited today.'

'The valuation?'

'Yes. They've accused you of stealing some money from the bedroom. They said they'd let you assess the flat alone, assuming that they could trust you to do that, but when they went to get some money later, a hundred euros was gone from a bedside cabinet. It's a very serious accusation, and as such, I have to take it seriously.'

'Well, yes, you would but. . .' Kate stared at her. Surely she didn't believe this? 'You can't possibly think it had anything to do with me?'

'I don't,' Shauna said. 'At least, my gut tells me so. But the accusation has been made and I can't just ignore it.'

'But I didn't steal anything!' Kate replied, a sense of panic bubbling up inside her, threatening to snatch away any logic. 'Why would I do that? A hundred euros? Would that be worth losing a job that you know full well I'm absolutely desperate for? I worked two weeks for free to get this job!'

'I know that. The problem is that I have to be seen to do something about it.'

'Are they going to the police?'

'I've asked them not to.'

'Shauna, you should have seen that place. They must be dodgy, be running some kind of racket or something. If anyone was worried about being robbed it was me not them!'

'I have only their word against yours. And I have to protect my business, my reputation and my other employees. Something like this could cause a lot of damage, and times are hard enough as it is. An estate agent. . . a client must be able to trust us completely if they're to let us into their homes—'

'But they can! I haven't done anything!'

'I really want to believe you, and deep down I think I do. That's not the issue; the issue is what might come of this.'

'So tell me what I can do. You want me to go and see them? Reimburse them?'

'And make it look like an admission of guilt? Perhaps not such a good idea.'

'I could give the money to you to take to them? You could say that you're just trying to set things straight. I could work in the office here with Nonna and not go out to homes. Nobody would be any the wiser.'

'Everyone would be wiser. I'm afraid Charles took the call.'

Kate's eyes narrowed. Suddenly it all made perfect sense. The slighted, jealous Charles. Had this complaint really come in, or had Charles made it all up? Did he know the youths who had been in the flat; set something up with them? If not, then it was the most incredible coincidence. He'd had a roasting from Shauna about his performance, and Kate already knew that he'd had it in for her, some vague and unfounded fear that she was out to usurp him clouding his judgement. The more she settled in and got on at Piccolo Castelli, the more he seemed to dislike her, and he'd made no secret of that in the last week or so.

'And what exactly did Charles say?'

'Simply what I've told you.'

'And you believe him?'

Shauna's expression hardened, from one of sympathy and pain for Kate's plight to one of displeasure. 'Are you saying I shouldn't? Are you saying it's a lie? Something that Charles would concoct?'

'No, I. . .' Kate's argument tailed off. How could she say any of this without making things look worse for her? Accusing a colleague of setting her up was bad enough, but this was serious stuff, and the colleague in question, though not Shauna's most reliable employee, was one who'd worked for her for years, one she knew well, liked and trusted. If Kate had been looking at it from the other angle, she'd have sided with the known quantity over the unknown every time.

'I just wonder if he's somehow mistaken the meaning of the call,' she added lamely.

'He's not that stupid,' Shauna said. 'Besides, I spoke to the clients myself and I can confirm that what Charles told me is true.'

'Yes, of course.' Kate ground her teeth, distracted by the screech of a horn outside on the road. If Charles had been here now, she'd have given him a slow round of applause. She had to hand it to him – as stitch-ups went, this was first rate. She turned back to Shauna. 'Where does that leave us?'

'As much as it pains me – and it does – I think you know where it leaves us.' Shauna paused. 'I have to let you go, Kate.'

She nodded. 'I thought as much. Will the police be involved?'

'The owner of the apartment is willing to forgo police involvement if I replace the stolen money and I fire you. I wouldn't recommend arguing with that, if I'm honest, because I think you'll find, under the circumstances, it's a pretty lenient deal.'

Kate reached under her desk and pulled out her handbag. 'I don't have enough cash to give it all. . .' she began, counting what notes were in her purse onto the desk, but Shauna scooped them up and handed them back.

'It's sorted. Nobody can prove it was you and what you said before was right – I know you wouldn't have risked this for a measly hundred euros. But I have to be seen to be doing the right thing by the client. You understand that, don't you?'

Kate nodded. What else could she do? Shauna was backed into a corner in the same way she was. 'I'd feel better if I tried to give you something towards the cost.'

'The business can stand it, but you can't.'

'So you don't want me tomorrow?'

Shauna raised her eyebrows. Kate knew it was a stupid thing to say; she simply didn't have anything else.

'No, of course not. I'll clear my stuff from the desk and go now, if that's OK.'

'It's probably for the best.'

Five minutes later Kate was standing on the street outside Piccolo Castelli as Shauna locked the door, unemployed again.

Seventeen

There were many tourist attractions that Kate still hadn't managed to see, despite how long she'd now been in Rome. Perhaps this was because her relationship with the city was now different as a resident, and she'd felt she ought to be using her time for more productive activities than wandering around museums and gardens. But Alessandro, once he'd seen how upset she was over her sacking from Piccolo Castelli, and in a bid to get her to loosen up and spill the whole story (which she'd told him at least a dozen times she didn't really want to talk about) had insisted she accompany him out to get some air. Having reluctantly agreed, she now found herself walking the gardens of Villa Borghese, hand in hand with him, and she had to admit that she did feel better for being out. In the flat she had been given too much time to mope, and she hadn't yet felt ready to talk to her sisters or anyone else about what had happened. It helped that the Borghese gardens were stunning and serene, with elegant statues, a tree-lined lake where the branches of the largest dipped into the crystal waters, immaculate, symmetrical landscaping and water features with glittering sprays that cast mini rainbows in the sunlit air. Because it was winter and early in the day, despite being mild, the gardens were near deserted, and Kate felt free to talk candidly. It was strange how being away from her apartment had somehow relaxed the way she felt about admitting the whole sorry episode to him, something that she hadn't wanted to do before simply because of the shame she felt about it. The old saying of no smoke without fire had come to mind, and, stupid as it was, she couldn't shake the notion. She had nothing to hide and had committed no crime, and yet she felt guilt in the accusation alone, and she couldn't help but worry that Alessandro might, somewhere in the back of his mind, question her innocence too. But he had been patient, and he had listened gravely as she told him everything, and when she finally finished, he paused for a long time, mulling the information over, before he finally spoke.

'I will see Shauna. I will speak to her—' he began, but Kate held up a hand to stop him.

'Please. It will only make things worse.'

'But this is not fair. You have committed no crime.'

'I know, but I don't need police involvement and that's what I'll get by trying to put things straight.'

'So you are happy to be falsely accused?'

Kate pinched the bridge of her nose and squeezed her eyes shut. 'Of course not. I just don't see what else I can do. I feel as if my right to be in Italy is tenuous enough, and something like this might draw attention from the wrong sort of people. And this way, at least I can bury the whole incident and move on – try to get work elsewhere without a conviction or doubts of innocence following me. Shauna has said she won't mention it in any reference I might need. It's a bitter pill, but I'll just have to swallow it.'

'I cannot swallow it. My nature will not allow me to see injustice such as this, and not when it is against the woman I love.'

'It's because you love me that I hope you'll go against your nature, just this once, and let it go. I don't want to think about it and I don't want to deal with it, because if I do, I might just fall apart and I need all my strength and positivity to pick myself up and start again. I need your strength and positivity too.' She gave a wan smile. 'Not directly, but I seem to recall you promising me once that your strength was mine to take if ever I needed it.'

'Always,' he said, halting on the shingle path to take her into his arms and hold her close. 'It pains me to see you treated so badly.'

She shrugged as she pulled away. 'Charles played a blinder.'

'A blinder?'

'He played the game cleverly, and he won. He wanted me out as soon as I started to perform well, to protect his own job, and he must have thought all his birthdays had come at once when the phone call accusing me came in. I get that, but what I still can't understand is why the client did it. I mean, did some money go missing and they assumed it was me? Or did the men deliberately lie, in which case, what reason could they possibly have had? I've never met them, I have no idea who they are and I don't see how they can know who I am. It makes no sense at all.'

'Perhaps they are friends of this Charles?'

'You mean they plotted it together?' Kate mused on this for a moment as they began to walk again. It wasn't the first time the idea had crossed her mind, but she'd dismissed it as a ridiculous notion. It was certainly a lot of trouble to go to, even if Charles did want her out, and there must have been less convoluted ways. But now, with Alessandro drawing the same conclusion too, she had to consider it again. The apartment had been something very different from the sort of property she'd visited before – which had usually been in affluent areas or with much more respectable owners. They were young too – perhaps Charles's age. Could he have cooked up such a plan? It seemed so unlikely, and yet it was the only answer that made any sense. And perhaps it was much easier to do that than she'd thought. All it took was a couple of mates with a flat willing to make a threat that Shauna couldn't ignore. She'd only just employed Kate, who was still on her probation period, and it was easier to lose her at this point than go through a potentially damaging legal process just to protect her, even if she did believe Kate was innocent.

'I should investigate this Charles,' Alessandro said thoughtfully.

When Kate had said she wanted to put it all behind her and move on, she'd been certain that was the best thing. But while it was the best thing for her, it was clear Alessandro wouldn't be able to forget it so easily. Perhaps it would help him understand things if she indulged him, let him do this one thing. She was certain he wouldn't find anything out of the ordinary about Charles – at least nothing criminal – so what was the harm? It was a case of sour grapes that had got out of hand, and when Alessandro realised there was nothing legal they could do about it, he would agree with Kate that they had to chalk it up to experience and move on with their lives. One thing was for sure, she'd be a lot more cautious in her dealings with people in the future. She'd never been stitched up in this way, had never imagined a scenario in which it would happen, and it had shaken her to her very core. The landscape of the world had shifted, friendships and acquaintances would have to be re-evaluated, and she had to wonder just who she could trust now.

'You can do that,' she said. 'But please don't get into trouble over it, and if you find he has no criminal past, nothing out of the ordinary, please let it drop.'

'*Va bene*. You have my word.'

'At least I have some dressmaking,' she added, forcing a smile that felt stiff and alien in her current mood. 'Perhaps Loretta will give me more orders if I do a good job.'

'She is paying you well?'

Kate's smile was more genuine this time. 'Good old Nunzia gave her the price so that I didn't have to, and it was the price she would have been paying had Salvatore not been up to his tricks. So I'm happy that it's fair.'

'That is good.'

'It is. I just hope I can get some more orders in now that I'm unemployed again.'

'Abelie and Bruno will help.'

'Abelie did say that. Bruno's very good with websites, so I believe. Are they actually dating again now?'

'Abelie will not say, but I think she likes him. She is playing a game. It is her way.'

'Treat 'em mean and keep 'em keen – that's what my gran used to call it. An old saying that means be horrible to them and they'll want you all the more.'

'Ah, so that is why you were so rude to me when we first met.'

Kate smiled. 'I was drunk when we first met. I didn't know what I was doing.'

He pulled her close and kissed her lightly. 'I have some good news – my request to work different hours of the day – it is being considered but I think I will get a good answer.'

'That's brilliant. You're happy with that?'

'Yes.'

'That's all that matters then.'

'God, Kate, I'm so sorry.' Anna's pain sounded genuine. It hadn't been Kate's intention to worry her – only to let her know what had been going on before Alessandro did it for her, and to let her know she was alright. She shifted on the sofa to get more comfortable, phone clamped to her ear as she gazed out at the creeping dusk.

'No need,' Kate said briskly. 'I wasn't that keen on it anyway, truth be told. A job's a job, eh? So I'll just get another one.'

'Really? You're OK with it?'

'Well, no, obviously. But I'd rather put it behind me and get on. Moping won't pay the bills.'

'Neither will that money in your bank account for much longer.'

'Yes, thanks for reminding me of that, because that's exactly what I needed.'

'Sorry.' Anna was silent for a moment. 'So, Alessandro hasn't found anything on this Charles?'

'Not a scrap. There's nothing on file for him at all other than the usual documents – work permits and such. He's never even got himself a traffic ticket, and everyone in Rome gets one of those from time to time.'

'Shame. Not because I want him to be a bad 'un, but because it doesn't really help you get to the bottom of the situation. You really think he had a hand in your sacking?'

'I don't see what else I can think. But I can't prove anything and I think it's a waste of time and energy me trying to. I've got things to keep me busy right now, so I won't have time to think about it anyway.'

'It's lucky you're getting dress orders. I still say you're on your way to getting that business going for real. Pretty soon you won't have time to think about a job because you'll have more orders than you can cope with. Have you sorted a website yet?'

'Bruno, Abelie's on-off boyfriend is designing it. I might find that most of my orders will come from there eventually. I'm doing some research now, thinking about niche clothing that I might be able to get involved in – forties and fifties recreations, that sort of thing.'

'There's certainly a market for that. I'm glad you're staying positive about things.'

'Not much else I can do, is there?' Kate took a sip of her cooling coffee. 'How's Lily?'

'Really good. Being careful, of course, but that's to be expected. She has a good feeling about the pregnancy this time. I don't like to say anything to jinx it, but I do too. She seems somehow healthier this time, y'know?'

'Let's hope you're both right. I wish I could be there; I feel terrible for my lack of support.'

'Don't be daft. You've got enough troubles of your own to worry about. If there's anything you need to know, we'd be straight on the phone to you.'

'I know that. Sometimes I just feel guilty.'

'It's in your DNA – the guilt gene. You can't help it, just like I can't and Lily can't. It's the way we're made.'

'We can blame Mum for that one.'

'We can,' Anna laughed. 'Would it make you feel better if I told you that Matt's wedding day was a bit of a disaster?'

'Who's told you this?'

'Someone told Christian at footie. Apparently the register office caught fire and they had to evacuate halfway through the ceremony. Nobody's entirely sure whether he's actually married now or not.'

Kate giggled. Not at Matt's misfortune, although that was funny, but just to let out the tension. It was good to see that she wasn't the only one having a tough time, though she did feel a bit sorry for her ex, despite everything. 'Poor Tamara.'

'That's who I feel sorry for really. She's a sweet girl by all accounts. A bit dopey but harmless all the same.'

'She must be dopey if she fell for Matt.'

'You did.'

'And I was dopey. Do you think Christian could get a message to him?'

There was silence at the other end of the line. 'What for?' Anna finally asked.

'Weird as it sounds, I might need a favour from him soon. And it's a huge one.'

'Now I'm intrigued.'

'I just need him to agree to a marriage annulment if the question arises. I don't think he'd kick up a fuss, but I want his assurance that he won't.'

'But you're already divorced.'

Kate let out a sigh. 'It's complicated. But if you have about three days I'll try to explain it to you now.'

'Maria?' Kate stepped back from the doorway to let Alessandro's sister in, drying her hands on a teacloth. 'This is a pleasant surprise.'

'Perhaps only a surprise?' Maria replied with a wry smile.

'No.' Kate smiled. 'I meant the pleasant bit too. But I am surprised to see you here. Is there anything in particular you wanted to see me about? I assume that you're not just looking for your brother, who isn't here, by the way, in case you were.'

'No, I am not looking for him. You are busy now?' she added, glancing at the cloth in Kate's hand.

'Nothing that won't wait. Come through and I'll make some coffee.'

Maria followed Kate into the kitchen. 'You have made your apartment very nice,' she said in an approving voice.

'I've done my best, but the budget has been a problem. Lovely as it is to get a compliment, I don't think you've come to talk about my décor, have you?'

Maria gave a wan smile. 'I am sorry – I should have come to visit before. I know my sisters have and now that I know you better I am sad that I did not.'

'It's OK; I won't hold it against you. And really, as you can see, you haven't missed anything.' Kate took two cups and saucers from the cupboard. It was quite strange to have Maria standing in her kitchen – it felt a little like she imagined it would feel to get a visit from a minor royal or a Member of Parliament. For Alessandro, she'd use her favourite chunky mugs, but somehow, what Maria thought of her now seemed to matter more than it had ever done before, and the best crockery she had (such as it was) came out. There was something quite momentous about the fact that Alessandro's awkward sister had made the effort to come and visit, although Kate did wonder vaguely whether she might take that sentiment back once Maria revealed the reasons for her unexpected call. They had been getting on better of late, but that didn't mean they were best friends by any stretch of the imagination.

'You have a divorce,' Maria said as Kate fiddled with the filter of a coffee maker that she usually overlooked in favour of instant when she was alone.

'I do.'

The room fell silent, and Kate had to wonder where this conversation was heading. But rather than pushing it, she simply let the silence run, turning her attention to making their drinks.

'Your husband – he was unfaithful?' Maria finally asked.

'My ex-husband,' Kate reminded her. 'Not my husband any longer. And in answer to your question, I don't know. He had a baby with another woman very soon after the divorce, but he says he wasn't seeing her when we were married.'

'You think he lies?'

'I don't want to think he was lying, but yes, I suppose I do. It doesn't really matter now.'

'You felt shame?'

'For his behaviour? Of course not. How was that my fault?' She paused in her task and looked squarely at Maria. 'Do you feel as if your husband's infidelity is your fault?'

'Perhaps I was not a good wife.'

'That's no excuse at all. If he felt that then he needed to talk to you about it, not go sheathing his sword in some other scabbard.'

Maria looked confused and Kate had to laugh. 'Sorry, what I mean to say is there's absolutely no excuse for his behaviour. He was unfaithful to you, he was unfaithful to your family life, he insulted your sacred marriage vows.' She wagged a finger at Maria. 'Ones you made before God, don't forget, and we all know how important that bit is to both your families – and that should be enough to reassure you that none of this is your fault.'

Maria nodded thoughtfully. 'Did you feel sad? All of the time?'

'After he left me? Yes. My sister once said that I was mourning the loss of a life I felt had been ripped from me. I think she was right.'

'My heart, she cries all of the time. I wake and I am sad, I eat dinner and I am sad, I play with the children and I am sad, I go to sleep and I am sad. I will never be happy again.'

Kate crossed the room and took Maria's hands in hers. 'Don't cry,' she said, feeling her own eyes fill with tears as Maria welled up. 'It feels like that now, but believe me – it will get better. You are gorgeous, and you are strong, and you have a wonderful family around you.'

'No man will want me.'

'Well. . .' Kate gave her a watery smile, 'perhaps when they see how much you don't need a man, it will make them want you all the more.'

'You are kind, but my children—'

'Families with children merge all the time. Perhaps not so much in your part of the world, but it still happens. The way I see it, though it seems tough now, you're doing the right thing. What's the point in spending your life tied to a lying cheat, letting him have his cake and everybody else's cake, while you wonder who he's with every time he's not around? It's not impossible that you'll find happiness again and you need to start believing that you deserve it. Your mamma doesn't like divorce, but there is nothing shameful in it when you're the wronged party. If anything, she should be proud that her daughter will not be treated badly and is willing to stand up for herself no matter what anyone else thinks.'

'You feel strongly.'

'You bet I do. I spent a long time blaming myself for Matt leaving me, but I see now that if he wasn't happy with the person I was, the answer wasn't to become someone else for him. I won't shoulder the blame for all that happened between us, and you have even less reason to than I did.'

Maria gave a weak smile. 'You are kind, as Alessandro says. I was not kind to you.'

'You were siding with your friend, and you didn't know me. I'm not interested in keeping grudges alive, and if you're happy for us to make friends from this point and put our bad start behind us then so am I.'

'I would like that,' Maria said, dabbing at her eyes with a handkerchief she'd just fished from her handbag.

Kate pulled her into a hug. 'I'm glad. I'm glad you came to see me too. You know that if you ever need to talk to someone who's been through what you're going through now, you can always come to me, any time.'

'*Grazie.*' Maria's gaze wandered the room as Kate finished their coffees. 'You are busy?' she asked.

'Huh?' Kate turned to face her.

'I see – you are making.'

'Oh!' Kate laughed as she followed Maria's gaze to where half a dress was laid out on her sofa, her machine idling on a table nearby and her sewing box open. 'It's just something I was messing around with for myself. I do have some work coming in but we have to go and buy the fabric first. Come to think of it, I'm going to have to think of a solution to that – I can't very well go fabric shopping with the customer every time I get an order if lots more start to come in.'

'It is beautiful. You are clever.'

'Thanks.' Kate handed a cup and saucer to Maria and gestured for her to sit at the table as she did the same.

'Your job at Piccolo Castelli – it is gone?'

'Hmmm. So Alessandro told you?'

'He told us all that the owner had asked you to leave.'

Kate took a sip of her coffee, wincing as it burnt her lip. But it was better than airing the reply that was dancing like a devilish sprite on her tongue. Why did he and his bloody family have to share *everything*? Some things were just too humiliating to share, and Kate would bet he'd shared every last sorry detail of her sacking with the lot of them. She should have asked him not to mention all of it – perhaps just tell them she'd left the job – but she often forgot that he saw nothing wrong in talking these things over with his mother, no matter how private anyone else would think they were. She wondered what Signora Conti had made of it all, whether she had been a lot less confident of Kate's innocence.

'Sadly it's gone.'

'What will you do?'

'For money? I'll have to start again, see what jobs are out there, try to grow my sewing business. . . The one good thing about the whole mess is that I was allowed to leave with an agreement that they wouldn't mention it to any prospective employer who might ask. Of course, I can't say that my ex-colleague, Charles, who landed me in the mess in the first place, will stick to that agreement, but it's all I have right now to stop me from driving myself mad with worry.'

'It is very sad. Why would Charles do such a thing?'

'I have no idea. I did nothing wrong to him, as far as I can tell. In fact, I was as nice as could be. But I guess he just didn't like me and there's nothing I can do about that.'

'This is very strong dislike.'

'You could say that. Who knows what sort of odd things go on in people's heads?'

'You will not leave Italy?'

Kate frowned. 'Why would I do that?'

'Because you will have no money to live here.'

'Ah, I don't give up that easily. Is that what everyone thinks will happen?'

'Not Alessandro. But Mamma. . .'

Of course she did, because Signora Conti was still obsessed with the idea that Alessandro's dalliance with an English woman would end the same way his Uncle Marco's had.

'I love Alessandro, and I love Rome, even though life here is hard sometimes. I'm not giving up either of those things without a fight.'

'I think Alessandro loves you very much. I hope to find a love such as yours one day.'

'And you will.' Kate was silent for a moment, studying Maria over the rim of her cup as she drank. 'What will you do for money? Will you get half of your husband's property? Is that how it works here?'

'He will tell the lawyer that he has not been unfaithful and I do not know what will happen then.'

'Have you ever considered he might be telling the truth? Perhaps it's been a misunderstanding?'

Maria's features hardened. 'I know my husband. I know when he lies, and I know when he has been with another woman. There is no misunderstanding and I have forgiven too many times before. There have been many more women than even my family know of – at first I would keep them secret because I thought I had failed as a wife and I felt shame. But now I will tell the world that the snake in his trousers cannot be tamed by me or any other woman, and that all women should stay away from him if they do not want their years to be filled with tears.' She made a spitting noise. 'He deserves to die lonely. I wish I did not have to see him at all, but the children. . . they are so young, and they want their papa.'

'It's hard,' Kate agreed. 'At least I didn't have that responsibility with Matt. I suppose that makes me lucky – that I could walk away and never have to see him again.'

'You have felt pain, as I have. Now I understand. I hope you do not have to go back to England – it would be very sad for you to part from Alessandro now that you have found another love.'

Kate sighed. 'Me too. I was trying to get on, find a good job, make some money, and I seem to have made things worse. It's like fate or karma or whatever was teaching me a lesson, because I have to admit that my heart wasn't always in the job, and if I'm totally honest, it wasn't really what I wanted to do. But it was a job that would've got me on my feet, and maybe I could have thought about changing things once I was financially settled. If I hadn't been passed Shauna's details at Lucetta's wedding, if I hadn't somehow pissed off Charles, if I hadn't got ahead of myself and started to do solo visits so soon, if I hadn't been the one to go to Via del Francese that day. . . it all feels like the universe somehow had it in for me.' She shrugged. 'Perhaps it has. Perhaps I'm not meant to be happy. I must have been a very bad person in a previous life.'

Maria's forehead creased into a frown. 'That street is not nice. You had to go there? To sell a house? I hope they gave you a gun to protect yourself.'

'Have you been there?' Kate asked, wondering what possible reason Maria would have had to visit such a down-and-out neighbourhood, especially if she disapproved of it so strongly.

'Only once – with Orazia. Her cousin owed her money.'

'Orazia's cousin lives on Via del Francese?'

'Yes.'

Kate went cold, her fingers on the coffee cup numb. She stared at Maria.

Orazia's cousin lived on Via del Francese! And what was the betting that Orazia's cousin was a youth who lived in a scruffy apartment block and sat playing computer games all day?

How could Kate have been so stupid? The truth had been staring her in the face the whole time.

Eighteen

'We must be calm,' Maria said as Kate paced the floor. 'Tell Alessandro – he will know what to do.'

Kate could hear the words, but she couldn't process them. Maria was asking her to be calm, but calm was an alien concept right now. Every nerve, every sinew, every synapse, everything was taut, like a violin string tuned too tight, and at any moment it could snap. Calm was for people who didn't have a vindictive, borderline psychotic bitch trying to ruin their life. Calm was for people who hadn't almost had everything dear snatched away from them by someone who treated it as a game, who abused their position of authority, who wanted everything Kate had for no other reason than to see if she could get it.

'Kate!' Maria repeated. 'Please, be calm.'

'I should have known,' she replied through gritted teeth. 'All that time I was blaming poor Charles, who was guilty of nothing more than being a cocky little shit. I should have known it wouldn't be anything more complicated than Orazia's hatred for me.'

'She is my friend – she would not do this.'

'I know you want to think the best of your friend – we all would – but you have to be logical about this. We know Orazia hates me, and we know that I was fired from Piccolo Castelli after being accused by the client I went to see on Via del Francese, and we know that Orazia's cousin lives in the very same apartment block there. I know you want to think the best, but all the evidence points to the very worst. I don't see how we can think anything other than Orazia using her cousin to set me up is what's going on here.'

Maria's gaze dropped to the floor. 'I know it looks bad for her.'

'It looks terrible for her! You can't seriously keep defending her, friend or not.' Kate stopped and held Maria in a frank gaze. Perhaps she was overstepping boundaries here, perhaps she was jeopardising a new and shaky understanding with Maria, but there was no other way to put it, and surely even Maria had to be able to see that.

'It seems I have been wrong about many things, and many people,' Maria said quietly.

'We've all done that,' Kate said, her tone softened all at once by the sight of Maria's obvious distress. 'People often show us a different face than their real one. I've been taken in plenty of times too.'

'But Orazia,' Maria began, clearly still unable to accept the only sensible conclusion available. 'I know she can say bad things, and she wants Alessandro, but she would not do this.'

'But she has!'

'But you would discover the truth—'

'Would I? Perhaps she thought I wouldn't, because only you knew that her cousin lived there and she thought that you were still unfriendly with me, in which case I was highly unlikely to find out. Who knows?' Kate threw her hands in the air and began to pace again. 'Maybe she wanted me to find out! Perhaps it's her way of taunting me, knowing that I can't do a bloody thing about it. She might follow me around to every new job, sabotage it in the same way, until I'm forced to give in and leave Italy, and she'd enjoy the fact that I knew it was her.'

Maria stood. 'We will find the truth. Orazia will tell us.'

'Just like that?' Kate's laugh was hollow. 'We knock on her door and she says it wasn't her and we smile sweetly and say thanks for being so honest?'

'She is my friend; she will tell me the truth for the sake of our bond.'

'She's nobody's friend, Maria! She's her own friend and nobody else matters! Anyone who can behave in the way she has cares little for friendship. You're supposed to be her friend, and yet she has no qualms about hurting Alessandro by hurting me, which in turn hurts your family and you, because you all care for him so deeply, no matter what you might think about me. Does that sound like friendship? Because it doesn't where I'm from.'

'Perhaps she does not understand how much Alessandro loves you. Perhaps she does not know how much she is hurting him when she hurts you.'

'Of course she does!' Kate wanted to shake Maria. She understood her stubborn defence of the woman she thought was her friend, but any fool could see the truth of this. 'In England, we would call her behaviour stalking, and it's a crime you can go to jail for. I've been told she's done it before too, with other men – did you know that?'

Maria looked uncomfortable but said nothing. If she did know something about it, Kate would be staggered that she'd let the woman anywhere near her brother. But perhaps Orazia had beguiled her, used their friendship to persuade Maria that this time things were different.

'Because Alessandro has too much respect for her connection to your family,' Kate continued, 'and to you in particular, he does nothing except keep quiet and suffer it. She has to be brought to account, Maria. She has to be told and she has to stop; it's gone too far now.'

Maria looked pained. Kate supposed it was one betrayal too many for her to take in – first her husband and then her friend – but she was too agitated and angry to care as much as she normally would have. Besides, exposing Orazia for what she really was would do Maria a favour in the end. A woman like that was poison, and Kate could see, now that she had spent more time getting to know Maria, that her poison had already been infecting Alessandro's sister. But then a horrible thought occurred to Kate, one she didn't dare voice for fear of the answer she might get, but one she knew wouldn't leave her alone until she had.

'You didn't know about any of this – did you?'

As Maria looked up, Kate saw a flicker of something. Was it guilt? It had gone in an instant. There was a pause that seemed all the longer for the reply that would follow it, and then Maria took a deep breath.

'I did not know it would be this.'

'But something?'

'That she would steal my brother from you.'

'But she didn't tell you how?'

Maria's gaze went to the floor. 'I thought perhaps she would use her. . . woman's charms. Do you understand?'

'That's about all I do understand. So she didn't say she was planning anything like this?'

'No.'

Kate regarded her thoughtfully for a moment. She supposed that Maria wouldn't have been here now, spilling the beans on Orazia's cousin and blowing her cover if they'd been in collusion. She had no other choice but to believe that Maria really had wanted to extend an olive branch, that this new devious development had nothing to do with her and that she'd had no knowledge of it before now.

'I'm sorry,' she said. 'It sounded as if I was accusing you just then, and I didn't mean to.'

'I understand. You are angry and hurt and I am Orazia's friend. I would think the same.' Maria made her way to the apartment door. 'Come,' she said, a new decisiveness in her voice. 'There is one way to settle this. Orazia is at home, I think, and we should speak to her to find out the truth.'

Kate had begun to wonder, as they made their way to Orazia's house, whether it would have been wise to let Alessandro, or any other member of the Conti family, know where they were going and why. They could even have asked someone to accompany them, but perhaps it would have looked too confrontational if they had arrived at Orazia's *en masse*, something that would have instantly had her on the defensive. Maria had expressed no anxieties about just the two of them visiting either, and so Kate had to assume that she felt she had the situation under control. Kate, on the other hand, had plenty of anxieties, not least her concern for the way Maria was driving. What was it about the Conti siblings that made them drive as if every road was the racetrack at Monaco? But Kate was spared abject terror by the distraction that turning her current situation over in her mind was providing. She had known Orazia to be devious, vindictive and just a little bit unhinged – but this? This was too far, surely? Even Kate was beginning to doubt her own conclusions as they travelled to her house to confront her. What if she'd got it very wrong? What if she was falsely accusing Orazia and all it did was piss her off even more? What if she made an official complaint, accused Kate of being the harasser? What if she treated the information of Kate's sacking and the circumstances around it as evidence and brought a prosecution for it, even without Shauna's say-so? Kate had no idea how the justice system worked in Italy, other than the few bits Alessandro had revealed when he talked about work, and she had no idea if that was even a thing that could happen, but she didn't like the possibility. Worst of all, what if Alessandro himself did not approve of their current course of action? What if it made him angry that Kate and Maria hadn't gone to him first? In vague terms, hardly able to express them perfectly herself, Kate had aired these doubts to Maria, who had waved them away and insisted that they were doing no wrong by simply going to talk to her. And then she would talk to Alessandro afterwards, if there was anything to tell. She wanted to get to the truth, didn't she? Of course, Kate had said, but, she argued, what if the information of the visit got to him from Orazia first? She would twist it and he would hear a very different version from theirs. But he would believe them over Orazia, wouldn't he, Maria had argued. And Kate had had no choice but to be content with that, because Maria had the bit between her teeth now, and it seemed that, whether Kate liked it or not, they were going.

Orazia's family lived in a suburb very much like the one Alessandro lived in. It was quiet, the pavements lined by evergreens and row upon row of balconies, like mini gardens, garlanding the terracotta apartment blocks.

'What if her parents are home?' Kate asked, casting a nervous glance up at the block as Maria pulled the handbrake on.

'She does not live with them.'

Kate couldn't decide if this was a good thing or not. 'She lives alone?'

'Yes.'

No mediation in the event of a row breaking out. No witnesses and no help. *Great.*

'You will wait here and I will talk to her,' Maria said, breaking into Kate's thoughts.

'I can't let you do that; it's not fair.'

'It is the easiest way.'

'But this isn't your battle to fight! You're as bad as Alessandro and Lucetta – always trying to shield me from everything, always trying to deal with everything for me. You've brought me here now and you can't expect me to sit in the car and wait while you sort a problem that's mine to sort.'

'It is mine also. Orazia will speak freely in front of me but she will not if you are there.'

'What will you say?'

'I will ask her if she has been playing tricks on you.'

Kate opened her mouth to reply. But they were spared further argument by the timely appearance of Orazia herself, stepping out of her apartment building, hair scraped back in a high ponytail, dressed for a run. As she stretched her legs on a low wall, the sight of her made all reason fly from Kate's mind, and before Maria had time to stop her, she'd yanked on the lock of the door and was out of the car.

'Kate!' Maria clambered out the other side and rushed round, but too late. Kate and Orazia were already squared up.

She'd tried being reasonable, and she'd tried being patient and understanding, and tolerant and diplomatic. She'd even tried ignoring the problem in the hope that, as her mother had always told her in the case of school bullies, it would go away. But nothing had worked, and instead Orazia had burrowed her way under Kate's skin, inch by inch, filling her thoughts, stealing her life, until it began to feel as if there were three people in her relationship with Alessandro. More often than not these days, Kate felt breaking point was on the horizon, and the tiniest thing would crack her wide open. It looked like that day had come.

'You,' Orazia said with a sneer. But then she seemed to check herself when she realised that Maria was looking far from happy as she tried to step between the two women.

'Is it true?' Maria asked.

'I do not know what you are talking about,' Orazia said. But from the look on her face, Kate could see that she'd already guessed the game was up.

'I think you do,' Kate cut in. 'So you can stop pretending.'

Orazia turned to Maria and said something in Italian that Kate couldn't catch. But then Maria frowned.

'In English,' she said. 'Kate must hear it.'

'Why should I speak English just for her?' Orazia said, although she did it anyway. 'She wants to live in Italy, she loves the Italian men then she can speak Italian too!'

'One man!' Kate cried. 'One man who loves me too and none of your games will change that!'

'I do not play games,' Orazia said. 'I am always serious.' She jabbed a finger at Kate. '*You* do not belong here, and I will make you leave.'

Despite the animosity of the situation, and Kate's increasing sense of indignation and simmering anger, her mouth fell open. 'I don't belong here? What gives you the right to say who does and doesn't belong here?'

'You are English – go and live in England with the English men.'

Kate held up a hand. 'I'm confused now so let me get this straight. Your reasons for hating me – are they simply about me being British, or are they about Alessandro?'

'Both!' Orazia spat. 'You are not welcome in my country and you have stolen my man.'

'He does not love you!' Maria cut in.

'You did not say that once before.' Orazia turned her venomous sneer on Maria now. 'You said you would persuade him; you said you would help me to win him. The witch has changed you too.'

'I saw that I was wrong about Kate. She has suffered, as I suffer now, and I saw that it was wrong to take away her happiness, to take away Alessandro's too. I did not understand how much he loved Kate at first, and how much she loved him. They will marry one day, and she will be my family. You must stop trying to break them apart and find love of your own elsewhere.'

'She has ruined everything!' Orazia squealed impetuously, flinging a hand in Kate's direction. 'She has taken my man and she has even taken my friend from me now!'

'I've done nothing!' Kate fired back. 'Everything you think you've lost was either not yours in the first place or lost through your own actions! Stop blaming everyone else for what you've brought on yourself! It makes no difference whether I'm here or not, because Alessandro is not yours and could never love you in a million years!'

'He would love me if you were not here.'

'If I wasn't here he would love someone else! You're not right for him so stop what you're doing!' Kate cried.

'I will make you leave,' Orazia growled.

'And then what? You can't make the whole female population of Italy leave, and even if you make me leave – which you won't – someone else will take my place, but that won't be you.'

'I cannot make them all leave, but I will be the one to win.'

'How? You sound ridiculous, and, frankly, mad!'

'Kate is right,' Maria put in. 'You must stop this now and accept he will never be yours.'

'No!' Orazia said. She turned to Kate. 'I will make you leave and you will be happy you are not here to see Alessandro come to me.'

Kate ground her teeth, her mouth set in a hard line. 'So you're going to do what? Follow me to every job I get and try to sabotage it so that I get fired? Make sure I never make enough money to stay in Rome?'

'If I must.'

Maria and Kate exchanged a brief glance. There was no surprise at the news of Kate's sacking and no question of what Kate meant. It was an admission of guilt that was impossible to mistake for anything else.

'So it *was* you!' Kate said.

'And I will do it again,' Orazia said. 'I will take Alessandro from you as you took him from me.'

'I did not take him! He was never yours, you crazy bitch!'

'When I have finished, he will want me, and he will hate you so much he will wish he had never found you lying drunken on the streets of Roma, and he will want to deposit you back with the trash where you belong.'

There was a silence. It lasted perhaps two or three seconds, but it seemed to stretch out, like time had been distorted, and everything around her was foggy, apart from bizarrely small and unimportant details – like the patterns on the bark of a nearby tree, and the spread of shingle in a paving slab – which were preternaturally clear and sharp. There was no rational thought, only a gut reaction to the extreme hatred that engulfed Kate, a feeling she'd never experienced so overwhelmingly before. And before she knew what was happening, she heard Maria's squeal echo in a street that was now strangely quiet and empty of the raised voices of only seconds before, and realised, with horror, that with her actions she had sealed her fate.

Nineteen

Kate had never punched anyone. She didn't even know she knew how to punch someone. But instinctively her hands had curled into fists, and from nowhere she'd swung a right hook that had caught Orazia squarely on the soft part of her cheek, knocking her off balance, a look of absolute shock on her face. Luckily for Kate she was a lot shorter than Orazia – a couple of inches higher and her fist would have connected with Orazia's cheekbone and she'd have broken a finger or two. And there wasn't enough force behind it to knock Orazia over, which meant she merely wobbled in an almost comical fashion, her eyes wide with the same disbelief that Kate herself was frozen to the spot by. *She'd just punched someone!*

Orazia stared at Kate as her hand flew to her cheek. Clearly she was as shocked by the turn of events as Kate. But then she found her voice. 'The dog bites after all.'

'I'm sorry!' Kate clutched her hand. She hadn't broken anything but it still hurt. And now the adrenalin had ebbed away, so had the anger, and she was consumed by fear. She hadn't punched just anyone – she'd punched Orazia, a policewoman with a serious grudge against her and the power to do something about it. 'I'm so sorry. I didn't mean to do it! You just . . . you . . .'

'You will be sorry!' Orazia spat.

Kate's eyes swam with tears. The harder she fought to keep them at bay, the more they threatened to fall. It was a sign of weakness that Orazia would revel in, and Kate hated herself for showing it. But Orazia had won. Whichever way Kate looked at it, Orazia had won. She had sabotaged the job that Kate had worked hard for, a job that she knew she could have been good at, and a job that she'd badly needed if she was going to stay in Italy. The estate agent job, the growing client base for her dresses, the gradual acceptance of Kate by Alessandro's family, the new understanding with Maria – it was all for nothing, wiped out in an instant with one impulsive, foolish act. Orazia had humiliated Kate, goaded her to react to the situation in a way that was totally out of character. Finally, just to top things off, she would have every right, and would no doubt know those rights very well, to prosecute Kate for assault. If the poverty didn't drive Kate back to England, a criminal conviction would.

'Come.' She felt Maria's hands on her shoulders, the voice of reason in her ear. 'We must leave. Now.'

Kate let Maria lead her away and sit her in the car, still staring at Orazia whose eyes, filled with loathing, followed them. But she didn't make a move to come after and retaliate. Perhaps, despite the look that said otherwise, she had already figured out that a full-blown altercation in the street wouldn't go well for her. This way, she was the victim, and nobody could argue that. All Orazia had to do now was keep her cool, bide her time, and the justice system would do the rest.

Kate was up the creek, not just without a paddle but with a bloody great hole in the boat. Orazia had won, and Kate's time in Rome was finished.

* * *

'You must be calm!' Lucetta scolded, handing Kate another tissue to dry her eyes. It wasn't like her to cry over every little setback, but these tears were out of sheer frustration at herself, her lack of control, the situation, and the fact that Orazia always seemed to come out on top. At least Maria had taken her straight to the Conti family home, and Kate took a crumb of comfort from the fact that its four strongest female members were now trying to help her figure out what to do next. She needed people thinking straight for her because she certainly wasn't managing to do that for herself. 'This crying does not help,' Lucetta added.

'I know; I can't stop it.' Kate looked helplessly from her to Maria, to Abelie, to Signora Conti and back again. All those times when Alessandro had wanted to go and speak to various people on her behalf to put things right, and she had been annoyed and forbidden it. Now she would give anything for him to be here to sort out the mess she'd created. If there *was* any sorting out to be done, because there might be no saving her this time. How could she have been so stupid? How could she have let Orazia wind her up like that? It had fallen so perfectly for Orazia, it was almost as if she'd guessed what Kate's reaction would be down to the nth degree, as if she'd planned for events to unfold in exactly this way all along. Perhaps she had, but whether this was the case or not, Kate had screwed everything up by failing to keep her cool.

'I will call Alessandro home,' Abelie said.

'No!' Maria replied. She glanced at Kate, who nodded in agreement.

'Much as I would love to have him here, there's no point in making him leave work. There's not a lot he can do anyway.' She looked at Maria. 'You say you don't think Orazia is on duty tonight?'

'I cannot be sure, but I think no.'

'Well, at least she won't get to Alessandro first to tell him her side of the story. Which won't be anything like ours.'

'He would not believe her.'

'But the courts might. Do you think she's reported it yet?'

'You did nothing,' Maria said.

'I punched her! That's assault! And she's a police officer!' Kate's lip trembled, and the tears began to fall again. 'What the hell am I going to do?'

'We are going to stay calm. There will be a solution,' Maria said.

'I don't know what that could be,' Kate replied. 'It's all a huge mess now – I have no job, a vindictive cow determined to see me off and now a possible criminal conviction hanging over me. I'm not exactly any government's most desirable citizen, and if I don't end up in jail here I'll be sent back to England.'

'You will not go to jail,' Abelie said and looked to the others, who all nodded.

They fell silent for a moment, and the silence almost told Kate they weren't really sure of that fact at all, even after they'd all said it. Kate stared miserably at her hands. Her knuckles were bruised from the blow she'd landed on Orazia's cheek, her fingers red. But then the sharp smell of lemons tempered with sweet honey and earthy whisky drifted her way, and she looked up to see Signora Conti holding out a mug for her.

'Hot toddy,' she said and smiled. 'Better.'

As Kate took it, touched by the gesture, she burst into tears again. Just when she had finally got Alessandro's family on her side, just when she finally felt like she might start to belong, she had to go and screw it all up with one act of supreme stupidity. How could she bear to lose all this now, when she had come so far?

Abelie pulled her into a hug. 'We will not lose you,' she soothed. 'You can trust us; you are our family now and we will make things right.'

'I don't see how you can,' Kate sobbed. 'Even you can't go above the law.'

'Orazia will not report you.'

'Of course she will.'

'You do not know Orazia as I do,' Maria cut in. 'It would make her look weak, and she would not like that. She will tell no one, and no one saw it happen.'

'How do you know?' Kate dragged the heel of her hand across her eyes. 'How do you know someone wasn't watching from a window? And she'll have a bruise, on her cheek – people will ask her about that.'

'She will lie.'

'But she said she was going to get me kicked out of Italy!' Kate cried. 'This is perfect for her so I don't understand why she wouldn't report me! I mean, I'd bloody well report me if I thought it would get what I wanted!'

'You must be calm!' Lucetta frowned, her tone rising with a sense of vexation now. Kate supposed she couldn't blame her for that, because she'd lost count of the number of times Lucetta had said it. But while it was easy to say, it was not so easy to do. But then Lucetta was distracted by something buzzing in her pocket, and she reached into it to produce her phone. Her expression became one of consternation as she looked at it, and then at Kate.

'Alessandro,' she said before swiping the screen to answer.

As Lucetta spoke to her brother, Kate put down her drink and reached into her handbag for her own phone. Five missed calls from him.

He knew. That was the only explanation for him calling while he was on duty – a thing he rarely did, and certainly not that desperately. Either Orazia had told him personally or the complaint had come in officially. The idea of the latter scenario made Kate feel sick. What if he'd been on desk duty at the time? What if the complaint had come to him directly through his daily work? She couldn't imagine a more horrifying turn of events, and yet it was more than possible. He would be shocked and ashamed, and it was no wonder he'd feel the need to call and find out just what the hell was going on.

In the time it took for these thoughts to coalesce in the storm of Kate's turbulent emotions, Lucetta had ended the call. She locked her phone and folded her arms.

'Orazia has told Alessandro she was attacked by you.'

Kate winced at the description. She had thought of it many ways since the event, but attack was not a word she'd associated with it. She wasn't the sort of person who attacked anyone – she'd never even had a catfight at school. But in the cold light of day, there was no other word you could use for it. Kate had attacked Orazia – provoked with words but certainly not with a reason that would stand up in court.

'She's going to press charges? Make a complaint to the police?' Kate asked, her head swimming as the room started spinning around her. She didn't know what was more terrifying now – the thought of losing Alessandro, her home in Italy, or being in trouble with the law. Her throat tightened, and her breath came in short gasps, and Lucetta's voice grew somehow distant as the roaring of her own blood filled her ears. Then everything went black.

Twenty

When her eyes opened again, the faces of Signora Conti, Maria and Lucetta were all staring down at her, while Abelie was cleaning. As Kate tried to lift her head and focus, she saw that the mug she'd been drinking her hot toddy from was lying on its side on the floor, its contents now being mopped up by Alessandro's youngest sister. She must have knocked it over as she passed out.

'I fainted?' she asked, though it was obvious. 'I haven't done that for a very long time – not since high school.'

'Too much fear,' Maria said.

'I know. I think my body needed to shut down to stop my brain from exploding.' Kate made a weak attempt at a smile.

'Should we call for the doctor?' Lucetta asked, looking distinctly worried by the prospect of Kate's brain exploding.

Kate shook her head. 'Was I out for long?'

'Perhaps a couple of minutes.'

'It's nothing to worry about then. Give me a few more and I'll be fine.'

It was strange, but Kate did feel much calmer, as if her system had somehow been rebooted. She was still stressed and anxious about the situation that had triggered the loss of consciousness in the first place, but the engulfing sense of blind panic had subsided into a grim acceptance of her now perilous position. She needed to do something about it, that was for sure, and what that thing might be was a huge question that seemed to have no answer, but at least now she felt able to process it better.

'You would like some water?' Maria asked.

Kate nodded gratefully and began to push herself to sit as Maria hurried to the kitchen.

'Would you like Alessandro to come home?' Lucetta asked.

'No. Absolutely not,' Kate replied. She half expected him to take it upon himself to try to finish his shift early and come back anyway, but she certainly wasn't going to ask him to. She was in enough trouble without making things awkward for him at work as well. Besides, it was probably sensible for him to be at work in case the official complaint from Orazia came in. He might be able to access the details (perhaps unethical, but Kate couldn't worry about that now) and they'd have some kind of warning about what to expect when the police did come calling. 'Did he sound angry?' she added.

'A little,' Lucetta admitted. 'But I think he was angry with Orazia and not you.'

Kate wanted to believe that was true, but she couldn't convince herself. More likely he was angry at the whole situation – at Orazia for her part in manipulating it, at Kate for reacting and at the fact it was about to make his professional life very difficult indeed, not to mention his professional relationship – such as it was – with Orazia. He was never happier than when he was working within well-defined moral parameters, but the personal nature of this turn of events blurred the edges of his black-and-white world until the picture was a mass of grey that he would have no hope of seeing the lines of right and wrong through.

'I just don't know where we go from here.' Kate ran a hand through her hair, gratefully accepting the glass of water handed to her by Maria. She took a sip and looked at them all in the vain hope that one of them would have a genius solution to sort it all out in one fell swoop. But they simply stared at her, and then at each other, and Kate's hopes were dashed. None of them had any more clue what to do now than she did.

'I will see Orazia,' Maria said finally. 'She will listen to me.'

'Excuse me for saying it but she wasn't exactly listening earlier,' Kate reminded her.

'I will make her see that she is wrong. If she makes this complaint against you, then we will make one against her.'

'What for? It was me who threw the punch – and I still can't believe those words are actually coming out of my mouth.'

'She has used her cousin to cause trouble for you.'

'We can't prove that,' Kate countered. 'Who's to say it wasn't a total coincidence that the apartment I visited just happened to belong to Orazia's cousin, who genuinely wanted to sell it, and that I didn't steal from him? Nobody can prove anything either way. She can, however, prove that I hit her.'

'She cannot prove that,' Maria said emphatically.

'Of course she can,' Kate said.

'No. There is no witness.'

'She'll have the bruise I gave her—'

'Pah!' Maria folded her arms. 'I have hit my husband harder than that playing games. There will be no bruise.'

'But I can see marks on my knuckles,' Kate insisted, inspecting her hands again. Looking at them now, perhaps they weren't quite as obvious as they'd seemed half an hour ago, but then, half an hour ago everything had looked a million times worse than it probably was. Was there a chance Maria might be on to something? It was more than she dared to hope for, and yet she clung to the notion like a shipwrecked sailor clinging to driftwood.

'They are not so bad,' Maria said, taking one of Kate's hands and inspecting it. 'I have worse from kneading dough.'

'She'll still try,' Kate insisted.

'She may.' Maria inclined her head in acknowledgement of Kate's argument. 'I have known her for many years. What she will not like most of all is to lose. So, we will make her think she has won.'

Kate frowned. So did Abelie and Lucetta.

'What do you mean by this?' Lucetta asked.

'I will tell her that you are willing to give Alessandro up, and that the family will give their blessing if she can make Alessandro love her.'

'I think that's pretty much what she's been trying to do for the past few months,' Kate said darkly. 'And look where it's got us.'

'You are the enemy,' Maria said. 'You are the reason, to her, that Alessandro does not love her, and she thinks that if he was free, he would love her – no?'

'I suppose so,' Kate said.

'She wants you to leave so that he is free.'

'Yes.'

'We will give her what she wants.'

'But I can't leave!' Kate squeaked.

'No,' Maria said. 'We will not ask it of you.'

'Then I don't understand.'

'We will tell her that you are leaving Italy. Alessandro will play along, and he will pretend he is heartbroken because you must leave and he has lost you. She will think she has won. When Alessandro does not want her still, she will see that nothing she does will win him, and she will give up.'

'I don't think she will,' Kate said.

Maria simply smiled. 'We will see.'

Kate didn't like Maria's plan. She didn't like it one bit, but she had agreed to it in desperation, unable to see a better solution. Alessandro had phoned briefly and spoken to her, but to her relief he hadn't chastised or blamed her, only asked if she was alright and told her that he believed her version of the story. But he'd had to work and she'd assured him that she expected nothing else, and they'd agreed that she would spend the night at his mother's place and wait for him to return the next morning so they could talk things over with the whole family.

Right now, Kate was curled up on the sofa while Signora Conti was in the kitchen making a light supper. Maria had gone to pick up her children from her mother-in-law's, where they had spent the day, and then she would return to put them to bed. Lucetta had gone home, and Abelie was making up Alessandro's bed with clean sheets for Kate to sleep there while he was at work, at Signora Conti's behest, despite Kate insisting that there was no need and she was perfectly happy to sleep in his unwashed sheets. There was a part of her that would have found his scent on the pillows comforting, because right now what she wanted more than anything else was to lie in his arms while he kissed her and told her everything would be alright. Despite Maria's confidence, the truth was she didn't think everything would be alright at all. If they couldn't make this work, she would have to leave Italy, and she couldn't possibly ask him to give up everything he knew for her and move to England. Even if he did, he would never be truly happy there, and worse than them splitting up now was the thought of him becoming bitter and resentful, forced to live a life he didn't want, and forced to live apart from the family that meant so much to him. It would mean the end for them, one way or another.

She glanced at her watch and wondered vaguely whether Anna was free. At times like this, her sister always had solid words of advice and encouragement, but then Kate didn't really fancy recounting the whole sorry turn of events to her – at least not yet. It was too painful, and Anna would either worry to distraction or be so incensed by it all that she'd be on the first plane over to throw a punch at Orazia herself. More out of habit than anything else, she pulled her phone from her pocket anyway and glanced at the screen.

New emails waiting to be read.

She didn't get that many but with nothing else to do, she opened the app and checked down the list. Only four, and mostly rubbish, apart from one Jamie had sent. Perhaps it would cheer her up. She opened the email and started to read.

Hey Princess,

How's it going? Are you the president of Italy yet?

I have some news. Please don't be angry with me, but Brad and I did something a little crazy. In fact a lot crazy. We got married. In Vegas. We got drunk, and Brad was like, hey, why don't we just run away to Vegas and do it? I thought he was joking, because he's always been all about the huge reception with all our family and friends, but the next day when the hangover was gone, the idea still didn't suck. So, we got in our car and we drove. We had a fun road trip along the way, and Vegas was so cool, I'm so glad we

decided to get hitched there. It was amazing, and I'm only sad that
our friends and family didn't get to share the day. But we're happy,
and I hope you're happy for us. We'll still get that party, one day, but
at least we're married now. I feel old already just saying that!

I've attached a video that a stripper we met took for us. She acted
as witness too, and she was really cool. She could twirl her nipple
tassels like you wouldn't believe.

I'll bring my husband over to meet you just as soon as I can. I still
can't get enough of calling him that.

Jamie x

Kate clicked on the link he'd attached. The video started. Jamie
and Brad were both in white lounge suits, laughing as the camera
shook, held clumsily by the unseen stripper. They stood outside a
pretty white building, set on emerald lawns, an incongruous red and
gold neon sign announcing it to be Cupid's Wedding Chapel casting
its lurid glow across their faces as they kissed. The camera followed
them inside, where the requisite Elvis look-a-like ushered them to
where the minister waited against a backdrop of white satiny curtains
and plinths of plastic roses. He began to speak, and then the camera
was deposited on a seat, facing the proceedings, so that Kate could
only see their legs with the red velour fabric of the chair in the fore-
ground, and could hear their voices as they made their vows.

After a few minutes, there was sparse applause and cheering, and
then the camera was lifted again as Jamie and Brad kissed to seal their
union, which was followed by confetti and more cheering. Whoever
was in the tiny audience sounded more than a bit drunk.

The camera followed them outside again, where it was handed to
Jamie, briefly showing the stripper in shot as it was exchanged. She
was much older than Kate had imagined a stripper to be – closer to

forty than twenty – and she had a face that spoke of a good soul but a hard life. Sadly, or thankfully, depending on which way you looked at it, the nipple tassels were nowhere in sight.

Jamie thanked her, and then the video was switched off.

Kate stared at the screen as it went black. They looked so perfect, so joyful in their union, and she wanted to be happy for her friend, who had found his prince at last and had his fairy-tale ending.

So why, as Kate locked her phone, were there tears of sadness, not joy, pouring down her cheeks?

Twenty-one

As bad as Kate felt that Alessandro had come home to so much trouble he wouldn't be able to sleep for a week, she was grateful for his arms around her, absorbing her sadness and turning it into strength. If ever she had needed that strength, it was now. Despite the entire Conti family wanting to contribute to the discussion, he had also realised that one thing they didn't need was crowding – at least, not until they had talked about what they were going to do next. He'd taken a huge blanket out onto the balcony, so that he and Kate could look out over the city, huddled under it together, and have a private conversation. Kate went over the events of the now previous day again and then over the plan that Maria had come up with where they would pretend to split up and Kate would lie low while Orazia got bored of the hunt. Maria believed that if Kate was no longer a threat then Orazia wouldn't bother pressing charges – it was easier not to get bogged down with the paperwork for a start, and Orazia was no fan of administration even when her own job demanded it. Maria had asserted that the only instance that would drive Orazia to go ahead with an official complaint against Kate was if Kate forced her into it by not giving up.

When she had finished telling him all this, Alessandro shook his head.

'It will not work.'

Kate felt herself relax. Though she'd been grateful for Maria's input, it wasn't a plan she liked, and she was relieved to hear Alessandro say it too. 'You think Orazia will press charges anyway? That she'll report me?'

He tipped his head this way and that, weighing the question up. 'Perhaps, perhaps not. But we cannot pretend to be apart forever, and when we are together again she will see that it was a lie and that will make her angry. If you think she is angry now, you should see her when she is very angry.'

'The kind of angry that tricking her into thinking we've split up will make her?' Kate gave an inward shudder. That was an Orazia she didn't want to meet. 'What if we could somehow prove that she framed me at work – lost me the job at Piccolo Castelli?'

'It would be difficult unless her cousin was willing to confess. And that would not excuse your actions.'

Kate gazed out onto the rooftops and streets below. The sun had been up for hours, but the street was still and peaceful. It was difficult to imagine the activity behind every window and door – families just like this one holding strong together through their daily rituals of discussions over meals and communal chores, supporting each other through everything that came their way, instilling the values of family and community into every new generation through word and deed without a clue they were doing it. They were out there, and Kate had felt so lucky to have finally been accepted into this one. Was it really about to be ripped away from her now, when she had worked so hard to become part of it?

'I don't suppose it would,' she said quietly. 'Then it looks as if I'm going to be leaving you soon.'

'There is another way.'

She looked up at him. The line of his jaw was set, and he gazed out onto the streets himself now as he paused. What was that expression on his face? Regret? Sadness? Kate's stomach lurched, and before he'd said it she'd already guessed.

'I will follow you to England.'

Kate stared at him. 'You can't do that!'

'You came to Italy for me.'

'That was different – I loved Italy anyway. And I didn't have anywhere near as much to lose by moving as you have.'

'I have the most important thing to lose, and that is you!' He pulled her close and kissed the top of her head. '*Ti amo troppo*, Kate,' he breathed. 'I cannot lose you.'

'But there must be another way!'

'No. If you go, then I go. This is the choice that Orazia will make for us. I will go to her, and I will tell her this, and we will see how far she is willing to go, but she will also see that she can never destroy our love, because no matter where she makes you go I will go too.'

'OK.' Kate took in a long breath. 'So, are we going to mention any of this to your family?'

'Yes,' he said after a heartbeat's pause. 'I think we must be honest with them.'

'Your mamma will not like it one bit – she'll blame me and hate me again.'

He ran a thumb down her cheek and smiled slightly. 'She has never hated you. Even Maria did not hate you, but you were. . .' His sentence tailed off. There were things even he couldn't deny.

'Different from the future they'd wished for you?' Kate finished for him.

'Perhaps, yes. But you are my future and they must accept this, even if that future is in England.'

'Your mother is upset enough by what happened to your Uncle Marco. It might finish her off if you tell her this.'

'She is strong, and she will understand. She has many children living close by.'

'You're her only son, though – I don't think she'll understand. If it comes to a fight, I'm still not convinced that she wouldn't come down on Orazia's side over mine, particularly if it meant you staying in Rome.'

'I do not love Orazia and I will never love her!' He took a moment to level his tone again. He was probably sick of Kate whining about Orazia and the threat she posed, and if she was honest, Kate was sick of hearing herself mention it. But that didn't make it go away. 'If Orazia was naked and covered in gold I would not want her.'

They were silent for a moment, and then Kate allowed herself a wry smile. 'Orazia, naked and covered in gold. . . now there's a mental picture I don't need.'

'My heart is your heart. It does not belong to anyone else. Mamma knows this, and you must remember it too.'

Kate nodded shortly before falling into silent contemplation of the distant rooftops again. It was easy to promise a heart but far harder to keep that promise. When the chips were down, and Alessandro was walking the streets of a cold, rainy Manchester suburb, the leaden skies pressing down on him, the sounds of boy racers zipping up and down in their souped-up hatchbacks, discordant house music blasting from oversized speakers in his ears, knowing that this was now his home, would he be happy? Would he still be quite as keen to follow Kate wherever she went? He could tell her that his heart belonged to her, but she had a rival, and it wasn't Orazia. Alessandro's heart belonged to Rome too, and try as Kate might to see the positives in the situation, she couldn't imagine him being happy anywhere else.

Hand in hand, they took the path to the entrance of Orazia's apartment building. Signora Conti had been horrified at Alessandro's suggestion that he was contemplating a move to England to be with Kate. She had screamed, she had pulled at her hair, swooned, and then regained the strength to scream some more. Ready for a slanging match, perhaps even physical violence, she'd threatened to go and sort the problem herself. But in the end, her children had managed to calm her enough to let Alessandro and Kate go to see Orazia, to try to talk some sense into her and end the campaign of obsessed manipulation and destruction that she seemed so intent on. Not only was it damaging to everyone around her, but if she didn't stop, she would doubtless get caught in the fallout herself. Alessandro said he owed her that much, as an old friend, to save her from herself, from this twisted version of the girl he once knew, and that was why they had decided to try and talk to her calmly, as friends instead of enemies, to see if they couldn't salvage something for all their sakes.

'Are you ready?' Alessandro asked as they paused at the doorbell.

Kate shook her head, afraid that if she spoke her voice would betray the churning of her stomach.

'It will be OK,' he replied, squeezing her hand. But then he stopped as his gaze tracked something in the distance, and his eyes narrowed. Before she'd had time to question it, his hand had slipped from Kate's, and without a word, he began to stride back down the path, away from the building.

'What's the matter?' Kate asked, chasing after him.

He stopped at a black car, parked a few metres away from the block. Squinting at the number plate, he sucked his breath through clenched teeth, muttering words Kate had never heard him use before, though walking the streets of Rome had taught her they weren't generally used in polite company.

'Donato's car,' he growled.

'Donato?' Kate frowned. 'As in Maria's husband?'

'Yes.' His gaze went thoughtfully to the building again, as if trying to x-ray every apartment wall.

'You think he's in there now?' Kate asked. 'I mean, it's a coincidence, but it's not really our concern now, is it?'

'It may be.'

Kate was silent for a moment. And then the realisation came crashing in on her. 'Wait – you don't think. . . surely not? You think he was having an affair with Orazia?' Kate's voice rose with incredulity. 'But she's caused all this trouble trying to get you. If she's already seeing Maria's husband, why would she do that?'

'Because she is crazy in the brain,' Alessandro said through gritted teeth, apparently forgetting any kind of forgiveness or understanding he'd been previously disposed to.

'I thought they were friends,' Kate insisted. 'I want to incriminate Orazia as much as anyone but it doesn't make sense.'

Alessandro turned to her. 'Whatever Orazia does makes no sense.'

'Do you think it was going on while Maria was with Donato? Or do you think it's started since they split?'

'Does it matter which?'

'I think it does.'

'It may be revenge because Maria made friends with you. The hair Maria found in their bed could belong to another woman – he does not care where he drops his trousers, but he likes to drop them often and with many women.'

They were silent again, watching the building side by side. Kate could feel the barely contained anger in the air between them, as if it was pulsing through Alessandro's skin.

'We don't actually know that's what's happening,' she said finally. 'It could be that he's visiting someone else – a friend, new girlfriend, family. . . there's a lot of conjecture going on here.'

'Come.' Alessandro started off towards the building, long purposeful strides that Kate was practically jogging to keep up with. 'We will find out.'

There was no reply from the buzzer.

'Perhaps she's not home,' Kate whispered, almost hopefully. This was turning into a showdown she was no longer sure she wanted.

'She is home,' Alessandro replied as he pushed at the main doors. With a click, they gave under his pressure and opened. The smell of cleaning products flooded out, strong in her nostrils. Either they hadn't been locked in the first place, or Alessandro was really bloody angry. She followed him inside and let the door close behind her again.

'How can you be so sure?' Kate asked.

Her only reply was the sound of his heavy steps as he took the stairs, two at a time, leaving her to run after him. For the first time ever, she almost felt sorry for Orazia, and even sorrier for Donato. If they really were up there together, she wouldn't wish Alessandro's fury on either of them. Chasing down a criminal was one thing, but when people messed with his beloved family, the law went out of the window, along with all its rules.

At the third floor he turned into the corridor and stopped at a door, thumping at it. There was no reply. He banged his fist again.

'I don't think she's in,' Kate said, catching his arm as he went for the door a third time. 'Wait.' Bending to the letterbox, she flicked it open and peered in. There were signs of someone having been in recently – or at least not cleaning up what they'd used last: an opened wine bottle on a table along with two half-full glasses, a jacket hanging over a nearby chair and, most tellingly, a tie draped over it. But all was quiet. 'Orazia,' Kate called tentatively. It wasn't that she relished the thought of facing her adversary again so soon after their last encounter, but the only way to be certain Orazia wasn't simply hiding from visitors was to present her with the one visitor she wouldn't be able to resist opening the door to. 'Are you in there?'

Kate stepped back and waited, casting anxious glances between Alessandro and the door. But then the sound of a chain being drawn back reached them, and the door was flung open to reveal a furious-looking Orazia, a dressing gown wrapped around her.

'What do you. . .' Her sentence trailed off as she caught sight of Alessandro. But then she rallied again, and the sneer reappeared. 'What do you want?'

'To talk,' Kate said. 'This business has got out of hand and we need to sort it.'

'I will!' Orazia spat. 'You will be leaving Italy soon, for good.'

Before Kate could reply, Alessandro shoved past Orazia and into the flat. Orazia hissed a curse in Italian and hurried after him. But he had already snatched up the jacket and tie, shaking it at her, his face twisted in disgust. 'What is this?' he growled.

She gave a nonchalant shrug, but nobody was fooled by it. 'You do not love me, so you will not care if I sleep with somebody else.'

For a moment, Kate was faced with the horrific possibility that Alessandro was going to hit Orazia, and a darned sight harder than she had. He stood, almost shaking with rage, and they squared up to each other in a way that was so tense Kate could barely watch for fear of what might happen next. But then Alessandro seemed to gain control, and he stepped back. Reaching into the inside pocket of the jacket, he produced a wallet and opened it. A quick check over the contents, and then he held it up with a sardonic smile.

'You would betray your good friend,' he said in a low voice. She ran to grab him, but it was too late. He was already at the bedroom door and threw it open to reveal Maria's husband, Donato, sitting on the edge of the bed. At least he'd had the decency to get his trousers back on and he looked up at them, half sheepish, half in abject terror, but there was no mistaking the guilt written on his face.

Alessandro regaled him with a choice array of swearwords, accompanied by quite a few gestures he must have learned on the seedier streets of Rome, but then, with a final look of absolute contempt, he simply closed the door again and turned to Orazia.

'You will leave Kate alone. You will leave me alone. That is all I have come to say.'

'Kate hit me!' she said, rubbing her cheek. Alessandro yanked her hand away.

'There is no mark,' he said. 'Kate will deny it.'

'I have witnesses!'

'Then let them come forward. But if they do, I will tell everybody about you and Donato.'

'You cannot prove anything,' Orazia said stubbornly. 'This is the first time we have been in the same room alone.'

'Neither can you,' Kate said, finding her voice for the first time, hope blossoming in her heart that they might just have found themselves a bargaining chip. 'And don't think we believe that crap for one moment. I think you have more to lose here than we do – your standing in the community, the goodwill between your families, not to mention a nice starring role in divorce proceedings. I imagine Maria will be able to get quite a lot more money from the settlement now that she can name a party to claim infidelity as the reason for the split.'

'You would not tell her – it would kill her and it would be your fault!' Orazia cried.

'No,' Kate said. 'It would be *your* fault! You are the betrayer and you are the sicko who seems to get off on destroying other people's relationships. When everything else comes out – all the other things you've done – it will look very bad and nobody will trust a word you say, even if it's true.'

'But we can make a deal,' Alessandro said, giving Kate a tiny but unmistakeably victorious smile. 'We will not talk about the things you have done to Kate, if you stop them and leave us in peace. We are in love, and you cannot kill that love. I do not think you know what being in love means, but understand that you will never have me, even if you make Kate leave. Why would I want you? You have destroyed my sister's marriage and insulted our families' friendship. God could command it and I would still refuse to touch you.'

'But you will tell Maria?' Orazia said, for the first time showing just a hint of fear.

'Yes,' he said. 'I do not keep secrets from my sisters.'

'She will be crazy.'

'She will hit much harder than Kate did,' Alessandro agreed. 'But it will be over quickly and we will keep our word that nothing else will be made public. Perhaps you can even marry Donato one day.'

'Although I wouldn't trust him to keep his trousers done up for you any more than he did for Maria,' Kate added, almost enjoying herself now. 'A leopard never changes his spots.'

Orazia stared at Kate, an expression somewhere between confusion and absolute loathing. There were no guarantees that this was over – not by a long way – but at least they had a weapon of their own now, something to fight back with. Orazia wouldn't want her affair with Donato to get out, no matter whether it had been instrumental in the break-up of his marriage to Maria or whether it had begun since then, and she certainly wouldn't want everything else she'd done to come out at the same time, because that would ruin her reputation in the minds of a community that had a collective memory longer than any elephant's and a strict moral code that made it very difficult to forgive that sort of behaviour.

The door to the bedroom opened and a sheepish-looking Donato peered out. Alessandro glared at him, and he quickly returned to the room and slammed the door behind him, clearly deciding that any attempt at a chivalric defence of Orazia was a bad idea. Then Alessandro turned back to Orazia.

'*Va bene*,' he said shortly. 'We understand each other at last. Stay away from Kate and from me, and perhaps we will spare your reputation.'

'She hit me,' Orazia said, now sounding like a sulky teen who knew she was beaten but refused to give up the last word.

'Yes,' Alessandro said. 'She did.'

'She will do it to others. She is dangerous.'

'No, she will not. You are the dangerous one, but perhaps not for much longer.'

He turned to Kate and offered his hand. Silently, she took it, and together they left Orazia staring after them as they walked away.

Twenty-two

Unashamedly, the dress owed more than a nod to the wedding dress Jackie Kennedy had worn for her marriage to JFK. Kate had endeavoured to lose a few pounds, if only to make the most of the fabulous cinched waistline that was a trademark of the style, but with so many of Signora Conti's good dinners on offer, and her pathetic willpower, it had been a lost cause before she'd begun. Right now, as Lucetta practically fought with Anna over which sister/almost sister could make the biggest fuss over arranging her veil, all that was forgotten.

Kate ran her gaze over the bridesmaids with a nervous smile. Lucetta, Anna and Abelie all wore soft lilac gowns that fell gracefully to their feet. They had all jumped at the offer to be bridesmaids, while Maria, Isabella and Jolanda had been happier taking a less active role as spectators in the congregation, all expressing the hope that it wouldn't offend Kate. She had reassured them that it wasn't going to offend her in the slightest. Lily, of course, now heavily pregnant and eventually allowed by the doctors to make the short flight to Rome, was the size of a semi-detached in Stockport, or so she said, and she'd been adamant she was sitting out bridesmaid duties too. Besides, there had been plenty of children to make up the numbers, and really, Kate had quite enough bridesmaid dresses to make in the end, particularly as her sewing business was now busy enough without making extra work for herself. But Nunzia had said what a great advert for her wares her own wedding would be, and Kate had to agree. It had taken her months, but she was proud of what she'd achieved.

When the truth had emerged about Kate's innocence, Kate had even received a phone call from Shauna at Piccolo Castelli (Maria had visited Orazia first to give her a good talking to, and then apparently went to see Shauna to put the record straight) offering to take her back. But Kate had realised during the time away from the estate agent's office that her heart had never really been in selling houses at all. She'd thanked her but politely declined. Like everything else, perhaps the only thing Kate had really needed to do was stand her ground and believe in herself, and it would all come right. And it did, as Kate now had a jazzy website displaying her handiwork, a rented studio space to work in and more orders than she could cope with. Alessandro complained that he never got to see her and when he did, her head was bent over a sewing machine, but it was only ever half-hearted. During their quieter, more intimate moments, he told her how proud he was of her strength and determination, though secretly she often thought that those qualities were ones she wouldn't have possessed without him. He had once told her that he was only half a man when she wasn't with him, and though she understood the sentiment, she often thought it wasn't that simple. They were whole people when they were apart, but so much more than the sum of their parts when they were together.

It was almost a year to the day since she'd first met Alessandro on the Spanish Steps, and some might have said far too soon to be married. But they'd been through so much together, had fought so hard for their love, that heartbeat of time was like an eternity. They knew each other, inside and out, and they belonged together, and nobody who knew them could deny it.

The early summer sun agreed, bestowing its reward on them today, wrapping them in gentle buttercup warmth as she stood on the steps of the Santa Maria church, her arm draped over that of her stepdad, Hamish, who looked resplendent in his kilt, and waited for her cue to go in. Her mother watched from the side lines, pride in her smile, Christian at one elbow and Joel at her other.

The whole of Alessandro's family was there, as was the remainder of Kate's rather smaller clan. Salvatore and Nunzia were in the crowd too. Kate was set to give up the apartment she was renting from them to join Alessandro in the new one they'd be sharing as a couple, but with Nunzia being Kate's best customer, and her efforts to help expand Kate's business so that it could finally support her financially, they had become firm friends.

And beside Nunzia, Jamie and Brad stood together looking impossibly handsome, the former fighting back tears that Kate couldn't help but smile at. Giving him a tiny encouraging wave, she made a note to grab him for a huge hug as soon as she could. After all, if not for him, none of them would have been standing there today.

Signora Conti was crying too. She'd had her role to play, showing more understanding than they could have hoped for when they'd finally come clean about Kate's divorce. She'd taken it upon herself to make the necessary arrangements with the local priest so that, with Matt's surprisingly cooperative help to gain the annulment she needed, Kate could be free to marry again. And despite all Kate's fears, she'd been as happy as anyone when Alessandro announced his intention to do just that. Alessandro's Uncle Marco stood at her side, and he gave Kate a brief nod of acknowledgement for the special bond he recognised existed between them. He also looked melancholy behind the faint smile. Perhaps he was thinking of his own English bride and how that had ended. But not once had he ever interfered in Alessandro's plans, despite that – he had only ever supported and encouraged the couple.

The guest list had grown exponentially. Alessandro's family was big enough by itself, and so any chance of a small, quiet affair had always been a slim one. But as more and more people had been added, and the preparations under Signora Conti's guidance had taken on titanic proportions, Kate had quite given up trying to control the beast and had, instead, let it rampage. Her mother had done what she could to help with costs, as had Anna and Lily, and Alessandro had found the rest. Kate didn't know where from, and as he was so insistent that it was necessary, and just how they were expected to do things, she'd decided she didn't want to know. She simply wanted to be married, to be tied to him by the most solemn bond, to know that she was his and he was hers, forever.

As the faint strains of wedding music floated out on the summer breeze, the gathered party began to cheer and clap. Kate took a deep breath. Inside, amongst the sumptuous marble and intricate gold idols of the famous church, Alessandro waited. The most unexpected, exceptional man, and he was about to promise himself to her. At times their relationship had felt like a dream, and sometimes the circumstances trying to tear them apart had been a nightmare she desperately wanted to wake up from. But from this moment, it was her future, one that she couldn't wait to begin.

'Are you ready, lass?' Hamish asked in his thick Highland accent and gravelled tones, his eyes creasing into a broad smile beneath unruly grey brows. Kate smiled and nodded. Not her father, the man she still missed so much it hurt to think of him, but as close as she was going to get, and a better substitute she couldn't think of. 'Good. You'll knock his socks off looking as beautiful as you do.'

Kate's eyes filled with tears and she fought to hold them back. *Not now.*

'Don't be nervous,' Hamish said. 'I'll be right here beside you.'

'I'm not nervous,' she whispered back, though in truth, her legs were shaking.

'Go on,' Lily said from over her shoulder, her favourite perfume – comforting scents of vanilla and honeysuckle – drifting into Kate's awareness. 'Your future is waiting in there for you, and I think you've both waited long enough. Go and get him.'

Kate turned to kiss her briefly, and then back again to face the entrance. 'OK,' she said, drawing a long breath. 'Let's go.'

They walked slowly, Kate trying to remember the pace she'd been advised to take during the rehearsal, but nothing would stay in her head and she was woefully out of step with Hamish. But he did his best, and nobody tripped, and that was the best Kate could hope for.

The sun was left behind, and the air was cool and perfumed as the ornate pillars of the church stretched before her, leading her down to the altar where Alessandro turned to watch her approach, a huge smile stretching his face and looking more handsome than Kate could ever recall. She had never loved him as completely as she did now, and the intensity of the emotion threatened to overwhelm her. *Deep breaths*, she kept telling herself. *Calm down*. But how could she be calm?

But as she reached him and they turned to face the priest, she felt his fingers brush against hers, as if to offer comfort and strength. The doubts and fears left her. Kate didn't believe in fate or destiny, but she believed in this, in him. Apart, they were ordinary, but together they were unbreakable. And as long as they were together, anything was possible.

A Letter From Tilly

I hope you've enjoyed reading *A Wedding in Italy* as much as I enjoyed writing it. I usually write stories firmly set in England, so working on the 'From Rome with Love' series has been an adventure, an excuse to lose myself in another culture. I hope that you'll enjoy getting lost there too with Kate and her new friends. If you liked *A Wedding in Italy*, the best and most amazing thing you can do to show your appreciation is to tell your friends. Or tell the world with a few words on a social media site or a review on Amazon. That would make me smile for at least a week. In fact, hearing that someone loved my story is the main reason I write at all.

If you ever want to catch up with me on social media, you can find me on Twitter @TillyTenWriter or Facebook, but if you don't fancy that, you can sign up to my mailing list and get all the latest news that way. I promise never to hassle you about anything but my books. The link is below:

www.bookouture.com/tilly-tennant

So, thank you for reading my little story, and I hope we bump into each other again soon!

Love Tilly x

Acknowledgments

The list of people who have offered help and encouragement on my writing journey so far must be truly endless, and it would take a novel in itself to mention them all. However, my thanks goes out to each and every one of you, whose involvement, whether small or large, has been invaluable and appreciated more than I can say.

There are a few people that I must mention. Obviously, my family – the people who put up with my whining and self-doubt on a daily basis. My ex-colleagues at the Royal Stoke University Hospital, who let me lead a double life for far longer than is acceptable and have given me so many ideas for future books! The lecturers at Staffordshire University English and Creative Writing Department, who saw a talent worth nurturing in me and continue to support me still, long after they finished getting paid for it. They are not only tutors but friends as well. I have to thank the team at Bookouture for their continued support, patience, and amazing publishing flair, particularly Kim Nash, Lydia Vassar-Smith, Lauren Finger and Jessie Botterill. Their belief and encouragement means the world to me. And special mention goes out to Peta Nightingale for always having my back. Heartfelt thanks go to my lovely agent too, Philippa Milnes-Smith at LAW literary agency.

As for this book in particular, I must thank my good friend Louise Coquio and her dad, who entered into many Italian lunch menu debates on my behalf so that Signora Conti always cooked the perfect lunch. I'd also like to thank Simona Elena Schuler for her help and patience with some of the Italian phrases that my poor command of the language failed to produce.

My friend, Kath Hickton, always gets a mention, and rightly so for putting up with me since primary school. I also have to thank Mel Sherratt and Holly Martin, fellow writers and amazing friends who have both been incredibly supportive over the years and have been my shoulders to cry on in the darker moments. Thanks go also to Emma Davies, Rob Bryndza and Christie Barlow – you have no idea how much I love our chats! Jack Croxall, Dan Thompson and Jaimie Admans also deserve thanks for ongoing friendship; not only brilliant authors in their own right but hugely supportive of others. My Bookouture colleagues are also incredible, of course, unfailing and generous in their support of fellow authors. I have to thank all the brilliant and dedicated book bloggers and reviewers out there, readers, and anyone else who has championed my work, reviewed it, shared it, or simply told me that they liked it. Every one of those actions is priceless and you are all very special people.